Girls Burn Brighter

ALSO BY SHOBHA RAO

An Unrestored Woman

Girls Burn Brighter

Shobha Rao

FLEET
2018

FLEET

First published in the United States in 2018 by Flatiron
First published in Great Britain in 2018 by Fleet

1 3 5 7 9 10 8 6 4 2

Copyright © 2018 by Shobha Rao

The moral right of the author has been asserted.

*All characters and events in this publication, other than those
clearly in the public domain, are fictitious and any resemblance
to real persons, living or dead, is purely coincidental.*

All rights reserved.
No part of this publication may be reproduced, stored in a
retrieval system, or transmitted, in any form or by any means, without
the prior permission in writing of the publisher, nor be otherwise circulated
in any form of binding or cover other than that in which it is published
and without a similar condition including this condition being
imposed on the subsequent purchaser.

A CIP catalogue record for this book
is available from the British Library.

Hardback ISBN 978-0-349-00682-6
Trade paperback ISBN 978-0-349-00683-3

Printed and bound in Great Britain by
Clays Ltd, St Ives plc

Papers used by Fleet are from well-managed forests
and other responsible sources.

Fleet
An imprint of
Little, Brown Book Group
Carmelite House
50 Victoria Embankment
London EC4Y 0DZ

An Hachette UK Company
www.hachette.co.uk

www.littlebrown.co.uk

For Leigh Ann Morlock

Indravalli

{ }

The most striking thing about the temple near the village of Indravalli was not readily apparent. No, one had to first climb the mountain and come close; one had to take a long, thoughtful look at the entrance. At the door. Not at its carved panels, or its fine graining, but at how the door stood so brave and so luminous and so alone. How it seemed to stand strong and tall, as if still a tree. It was the wood, lumbered from a grove of trees northwest of Indravalli. The grove was cultivated by an old woman—they said more than a hundred years old—who was childless. She and her husband had been farmers, and when she'd come to understand that she would never have children she'd started planting trees as a way to care for something, as a way to nurture something fragile and lovely. Her husband had surrounded the young saplings with thorny bushes to keep out wild animals, and it being a dry region, she'd had to carry water from many kilometers away to water them. Their grove now boasted hundreds of trees. All of them steady and swaying in the dry wind.

A journalist from a local newspaper once went to interview the old woman. He arrived at teatime, and he and the old woman sat in the shade of one of the trees, its wide leaves rustling high above them. They sipped their tea soundlessly; even the journalist, forgetting all his questions, was overcome by the quiet green beauty of the place. He had heard of her child-lessness and her recently dead husband, and so, to be delicate, he said, "They must keep you company. The trees."

The old woman's gray eyes smiled, and she said, "Oh, yes. I'm never lonely. I have hundreds of children."

The journalist saw an opportunity. "So you see them as children?"

"Don't you?"

There was silence. The journalist took a long, deep look into the grove of trees, their thick trunks, their strength, despite drought and disease and in-sects and floods and famine, and yet shining with gold-green light. Radiant even in the heat and heaviness of afternoon. "You're a fortunate woman," he said, "to have so many sons."

The old woman looked up at him, her eyes on fire, her wrinkled face taking on the glow of her girlhood. "I am fortunate," she said, "but you're mistaken, young man. These aren't my sons. Not one. These," she said, "are my daughters."

1

Poornima never once noticed the door of the temple. Neither did Savitha. But the temple watched them closely, perched as it was on the mountain that towered over Indravalli. The village itself was near the banks of the Krishna River, a hundred or so kilometers inland from the Bay of Bengal. Though it was situated in a level valley, the hamlet was shadowed by one of the largest mountains in Andhra Pradesh, called Indravalli Konda, with the temple halfway up its eastern face. It was painted a brilliant white and looked to Savitha like a big boll of cotton. To Poornima, the temple looked like the full moon, perpetually embraced by the sky and the branches of the surrounding trees.

Poornima was ten years old when she stood outside her family's hut, staring at the temple; she turned to her father, who was seated on the hemprope cot behind her, and asked, "Why did you and Amma name me after the full moon?" Her mother was sitting at the loom, working, so Poornima didn't want to bother her with the question. But she might've—she might've thought nothing at all of bothering her, of clinging to her neck, of breathing in every last trace of her scent—had she known her mother would be dead in another five years. But her father didn't even look up when she asked

him. He just went on rolling his tobacco. Maybe he hadn't heard. So Poornima began again. "Nanna, why did you—"

"Is dinner ready?"

"Almost."

"How many times do I have to tell you to have it ready when I come
in?"

"Was it because I was born on a full moon night?"

He shrugged. "I don't think so."

Poornima then imagined the face of a baby, and she said, "Was my face
round like the moon?"

He sighed. He finally said, "Your mother had a dream, a few days after
you were born. A sadhu came to her in the dream, and he said if we named
you Poornima, we'd have a boy next."

Poornima looked at him as he lit his tobacco, and then she went back
inside the hut. She never again asked about her name. On full moon nights,
she tried her hardest to not even look up. It's just a stone, she decided, a
big gray stone in the sky. But it was hard to forget, wasn't it? That conversation. It would pop up out of nowhere at times, seemingly out of nothing.
While she tasted for salt in a pot of sambar, for instance, or while she
served her father tea. The sadhu had been right, of course: she had three
little brothers. So what was there to be sad about? Nothing, nothing at all.
She even felt pride at times, and said to herself, I was their hope and I came
true. Imagine not coming true. Imagine not having hope.

At fifteen, Poornima came of marriageable age, and she stopped going to
the convent school. She began to sit at the spinning wheel, the charkha, in
her free time to help the household. Each spool of thread she completed—
the thread sometimes red, sometimes blue, sometimes silver—earned her
two rupees, and this seemed like a fortune to her. And in some ways, it was:
when she'd begun menstruating at the age of thirteen, she was gifted the
most expensive piece of clothing she'd ever worn, a silk langa costing a hun-

dred rupees. I can earn that in less than two months, she thought breath-lessly. Besides: that she, a girl, could earn anything, anything at all, lent her such a deep and abiding feeling of importance—of *worth*—that she sat at the charkha every chance she got. She woke early in the morning to spin, then spun after the breakfast dishes were washed, after lunch was prepared and served, and then again after dinner. Their hut had no electricity, so her spinning was a race against the sun. Full moon nights were also bright enough to continue, but they only came around once a month. So on most nights, once the sun went down, she'd put her charkha away, look impa-tiently at the crescent moon or the half-moon or the gibbous moon, and complain, "Why can't you always be full?"

But sunlight and moonlight weren't Poornima's only considerations. The other one, *the main one*, was that her mother was ill. Cancer, as far as the doctor at the American hospital in Tenali could tell. Medicine was expen-sive, and the doctor put her on a diet of fruits and nuts—also expensive. Her father, who made the homespun cotton saris that their region of Guntur district was famous for, could barely keep his wife and five children fed on government-rationed rice and lentils, let alone the luxury of fruits and nuts. But Poornima didn't mind. She relished—no, not just relished, but de-lighted, actually *savored*—the food she was able to buy for her mother every day: two bananas, a tiny apple, and a handful of cashews. By savor-ing, it was not that she actually ate any of the fruit or nuts. Never did she take even a single bite, though her mother did, once, coax her into accept-ing a cashew, which, when her mother turned away for an instant, Poornima placed back on the pile. No, by savoring, what Poornima did was watch her mother slowly eating the banana, even chewing such a soft thing exhaust-ing her, but Poornima watched her with such conviction, such hope, that she thought she could actually *see* her mother getting stronger. As if strength were a seed. And all she had to do was add her two rupees' worth of food and watch it grow.

It got so that Poornima almost made as much as her father. Here is what she did: she'd get loops of raw thread, undivided and in thick bundles, and by using the charkha, her job was to spin the thread so that it separated, and as it did, wound around a metal canister. She once looked at the thread wound around the canister and thought it looked just like a tiny wooden barrel, nearly the size of her littlest brother's head. This thread would then eventually end up on the loom where her father made the saris. It was treated further before it got to the loom, but Poornima always thought she could spot the lengths of thread that she had spun. The canisters that she had wound it around. Anyone would've laughed if she'd told them this— they all look the same, they'd have said—but that wasn't true. Her hands had felt the canister, known the places it was dented, the contours of its body, the patterns of its rust. She had held them, and it seemed to her that anything a person has held is a thing they never really let go. Like the small wind-up clock her teacher had given her when she'd left school. It had a round blue face, four little legs, and two bells that chimed every hour. When her teacher, an old and embittered Catholic nun, had given it to her, she'd said, "I suppose they'll get you married now. With a child a year for the next ten. Hold this. Hold *on* to this. You won't know what I mean now, but you might one day." Then she'd wound up the clock and let it chime. "That sound," she'd said. "Remember: that sound is yours. No one else's but yours." Poornima had no idea what the old nun was talking about, but she thought the chiming of the clock was the most exquisite sound she'd ever heard.

She began carrying the clock everywhere. She put it next to her charkha while she worked. She placed it beside her plate when she ate. She put it by her mat when she slept. Until one day, just like that, the clock stopped chiming, and her father exclaimed, "Finally. I thought that thing would never stop."

A few months after the clock stopped chiming Poornima's mother died. Poornima had just turned sixteen—she was the eldest of the five children—and watching her mother die was like watching a fine blue morning turn to gray. What she missed most about her mother was her voice. It was soft and mellifluous and warm against the rat-chewed walls of the small hut. It pleased Poornima that such a lovely voice should reach for her, that it should cut through the long hours, when all those hours really amounted to were two bananas, an apple, and a handful of cashews. Her mother's was a voice that could make even those few things seem like the ransom of kings. And now Poornima had lost both her mother and the clock.

With her mother dead, Poornima slowed her charkha; she put it away sometimes even in the middle of the day, and she would stare at the walls of the hut and think, I'll forget her voice. Maybe that's what that old nun had meant, that you forget a sound you don't hear every day. I don't think I will now, but I will. And then I'll have lost everything. Once she thought this, she knew she had to remember more than a voice, she had to remember a moment, and this is the one that came to her: In the course of her mother's illness, she had been well enough one morning to comb Poornima's hair. It had been bright and sunny outside and the brush strokes had been so gentle and light that Poornima had felt as if the person holding the comb were not a person at all but a small bird perched on its handle. After three or four strokes her mother had stopped suddenly. She'd rested her hand on her daughter's head for a moment, and Poornima turned to find her mother's eyes filled with tears. Her mother had looked back at her and with a sadness that had seemed old and endless, she'd said, "Poornima, I'm too tired. I'm so tired."

How long after that had she died?

Three, maybe four months later, Poornima guessed. They'd woken up one morning and her eyes had been open and empty and lifeless. Poornima hadn't been able to cry, though. Not when she'd helped bathe and dress her mother's body. Not when her father and brothers had carried her, jasmine-laden, through the streets of the village. Not even as the funeral pyre had burned down to a cold ash. Nor when she'd strung the last chrysanthemum on the garland that hung from the framed portrait of her mother. Only later, when she'd walked out into the season's first cool autumn morning, had she cried. Or tried to cry. The tears, she recalled, had been paltry. At the time, she'd felt like a bad daughter for not crying, for not *weeping*, but no matter how sad she'd felt, how profound her sorrow, she'd only managed to squeeze out one or two tears. A vague reddening of the eyes. "Amma," she'd said, looking up at the sky, "forgive me. It's not that I don't love you. Or miss you. I don't understand; everyone *else* is crying. Buckets. But tears aren't the only measure, are they?"

Still, what she had imagined came true: as the months wore on she forgot her mother's voice. But what she *did* remember, the only thing that truly stayed with her, was that for a short time—while combing her hair—her mother had rested her hand on her. It was the slightest of gestures, and yet Poornima felt it, always: the weight of her mother's hand. A weight so delicate and fine, it was like the spatter of raindrops after a hot summer's day. A weight so small and tired, but with strength enough to muscle through her veins like blood.

In the end, she decided, it was the most beautiful weight.

Once a month, Poornima went to the temple on Indravalli Konda to offer prayers for her mother. She stood in the incense-choked anteroom and watched the priest, hoping the gods would speak to her, would tell her amma was with them, though what she truly yearned to reach was the deepa, more a small lantern, that was perched at the very summit of the mountain. Sometimes she'd stand outside their hut and look up, on a Sunday or a festival day, and it would glow, distant and yellow and blinking, like a star. "Who lights it?" she once asked her father.

"Lights what?"

"The deepa, on the summit."

Her father, sitting outside the hut after dinner, his arms fatigued, his body hunched, glanced at Indravalli Konda and said, "Some priest, probably. Some kid."

Poornima was quiet for a moment, and then she said, "I think Amma lights it."

Her father looked at her. His look was dark, ravaged, as if he'd just walked out of a burning building. Then he asked for his tea. When she handed it to him, he said, "Another ten months."

"Ten months?"

"Till her one-year ceremony."

Now Poornima understood what he was saying. After a family death, it was inauspicious to have a celebration of any sort, let alone a wedding, for a full year. It had been two months since her mother's death. In another ten—her father was saying—she would be married.

"I've already talked to Ramayya. There's a farmer near here. A few acres of his own, and a good worker. Two buffalo, a cow, some goats. He doesn't want to wait, though. He needs the money right now. And he's worried you won't take to being a farmer's wife. I told Ramayya, I told him, Look at her. Just look at her. Strong as an ox, she *is* an ox. Forget the oxen, *she* could plow the fields."

Poornima nodded and went back inside the hut. The only mirror they owned was a handheld mirror; she couldn't even see her entire face unless she held it at arm's length, but she held it up to her face, saw an eye, a nose, and then she moved it down to her neck and breasts and hips. An ox? She was overcome with a sudden sadness. Why, she couldn't say. It didn't matter why. It was childish to be sad for no reason at all. She only knew that had her mother been alive, she would've probably already been married. Maybe even pregnant, or with a baby. That was no cause for sadness either. She was concerned about this farmer, though. What if he *did* make her pull the plow? What if her mother-in-law was cruel? What if all she had were girls? Then she heard her amma speak. None of those things has even happened yet, she heard her say. And then she said, Everything is already written in the stars, Poornima. By the gods. We can't alter a thing. So what does it matter? Why worry?

She was right, of course. But when she lay on her mat that night, Poornima thought about the farmer, she thought about the deepa on top of Indravalli Konda, she thought about beauty. If her skin had been lighter, her hair thicker, or if her eyes had been bigger, her father might've found a better match for her: someone who wanted a wife, not an ox. She'd once heard Ramayya saying, when he'd come to see her father, "Your Poornima's a good worker, but you know these boys today, they want a *modern* girl. They want fashion." Fashion? Then she thought about her mother; she thought about her last days, spent writhing in pain; she thought about the weight of her mother's hand on her head; and then she thought about the two bananas, the apple, and the handful of cashews, and as if *this* were the moment her heart had been waiting for, it broke, and out poured so many tears that she thought they would never stop. She cried silently, hoping her sleeping father and brothers and sister wouldn't hear, the mat she lay on soaked so thoroughly that she smelled the wet earth underneath, as if after a rainfall, and at the end of it, her body was so wracked with sobs, so drained of feeling, so exquisitely empty, that she actually smiled, and then fell into a deep and dreamless sleep.

2

It was around this time, around the time of the death of Poornima's mother, when Savitha's mother—much older than Poornima's mother would've been, far poorer, and yet who hadn't been ill a single day of her life—came to Savitha, her eldest daughter, of seventeen or so, and confessed that they had no food for that night's dinner. "No food?" Savitha said, surprised. "What about the twenty rupees I got for the bundles yesterday?" By bundles, she meant the bundles of discarded paper and plastic she'd collected at the garbage heaps outside of town, next to the Christian cemetery. It had taken her three days of crawling over stinking and rotting and putrid scraps, fighting off the other garbage pickers, along with the pigs and the dogs, to make the twenty rupees.

"Bhima took it."

"He *took* it?"

"We still owe him thirty."

Savitha sighed, and though the sigh was slow and diffuse, her mind was alert and racing. She thought of her three younger sisters, who also scoured the garbage heaps; her mother, who cleaned houses; and her father, who, after years of drinking, had finally given it up when his rheumatoid arthritis had gotten so bad that he could no longer hold a glass in his hand. He might get a handout from the priests at the temple, where he begged most days, but it would hardly be enough for him, let alone his wife and four daughters. She also had two older brothers, both of whom had gone to Hyderabad looking for work, with promises of sending money home, but there had not even been a letter from either in the two years since they'd gone.

She stood in the middle of their meager hut and tallied all the ways in which she could make money: she could collect garbage, which clearly wasn't bringing in enough; she could cook and clean, as her mother did, though there were hardly any families rich enough in Indravalli to keep even her mother employed; she could work the charkha and the loom—she did belong to the caste of weavers, after all—but money from making cotton saris was dwindling each year, and given how little each sari brought in, if a family owned a charkha or a loom, they kept the work within the family, to keep the money there as well. Savitha looked at their charkha, broken, draped with cobwebs, slumped in the corner of their hut like a heap of firewood waiting for a match. For five years now, they hadn't had the money to get it fixed. If only it were fixed, she thought, I could make us more money. She was, of course, aware of the absurdity of the thought: she needed money to make money.

But thread! To hold it again between her fingers.

She still remembered clutching a boll of cotton in her tiny hands when she'd been a little girl and being amazed that such a bit of silly fluff, filled with dark and stubborn seeds, could become something as lovely and smooth and flat and soft as a sari.

From boll to loom to cloth to sari, she thought.

She left the dark hut, the broken charkha, and her mother, staring list-lessly at the empty pots and pans, and wandered into the village. She walked past the huts of the laundresses and past the train station and past the to-bacco shop and the dry goods shop and the sari shop and the tailoring shop and past even the Hanuman temple, in the middle of Indravalli, and found herself in front of the small gated opening to the weaving collective. She heard voices and the whirring of a fan. And just there, if she put her face to the gate, she could smell the faint aroma of new cloth, a mingling of freshly cooked rice and spring rain and teakwood and something of those hard seeds, so unwilling to let go. More captivating to her—this slight scent, lost so soon in the wind—than the most fragrant flower.

With hardly a thought, she opened the creaking gate with a firm grip and went inside.

Poornima's father owned two looms. One was where he worked, and the other was where her mother had worked. They'd each taken two or three days to complete a sari, but now, with only one person at the loom, there were only half the number of saris. That meant half the money. Poornima was too busy with her charkha and the household chores to take over the second loom, her brothers and sister too small to reach the treadles, so her father began looking for help. He asked everyone he knew, he inquired at the tea shop he frequented in the evenings, he went to the weaving collective and announced he was willing to offer a quarter of the proceeds of every sari that was made, along with meals. There were no takers. Indravalli was a village composed mainly of sari makers, and most of the young men were busy helping their own families. The village was purportedly founded in the time of the Ikshvakus, and ever since, had been weaving cloth—in ancient times, clothing for the royal courts, but now simply the cotton saris worn by the peasantry and, occasionally, the intellectual elite. The Quit India Movement, along with the image of Gandhi sitting at his charkha, spinning, and his inception of the homespun ideal, had improved Indravalli's prospects considerably, especially in the years leading up to independence. But now it was 2001, a new century, and the young men of Indravalli, those who were born into the caste of weavers, to which Poornima and her family also belonged, were struggling to feed their own families. In fact, many had abandoned weaving and taken up other occupations.

"Weaving is dying. It's death," her father said. "I heard they have fancy machines now." Poornima knew that was why her father was looking to marry her off to the farmer. He laughed bitterly and said, "They may have invented a machine to make cloth, but let's see them invent a machine to grow food."

Poornima laughed, too. But she was hardly listening to him. She was thinking that if she could get her father to buy more kerosene, she could weave at night, by lantern light, and then he wouldn't have to hire someone.

But the following week, a girl leaned into the doorway of the hut. Poornima looked up from her cooking. She couldn't see the girl's face—the sun was behind her—but by the curve of her body, by the way it bent into the low doorway with the grace of a strong and swaying palm, she knew she was young. Her voice confirmed it, though it was more gentle, and older, than she expected. "Your father?"

She could obviously see Poornima. "Come back in the evening," she said, squinting. "He'll be home before dark." She turned away and reached to take the lid off the pot of rice; as she did, the edge of it burned her finger. She snatched the hand away—the finger was already turning red—and put it in her mouth. When she looked up again, the girl was still there. She hesitated, and the image of the palm came back: but now it seemed like a young palm tree, just a sapling, one that wasn't quite sure which way to bend, which way the sun would rise and set, which way it was *expected* to grow. "Yes?" Poornima said, taken aback that she was still there.

The girl shook her head, or seemed to, and then she left. Poornima stared at the place she had just been. Where did she go? Poornima nearly jumped up and followed her. Her leaving seemed to empty them in some way—the entrance to the hut, and the hut itself. But *how*? Who was she? Poornima didn't know; she didn't recognize her from the well where she went to draw water, or as one of the girls in the neighborhood. She guessed she was from the temple, come to ask for donations, or maybe just a peddler, come to sell vegetables. Then she smelled the rice burning, and forgot all about her.

A week later the girl was seated at her mother's loom. Poornima knew it was her because the room filled again. She'd forgotten it was even empty.

Filled, not with a body or a scent or a presence: that was her father, seated at the other loom. No, *she* filled it with a sudden awareness, a feeling of waking, though it had been light for hours. Poornima set a cup of tea down next to her father's loom. He glanced at her and said, "Set another plate for lunch."

Poornima turned to go. She was now standing behind her. The girl was wearing a cheap cotton sari; her blouse was threadbare, though still a vivid blue, the color of the Krishna at the hour of twilight. There was a large round birthmark on her right forearm, on the inside of her wrist. Striking because it was at the exact point where her veins seemed to meet, before they spilled into her hand. The birthmark seemed to actually gather them up—the veins—as if it were ribbon that tied together a bouquet. A bouquet? A birthmark? Poornima looked away, embarrassed. As she hurried past, the strange girl pulled the picking stick of the loom out toward her, and in that moment, Poornima couldn't help it: she saw her hand. Much too big for her thin body, more like a man's, but gentle, just as her voice had been gentle; though what truly struck Poornima was that her hand gripped the picking stick with such force, such solidity, that it seemed she might never let go. The pivot of her entire body seemed to be pulling the picking stick. To hold it tight. Poornima was astonished. She'd never known a hand could do that: contain so much purpose.

That night, after dinner, was when her father first mentioned her. The deepa on Indravalli Konda was dark, and Poornima was putting her siblings to bed. Her youngest brother was only seven years old, her sister was eleven, and she had a set of twin brothers, twelve. They were relatively good children, but sometimes Poornima thought her mother might've died from tiredness. She was unrolling their sleeping mats and telling one of the twins to stop pulling his sister's hair, when her father, rolling tobacco, said, "You eat with her. Make sure she doesn't take more than her share."

Poornima turned. "Who?"

"Savitha."

So that was her name.

Poornima stood still, a mat half unrolled. "She's all I could find," her father said, lying back on his hemp-rope bed, smoking. "The weaving collective said I should be happy. As if my wages are low. Besides, she should be grateful. That father of hers, old Subbudu, can hardly feed himself, let alone that miserable wife and those four daughters." He yawned. "I hope she's not as weak as she looks."

But Poornima, smiling into the dark, knew she wasn't.

Savitha was quiet around Poornima at first. She was a year or two older, Poornima guessed, though neither truly knew their exact ages. Only the birthdates of the boys were recorded in the village. Still, when Poornima asked, over lunch one day, Savitha told her just what her mother had told her: that she was born on the day of a solar eclipse. Her mother had said that while in labor with her, she'd looked out the window and seen the sky darken in midday, and was paralyzed by it. She was convinced she was about to give birth to a rakshasa. She'd told Savitha that in that moment, all her labor pains had subsided and were replaced by fear. What if she *was* giving birth to a demon? Her mother began to pray and pray, and then she began to tremble, wishing her new baby dead. Wondering if she should kill it herself. That was better, she'd told Savitha, than unleashing evil into the world. Anyone would do the same, she'd told Savitha. But then the eclipse had ended, and her baby was born, and it was just a regular, cooing little baby.

"Your mother must've been relieved," Poornima said.

"Not really. I was still a girl."

Poornima nodded. She watched her while she ate. Savitha had a healthy appetite, but no more than anyone else who sat at the loom for twelve hours a day.

"That's why she named me Savitha."

"What does it mean?"

"What do you think? She thought that if she named me after the sun, it wouldn't go away again."

She licked her fingers of rasam, the birthmark on her wrist swaying between her mouth and the plate like a hammock, and then she asked for another helping of rice to eat with yogurt.

"Do you want salt?" Poornima asked.

"I like it sweet. To tell you the truth, what I love with yogurt rice is a banana. I squish it up and mix it in with the rice. Don't make that face. Not until you try it. It tastes like the sweetest, loveliest sunrise. And I'm not just saying that because of my name. It just does; you should try it."

"But bananas," Poornima said, thinking now of her own mother and the two bananas she'd bought for her every day, and how, in the end, they hadn't made a bit of difference.

"I know. Expensive. But that's the thing, Poori—do you mind if I call you that?—you *shouldn't* eat it at every meal. It's too good. Too perfect. Would you want to see the sun rise every morning? You'd get used to it; the colors, I mean. You'd get so you'd just turn away."

"And that's the same with too much yogurt rice and bananas? I'd just turn away?"

"No. You'd still eat it. You just wouldn't think of it."

Think of it?

No, she wasn't quiet anymore, Poornima thought. Not at all. And she was strangely obsessed with food: the thing with the bananas and yogurt rice, calling her Poori, the way she licked her fingers, as if she would never eat another meal. Poornima's father had said her family was poor, poorer even than they were, which was hard to imagine. Six children in all, her father had told her, old Subbudu so frail that he'd long ago given up sitting at the loom, her mother cleaning, cooking for other families, no better than a common *servant*, he'd said derisively, and her older brothers moved to Hyderabad, promising to send money home, though the family hadn't yet received a single paisa. And with four daughters unmarried. "Four," her father had exclaimed, shaking his head. "The old man's done for," he'd said. "He might be better off finding four big rocks and a rope and leading them to the nearest well."

"Which one is Savitha?"

"Oldest. Of the girls. Not even enough for *her* dowry." So her marriage was delayed, too, just like Poornima's. Her father narrowed his eyes then and looked at her. "Not eating too much, is she? Tucking a little away for her sisters?"

"No," Poornima said. "Hardly anything."

What Poornima liked most about Savitha—in addition to her hands—was her clarity. She had never known anyone—not her father, not a teacher, not the temple priest—to be as certain as Savitha was. But certain about what? she asked herself. About bananas in yogurt rice? About sunrises? Yes, but about more than that. About her grip on the picking stick, about her stride, about the way her sari was knotted around her waist. About everything, Poornima realized, that she herself was *unsure* about. As the weeks went by, Savitha began to linger a little longer over her lunch; she came earlier to help with the morning chores, though she must've had chores to do at her own house beforehand. She and Poornima also began to go to the well together for water.

On one of these trips, as they were walking back together, the clay pots of water balanced on their hips, they came across a crowd of young men about their age. There were four of them, clustered around the beedie shop, smoking, when one of them, a boy of about twenty or twenty-two, thin as a reed but with a thick shock of hair, noticed Poornima and Savitha and pointed.

"Look over there," he called to the other men. "Look at those hips. Those curves. Such fine examples of the Indian landscape."

Then another of the men whistled, and another, or maybe the same, said, "Not even Gandhiji could've resisted." They all laughed. "Which one do you want, boys," he continued, "the yellow or the blue?"

Poornima discovered he was talking about the color of their saris.

"The blue!"

"The yellow," another yelled.

"*I* want to be the clay pot," another said, and they all laughed again.

There was no way to get around them, they realized. The men came closer and surrounded them. The circle they formed was porous but menacing. Poornima looked at Savitha, but she was looking straight past them, as if the men weren't even there. "What do we *do*?" Poornima whispered.

"Walk," she said, her voice firm, steady and as solid as the temple on Indravalli Konda, the one on which Savitha's gaze seemed to be fixed.

Poornima glanced at her and then she glanced at her feet.

"Don't look down," Savitha said. "Look up."

She lifted her gaze slowly and saw that the men were now in a tight huddle. They were jumping up and down like crickets; one grabbed Savitha's pallu and yanked it. She slapped his hand away. This brought out a long howl from them, and more dancing and laughter, as if the slap had been an invitation. Poornima was mildly aware of other women, standing at the entrance to their huts. Boys, they would be thinking, shaking their heads. Poornima felt a rising panic; this was a common occurrence in the village, but the men usually left them alone after a little teasing, a few winks. *These* men were following them. And there were four of them. She looked at Savitha. Her face was as determined as before, staring ahead of her, straight at the temple and Indravalli Konda as if she could bore a hole through both. The men seemed to sense something in her, something like defiance— and this defiance, its *audacity* seemed to enliven them even more. "Darling baby," they said in English, and then in Telugu, "why don't *you* choose." They were talking to Savitha.

And this. This was the signal she was waiting for.

She set down her pot of water, straightened her back, and stood still. Absolutely still. And with her stillness came an even greater stillness. The people standing at the entrances to their huts, the bend of the street leading to Indravalli Konda, the fields of rice all around, and even the clacking of the looms, ubiquitous in the village at all hours, were strangely quieted. They could almost hear the Krishna, a few kilometers away—the lapping of its waters, the flapping of the wings of water birds.

"I know who I want," Savitha said.

The first man, the thin one with the abundant hair, whooped and hollered and skipped around the circle like a child. "She knows. She knows. Sorry, boys, better luck next time."

"Which one? Which one?" they chirped.

Savitha looked at each of them in turn, met their eyes, and then she walked a step or two in each of their directions, as if taunting them with her choice, and then she smiled—her flash of teeth as gleaming and virtuous as the white of the distant temple—stepped toward Poornima, took her hand, and said, "I choose her." With these words, she picked up her pot of water, tugged at Poornima's arm, and pulled her out of the circle. The men let them go but hissed and growled. *"Her?"* they groaned. "She's uglier than you are."

When they got home, Poornima was trembling.

"Don't," Savitha told her. "It's no good."

"I can't help it."

"Don't you see? I could've chosen a tree. A dog."

"Yeah, but they could've hurt us."

"I wouldn't have let them," she said.

And so, there they were: those five words. They were a song, an incantation. Poornima felt a weight, an awful and terrifying weight, erode. Had the weight been borne from her mother's death? Or from being an ox? Or was it from something less obvious, like the passage of time, or the endless spinning of her charkha? Though, when she thought about it, they were the same thing, weren't they? It hardly mattered. She and Savitha became such close friends that neither could eat a single meal without wondering if the other would've preferred more salt, or if she liked brinjal with potatoes. Breakfast was suddenly their least favorite meal, and Sunday their least favorite day. Poornima even saved a paisa here and there and began to buy bananas whenever she could. The first time she did, she presented one to Savitha at lunch, when she served her the buttermilk. There had not been enough money for yogurt that morning. Savitha didn't seem to mind. She mixed her watery buttermilk and rice with as much relish as if it were the thickest, creamiest yogurt she'd ever eaten. Poornima watched her, and then she held out the banana.

Savitha gasped. "Are you sure?"

"Of course. I bought it especially for you."

She was so delighted that she became curiously shy. "My mother says if I'd eaten fewer bananas in my life, they would have had the money for my dowry."

Poornima smiled and looked down.

Savitha stopped eating. "When did she die?"

"Four months ago."

Savitha mixed the banana into her rice. First she took off the entire peel then mushed it with her thumb and fingers into the rice. The banana ended up in unsightly lumps, strewn across the carpet of rice like wading bandicoots. It was all a gloppy, unappetizing mess.

"You *like* that?"

"Try some." She raised a handful toward Poornima. Poornima shook her head vigorously. Savitha shrugged and ate the rice-and-banana concoction with great relish, closing her eyes as she chewed.

"You know what's even better than this?"

Poornima wrinkled her nose. "Most things, I would imagine."

Savitha ignored her. She leaned toward Poornima, as if revealing a secret. "I don't know for sure, I've only heard, but there's supposed to be this rare fruit. Unbearable, Poori. Pink inside, almost buttery, but with the sweetness of candy. Sweeter. Better even than bananas, better even than sapota. I know, I know, you wouldn't think it possible, but I heard an old woman talking about it in the marketplace. Years ago. She said it only grew on some island. On the Brahmaputra. Even the way she described the island was lovely. She looked at me, right at me, and she said, 'You know how Krishna plays the flute for his Radha, wooing her at twilight, just as the cows are coming home? It is that sound. That is the sound of the island. Flute song. Everywhere you go there are the fruit, and there is flute song. Following you like a lover."

"That's what she said?"

"Yes."

"Like flute song?"

"Yes."

Poornima was silent. "What's the name of the island?"

"Majuli."

"Majuli," Poornima said out loud, slowly, as if tasting the word on her tongue. "And you believed her?"

"Of course I believed her," Savitha said. "Some of the crowd didn't, but I did. They said she was senile and had never been north of the abandoned train depot, let alone to the Brahmaputra. But you should've seen her face, Poori. How could you *not* believe her? Lit up like a star."

Poornima thought for a moment, perplexed. "But how can an island be like flute song? Did she mean she loved the island? Like Krishna loves Radha?"

"No. I don't think so."

"What then? It's a song of love, after all."

"Yes," Savitha said, "but it's also a song of hunger."

Now Poornima was even more confused. "Hunger?"

"Maybe what she meant was that the island was the end of hunger. Or the beginning of it. Or maybe that hunger has no beginning. Or end. Like the sound of Krishna's flute."

"But what about love?"

"What is love, Poori?" Savitha said. "What is love if not a hunger?"

3

The following week, Savitha invited Poornima to her house. It was a Sunday. Her father didn't mind as long as she first cooked and fed her brothers and sister and laid his tobacco and mat out for his afternoon nap. The day was hot; it was March, though already they had to keep to the shade—Savitha ahead, Poornima following close behind her—skidding along under the trees and the overhanging thatched roofs of the huts to keep out of the sun. Savitha lived on the other side of the village, farther from Indravalli Konda but closer to the Krishna. Many of those belonging to the caste of laundresses lived on that side of town, because of its proximity to the water. There were also—discovered on that side of the village— inscriptions dating back to the time of the Cholas, though, being close to the railroad tracks, it was also the village's primary bathroom, and the in- scriptions mostly ignored. Still, the majority who lived there belonged to the caste of weavers, Savitha's family among them.

Their hut was on a small ridge. The road—more a dirt path—leading to it was lined with scrubs, their leaves and branches already withered and gray from the heat. When Poornima reached down and touched one, a silky film of gray came off the leaf, and she realized it was ash, from the wood fires that were built outside the huts along the path—they being too poor to have even a cooking area inside their huts. Piles of trash also lined the huts, sniffed occasionally by a stray dog or a pig hungry enough to withstand the heat. It was almost time for tiffin, four in the afternoon, but no one seemed to be home. By now, the sky was white, glowing like a brass pot lit from within. Beads of sweat dripped down Poornima's back. Clung like mist to her scalp.

When they reached the hut, Poornima realized her family was wealthy compared to Savitha's. They couldn't even afford palm fronds for the roof of their hut; it was a discarded sheet of corrugated tin. The outside walls of the hut were plastered with cow dung, and a small area of dirt was cleared in front of the scrubs, though it was still scattered with trash—bits of old yellowed newspaper, disintegrating, blackened rags, vegetable skins too rotted even for the tiny piglets that roamed freely from hut to hut. Poornima stepped over these, and when she followed Savitha into the hut, the first thing that overcame her was the smell. It smelled like old, unwashed clothes and sweat and pickled food. It smelled like manure, woodsmoke, dirt. It smelled like poverty. And despair. It smelled like her mother dying.

"We don't have any milk for tea," Savitha said. "Do you want one of these?" She held out a tin of biscuits that were clearly meant only for company. Poornima bit into one; it was stale and crumbled into a soft yellow paste in her mouth. "Where is your mother? Your sisters?"

"My mother cooks today. For the family that owns that big house, the one near the market. My sisters go collecting in the afternoons," Savitha said.

"Collecting what?"

She shrugged. "I usually go with them."

"Where?"

"Edge of town. By the Christian cemetery."

Poornima knew that was where the garbage dumps were. Not the small heaps that dotted the village, practically on every doorstep, but the massive ones, three or four in all, where the small heaps were eventually deposited. Poornima had seen them only from a distance—a far mountain range on the southern horizon that only the poorest climbed. Seeking discarded cloth or paper or scraps of metal, food, plastic. Usually children, she knew, but sometimes adults. But always the poorest. She remembered her mother saying once, as they passed them, "Don't look," and Poornima had not known whether she meant at the cemetery or at the children scrambling up the heaps. But now, standing in Savitha's impoverished hut, and with her mother long dead, she thought she understood. Her mother had said don't look and she'd meant don't look at either the cemetery or the garbage heaps. She'd meant, don't look at death, don't look at poverty, don't look at how they crawl through life, how they wait for you, stalk you, before they end you.

"*You* go?"

"Not anymore. Not since I started working for your father."

Poornima looked out the one window of the hut. It looked out onto Indravalli Konda, and she looked at the temple and felt pride for the first time toward her father; he'd given Savitha a livelihood and led her away from the garbage heaps. She had never thought of him as generous, but she realized generosity could be a quality that was hidden, obscured, veiled as if by ash, like the true color of the leaves on the scrubs outside Savitha's hut. "But how did you learn to weave?" she asked.

"My parents used to. My mother still has her old charkha," she said, pointing to a pile of wood in a corner. Pinned above it was a calendar with Shiva and Parvati, with Ganesha and Kartikeya seated on their laps. Next to the broken charkha was a large bundle wrapped in an old sheet, maybe a shawl. A few dented aluminum pots and pans lay in another corner, below a hanging vegetable basket that contained a stray piece of garlic, a distended onion, and a round orange squash. Poornima saw a leftover clump of rice swarming with flies. A frayed bamboo mat leaned next to them. "We used to have a loom. But my father drank it away. A small beedie shop. Not here. In the center of town. He drank that away, too."

Poornima had never heard of such a thing. The word for alcohol in Telugu was *mondhoo*, which could mean medicine, or poison. It was considered taboo to even mention the word, and never around women and children.

Drinkers were spoken of in hushed voices and considered leprous, or worse. To be standing in the *home* of a drinker—Poornima shuddered. "Where is he now?"

Her eyes turned to the window. "Up there, probably."

Poornima followed her gaze. There was Indravalli Konda, the temple, sky. "The temple?"

"He goes and begs for handouts. Usually the priests feel sorry for him and give him half a coconut, a laddoo if he's lucky." She said it so offhandedly that Poornima was amazed. "It's enough to keep him."

They both stood, looking out at the temple. The story—not a myth; it couldn't be a myth because it actually happened, Poornima had seen it—was that once a year, inexplicably, nectar would run from the mouth of the deity. A sweet, thick nectar flowing freely. No one knew where it came from, why it started, or why it stopped, but Poornima looked around at Savitha's hut, at the one clove of garlic and the rotting onion and the squash that she knew was the entirety of their provisions, maybe for the week, and thought, It should run all the time. If we are truly God's children, like the priests say, then why doesn't it run all the time?

"I won't give him my earnings. He thinks I'm saving for my own dowry. But I'm not. I'm saving it for my sisters' dowries." Savitha looked at Poornima. "I'm not getting married, not until they are."

"No?"

Savitha looked past her, as if into a cave, and said, "No."

The farmer was no longer interested. He sent word to Poornima's father. He said he couldn't wait the remaining eight months, and besides, he said, he had heard his daughter was as dark as a tamarind. Poornima's father was crestfallen. He prodded Ramayya, who'd brought the news, with question after question. "What else did he say? Any chance he'll change his mind? A tamarind? Really? She's hardly as dark as a tamarind. Do you think she is?

It's a curse: daughters, darkness. What if I buy him another goat? A few chickens?"

Ramayya swung his head and said it was hopeless. He took a sip of his tea and said, "We'll find her another. I already have a lead."

Poornima's father's eyes lit up. "Who?"

It was a young man who lived in Repalle. He had passed his tenth-class exams and was now apprenticed at a sari shop. His parents were both weavers, but with their son working, and in anticipation of a daughter-in-law who would bring in a dowry and hopefully extra income with a charkha, they were slowing down and focusing on getting him married. "There's a younger daughter, too, so it's unclear," Ramayya said. He was referring, of course, to the fact that the young man couldn't get married until his sister was married and settled. But, according to Ramayya, the younger daughter's marriage was already fixed. Only the muhurthum—the most auspicious date and time of the wedding—remained to be arranged. Poornima's father was delighted. "Plenty of time, then," he said, smiling. "And what about the dowry?"

Ramayya finished his tea. "Within our range. He's still an apprentice, after all. But one thing at a time."

The next afternoon, Poornima told Savitha what she'd overheard. She'd come in for lunch. They always ate after Poornima's father, and he'd asked for a second helping of capsicum curry, leaving Poornima and Savitha with only a small spoonful to share. They ate their rice mainly with pickle. "Where did you say?"

"Repalle."

Savitha was silent for a moment. "That's too far."

"Where is it?"

"It's past Tenali. It's by the ocean."

"The ocean?" Poornima had never seen the ocean, and she imagined it to be just like a field—a field of rice, she thought—with ships in the distance instead of mountains, blue instead of green, and as for waves, she'd discussed them with a classmate once, when she was in the third class. "But what *are* they? What do they look like?" The other girl—who'd also never seen the ocean—said they were the water burping, and they looked like a cat when it's stretching. A cat? Stretching? Poornima was skeptical. "Will you visit me?"

"I told you. It's too far."

"But, a train."

Savitha laughed out loud. She held up a bit of capsicum. "You see this? You see *this*?" she said, indicating her full plate of rice and a fingertip's worth of last year's tomato pickle. "This is a feast. How do you think I will ever afford a train ticket?"

That night, Poornima lay on her mat and thought about Savitha. It was vaguely unsettling, but it seemed to her that she couldn't possibly marry a man who lived too far away for Savitha to visit. So that, essentially, *Savitha* was more important than the man she would marry. Could that be true? How had this happened? Poornima couldn't say. She thought about the fierceness that sometimes flooded Savitha's eyes. She thought about the view of the temple from the window of her hut. She thought about her mixing rice and buttermilk with banana, and how, when she'd finally asked her for a bite, Savitha, with a wide grin, had rolled a bit of dripping rice into a ball between her fingers, and instead of handing it to her, she'd fed her. Raised the bite to Poornima's mouth, so that she'd touched the very tip of her fingers with her tongue. As if she were a child. As Amma might've done. But with Savitha, there was no illness to mar the gesture, no dying; she was alive, more alive than anyone she'd ever known. She made even the smallest of life seem grand, and for Poornima, who had always ached for something more than the memory of a comb in her hair, more than the chiming of a blue clock, or a voice that she tried so often to conjure, watching Savitha, watching her *delight*, was like cultivating her own. And even in her daily duties—cooking, going to the well for water, washing dishes, scrubbing clothes, sitting for endless hours at the charkha—she found a sudden and glimmering satisfaction. Perhaps even joy. Though what surprised her most was that she could no longer imagine her life without her. Who had she talked to at meals before Savitha? What had she done on Sundays? Who had she cooked for? Her father, who was slow to notice most things, had said the previous evening, "That Savitha seems like a good girl. She's a hard worker, that's for sure." Then he'd turned back to his tobacco and said, "Shouldn't let a girl like that run around. Should get her married. How old is she? Too old to run around, I'd say. No telling."

No telling, Poornima repeated to herself. No telling what?

Her father looked at her. "They'll be here tomorrow. Probably in the afternoon."

"Who?"

"The boy from Repalle. His family."

"Tomorrow?"

"Here." Her father handed her a few rupees. "Send your brother out for snacks in the morning. Pakoras, maybe." Poornima stared at him. "Don't just stand there. Take it."

In the morning, when Poornima told her, Savitha only smiled. "It'll come to nothing," she said.

"How do you know?"

"Because these things always do."

"What things?"

Savitha pointed at the sky. "Things that are not ordained. That are broken before they ever begin."

"But—they're on their way. Gopi is out buying pakoras."

She smiled again. "A few mornings ago, I was on my way to your house. I was crossing Old Tenali Road, you know, where all the lorries pass on their way to the highway. As I was crossing by the paan shop, I heard a thump. More like a quick thud. I didn't think much of it. But I did turn around to look, and when I did, I saw an owl on the road. It had obviously been hit. One of its wings looked wrong, just *wrong*. Do you know what I mean? It looked dead. Or sleeping. But no, it was awake, Poori. *Awake*. More awake than anything I've ever seen. It was not making a sound. No calling, no whimpering. Do birds whimper? Anyway, none of that. It was just sitting there, fallen there, in the middle of the road. With all the bicycles and people and lorries whisking by it. One lorry even went right over it. But the owl just sat there. Its eye—the one facing me—like a marble. A perfect black-and-gold marble. Reflecting everything. I was now close, you see, bending over it, wondering what I could do to help it. But what could I do? Its shattered wing was awful. Like a lonesome day. Like hunger. But as I looked at it, I realized it was *saying* something to me. It was trying to tell me something. I swear. And you know what it was? What it was trying to say?"

Poornima said nothing.

"Owl things. Things I couldn't possibly understand. They were dying words, the words of the dying, but spoken in an another language. A silent one. But it was also saying something else, something to me. It was saying, The man from Repalle doesn't matter. You'll be together. (He was talking about you and me, of course.) That's the way it is: If two people want to be together, they'll find a way. They'll *forge* a way. It may seem ludicrous, even stupid, to work so hard at something that is, truly, a matter of chance, completely arbitrary, such as staying *with* someone—as if 'with' and 'apart' have meaning in and of themselves—but, the owl said (and by now, Savitha added, the owl was sighing, maybe wheezing, nearing death), But that's the thing with you humans. You think too much, don't you?"

"Wait," Poornima said. "The owl said all this to you?"

"Yes."

"So, it knows me? It knows you? It knows the man from Repalle?"

"Knew. It's probably dead by now."

"Okay. Knew."

"Yes."

"Yes?"

Savitha returned her gaze, unblinking, and said, "Yes."

The marriage viewing took place that evening. They arrived a little after six o'clock. There was the groom, who was apprenticed in the sari shop, along with his mother, father, Ramayya, and an uncle and aunt. Though the uncle and aunt could have been an older cousin and his wife. It was hard to tell, and Poornima never found out for sure. She was in the weaving hut, where the looms were located, when they arrived. Her father's sister was helping her with her sari—cream-colored cotton with a green border, which had belonged to her mother—and tying a garland of jasmine to her hair. Poornima had oiled it that morning, the coconut still scenting her fingertips, and the kumkum leaving a thin film of powder on them as if she'd caught a red butterfly. Her aunt yanked at her hair as she braided it, pulling the strands with such force that Poornima squealed in pain.

"Shush," her aunt scolded. "One boy already fallen through. The shame. How do you think it looks for a girl? Huh? Thank the Lord Vishnu he never laid eyes on you. That would've been the end. Your poor father. First he loses a wife, five kids on his own, and now *this*. Working his fingers to the bone. But this one will work out. You'll see." She lathered Poornima's face with a thick coating of talcum powder. She reapplied the kumkum and kajal. And then she took the gold bangles off her own wrists and squeezed them onto Poornima's. "There," her aunt said, taking a step or two back. "Now, keep your eyes down, and only speak when spoken to. Don't get frisky. Just answer their questions. And try to sing. If they ask you, sing something. A devotional ballad is good. Simple, so you don't mess it up."

Poornima nodded.

Her aunt then led her out of the weaving hut, around the back of the main hut, and into the front, where they were all seated. She nudged Poornima onto the straw mat, on which were also seated the groom's mother and aunt or cousin. The groom's father was seated in the chair, while all the other men were seated on the edge of the hemp-rope bed. Pleasantries were exchanged with Poornima's aunt, whom the aunt or cousin seemed to be acquainted with. Then the groom's mother reached over and touched the gold bangles. "Not very thick," she said.

"Yes, well," Ramayya said lightheartedly, "all that can be discussed later."

The woman smiled, let go of the bangles reluctantly, and said, "What's your name, dear?"

Poornima lifted her gaze to the woman she assumed would be her future mother-in-law. She was fat, well-fed, her stomach above the waistline of her sari rested as round and moist as a clay pot. Her nails and teeth were yellow. "Poornima," she replied. She liked that she'd called her dear. But she disliked the timbre in her voice, was suspicious of it; it'd gone too easily between the thickness of the gold bangles and her name, as if they were one and the same, as if they were part of the same inquiry, the same pursuit.

"Ask her, Ravi," the groom's aunt or cousin said. "Ask her something."

The groom was sitting on the edge of the bed; Poornima saw only his shoes (brown sandals) and the cuff of his pants (gray, with pinstripes). His ankles—the only part of his body that was in her view—were dark, the hair on them wiry and thick. "Can you sing?" he said.

She cleared her throat. A devotional song, she told herself. Think of a devotional song. But then her mind drew a blank. Not a blank, not exactly. What she thought of was the owl. The dying owl that had spoken to Savitha. What had it said? Something about finding a way, forging it. What would she do in Repalle, alone, without Savitha? That question seemed greater than any other question she'd ever been asked. Greater than all other questions put together. "I can't," she said. "I can't sing."

Her aunt gasped. "Of course you can," she said, laughing nervously. "Remember that one. That one we sing at the temple. About Rama and Sita and—"

"I remember it. I remember it perfectly. I just can't sing it. Like I said, I can't sing."

Ramayya rose a little, his eyes wide. "Shy. That's all. Such a shy girl."

The groom cleared his throat. The aunt or the cousin said, "Well, that's all right. Singing's not all that important. She can cook, right? How many canisters can you spin on the charkha per day?"

"Four, five."

"Now, see," the woman said, "that's not bad."

"Swapna can spin eight," the groom's mother said. "And that's *with* the baby."

The conversation went on like that. They finished their tea, all the pakoras, and most of the jilebi, leaving only bits of sugar syrup on the plate. They talked about the lack of rain, and about how the trains from Repalle were always late, they talked about the price of peanuts and mangoes and rice, and then they talked about the new government, and how prices had been cheaper, and the quality of the produce better, when the Congress party had been in power. Her aunt then led Poornima out of the room. She was scolded, as she knew she would be. "You fool," her aunt said. "Who'll marry some-one like you? Who'll marry someone so wicked? Thank the Lord Vishnu your mother wasn't here. It would've killed her. A daughter so terrible. Don't you see? It has nothing to *do* with whether you can sing, you fool. They just want to make certain that you will *listen*. That you'll be obedient. And now they know. They know you're wicked."

When Poornima told Savitha the next day, she laughed. "That's it! That's how we do it." Then she pushed a strand of hair that had fallen across Poorn-ima's face and said, "That's it. We're safe."

4

A heat wave settled into Indravalli in the days after the marriage viewing. Poornima began getting up in the dark to do the morning chores. Getting water at the well, cooking for the day, sweeping and washing—all of it had to be done before the sun came up. Once the sun touched the horizon, licked even the mere tip of it, the earth burned as if lit on fire. The air, through the mornings and afternoons, was still and hot, searing; a thin breeze drifted along in the evenings, but that too was hardly a whimper. Poornima sat at the charkha in the afternoons, spinning listlessly, and waited for dinnertime. She couldn't visit Savitha during the day, while she was at the loom: her father was in the weaving hut, too, watching them from his own loom. In the afternoons, she took their tea to them, but she and Savitha hardly exchanged a glance. Besides, Poornima's father was furious. The Repalle family was now demanding an even larger dowry, *double* what had previously been discussed. "Double," her father hissed, "for your insolence." They'd also asked for a set of gold bangles for their daughter, the groom's younger sister. "*Gold,*" her father repeated, "gold, gold, gold. Do you understand? Gold. How do you suppose I get the money to buy gold?" His eyes, already bloodshot and inflamed from the heat, gaped at his daughter. "And I've got another one after you. In what? Two or three years? And that friend of yours. Savitha. What do you think she asked me the other day? She asked me if she could use the loom, after work. Come in early, leave later. *My* loom. And she asked, just like that, as if I owed it to her." He shook his head, swiping at a mosquito on his arm. "It's your audacity," he said. "It's the audacity of you girls, you modern girls, that will be your ruin. That will be *my* ruin."

"Why?" Poornima asked.

"Why what?"

"Why does she want to come in extra?"

"How should I know?" her father said. "Why don't you ask her?" Poornima stood looking at him. He slapped at another mosquito. "Well, don't just stand there. Get me the swatter."

She asked Savitha the next day at lunch. The air in the hut was liquid; it throbbed white and raw with heat. Flies buzzed listlessly, lifting a little off the ground and then settling back, as if exhausted from the effort. Savitha was sweating from sitting at the loom. Beads of perspiration stood at her hairline, studded her collarbone. Poornima could smell the scent of her body: jungled, musky. Not the slightest whiff of laundry cake or a bit of sandalwood soap or even talcum powder. Animal: that was her scent.

Savitha stopped eating and listened as Poornima told her about the Repalle people, and how they were asking for more dowry. "Can your father give it to them?"

"I don't think so. He can barely afford the dowry he's offering now."

"So it's done."

Poornima shrugged. "Maybe. Everyone is furious, though."

"Because you wouldn't *sing*? What are we? Trained monkeys?"

Poornima didn't answer. Instead, she said, "Why do you want to work longer at the loom? Why did you ask my father if you could?"

Savitha took a bite of her rice and sambar. Her eyes twinkled. "I'm making you something. I'm making you a sari. That's why I asked your father if I could use the loom. Do you think he'll let me?"

"A sari? But how? Where will you get the thread? How will you make two saris at once? You can't."

"That's why I wanted to come in extra. I'll finish the sari for your father by working after hours. And then, when that's done, I can start yours on a Saturday night, work all day Sunday, and have it done by Monday morning. And the threads? I got those from the collective. They had extra. Apparently somebody dyed them the wrong color. Indigo. They can't dye over it, or they don't want to. Either way, they gave it to me for cheap."

"A sari in *one* day?"

"Two, if I work day and night."

"That's ridiculous. You can't work without sleeping for two days. Besides, why? Why do you want to make me a sari?"

"It'll be my wedding present to you. You will eventually get married, you know. Not to this guy in Repalle, I hope. I hope it's somebody in Indravalli. But when you do, I can't afford to give you anything else. Besides, look at this," she said, holding up a handful of rice. "No one has ever cooked for me. My mother must've, but I don't remember it. As long as I can remember, I've cooked for myself, and for my parents and brothers and sisters. And the bananas. I know you save your money to buy them for me. But it's not just the cooking. It's everything. Everything. From the way you sit and spin the charkha, as if you weren't spinning thread at all, but as if you were spinning the strangest stories, the loveliest dreams. And the way you set the tea down next to me when I'm at the loom. And the way you hold the pot of water when we're walking back from the well, as if nothing, nothing in the world, could match the finery, the fineness, of that pot of water. Don't you see, Poori? Everything else is so bland, so colorless, except you. But that indigo." She smiled. "The least I can do is make you a sari. I *know* how to do that. And a few sleepless nights won't matter. Imagine when I see it on you."

Poornima wanted to get up, pull Savitha up from her plate, and embrace her. No one—not ever—had thought to *make* something for her. Her mother, of course, but she was dead. And the weight of her mother's hand, holding the comb in her hair, was all she had left of her. At times, many times, she gripped that memory, that weight, as if it alone could guide her through dark and savage forest paths, and eventually, she hoped, into a clearing, but it wasn't true. It couldn't. All that memory could do was give small solace. One drop after another after another, like the glucose drip that had punctured and bled her mother's arm when she'd been in the hospital. It had been nothing. Not really. Sugar. They had dripped sugar into her. "To keep her strength up," the doctors had said. As if sugar were a stand against cancer. But *Savitha*, Savitha wanted to make her a sari. A sari she could wind around her body and hold to her face. Not a memory, not a scent, not a thing that drifts away. But a sari. She could take that sari and weep into it, she could stretch it across a rooftop, a hot sand, wear it to the Krishna and wade into its waters, she could wrap herself in its folds, cocoon herself against the night, she could sleep, she could dream.

5

The owl was right: negotiations with the family from Repalle fell apart. They refused to budge from their dowry demands, though Ramayya did get them to agree to accept one gold bangle for the sister instead of two. "One, two. What does it matter? I can't afford half a gold bangle. Let alone the dowry," her father said.

"They've seen her. That's the thing," Ramayya said. When Poornima brought Ramayya his tea, he looked at her with such distaste that she thought he might fling the tea back in her face. She moved away. "Shy," he said with disgust. "You're not shy. You're rude. You and your father are lucky I'm still willing to help. Word's gotten around, you know. Everyone between here and the Godavari knows about you. Who would want you now?"

When Ramayya left, Poornima's father slapped her, hard. Then he grabbed her by the hair. He said, "You see this? You see what you've done?" His grip on her hair tightened and he said, "The next time somebody asks you to sing, what're you going to do?"

Poornima blinked. She held back tears. Her scalp burned, hairs snapped like electric wires. Her brothers and sister crowded around the door of the hut to see. "What?" he growled. "What will you do? Say it. *Say it.*"

"Sing," she whispered, wincing in pain. "I'm going to sing."

He let go with a shove, and Poornima fell forward. She knocked against the steel cups in which she'd served the tea, and her hand split open. One of her brothers ran to get a rag, and she tied it around her hand. The blood soaked through, and there was still dinner to prepare. She sent them out to play and leaned against the wall of the hut. It was the eastern wall. Across from her was a high window. Through it, beyond Indravalli Konda, she could see the setting sun. Not the sun itself, but pink and yellow and orange clouds, thin, their ends sharp as knives, rushing toward the mountain as if they meant to bring it to its knees. How delusional, she thought: as if those useless bits of fluff could maim a mountain.

She closed her eyes. The pain in her hand, her scalp, her face where he'd slapped her, none of them she even noticed. They were still there, but she could no longer feel them. Her body swam, slowly, as if through a thick and sedimental sea. It's the heat, she thought, but the heat wave had passed. It was April, and though the temperatures had lessened some—although stepping outside in the afternoons was still unwise—the heat would not completely abate, not until July when the monsoons arrived. Until then, the air was stifling. The hut was stifling. Poornima could hardly breathe. She wanted to cry, but her body felt as dry as a coconut husk. The heat having sapped everything, even tears.

And it was only April.

Savitha saw the cut on her hand, the bruise on her face when she came in for lunch the next afternoon, and was livid. "Don't you worry," she said, fuming.

"Worry about what?" Poornima asked.

"Nothing. Don't you worry about a thing." Then she laid Poornima's head in her lap, she brushed the hair from her face, and she said, "Do you want to hear a story?"

Poornima nodded.

"What kind of story?"

"You're the one who asked."

"All right, but an old story or a new one?"

"A new one."

"Why?"

Poornima thought for a moment. Savitha's lap was warm, though a little uneven, like sleeping on a lumpy bed. "Because I'm sick of old things. Like Ramayya. And this hut." She raised her hand to her face, the cut still open on her palm. Curved, like a clay pot. "I want something new."

"In that case, once upon a time," Savitha began, "though not very long ago, since you want a new story—once upon a time, an elephant and the rain had an argument. The elephant was proud. It walked proudly around the forest. It ate whatever it wanted, reaching high into the trees, scaring away all the other animals. It was so proud that one day the elephant looked up, saw the rain, and declared, 'I don't need you. You don't nourish me. I don't need you at all.' The rain, after hearing this, looked sadly back at the elephant and said, 'I will go away, and then you will see.' So the rain went away. The elephant watched it go and had an idea. He saw a nearby lagoon filled with water and he knew that without rain, it would soon dry up." Here, Savitha stopped. Poornima lifted her head from her lap and sat up.

"So what was it? What was his idea?" Poornima asked.

Savitha turned to face her. She smiled. "The elephant, you see, saw a poor old crow walking along the forest path, looking for grubs, and ordered him to guard the lagoon. 'Only *I* may drink from the lagoon,' he told the crow. So the old crow sat and sat and guarded the lagoon. Eventually there came a monkey and said, 'Give me water!' and the crow answered, 'The water belongs to elephant.' The monkey shook its head and went away.

"Then came a hyena and said, 'Give me water!' and the crow answered, 'The water belongs to elephant.'

"Along came a cobra and said, 'Give me water!' and the crow answered, 'The water belongs to elephant.'

"Then came a jungle cat and said, 'Give me water!' and the crow answered, 'The water belongs to elephant.'

"Then came a bear and a crocodile and a deer. They all asked for water and the old crow always gave the same answer. Finally, there came a lion. The lion said, 'Give me water!' and the crow answered, 'The water belongs to elephant.' When the lion heard this he roared; he grabbed the poor crow by the neck and beat him. Then he took a long, refreshing drink from the lagoon and walked away into the forest.

"When the elephant returned, he saw that the lagoon had dried up. 'Crow,' he said, 'Where is the water?' The old crow looked down sadly and said, 'Lion drank it.' The elephant was enraged. He said angrily, 'I told you not to let anybody else drink from the lagoon. As punishment, shall I chew you up, or simply swallow you whole?'

"'Swallow me whole, if you please,' the crow said.

"So the elephant swallowed the crow. But once the crow entered the elephant's body, the crow—our little crow—tore at the elephant's liver and kidneys and heart until the elephant died, writhing in pain. Then the crow simply emerged from the elephant's body and walked away."

Savitha was silent.

Poornima looked at her. "What about the rain?" she said.

"The rain?"

"Did it come back? Did it fill the lagoon again?"

"The rain doesn't matter."

"No?"

"No."

"But what about—"

"That doesn't matter either."

"It doesn't?"

"No," Savitha said. "Here's what matters. Understand this, Poornima: that it's better to be swallowed whole than in pieces. Only then can you win. No elephant can be too big. Only then no elephant can do you harm."

They grew silent.

Savitha went back to her loom, and Poornima, washing up after lunch, looked at the wound on her hand, open again now from scrubbing dishes, and she thought about her father, she thought about the old crow, and then she thought, Please, Nanna. If you swallow me, swallow me whole.

6

Savitha began working longer hours. She was fast, but orders for the wedding season were even larger than expected. She came in early in the morning and left late at night, working harder than any man Poornima's father had known. Sometimes, Savitha caught him eyeing her greedily—as if he were already counting the coins she was minting for him. She didn't mind. "He's paying me extra," she said to Poornima. "Besides, once the rush ends, I'll be able to make yours." She was trying to cheer her, but Poornima only looked back at her sadly. Ramayya arrived every evening at teatime and proclaimed defeat. One night, she told Savitha, she'd stood behind the door of the hut and listened. "No one will have her. No one," he declared to her father. "They've all heard. The minute they hear her name, *your* name, they shake their heads and say they're not interested. And dark, on top of it. Word travels, after all. No, we might have to increase the dowry. *Some* poor fool will need the money."

Savitha said to her, "Come over tomorrow. I want to show you something." When she did, Savitha showed her the bales of indigo thread for her sari. "It's not completely paid for, but the collective gave me credit." She held it against Poornima's skin. "Like the night sky," she said, smiling. "And you the full moon." Poornima, too, managed a smile. She offered her tea, and when Poornima refused, Savitha turned to a corner of the hut and said, "Nanna, do you want some?"

Poornima swung around. There was an old man sitting in the corner of the room. Huddled. He'd been quiet all this time, invisible. There seemed to be movement, and Poornima thought to say, No, please don't get up on my account, but then she saw that he was trembling. Then there came a grunt, maybe the broken half of a word, and, as if in response, Savitha poured out some tea into a steel cup. She went over to her father and cradled his head as she held the cup to his lips. He caught Poornima's eye. He said, in a hoarse whisper, but strong, stronger than Poornima would've thought possible in a man who looked so weak, "You see that? You see the temple?" He was pointing out of the small window, at Indravalli Konda. "They can see us, just as we can see them. I've looked. I've stood on the steps of the temple and looked. The door of this shithole looks just as mysterious, just as inviting as that door does from here."

"Drink," Savitha said.

The old man—too old to be Savitha's father; he looked more like her grandfather—said, "I did too much of that. Too much, don't you think?"

Savitha tipped the glass. A drop of tea dribbled out. He pulled his hand out from under the blanket, instinctively, and Poornima stepped back in horror. It was a bundle of broken twigs, the fingers smooth but twisted. Savitha saw the look on Poornima's face. "Joint disease," she said.

"That's not right. Not joint disease. That's too easy. You see this here?" He raised his hand into the air and sunlight touched its very tip, like the top branches of a tree. "This is freedom. This is the human spirit, perfected. If we were all born like this there would be no war. We would live like brothers, afraid to touch each other. Do you know, Savitha, what I saw the other day? And what is your name?" When Poornima told him, he said, "Do you know there are some places in the world where people's names have no meanings? It's true. Can you imagine? What kind of places are they? Empty, that's what I say. Empty and sad. A name without *meaning*, it's like having night without day. There are places like that, too, I've heard. Now, what was I saying? Savitha, the tea's cold," he said, laughing. "You see. I talk too much. Far too much. Mondhoo kept me quiet. Mondhoo kept the words quiet, chained to a tree. Oh, yes! What I saw the other day. Why, now I can't remember." He laughed, copiously and happily, like a child.

Poornima liked him. She didn't care what he'd meant to say, nor did she have any idea what he meant by words being chained to a tree, but she liked him because he was so unlike her own father. Unlike Ramayya, unlike any man she'd ever met. She forgot, then, and for the entire walk home, that she was dark, that she was unmarriageable, that there was not enough money for her dowry, that there was a poverty even greater than her own.

Ramayya was jubilant when he came over the following week. He nearly danced through the door. It was the beginning of May. The wells were dry. The streams were choked with dust. The level of the Krishna was so low that laundresses from either shore walked to the middle of the river to share gossip. After two weeks, and after a few children had died of dysentery, the municipal government brought in water in massive tanks. Lines formed around the tanks—sometimes a hundred, two hundred people long. People watched the sky for the slightest hint of a cloud. Even a thin one, the most trivial strip, would have them holding their breath, waiting for rain. Everyone knew the monsoons wouldn't come until June or July, but someone had heard of a bit of rainfall in Vizag, just enough to fill the streams. Maybe it would come down the coast.

But Ramayya seemed unconcerned. "Poornima," he yelled out as soon as he was within earshot, "bring me a glass of water, would you? My throat is parched. And for my feet. Enough to wash my feet. Look at all this dust. I practically ran here."

Water? Poornima wondered. She looked into each of the empty clay water pots and scraped the bottom of one to fill a small glass. When she took it to him, he was already engrossed in conversation with her father. "He's perfect. I haven't talked to the family yet, but he's perfect."

"Who's perfect?" Poornima asked.

"Who do you think? Go do something. Go find something to do."

Poornima walked back into the hut and stood just inside the door.

"Would you believe it? I didn't even have to go very far. Just to Namburu. The boy's grandparents were weavers. Did well, it seems. Bought up a sizable chunk of land around Namburu. They were farmers, before independence, but now they've sold most of it. Made plenty, too. He has two younger sisters. They're looking for matches for the older one, our Poornima's age, but seems she's a bit picky. Well, they can afford it."

Poornima heard her father say, "What does the boy do?"

"An accountant!" Ramayya said jubilantly. "He studied. There's no money in weaving. You know that. None at all."

"How much do they want?"

"That's just it—they're within our range. Well, almost. But I've heard we might be able to talk them down."

"Talk them down?"

Here, Poornima heard shuffling. When Ramayya finally spoke, his voice was lowered. "There's nothing *wrong* with him. Nothing like that." More shuffling, a further drop.

"But what *is* it?" Poornima's father's voice rose with suspicion.

"Our girl's no catch, you know. So no need to be so dubious. Just a small affectation. An *idiosyncrasy*. Nothing to worry about. That's just what I heard, mind you, and really, who knows."

Savitha squealed with delight. She took Poornima in her arms. "So you're getting married! *And* he lives in Namburu. That's not far at all. It's right here. I could *walk* there."

"Yes," Poornima said. "Maybe." Then she was silent. Then she asked, "What does *idiosyncrasy* mean?"

Poornima stood outside her hut and looked at the palm trees. They caught the breeze, a slight one, just enough to rustle the topmost fronds. The other plants that surrounded the hut—a neem tree, a struggling guava, a vine of winter squash—all looked exhausted. They drooped. They sulked hopelessly in the heat. There had been no rain—it was absurd to think there would be. It was only mid-May. The temperature hovered somewhere near thirty-nine degrees Celsius in the mornings, rising to forty-one or forty-two in the afternoons. Shade—that elusive place—was without meaning. The hut broiled like it was set on a frying pan.

Information, as Ramayya learned of it, trickled in. He'd talked to the parents and they had said their son would not be ready to marry for another two months; exams, they'd said. The timing was perfect. That would be just after Poornima's mother's one-year death ceremony. The son's name was Kishore. He was twenty-two years old. "I haven't met him yet," Ramayya said, "but there's no condition that *they* mentioned. He seemed perfectly fine. College. An accountant. What else could our Poornima possibly hope for?"

"Do they want to see the girl? They must. Don't they?" Poornima's father asked.

"Of course. Of course," Ramayya assured him. "No telling when the boy will be able to come, though. Like I said, exams."

"And the dowry?"

"Settled."

It was decided that they—the parents, at least—would come at the end of May. If the visit went smoothly, there would be a full month to plan the wedding, and then, at the end of June, would be the ceremony. June! "But it's so *soon*," Poornima said.

Savitha was already busy with plans. "Exactly. That's just it. I hardly have time to finish all the saris. And I still have to make yours. What do you think of a red border? I think red would be nice with the indigo. I can hardly wait! You. Married. Do you mind if I spend the night sometimes? That would make things easier. I could stay at the loom as long as I wanted."

Poornima asked her father later that evening, and he said, "Fine, fine," hardly hearing her as he rolled his evening tobacco.

And so Savitha began spending nights. They slept together on the same mat—they had none to spare. Despite the sweltering nights, Poornima liked the feel of Savitha's body close to hers. She liked how Savitha seemed to savor everything, even the most mundane. "Look at the sky!" she would exclaim. "Have you ever seen so many stars?"

"It's too hot to look at the sky."

Savitha would then take Poornima's hand and squeeze it. "My amma said we might have enough money by next year. For my sister's dowry. Two more after her, but that's *something*, don't you think?"

Poornima nodded into the dark. She thought then she might tell Savitha about her mother, and the chiming clock with the blue face, but she didn't. Her father might hear. She lay still and listened to the breathing of her brothers and sister, and it occurred to her that she might've never met Savitha had her mother been alive. She saw no betrayal in it: her mother had died, and here was Savitha. But what she did wonder about was Kishore, her future husband. They had sent a photograph. Ramayya had brought it and showed it to them. But it was of him as a boy, maybe eight or nine. He was standing in a row with his sisters, one on either side. They were posed in front of a photographer's canvas of a glowing white palace and fountains and gardens. Above them was a crescent moon. Clouds approached the moon, wispy and romantic. Poornima stared intently at the little boy's face. It was a perfect oval. The mouth a small almond. One of his hands hung listlessly at his side, as if his fingers ached for the toys or the marbles or the toffee he'd been forced to set aside. The other hand was behind his back. His face was the most childlike. Soft, with the features of a baby still clinging to it. Poornima liked that. She then studied his eyes, trying to see into them, or at least see something *in* them, but they were empty. Barren. As if he were looking into an abyss. A strange land. "It's a *photo*," Savitha scolded. "What *do* you expect to see? His heart?"

Yes, Poornima wanted to reply. I want to see his heart.

This time, during the viewing, Poornima was allowed no mistakes. She understood—dressed again in the same silk sari belonging to her mother, though the blooms of jasmine were different, garlanded this time with an alternating row of orange kankabaram—that she was absolutely being monitored. Her aunt sat closer to her. Instead of being led out by the elbow, like the previous viewing, her aunt placed one hand on her braid, as if prepared to yank it at any moment. When she sat down on the mat, her father smiled at her. Smiled. But it was not a smile of encouragement or love or paternal feeling. The smile said only one thing: I'm watching. I'm watching, and the first sign of defiance—the first glimmer in your eyes *leading* to defiance— will be acted upon. Acted upon how? Poornima bent her head and shuddered to think.

Still, she had no plans of ruining this viewing. The groom wasn't there—studying for exams, his father said—but his parents, the middle sister, and a distant cousin who lived in Indravalli were there. Poornima raised her eyes just enough, after looking at her father, to see that *his* father seemed small next to hers, shy and hesitant. The mother, seated across from Poornima, was fat and boorish, maybe from the heat or the bus ride from Namburu to Indravalli, though her eyes were flinty and exacting. The sister, who sat to Poornima's side, looked at her askance and hardly said a word. Her gaze was like her mother's: scrutinizing, vain and impatient, cold. But they were both plump, and Poornima liked that; fatness indicated to her a certain jolliness or abandon, certainly a richness. The sister reached out and took Poornima's hand and rubbed the fingers roughly, one after another, as if counting them. Then she let go and smiled coolly. The men continued to chat, and Poornima, silent and awkward for the remainder of the viewing, nearly embraced her future mother-in-law when, just before they were to leave, she took Poornima's chin in her hand—not gently; no, she couldn't say it was gentle, but it was with what Poornima thought was genuine feeling—and said, "No, you're not nearly as dark as they said."

The sister snorted, or was it a guffaw? Then they left.

She told Savitha about the viewing that night. Savitha had gone home to help her mother with the cooking and had returned before dark. She sat at the loom for another hour, and when she came in for her dinner, Poornima already had her plate ready. She'd made roti, with potato curry. There was a bit of yogurt and leftover rice from lunch. "But they didn't ask you to *sing*," Savitha said. "I like them already. Is there any pickle?" When Poornima rose to get it, she said, "And what about the groom? What about him?"

"Exams," Poornima said. Then she grew quiet. "What if we have nothing to talk about? I mean, he's in *college*, after all. He'll think I'm stupid, won't he? He'll think I'm just a villager. A bumpkin. And what *is* accounting? That thing he's studying?"

"Numbers," Savitha said. "It's numbers. Your father gives you money, doesn't he? To buy food. And you go to the market, don't you, and get change. And you keep a log. I've seen it. A log of all the expenses, so you can show them to your father every week? That's accounting. That's all it is. Besides, Namburu is smaller than Indravalli. He's more of a villager than we are."

Poornima was unconvinced. That couldn't be *all* it was.

The wedding preparations began. There were still details of the dowry and wedding gifts to work out, but Ramayya was confident he could convince them to lower their demands. Savitha raced to finish the sari orders so she would have enough time to make Poornima's. Kishore, her groom, was scheduled to take his exams at the end of the month. But first, there was Poornima's mother's one-year death ceremony. It was set for the beginning of June. It included a day of feasting. A goat would be slaughtered, and the priest would conduct a puja. Her father would perform a ritualistic lighting of a funeral pyre. During the days that followed, Poornima watched her father anxiously: his mood darkened. She guessed it was from the memory of her mother's death, or the dowry demands. He said it was because they were falling behind on the sari orders. "Doesn't she know we have work to do?" he'd say if Savitha went home for even an hour or two in the evenings. "Tell her I'll pay her extra for staying longer. I can't afford much. Hardly any to spare. But some," he said.

The day of the ceremony, when it arrived, brought a drop in temperature along the entire coast of Andhra Pradesh. Poornima woke that morning and realized there was a breeze. Not a cool breeze, not really, but she rejoiced. Her mother must be watching. She must be speaking. She must be saying, Poornima, I'm happy. Your marriage will be a good one. She must be saying, I miss you, too. And that comb, she must be saying, I hold it still.

The young goat to be slaughtered was tethered to a pole outside the hut. It was brown and white; the white in bands, one around its midsection, around each hoof, and another patch dropping down its head and between its eyes. Poornima tried to feed it some dry, dead grass she'd plucked outside the hut. The goat sniffed it and then looked at her. Its eyes were dark globes, and its gaze curious—to see if she had any other food—but when it saw that she didn't, it looked away. Poornima knew she shouldn't look at it for too long, that looking would only increase her sympathy for the doomed goat, but its smell was what kept her there: urine and wilderness and hay.

She thought of its smell when she watched it being slaughtered. The knife—clearly not sharp enough—had to be run back and forth across its neck as if it were a loaf of tough bread. In order to hold it down, they forced the goat onto its side, and one man sat on the hind part of its body, while two others each held a pair of legs. Another man held a bucket under its neck. But there was no need to have done all that. The goat, struggling at first, and then seeing the knife, or perhaps *sensing* the knife, let its body go limp. Losing hope, Poornima thought, or maybe losing nerve. The first slice of the knife left it bucking in pain, one quick surge that ran the length of its body and then came to rest. The knife drove deeper, but the goat still blinked, looking now into a grayness, Poornima guessed, a falling darkness, the globes now losing their light. Its tail wagged one last time, the muscles no longer beholden to their master, and the man who was sawing its neck put his thumb into the mouth of the young goat. Poornima wondered whether he meant to do it, to give the goat one last comfort, one last suck-ling, or whether it was simply accidental. The goat was dead a moment after. First its body, then its blinking. But something of it seemed to Poornima to go on for a moment longer, an energy, a feeling of life; and then that, too, went away.

The smell—the urine and wilderness and hay scent of the goat—was drowned out by the scent of copper and other metals Poornima couldn't exactly name: the smell of her hands after she'd lifted the bucket at the well, the smell of the freshly scrubbed pots, the smell of river water and silt. It was also hot, the scent, and flies gathered around the goat in great armies. They drank and drank, as armies do, and then they settled on the flesh.

That night, Poornima lay awake for a long while. She thought she would be kept awake by images of the goat, the globes of its eyes, but she wasn't. She was instead thinking of her mother. They had, when she was nine or ten, set out to visit Poornima's maternal grandparents' village. Kaza was a two-hour bus ride away, and she and her mother had started early, hoping to be back by nightfall. Her mother had woken her while it was still dark and washed Poornima's hair, then scrubbed her with a cleansing powder that left her skin red and tender. Then she'd had Poornima put on her best langa, red bangles, and silver anklets, which had been part of her mother's dowry; on the way to the bus stop, her mother had splurged on two pink roses, one for each of their braids. The bus ride had started a little after seven A.M. It was packed with people. They sat in the front, in the women's section, with the back reserved for men. Poornima stepped over chickens, over bundles of produce and kindling that cluttered the aisle; babies wailed and fussed. She sat next to her mother and looked out the window. She'd rarely been on a bus, and the speed with which the fields spun past her window delighted her. She looked out and tried to count all the dogs and the pigs and the goats they passed. But there were so many she lost count, and started over with huts, and when even those became too many, she laughed and thought, Mountains, I'll count mountains.

But then, with a loud clank and a screech, the bus came to a halt. Everyone looked at everyone else. A few of the men in the back yelled out. The bus driver, seated calmly, upright, with a neat mustache and a freshly pressed khaki uniform, turned the engine. It ground but didn't catch. The voices in the back rose. "Aré, aré, maybe the RTC will send a car." "Sure they will," someone yelled back, "its name is Gowri and she runs on grass." The driver told them to shut up.

The bus driver got out—along with most of the men—and looked under the hood. Poornima heard the sound of a wrench or a metal pick clanging against the engine, maybe, and then it went still. The bus dropped. Actually sagged, as if it were suddenly too exhausted to go on. The women, too, exited the bus. The babies quiet now, alert.

The day was cool, late in October, and the morning chill still hung in the air.

Poornima got down with her mother. She'd brought a shawl with her and this she wrapped around Poornima. Most of the mothers had already settled on the side of the road, their children running or playing in the dirt. The men huddled around the open hood.

Poornima looked up and down the road. There was a bullock cart in the far distance, almost a haze, coming toward them. Women in colorful saris tucked between their legs dotted the fields, bent over the flooded rice paddies. There was a small temple, white against the emerald stalks of rice. She thought of that temple, and of the black carved deity inside, and the simple offering of a flower—maybe a pink rose, the kind that was in her hair—left at its feet. She settled, then, beside her mother. The men were now smoking their beedies, spitting, laughing, and the women minded the children. Another bus was due to go past in an hour or two, and they would all pile into that one, space allowing. Some would probably have to climb on top of the bus, or hang by the bar on the door. But for now, everyone seemed perfectly content to sit there by the side of the road. The sun like a small yellow bird, fluttering awake.

Poornima turned to her mother. She had never been alone with her; her father or brothers or sister had always been nearby, or just outside the hut. She was sent on errands for her mother, but never *with* her mother, and when they'd traveled to her grandparents' house in the past, one or more of her siblings had always been with them. In a kind of revelation—in the morning light, sitting on the red dirt by the side of the road—she saw that her mother was beautiful. Even with all the other young mothers crowded around, and the blossoming adolescent girls, youthful and lovely, giggling among themselves, her mother was still the most beautiful. Her eyes were deep black pools, with tiny silver fish gleaming in them when she laughed. Her hair curled at the nape of her neck in ringlets, and her lips were the pink of the rose. Even the dark circles under her eyes had a certain prettiness, as if they were gray crescents, moonlit, pulling in the light.

"Are you hungry?" her mother asked, opening the bundle of last night's rice and spiced yogurt and the dollop of mango pickle she'd brought from home.

"Yes," Poornima said.

And her mother, unthinkingly, her gaze not even on Poornima, but on the distant horizon, watching for the second bus, perhaps, or maybe the approaching bullock cart, took handfuls of rice, rolled them into balls in her palm, and—as she had when Poornima had been a small child—fed them to her. Poornima chewed. The rice, having been cradled in her mother's hand, tasted better than anything she'd ever eaten; she couldn't imagine a greater food. Her mother, though, still paid her no attention. Her thoughts were elsewhere. On her husband, maybe, or the children she'd left behind, or the chores she'd left undone. But for now, for these few moments, Poornima thought her mother's body was enough. It was more than she could ever ask for. To be fed by her hand, to sit next to her, so close she could feel the warmth of her skin in the chill of an October morning, and to know that life, its crowds, would soon separate them. But not now. For now, just until the next bus, her body belonged to Poornima. And when her mother finally noticed the tears brimming in her daughter's eyes, she stopped, looked at her quizzically, and then she smiled. "The bus will *be* here. Any minute now. There's no need to cry, is there? We won't be out here for much longer."

Poornima nodded, the rice having caught in her throat.

7

Savitha shook her awake early the next morning, while it was still dark. "Will you make tea?"

Poornima rolled off their mat. She folded the blankets, placed them on top of her pillow, and stacked them in the corner of the hut. Her father and brothers and sister were asleep.

"So early," she said, yawning, gathering her hair into a knot. "Why are you up so early?"

"That sari isn't going to make itself. Besides, your father said I could make extra if I finished six by your wedding day."

"*Six*? That's one sari every three days."

"Seven. I still have to make yours."

Poornima shook her head. She cut a branch off the neem tree and chewed on it. By the time Savitha was settled at her loom, Poornima brought in the tea. Savitha took a sip. She took another. "No sugar?"

"My father's saving everything for the wedding."

"Has he even seen you yet?"

Poornima shrugged. "I told you. He has exams."

"Exams, Poori? How can he dream of you if he hasn't seen you?"

Poornima blushed. And then she was confused. Her mother's one-year death ceremony had kept her occupied, for a time, but now she was back to wondering. It was not uncommon to marry someone without first seeing them, or hearing their voice, but it struck her as strange that Kishore, her groom, showed no *interest* in meeting her. His parents had already come twice to handle the dowry negotiations, the Indravalli cousin had stopped by last week for evening tea, and her father and Ramayya were going to Guntur in a few days to shop for the wedding, and yet he had never arrived, not even on his way home to Namburu from college. Not once. He actually had to pass *through* Indravalli to get there! She shook her head. It would be nice, she thought, to see him, but she couldn't insist. Insist to *whom*? Besides, it was a good match, as everyone said. A college-educated match; Poornima couldn't hope for more. And that idiosyncrasy that Ramayya had alluded to: no one had mentioned it again. It was probably nothing.

Poornima looked around her. Savitha had finished her tea; the empty cup rested on the dirt floor of the hut. She was working away at her loom. Sunlight flooded in, through the open eastern end of the hut, and Poornima wondered what he was doing this very instant, her groom. Was he watching the sun rise? Was he thinking of her?

She also wondered, at times, whether her father would miss her when she married and moved to Namburu, or wherever her new husband would find a job. Because it occurred to her, despite what Savitha said, that she could possibly move farther away than Namburu. Maybe to Guntur. Maybe as far away as Vizag. Regardless, she would no longer be here. Would her brothers and sister miss her? Her sister was now old enough to cook and clean; she was twelve, and she could perhaps, after a time, begin working on the charkha. At least for two or three years, until she, too, got married. Family—the thing that she and her father and her siblings were bound by— suddenly seemed strange to her. What had collected them like seashells on a beach? And placed them together, on a windowsill?

She thought, in the weeks leading to her wedding, that she would ask her father. Not whether he would miss her—*that* she obviously couldn't ask—but whether he would miss her mango pickle, say, or the stuffed egg-plant she made, his favorite. But then, Poornima thought, she didn't have to; she already knew the answer. It had come to her when she'd overheard him and Ramayya talking, and her father had told him a story Poornima had never heard before.

The story was about when she was little, just over a year old, and she and her parents had gone to the temple in Vijayawada. It had been raining all morning. It had been the day of her mundan, the offering of a baby's hair to the gods, and afterward, they'd found a covered spot, a fisherman's palm-frond shelter, on the shores of the Krishna. Poornima's mother had laid out the food for their lunch. By this time, the rain had slowed, he told Ramayya, but it was still gray, the mist still hovering over the river, which was only a few yards away. According to her father, while they had been busy laying out the lunch, Poornima had squirmed away. "Straight into the water," her father said. "Probably she followed a boat or some other kid into the water. She did that a lot. Followed whatever caught her eye." Within seconds, he continued, she was up to her neck. "Her mother panicked. I jumped up and ran as fast as I could. It was only a few steps, but it seemed to take ages. Ages. I held her in my sight, I willed her to stay right there. If I even said, if I even whispered, 'Don't move!' I was afraid she would move. Fall. Be taken by the river. So I didn't say anything. I just looked at her and willed her to be still." And she was, he told Ramayya, she was as still as a statue. Her newly shorn head gleaming under a break in the clouds.

When I got near the waterline though, he said, I stopped. I know I should've plucked her up and given her a slap, but I couldn't. You see, he said, she looked like she was nothing. Just a piece of debris. In that mist, in that gray, in that vast, slippery rush of water, she looked like nothing. Maybe the head of a fish tossed back in the water. Or a piece of driftwood, not even very big. I looked at her, he said, I looked and I looked, and I could hear her mother shouting, running toward me, but I couldn't move. I was standing there, and I was thinking. I was thinking: She's just a girl. Let her go. By then, her mother had come up from behind me, and she'd snatched her out. Poornima was crying, he said, her mother was crying, too. Maybe they both knew what I had thought. Maybe it was written on my face, he told Ramayya. And then her father had let out a little laugh. "That's the thing with girls, isn't it?" he'd said. "Whenever they stand on the edge of something, you can't help it, you can't. You think, Push. That's all it would take. Just one little push."

A week before the wedding, Ramayya brought an urgent message from Namburu. "What is it? What is it?" Poornima's father asked him, sitting on the edge of the hemp bed, holding a cup of weak, unsweetened tea, his eyebrows raised.

"It's the dowry," Ramayya said, shaking his head. "They want twenty thousand more." Ramayya's tea was sweetened, but he still looked up at Poornima as if she were the reason for this sudden demand.

"Twenty thousand! But *why*?"

"They must've heard. Something. Maybe from the Repalle people. Who knows what they've heard. But they know it's too late. You've committed, and you'll have to pay up."

Her father gave Poornima a look of such loathing that she backed into the hut. She thought of the mother from Namburu, and how her kind words had turned so quickly to dust; she thought of the resignation in the father's eyes, the sister's laugh. But where was *he*? she wondered. Where was the groom? And what had he to say about this sudden, inexplicable demand?

The next morning, Savitha announced with a smile, "I'm starting it this afternoon."

"Don't bother," Poornima said gloomily. Then she told her about the increased dowry demand, and how her father had said that even if he sold both of his looms, he'd still barely have enough.

"What will he do?"

Poornima shrugged and looked out at the blazing light of late morning.

The heat—after a slight cooling—had risen again like a wounded beast. Dripping, thrusting, moving across the plains of Andhra Pradesh with a hatred so intense it had killed more than three hundred people the previous week. Anytime after midmorning was far too hot to work; by afternoon, everyone slept from exhaustion, waking with sweat pooled around their bodies. Even so, and even with the heat, just as she'd said she would, Savitha began making the sari that afternoon. After lunch, while everyone else spread out their mats, she strung the loom with the indigo thread, with red thread along the border. "Sit with me," she said to Poornima. "Bring your mat in here." Poornima sat against one of the wooden poles until her eyes nearly closed, and then she dragged her mat inside.

They talked; Poornima stayed awake as long as she could, until her eyelids, in the searing heat of midday, closed like lead. Mostly, she listened to Savitha talk. She told Poornima that her father was sick. Sicker than he had been. She said most of the extra money she'd made over the past few weeks had gone toward his medicines. "But we may still have enough by next year," she said. Her face soft and ochered against the surrounding bright white of the sun, her braid pulled into a knot at the back of her head. Concentrated now, focused on the working of the loom.

Poornima heard it clattering, repetitive, and yet so like a lullaby. The swooshing of the shuttle felt like water washing over her, and Poornima closed her eyes. Savitha was telling her something. Something about one of her sisters, and how she'd scorched a pot of milk. And then she heard her saying that they were building a cinema hall in Indravalli. Maybe we can go to a cinema when you come to visit, she was saying. Floor seats, of course. But imagine, Poori, a cinema!

Poornima felt herself sink, sink like a stone. She knew she was asleep, but she could still hear Savitha's voice. It seemed to go on and on. Like the murmuring of wind, the fall of rain. And she heard her say, Don't forget a thing. Not one thing. If you forget, it's like you've joined the stone at the bottom of the sea. The one we're all tied to. So remember everything. Press it. Press it between the folds of your heart like a flower. And when you want to look, *really* want to look, Poori, hold it up against the light.

That night, Savitha let Poornima sleep. She sat at the loom alone. She adjusted her lantern so that the light fell on the sari, half done nearly. The indigo thread was simply the night, weaving itself into the sky, the stars. Her hands and her feet merely the day, watching it fall.

Her mind wandered. The clacking of the loom led her away. Back to her childhood. Back to what she had pressed into the folds of her own heart. What she now held up against the light.

And it was this: She was three, maybe four. Her father was doing odd jobs at the time, and on some days he would take her along, whenever her mother was busy cleaning or collecting. On this day, he was working for a rich family whose daughter was getting married. Her father's job was to make the tiny sugar molds shaped like birds. Savitha had no idea what the birds, hardly bigger than her hand, would be used for (decoration, her father told her, but how *could* they, she wondered, when they looked so tasty), so she sat quietly and watched the pot, and then the molds, hoping some of the sugar would dribble out. Her father had only been given a dozen molds, so the pot was left to simmer while they waited for each batch to harden. Once they set, he carefully lifted out each of the white sugar birds, their wings outstretched, and placed them in the sun to dry. She wondered whether she could lick one, just once, without anyone noticing, but when she looked over, her father was watching her. By now, he'd made nearly a hundred or so. She sat hunched by the birds for some minutes when she heard her father gasp; his eyes grew wide when she turned to him. He pointed. "Look. Look at that one. Its little wing is broken."

Savitha followed his finger. There! One of the birds, drying in the middle of the grid of birds, *did* have a wing that had broken off. She jumped up, alarmed. "What will we do, Nanna? Will they make us pay for that bird?"

Her father shook his head solemnly. "No, I don't think so. But we'd better eat it, just to be sure."

Savitha thought about that statement, and then she smiled. Laughed. "I'll get it, Nanna. I'll get the bird." She ran to the edge of its row and leaned over, carefully, carefully, but she lost her footing and fell, crushing all but one or two of the birds beneath her. Savitha lay for a moment on the broken birds. Her eyes flooded with tears. She knew she was in for a scolding, maybe even a beating, and what was more: her father would have to make all those birds all over again. She finally got up, gingerly, her arms and legs and frock and even her face studded with splintered pieces of sugar. Her cheeks hot with tears. She was afraid to look at her father, afraid to raise her gaze, but when she did, to her surprise, he was laughing. His eyes were shining. She couldn't understand it. "But Nanna, you'll have to make them all over again." Her father still laughed. Now he pointed at her. "And I thought you were sweet before," he said.

It took her a moment to understand, and when she did, she flew into his arms; he laughed some more and hugged her close and lifted her off the ground. "Forget those birds," he said. "You, you, girl of mine, *you're* the one with wings."

Sitting at the loom now, on a hot June night, she considered those two wonders: a girl bejeweled with sugar and the words *you're the one with wings.*

A darkness fell over the lantern light.

Savitha turned and saw Poornima's father. He smiled, and she thought, But he's never smiled. And then he said, "Come with me."

8

Poornima was asleep. A sound reached her. Cut through her dreams. She thought the sound might be an animal, a stray dog or a pig. Poornima listened. Then it came again. A cry.

From where? From where?

The weaving hut.

Poornima jumped up. She ran.

The weaving hut, she saw, was dimmed by shadows. A lantern burned. "Savitha?" she whispered.

At first only silence, except heavy, as if it had grown viscous in the heat, the dark. And then a low moan.

"Savitha?" She walked toward the sound. From the corner of the hut. Her eyes adjusted, and she saw a bundle, a shadow deeper than the surrounding shadows. She passed both looms. They looked massive, sinister in the dark, as if they were giants, hunched and full of hunger. But the bundle—she could see now that it was weeping, this bundle, sobbing so quietly, so achingly, that Poornima wondered if it was human, if the creature before her was born with anything besides this weeping.

She stumbled. She bent down.

Then she stilled. For a single moment, fleeting, she thought, Maybe I'm dreaming. Maybe my eyes will open. But when she reached out her hand, she touched bare skin. Hot, heat like sunburned earth. Like desert sand. It was then that she saw Savitha's clothes, ripped. Some on, some off. Lying around her like torn sails. "Savitha. What is it? What's happened?"

The sobbing stopped.

Poornima knelt and took her shoulders. She felt the bones, the sharpness of them. The bones of a small animal. The hull of a tiny ship. Savitha shrank away. As she did, Poornima saw the part in her hair. The lantern lighting a river. Her braid undone, her long hair in disarray, but her part untouched. Silver. Waters pulsing through a mountain pass.

It was then that her grip on Savitha's shoulders loosened. "Who?"

Savitha—whose head was bent over her knees, let out a wail. Low and tender and broken.

"*Who?*"

Her eyes filled with tears.

Savitha shook so violently that Poornima held her body against her own. She clasped her head to her chest and they rocked like that. Poornima thought she should get help, rouse her father, the neighbors. But when she made a move, the slightest stirring, Savitha gripped her hand. Gripped it so tightly that Poornima looked at her in astonishment.

"Who?"

Their eyes met.

"Poori," she murmured.

And it was then that she understood. It was then that Poornima knew.

She let out a scream so loud that no less than ten people came running. By now, Savitha had shrunk. Retreated like a wounded animal. Scraps of her blouse fell from her shoulders. Her shoulders brown and denuded like distant hills. They stood around them; the questions and gasps and exclamations singing past Poornima like arrows. She dropped to her knees. A neighbor stood over her and said, "What is it? What? What's wrong with you girls?"

"Bring a sheet," someone yelled, trying to lift her up, but Poornima refused, covering Savitha's body with her own. What other use could it have, she thought, this body of mine? What other use?

The sky the next morning was white with fever. The air so thick and hot it tasted of smoke. Poornima blinked awake, her eyelids wretched and unbelieving. Savitha was seated just as she had been, the sheet thrown over her, and Poornima eyed her desperately, thinking, No, this is no dream. Why couldn't it be a dream? A moment later, Poornima's brother sidled past the door, averted his eyes, and said, "Nanna wants his tea."

Poornima looked at her brother, and then, when he'd gone, she looked at the empty doorway.

"Nanna wants his tea," she parroted in a whisper, as if not only those words but all of language were a stranger to her.

She sat with those words, thinking through each one, and then slowly rose to her feet. Savitha didn't move. She didn't even seem to be awake, though her eyes were open.

Poornima moved through the heat, dazzled by the light, dizzied, from the weaving hut into the main hut, and set the water to boil. She added the milk, the sugar, the tea powder. She watched the blaze. It didn't seem possible: it didn't seem possible that she could make tea, make something as ordinary as tea. The world had reordered itself in the night, and to make tea, *tea*, for her father, seemed, in some way, a more fundamental offense than the one he had committed. She watched it with disgust, first simmering, then boiling, and then held the cup away from her, as though the wound he had opened, induced, was already festering, maggoted; as though she held that wound in her hand.

He was seated on the hemp-rope bed, just outside the hut. The elders were some distance away, and she could see that he was straining to hear them. When he saw her, he straightened his back and held out his hand, callous in its reach. A hot venom shot through her; she recoiled. She took steps toward him but her feet didn't seem to be striking anything solid, anything sturdy. The ground is so soft, she thought, so like cotton. But then the venom turned to nausea, the heat, the glare of morning made her sway, her vision suddenly swam with iridescent dots, flashes of lurid light.

She was only a step or two away from him when her body gave out, gave in to the vertigo, the pull of the earth. She stumbled, a drop or two of tea splattered, her other arm reached to break her fall, and it was this arm that her father caught. It was this arm—the one he had never before touched, never in her memory—that he touched now. She felt the sizzle of his skin. The serpent curl of its claws, tongues, fingers. Scales like burning coals. She pulled away with a kind of violence, horror, and fled back to the weaving hut.

Back to Savitha.

She huddled against her, burrowed against her body, as if she had been the one who had been wronged. Wronged? It was a father, steadying his daughter. And yet, to steady her in this way, at this time, with its sickening glint of kindness, seemed to Poornima a greater affront than if he'd simply let her float away on the Krishna, all those years ago. Why, she wanted to ask, Why didn't you?

It was then that Savitha's father arrived. His hands—those gnarled fingers, bent and misshapen—no longer hidden. But held out in front of him, as if beseeching. Begging. Waving before him like wild branches. Twisted by lightning strikes, bugs, disease. But his face, his face, Poornima saw, was frozen. Such despair as she had never seen.

"My girl," he said simply, his eyes red, shattered. His voice in ruins.

He tried to lift Savitha—to take her with him—but she gripped

Poornima's arm. "Leave her," someone yelled through the door. He tried lifting her once more, but Savitha gripped harder, and finally, watching his struggle, Poornima looked at him as she would at an empty field, and said, "She wants to be left."

The afternoon brought swirls of chaos and maddening commotion. Neighbors, elders, onlookers, children hushed and sent away, men, everywhere men. But Savitha—Savitha remained still. Not since she'd gripped Poornima's arm had she so much as turned her head. She'd simply pulled the sheet up to her neck, blinked once, and then stayed sitting, stonelike, exactly as she was. Poornima sat beside her and at one point, panicked and unnerved by her stillness, held her fingers under her nose for a moment to make sure she was still breathing. The dewy warmth of her exhalation, its delicacy, countered all the voices, the noise, the endless *people*.

Hands, sometime in the afternoon, tried to pull Poornima away. Tried to pry her away from Savitha. But this time, Poornima clung to *her* with a kind of madness, frenzy. She heard someone say, not even in a whisper, "It'll taint her. These things always do. And so close to her marriage being settled." Another said, "A dung heap is a dung heap. If you step in it—"

Poornima, though, felt like a blade of grass bent viciously by wind. She spoke to the wind. Please, she said to it softly, please stop. But when it did, just for a moment, she was stunned by the silence. Afraid. Afraid it would reach through the smoke, the heat, the numbness, and swallow them, she and Savitha, piece by piece.

The day wore on. The heat still savage. Clawing. Invading everything. Even Poornima's tongue and her ears and her scalp were coated in a layer of dust. She paid it no attention; evening drew to a close. She listened. She heard everything. The village elders were still gathered outside the hut, debating what to do. Late in the evening, Savitha's father joined them, and every now and then, Poornima heard shouting, and they seemed to her the shrieks of strange and startled birds, caught in nets.

"*You*," a voice said.

Poornima looked up. Standing in the doorway of the weaving hut was a woman she didn't recognize. But she seemed to know her.

"You," she seethed. "It's *your* fault."

Poornima shrunk farther into her corner. The wall behind her hard and rough and unforgiving. She knew now: Savitha's mother.

"Your fault. Your fault."

"I—"

"If it wasn't for you, if it wasn't for your *friendship*, my Savitha would've never come here. She would've never stayed here. In this house of demons. In this house. Never. You're a demon. Your house is demonic. And that sari." The tears began; her voice failed. She slid to the ground. She clutched at the doorpost. She crawled toward Poornima like an animal. "That sari. That sari. That she was making for *you*. This would've never happened otherwise." Now she had crept so close that Poornima felt her breath against her face. Hot, rancid, poisoned. "My child. My *child*, you understand? No. No, you don't. You couldn't, you demon."

Someone came in. They saw her. They pulled her away. She screamed— wretchedly, without form, as if a stake were being driven into her heart. She kicked as she was dragged away. Dust flew into Poornima's eyes. She blinked. In the quiet that followed, a pall descended over the hut. Over Savitha and Poornima. A great and unendurable silence. As if Savitha's mother had opened a portal, and air had rushed in. It was then that the tears started. And once they started, Poornima saw, they had no end. They came in great and uncontrollable sobs. If her mother's death had brought a storm, *this* could drown the earth and everyone with it.

No one paid her any attention. They went in and out of the weaving hut. All manner of people. Late in the evening, a child—a little boy—peeped through the doorway, and one of the village elders grabbed his arm and pulled him away. He admonished him. "What is there to see?" Poornima heard him say. "Spoiled fruit is spoiled fruit."

The tears kept coming.

At one point Poornima choked with her weeping, and when she did, she realized she'd forgotten to breathe. Forgotten that there was such a thing as air. That there was anything other than pain.

She took Savitha's limp hand and held it in hers—and youth and middle age and senescence passed before her like the cinema she had never seen, like the cinema Savitha had delighted in one day seeing.

"Savitha?"

Nothing.

"Savitha?"

Not the slightest movement. Not a twitch or a breath or a blink.

"Say something."

Deep into that night, the village elders came to a decision: Poornima's father was to marry Savitha. They all agreed: it was to be his punishment, and it was just.

No one bothered to tell Savitha the decision. Poornima only heard of it when Ramayya walked by the door of the hut and hissed, "She'll get married before you. The trash picker. And without even having to give your father a dowry."

Poornima stared at him. She turned from the doorway only when she felt movement; Savitha had blinked. For the duration of the second night, Savitha sat again, motionless. "Savitha," Poornima tried one more time, shaking her, pleading once more for so much as a word, a gesture, before falling finally into a disturbed and plagued sleep. Mostly by dreams, nightmares, visions, and premonitions, but once by Savitha's voice.

"Do you remember?" her voice said.

Poornima rolled her head in her sleep; she mumbled, "What?"

"About Majuli. About flute song. And that perfect fruit. Do you remember?"

"Yes."

There was silence. Poornima shifted again in her sleep, felt for Savitha's hunched body but found only air.

"I'll be many things, Poori, but I won't be your stepmother."

"Okay."

A shuffling.

"Poornima?"

"Yes?"

"I'm the one with wings."

In the morning, Poornima woke to screams and clamoring and calls for a search party; she looked around the weaving hut and found it empty. Savitha was gone.

Poornima

1

Poornima's wedding was postponed indefinitely. The groom's side wouldn't budge from their demand for twenty thousand more rupees. Especially now with rumors swirling as to the fouled runaway girl, her friendship with Poornima, and suggestions—by people whom Poornima had never even met, by people not even from Indravalli—that Poornima had helped her to run away. And what could be said about a girl like that? they said. What good would she be as a wife?

Not only that, but every day, more details dribbled in from Namburu confirming their hesitation. The father sent word that his son—in addition to the twenty thousand—would need a watch and a motorcycle. The older of the groom's sisters, whose name was Aruna, wondered aloud, in the company of some of the other village women in Namburu, whether it wouldn't be difficult for her to have a sister-in-law so clearly beneath her. Beneath you? one of them had asked. Beneath you how? Supposedly, the sister had looked at her gravely and said, "Beneath me in the way a monkey is beneath me."

Still, it was the mother's comment that most agitated Poornima. She'd told one of Poornima's distant cousins, while bemoaning her college-educated son's marriage to a village girl, "What can one do? That's the thing with a successful son: you either have to get him married to a modern college girl who'll ruin him with her excesses and demands, demands of makeup and fashionable saris and jewelry every time she so much as passes gas, or the village bumpkin who is as dark as a mustard seed, with the social graces of a mama pig in mud." But hadn't she said Poornima was not as dark as she'd thought? Hadn't she taken Poornima's chin in her hand?

She wished Savitha were here, so she could talk to her about it. Savitha? Her heart blazed with pain. And then gave out like a candle.

She had been gone for a month now. Thirty-three days. The search party that had gone to look for her—made up of a group of young men from Indravalli (there had also been a local police constable in the beginning, but he'd returned within two hours of starting the search and declared, wiping his brow in the heat, "The last time I spent more than an hour looking for a girl was the daughter of an MLA. We ended up finding her at the bottom of a well, not two hundred yards from the MLA's house. It's always the same; take my word for it. In this heat, I give it a day or two. Maybe three. And there she'll be, floating, puffed up like a puri.")—had gone as far as Amravati to the west, Gudivada to the east, Guntur to the south, and Nuzividu to the north. Nothing. They'd come back without so much as a rumor as to her whereabouts. Where could she have gone? the women in Indravalli wondered. Where is there to disappear to?

Poornima looked in the direction of the Krishna, east, and wondered the same thing.

After two months of back and forth, Ramayya and Poornima's father finally reached a compromise with the Namburu family. Poornima's father would add an extra ten thousand to the dowry, paying out five thousand now and five thousand within a year of the marriage, along with a scooter instead of a motorcycle—Ramayya suggesting to them that a scooter would be more convenient as Poornima began having children (sons, he was careful to add). The Namburu family, after a tense week of silence, finally agreed, grumblingly, bemoaning the generosity of their discount. Ramayya was overjoyed that the match had finally been settled, but Poornima's father was miserable. "But you won't have to sell the looms," Ramayya said, trying to cheer him. "And just think, you only have one more to go." Poornima's father raised his dark gaze to her, when she handed him his tea, and eyed her with contempt. And Poornima, surprising even herself, eyed him right back.

The wedding was set for the following month. Poornima spent most of that month inside the hut. It was considered gauche for a girl to be seen out and about in the village after her betrothal, and there was also the matter of the evil gaze of the other villagers, putting a hex on Poornima, envious of her good fortune in marrying a college-educated boy. "Besides," her aunt said, staying with them for the month to help with the preparations, "we don't need you getting any darker." It didn't matter either way to Poornima: light and dark, inside and outside, hope and hopelessness slowly started to lose meaning for her.

Sometimes, while sitting listlessly at her charkha, or combing her sister's hair, she would look up through the open door of the hut and wonder, What is that shining thing out there? What is it, so painful, so bright? People, too, lost their place in her mind; they were no longer moored to anything Poornima recognized or controlled or even understood as *herself*. Once, early in the month, her younger brother ran inside with a cut on his arm. He held it up to her, crying, waiting to be bandaged, but Poornima only looked down at him and smiled kindly, distractedly. She handed him a fifty-paisa coin and nudged him back out the door, drops of blood trailing him, and said, "Go. A banana. Quick. Savitha's on her way." Later in the month, her aunt asked her to put rice on the stove for dinner, and Poornima looked up from the corner where she was seated, stared at her aunt, and with her eyes as empty as an open field, she asked, "Who are you?" Twice, maybe three times, Poornima felt a flash, a stab of something she couldn't name. Something akin to a shard of bitter cold, or blinding heat. What was it? What was it?

She thought that it might be illness, that she had caught something. Malaria, maybe. But then it settled. It settled in her chest, on the left side, just above her heart. At first it was only a sprinkling, like a few grains of rice that might've spilled onto a stone floor. And all she had to do was bend to pick them up, one by one. But then the sprinkling of rice grew into a weight. A density. It became a *mound* of rice. She tried to press her palm against her chest, in an attempt to soothe it away. But it wouldn't slacken, it wouldn't loosen; it simply sat there, tight as a fist. She thought of the weight of her mother's hand, resting against her hair, and now, in her chest this time, was yet another weight. But this one ravaged, conjuring no memory, no longing, no lost childhood or honeyed voice or a hand raised to feed her, conjuring nothing, nothing at all except the two words: *she's gone.*

2

More aunts and uncles and cousins started arriving the week before the wedding. The hut was bustling. A tent was erected, blue and red and green and gold. Mango leaves had been bought and garlanded together, strung across the doorway to the hut and all along its edges. Various items for the ceremony—turmeric, kumkum, coconuts, rice and dals, packets of camphor and incense and oils—came in every few minutes. It all had to be stored, put away. And then there was the cooking. All those relatives, there must've been more than thirty by Poornima's last count. They all had to be fed, bright green banana leaves spread before them as plates, the dirty ones collected and thrown to the pigs. Her aunts and cousins helped, but every few minutes someone would turn to Poornima—usually one of her young cousins—and say, Where do you keep the salt? or, Imagine, you'll be the wife of a fancy man, or, What is it, why are looking at me like that? To which, to all of which, Poornima would place her hand above her heart, and wonder at the hardness, and the ache.

The days passed.

When the morning of the wedding came, it came like an invader. The sun rose in a clamor of paint strokes—pink and purple and orange and green—then rested angrily against the horizon, waiting for land, women, villages on fire. Early in the day, all her female relatives gathered around Poornima, along with her future sisters-in-law and a few neighbor women, for the bridal ceremony. They oiled her hair and then they rubbed turmeric over her body. Each one, in turn, then blessed her with rice soaked in turmeric and kumkum and sandalwood. With the older women, Poornima rose and bent to touch their feet. Aruna, the sister who'd compared Poornima to a monkey, stood a little apart, watching, as if she were bored by it all. When her turn came to bless Poornima and sprinkle her bowed head with turmeric-soaked rice, it felt to Poornima that the grains landed on her head with a kind of jab, like hail, but they also served to wake her up, and, as if she were coming out of a long and complex dream—so convincing it was, so utterly irrefutable, that the waking world, the one in which she was surrounded by twenty women, all smiling, all with yellow teeth, seemed to her the fraudulent one—she blinked and bowed her head lower, saw the throw of rice, and thought, Rice. Is there anything else in the world besides rice?

The muhurthum—the exact time the marriage ceremony would start, based on the bride's and groom's horoscopes—was set for that evening at 8:16 P.M. It was a little after seven P.M. and Poornima was seated on the veranda with the priest—without the groom—conducting the Gauri Puja. It wasn't until *after* this that she would be led to the mandapam, the wedding dais, and seated next to Kishore in order to go through more pujas, and then have him tie the wedding necklace, the mangalsutra, around her neck. Poornima sat listening to the priest, following his instructions, but everything still felt to her like a mirage, a distant and unreachable place. She listened to the drone of the priest's voice; she stared into her lap—her head bent, just as a bride's should be—her hands folded in prayer.

She was wearing a red-and-green sari, made of heavy silk. She wore a few jewels, mostly fake or borrowed, the row of bangles on each wrist glittering in the camphor flame. The henna crawled up her arms and her feet like moss, smothering and airless.

Everything—everything from the bridal ceremony to the dressing in the shadows of the hut, helped by her aunts, the pujas, the young priest yawning as he incanted them, and the constant rush of color and noise and people—all of these were things Poornima could in no way feel, only see, as if she were peering through a window.

Through this window, the priest looked at Poornima, who was squirming a little, incense smoke choking her, and said, "Pay attention." Then he said, "Get up." It was time to go to the mandapam, where her groom was waiting.

Her father waited beside her, to lead her to the dais. Poornima looked at him, his face set hard against her, or maybe against her dowry-raising in-laws, or maybe his own frailty—although she saw none of it; she saw only madness, her own—and he said, "Let's go," and she said, "Where?"

The sun was beginning to set by now, the western sky blazed green and orange and red. The line of the eastern horizon was once again white with heat. Where am I being led to? Poornima wondered. Wherever it was, she didn't mind. Not really. She noticed the sunset, with wonder, and thought, It is such a lovely evening, and such a lovely sari I am wearing. It delighted her. That window she was peering through: so much loveliness behind it. And yet, somewhere deeper, she thought, No, I don't want this sari. I don't want this day. I don't want this father. What do I want—what do I want? She was not able to answer, and so all of it remained, and she walked on, pretending to be delighted.

Her head was down, of course. She didn't look up, but she knew she was nearing the tent when the heat, the air around her, grew heavier. Her father didn't seem to notice; he seemed entirely focused on the dais, leading her to it. But the air was stifling, no longer lovely, and Poornima felt a rising panic. She tried to stop him, she tried to buck him off, but he kept his grip on her elbow and steered her toward the dais.

"I want to stop," she said to her father.

Her father tightened his hold on Poornima's elbow. He said, "Don't be stupid."

Don't be stupid, Poornima thought, and the words seemed decent enough. And so that's what Poornima chanted to herself, Don't be stupid. Don't be stupid. Don't be stupid. Don't be stupid. Don't be stupid. Don't be stupid. Don't be stupid. Don't be stupid. And she kept chanting this, over and over and over again, until she arrived at the mandapam, climbed the two steps, and was seated next to her groom.

Don't be stupid, she told herself.

Her father placed Poornima's hand in the groom's. She didn't look. Why look? Who was this strange man? He barely held it, anyway. More pujas. The priest handed her two bananas and an apple. Two bananas and an apple. Poornima looked at them. They seemed so familiar. So enticing. As if she'd waited her whole life to be handed this exact number and variety of fruit.

Why?

She wanted to ask the man sitting next to her. He might know. She was about to turn and do exactly that when the priest, impatiently, as if he'd already told her many times, said, "Ammai, can't you hear? I said, give him the fruit." And so Poornima decided she would ask later, after handing him the fruit. His hand came closer, closer and closer, and this time, Poornima raised her eyes. Just enough. She gasped. His right hand: it wasn't whole. He was missing two fingers. His middle and most of his index. The nub of his index finger looked like dry shredded meat, still pink, and the end of where his middle finger should have been was closed up, turned inward, like the mouth of a toothless old man. She shrank away.

So this, she thought with disgust, this is what they meant by idiosyncrasy. She recalled that she'd once known someone else with these hands, with hands just as grotesque (someone's father, but whose?). And then she thought, But who is *this* man? And why am I to hand him these two bananas and an apple? They're mine. These fruits. I don't want to place them in that hand, she thought; I don't want to place them in a hand so harmed.

It was not the fruit. Or perhaps it was the fruit. Either way, by the time Kishore had tied the mangalsutra around her neck and they'd walked the seven steps around the fire—her five fingers held in his three (and a half)—she understood. And that window? She understood now that there was no window. There never had been. Or, if there had been, it had broken, a rock had crashed through it: and here she was, staring at the rock, the shards, the air rushing in. She understood, in that moment, that she was married.

3

Her husband's home, in Namburu, was not at all a hut. It was a real *house*, made with concrete and with two floors. It had four rooms on the first floor and one large room on the top floor, with the remainder of the flat roof serving as a terrace. Here, laundry was hung, and on the hottest summer nights, everyone brought their mats up and slept under the stars. But not anymore. Here was where Kishore and Poornima would live, and here was where Poornima was escorted for their first night together. Poornima's young cousin accompanied her, serving as a chaperone, and her new mother-in-law and sisters-in-law greeted them at the door with a glowing aarthi. Poornima looked down at her toes.

They played a game, she and her new husband, while all the relations cheered them on. It was a game that had been played since ancient times: the same game, in the same way. Water was poured into a brass vessel, narrow at the top. A ring was dropped in. Plop. Into the water. They were to reach their right hands, only their right, into the vessel, and whoever came up holding the ring was the winner. The narrow opening was the key—their hands were meant to touch. The fingers meant to interlock. The foreplay—between these two strangers—meant to lead to sex. The first sex. Poornima reached her hand in and felt an immediate disgust. Instead of five, she felt three fingers. The thumb and pinkie hardly fingers, so that left only one. And this one rubbing against hers, the nub of the other—the index, the one that was minced—like moist, undercooked meat. And then nothing. The middle finger just an absence. An omission. She smiled shyly, trying to hide her revulsion. This is your new husband, she told herself. This is your new life. And then she looked up. Her new husband was looking right back at her. At her? Maybe through her. But he had a peculiar look in his eyes. Poornima recognized the look; what was it? She went through all the recollections of her youth, and her girlhood, the whole of her life, really, and it seemed to her that it was not at all peculiar, or unfamiliar. It was, in fact, the most familiar look of all. It was the look of a man: undressing her, teasing off her clothes, her innocence, ripping it with his teeth, biting at the tender heart of it, and then laughing and cruel, savoring the completeness of his incursion, its terror and its desire, and here she was, already half spent, half spoiled, half naked.

And here she was: already half swallowed.

And it was then that the tears started—before she could stop them, while her fingers still searched for the ring, but not really, because she already knew he would win; or rather, that she would lose—but they didn't matter, because hardly anyone noticed, and if they did, they mistook them for tears of joy.

That evening, after the afternoon filled with games and gentle teasing of the bride and groom ended, Poornima was bathed and dressed in a white sari and her hair adorned with blooming jasmine. She was handed a glass of warm milk for her new husband, scented with saffron, and she climbed the steps to the rooftop room. Slowly. So slowly that her young cousin, who accompanied her up the stairs, along with a few of Kishore's female relations, looked at Poornima and thought she might cry again. This young cousin, named Malli, knew nothing of what had happened back in Indravalli—only that there was a strange hush over the ceremony, one that she guessed was associated with the crazy-looking woman curled up in the weaving hut all those weeks ago, nestled under Poornima's arms, the one she'd only gotten a glimpse of, though a boy cousin, who'd gotten a better look, had told her she was a rakshasi come to devour new babies. "But why new babies?" she'd asked him. "Because, stupid, they're the tenderest." That seemed to make sense. "So we're too tough?" He'd looked at her and sighed impatiently. "*I* am. I don't know about you. Let me see." He'd squeezed her arm, and said, "Probably you're all right." Still, Malli was happy to join Poornima on her journey to Namburu. It was the custom—a young female relative joining the bride to her new home, a way to ease the journey to the strange, unfamiliar place—and Malli had jumped at the chance. But now that she was here, climbing the stairs beside Poornima, a cousin she barely knew but who struck her as being in an awful, pounding sort of pain, Malli wondered whether it wouldn't have been better to take her chances with the rakshasi.

Outside the door to the room, Malli and the other relations left her, giggling as they hurried away.

Poornima watched them go.

She looked at the doorway. There was a garland of young green mango leaves strung across the top of the doorframe. The door itself had a fresh coat of green paint and was blessed with dots of red kumkum and turmeric. She stood against it and listened. Not for sounds of her new husband, who, she knew, waited beyond, but for something else, something she could not name. Maybe a voice leading her away, maybe to the edge of the roof, maybe to its very edge. But there was nothing. The glass of milk in her hands grew cool. She looked down and saw the layer of skin on its surface. It had appeared out of nowhere: thin and creased and floating. Cunning. How did milk do that, how did it *know* to do that? she wondered. To protect itself? How, she thought, could it be so strong?

She set the glass down next to the door and walked to the center of the terrace. The concrete burned her bare feet, but she hardly noticed. She saw something shining toward the middle of the roof, but when she reached it, she saw that it was only a piece of wrapper, for a toffee. What had she thought it was? A coin? A jewel? Poornima didn't know, but she was so disappointed that she sat down, right next to the wrapper, and stared at it. "You could've been a diamond," she said to it. Then she said, "You could've been anything." The wrapper stared back. It was nearly dark by now. It had cooled some, but the afternoons were still hot, in the high thirties, and the concrete that Poornima sat on held the heat. She didn't mind. What she minded was that when she was small, three or four years old, one of her earliest memories, she'd gone with her mother to the market to buy vegetables. While they were walking back home, her mother had stopped in a dry goods shop to buy a gram of cloves. Poornima looked at all the tins on the counter of the shop, filled with chocolate candies and biscuits and toffees, and asked her mother to buy her one. Her mother hardly looked at her. She said, "No. We don't have the money."

Poornima waited, watching the tins.

Another customer—a fat lady with her fat son—came into the store. The boy—even to Poornima's young gaze—struck her as spoiled. He was older than her but seemed slower, as if he'd been fed all his life on butter and praise. *He* didn't even ask for a candy. He simply pointed at the toffee he wanted and yanked on his fat mother's pallu. The owner obliged him by opening the tin, and then, laughing obsequiously, he said, "Take as many as you want, Mr. Ramana-garu." The boy grabbed a handful and walked away. The owner was busy helping the mother, and so he, too, walked away. Poornima's mother was bent over the jars of spices, examining a handful of cloves. Poornima turned back to the tin.

Its lid was still open.

She didn't eat it until she got home. She'd clutched the toffee in her little fist all along the walk home and then she'd waited until she was alone—while her mother was making dinner and her brothers were playing—and then she'd slowly unwrapped it, the red toffee in the middle of her palm nearly as *big* as her palm, and sparkling like a gem, a smooth and sugary gem. She licked it, once, twice, until she could no longer stand it. Then she popped it into her mouth. She'd had toffee before, but never a whole one; her mother had always broken them into pieces so she could share them with her brothers. The worst part of it was the shattering, Poornima thought: to take a perfectly luscious round gem and to break it into shards. It was indecent. She resented her mother even more than her brothers. But *this*, this one was whole. She sucked on it and sucked on it until the sweetness flooded her mouth, tickled her throat. It was down to nothing, barely a sliver, when she heard her mother calling for her. She swallowed it down, and when she went to the back of the hut, where her mother was cooking, she started to cough from the woodsmoke.

"What is that?" her mother said.

Poornima looked at her.

"Come here," her mother said.

Poornima took a small step toward her mother. She grabbed her daughter's cheeks and squeezed. Poornima puckered her mouth like a fish. "Open up," her mother said. "Don't think I don't see you."

Poornima finally opened up, a little, and then when her mother squeezed harder, her entire mouth gaped open, red and shining and slippery like the inside of a pomegranate.

"Did you steal it?" her mother asked.

Poornima said nothing, and then she nodded.

Her mother sighed. She said, "Stealing is wrong. You know that, don't you, Poornima. You should never, ever do it." Poornima looked at her mother and nodded again. "You've already eaten it, so we'll have to go tomorrow and give him money. I won't tell your father, you understand, but it wasn't yours. Remember that, Poornima: never take what isn't yours. Can you remember that?"

Poornima remembered, but she no longer agreed. Sitting in the middle of the terrace, on the evening of her wedding night, she looked at the wrapper and she thought about her mother. She thought about the red toffee; she could taste it still on her tongue, feel the sweetness, still, traveling down her throat. But she didn't agree. Amma, she said to the wrapper, if only I *had* taken what wasn't mine. If only I had taken a moment to insist, insist on meeting him before the wedding, I could've counted his fingers like they counted mine. If only I'd refused. Refused it all: to let you die, to let the goat die, to let that blue clock stop chiming. If only I'd said, *You* are flute song. She picked up the wrapper. She said, Don't you see, Amma, if only I had taken the things I wasn't meant to take. If only I'd had the courage.

She dropped the wrapper and watched it blow away.

She walked to the door, behind which her new husband was waiting, probably asleep by this time, and picked up the glass of now cold milk. She saw on its surface specks of dust that had blown in, sailing on the wrinkled layer of milk. She looked at them, the specks, and decided to let them convince her: hold fast, they said, stay on the surface, and these waters, these creamy, sumptuous white waters, let them carry you. Where would they take her? She had no idea, but behind that door was a man who was not her father. And to whom she now belonged. That seemed an improvement; that alone was a better place.

Inside the room was a bed, a wooden armoire with a long mirror fringed with a design of berries dangling from curling vines, a desk, and a television. A television! No one in Indravalli had a television. Kishore saw her staring at it, and said, "Don't get excited. It doesn't work." Her eyes left the television and returned to the glass of milk in her hand. He took it and placed it on a small round table beside the bed. The thin yellow sheet on the bed was covered with rose petals arranged in the shape of a heart, and Poornima wondered who'd done that: shaped them into a heart. It was a gesture so enchanting, so unexpected, that she wanted to sit on the edge of the bed—gingerly, so as not to disturb the petals—and look at it. Just look at it. But Kishore seemed not at all interested in the heart, because without prelude, he pulled her onto the bed, tugged at the folds of her sari, and burrowed his head, his wet lips, into the dip of her blouse, his fingers stabbing at her breasts like the ends of a potato. In the ensuing confusion, Poornima missed whatever it was that lanced into her. She let out a whimper, too scared to scream, but by now, Kishore was grunting away on top of her. She couldn't decide—as she watched his face, its grimace, its shudderings— what hurt more: the thing coming in or the thing going out. But then it ended. Just like that. After one final push, Kishore looked down at her and smiled. A true smile. And she thought, Yes, after all, yes, you are the one I belong to now. Then he rolled off her, and in the dark, just as Poornima felt for the first time the velvet of the rose petals against her back, cool and forgiving like rain, he said sleepily, "I like two cups of coffee. One first thing, when I wake up, and one with tiffin. Do you understand?"

She nodded into the dark. And tried her very hardest to understand.

4

At the end of their first month of marriage, on a Sunday, Kishore took Poornima and his sister Aruna, seventeen and younger than Kishore by six years, to Vijayawada. His other sister, Divya, who Poornima saw for the first time at the wedding, was ten years younger than him, and studious. She was quiet, the opposite of Aruna, and didn't want to come along to Vijayawada because she had exams. So Poornima and Kishore and Aruna set out after breakfast. Poornima wore her best sari, an orange one with a pink border that she'd gotten as a wedding gift. They ate masala dosas at a restaurant near the bus station. Aruna and Kishore didn't enjoy their dosas—Aruna said the curry was flavorless and that the waiter was insolent; Kishore added that the restaurants near the company where he worked, on Annie Besant Road, were far better—but Poornima had nothing to compare hers to; she'd never been to a restaurant before. Afterward, Kishore took them to the cinema.

This was also a first for Poornima.

Her eyes warmed with tears as she and Aruna waited for Kishore to buy the tickets, wishing she were here with Savitha, as they'd once planned, but Poornima gasped and forgot all about her when she entered through the balcony doors. She'd never seen a room so big. It was like entering an enormous cave, but one that was chiseled and glamorously lit. She stood in awe—looking at the red plush seats, some of them ripped but still luxurious, and the droplets of golden light along the walls where the lamps were hung, and the crowds of people, rushing to find seats. Kishore and Aruna must've been to this theater before because they pushed past Poornima to a row of seats in the middle of the balcony.

Then the curtain parted, the screen filled with light, and Poornima was astonished again. The people were huge! They seemed to be bearing down on her, ready to lunge. Her eyes grew wide, a little afraid, but when she looked anxiously at Kishore and Aruna, they were already engrossed in the film—a sad tale of two lovers separated by the disapproval of their parents, especially the girl's parents, because the boy was penniless, and he had no job (as far as Poornima could tell), but he was strikingly handsome, and he had a handsome motorcycle, even though he was poor. The girl's parents, in an effort to keep them apart, went so far as to lock her up in a remote mountain home. It was sad, but there were song and dance sequences of the lovers in Kashmir, and Shimla, and Rishikesh, dancing and frolicking in the snow. The actress was wearing only a shimmering, diaphanous blue sari against the white of the snow, and Poornima leaned over and asked Kishore, "Isn't she cold? Isn't snow supposed to be cold?" He ignored her, or maybe he didn't hear.

At the end of the movie, the hero won over the girl's parents by rescuing their family business from a greedy relative who was plotting to overtake it and throw them out of their mansion. If the hero hadn't exposed him, and if he hadn't held the bad relative at gunpoint, the girl's family would have lost everything—money, jewels, cars—and would've been left homeless. The girl's parents, in that instant, recognized the boy's cleverness and quick-wittedness, and the movie ended with the girl's parents placing their daughter's hand in his.

Poornima was so touched by the radiant faces of the hero and heroine, by all they'd had to overcome, that she began to cry. Kishore and Aruna looked over at her and laughed. "It wasn't even that good," Aruna said. Poornima didn't agree; and on the way home, as the bus wound through the darkening paddies of rice and the fading fields of cotton and peanuts that lined the road from Vijayawada to Namburu, and as the outlines of the distant hills bled into the night sky, she realized she wasn't crying because of the film, she was crying because she *hadn't* forgotten. Not for an instant. Savitha had been there, seated next to her, in some way. In some way more essential than even Kishore and Aruna had been there. She could picture it: Savitha would've grasped her hand when the hero pulled out the gun, and she would've liked him, the hero, because he was poor like they were, and because he loved the heroine with such sweetness, such guileless longing. Imagine, Poori, she would've said, shaking her head, imagine how cold that poor girl must've been, in that thin sari. All that snow, she would've said, it looked just like yogurt rice, don't you think?

In the days and weeks after going to the cinema, Poornima thought more and more about it. Not the film itself. Not exactly. What she thought about were the faces of the other people in the theater, especially Kishore's and Aruna's. She'd never seen such a thing: lights flashing, changing colors, illuminating the rapt faces of people in an audience. She'd not even seen the lights of a television shining and shifting, let alone the lights of a movie screen. It seemed to her, as the months wore on, that the quality of that light, distant yet penetrating, menacing yet harmless, was how the events of her own life felt.

For instance, one evening, while she was cooking dinner for the family, her mother-in-law walked into the kitchen (which was actually a separate room, much to Poornima's astonishment) and demanded to know where her garnet earrings were, the ones in the shape of a flower; she wanted to wear them to the temple, she said. Poornima, who hadn't even known her mother-in-law owned a pair of garnet earrings, said she didn't know, and went back to making the eggplant-and-potato curry on the stove. Her mother-in-law, watching closely as Poornima added salt to the curry, sighed loudly and muttered, "The poor. You never know around them." Poornima put down the spoon, watched her mother-in-law leave the kitchen, and wondered, You never know what?

But then the lights of the cinema moved closer, became more menacing.

This time, it was while the family was having tea and pakora on a Sunday afternoon. Poornima had just sat down to drink her tea when Aruna eyed her closely, turned to her mother, and said, "*Somebody* discolored my silk shalwar. Amma, do you know who it could've been?" It had been a delicate pink, but was now apparently splotched with blue and purple. They both turned to Poornima. Their gaze took on a kind of hatred, sudden and smoky. "You soaked it with something blue, didn't you? Was it that blue towel? I bet you soaked it with that towel. Amma, can you believe it? You're jealous, aren't you? It's impossible to have nice things around some people. I know you soaked it with that towel. How can you be so stupid?"

Poornima opened her mouth to protest, but she honestly couldn't remember. She did the entire family's laundry, so maybe she had soaked it with the blue towel. But not on purpose, and certainly not because she was jealous. She looked at Kishore, but he was busy chewing an onion pakora. She turned to her father-in-law, who rarely said anything in front of his wife, and had a habit of slinking off whenever a discussion became heated or turned to him. Today he simply sat with his hands folded, staring into them as if into a deep well. Only Divya was an ally—a serious girl who Poornima had grown to like, but who had no voice, being the youngest, and was often shouted down.

But before Poornima could even turn to Divya, her mother-in-law was at her side, yanking her head back by her braid. "Ask forgiveness," she growled. "Ask." Poornima was so surprised she couldn't get any words out, not even a scream. Her mother-in-law finally let go, and Poornima did ask forgiveness, but then, that night, as she was falling asleep, she thought, It was absurd of me. It was cowardly of me. I should've never asked for forgiveness when I'm not even sure I had anything to do with it. I don't remember ever even seeing that silk shalwar. What did it mean to ask forgiveness, she wondered, not knowing the crime, or who committed it. It meant nothing, she realized. Nothing at all. And so she decided in that moment—decided, yes, decided, astonished that she could even do such a thing as *decide*—that she would never again ask forgiveness for a thing she didn't do, for crimes she could in no way recall committing. And so she fell asleep smiling, and drifted into a dream.

After six months of marriage, the days took an even darker turn. Poornima's father had been able to give them the first five thousand rupees at the wedding. He'd taken a loan from the weaving collective, at an exorbitant interest rate, but had been able to keep both of his looms, and even hired a boy—young, hardly able to reach the treadles—to work the second loom. But he still hadn't managed to buy Kishore a scooter, nor had he any way to pay the remaining five thousand. Poornima would've known nothing about this, since she hardly had any contact with her father, had it not been for the fact that her in-laws began to mention it more and more. *Mention*? That wasn't quite the right word. *Hound* was a better word. They began to hound her about it.

At first, Poornima didn't even know they were talking about the five thousand. They were circumspect, and they would say things like, Some people. Some people are just too lazy to pay their debts, or, You can't trust anyone, especially not the poor, the ones with daughters. Why should their bad luck cost *us* money? or, Liars—if there's one thing I can't stand, it's a liar. But after a few weeks, the grumbling became more pointed. While Poornima was eating dinner one night, after all the others had finished—first Kishore and her father-in-law, and then her mother-in-law and Aruna and Divya had to be served—her mother-in-law walked into the kitchen, where Poornima was sitting on the floor and eating, and said, "Did you get enough to eat, my dear?"

Poornima looked up at her in astonishment. My dear?

"It's just as well," she continued. "Eat your fill. *You* can live off of us. But who are we going to live off of?"

Poornima tried to talk to Kishore about it. She brought it up one night, after they'd climbed to their upstairs room. The nights were cooler now. It was January, and they'd had to switch out the thin sheets for the woolen blanket. The sky was a deep and distant blue; winter stars pierced it with cold indifference. Poornima stood on the terrace for a moment, looking out at the other houses in Namburu, most of them only thatched-roof huts like the one she'd grown up in. Golden lantern light spilled onto the dirt passageways between the huts, and there was the smell of woodsmoke, cooking fires setting rice to boil, round wheat pulkas browning directly over the flames. Poornima looked in the direction of Indravalli and knew this same cold night air must hang over Indravalli, too, this exact night air, probably, and yet she felt no kinship with it. No affection. It was as if the winter had turned the season of her heart, too, and left it filled only with smoke and distant, frozen stars.

Kishore asked her to come to the bed when she entered. He was lying on top of the covers. "Take off your blouse," he said. Poornima took off her blouse and wrapped her pallu around her shoulders, though the shadowed curves of her breasts, her thin arms, could still be guessed through the fabric of her sari. "No," he said, "take that off, too." She did so reluctantly, shy, unaware, even after six months of marriage, and even with Kishore on top of her practically every night, of her adolescent body, and of the crude brutality it could inspire. "Massage my feet," he said. She moved to the end of the bed. Her fingers, though they'd already been rough in Indravalli from the charkha and the housework, were now calloused and cracking from the constant work, her hands the only part of her that seemed to absorb the daily disgraces, the accusations, the domesticity of everyday cruelty. When she lifted her eyes, she saw that Kishore's were closed, and though her bare chest was cold, she didn't dare to cover it again. She thought he might've fallen asleep, but when she slowed the massage a bit, he called out, "Keep going. Who told you to stop?" She heard him snore lightly, or maybe he grunted, and then, after a moment, he said, "Come here." He took her while she was on her back first, and then he turned her over onto her stomach and took her again. When he finally came, he collapsed on top of her and lay there for so long that Poornima watched as three different mosquitoes bit her and flew away, drugged, heavy and bloated with her blood.

She waited a moment, once he rolled off, and then she took a deep breath. She said, "I can't help it. I can't help it if my father doesn't have the money."

Silence. She slapped away another mosquito, the room now thick with them, attracted by the heat of their bodies.

"Yes, you can," he said.

Poornima stopped. She stared at him in the dark. "I can?"

His voice grew cold. The room, too, grew suddenly cold. All the mosquitoes wandered off. "Tell him there's worse to come," he said, "unless he pays up."

"Worse? Worse how?"

But Kishore didn't say anything, and after a moment, he was snoring. Fast asleep. Poornima lay awake, the returning mosquitoes now a welcome distraction, the loss of blood an offering.

It wasn't that conversation. Or maybe it was. Regardless, Poornima, a few weeks after that night, began to sneak upstairs between her chores, or race to finish them, or find any excuse to leave the main part of the house and climb to the second floor, close the door to their room, and sit on the edge of the bed. She never lay down; lying down reminded her of Kishore, and she didn't want to be reminded of him. She didn't want to be reminded of Savitha, either, so she didn't close her eyes.

Instead, she studied the room. The walls were painted a pale green. There were watermarks on two of the walls, but none on the third and fourth. Two windows on either side of the door looked out onto the terrace, and these had bars and shutters across them, to keep out thieves. There was a lot to steal, Poornima thought: the wooden armoire was handsome; nothing in their hut in Indravalli was as handsome as the armoire. Inside it were mostly Kishore's work clothes, along with her wedding sari, some papers and jewelry and cash that Kishore kept in a locked metal box, and a doll that was wrapped in crinkly plastic, which a distant relative had brought back from America. There was also, in the armoire, a bronze statuette Kishore had gotten for being the best student at his college each of his four years there, and this he kept especially protected, in a designated place nestled between some clothes. Tucked in between everything were mothballs. Against the other wall were the television and the desk. The television still didn't work— Poornima wondered whether it ever had—but the room felt rich for having it there, a piece of muslin cloth covering it to keep out the dust.

Next to the television was the desk, and on the desk were Kishore's papers. These papers were different than the papers in the armoire, he'd told her. These papers were just his work papers, he'd said, while the ones in the armoire were government papers and bankbooks. Poornima looked at them, and seeing that they were in disarray, she got up from the bed and went to the desk to straighten them. As she did, she saw that they were filled with columns—six of them, with many, many rows underneath filled with lots of numbers and scribbles that she couldn't possibly understand, so she laid them back down on the desk. But something caught her eye: she saw that the first row on the topmost page *did* make sense. It was simply the numbers in the second, third, fourth, and fifth columns added up, and listed in the sixth column. The first column was just a date. That was easy enough; she'd learned addition well before the fifth class, which was the last year she'd attended school. Then she checked the remaining rows, and they, too, were the same: simple addition, that was it.

Was *this* what Kishore did at work all day? She nearly laughed out loud. Asking for foot massages, demanding that she press his shirts every morning, yelling for a glass of water as soon as he walked in the door: as if he'd crossed a desert, as if his labors had utterly parched him, when all he was really doing was adding up numbers! But then she checked the other sheets of paper, and it wasn't true. Those columns weren't added up; something different was happening in those columns.

Poornima sighed and went back downstairs. There were the lunch dishes

to wash and dinner to prepare. Her mother-in-law and Aruna liked their
tea at four o'clock, and it was already ten past. Poornima hurried to the
kitchen. But as she boiled the water and milk, and raced to add the tea powder, and brought down the sugar things, she wondered about those other
pages. What *were* those columns doing? Maybe Savitha had been right, she
thought. Maybe, in the end, accounting was not much more complicated
than when her father gave her money to go to the market, hardly any money
at all, and she'd still had to buy enough vegetables and rice for all of them,
and even so, he'd demanded that she bring back change, along with a full
rendition of all she'd spent and where. If she'd bought a kilo of potatoes for
five rupees, he'd say, "I could've gotten them for four," and if she did get
them for four, he'd say, "They're small. Pockmarked. No wonder."

Still, as she was scooping the sugar into the cups, Poornima suddenly
put down the spoon. She put it down and looked up. She was amazed. She'd
just thought of Savitha, and yet she had felt none of the usual blunt, dreary
pain or confusion or longing that she always felt, nor even the gleaming,
sharp hatred toward her father. None of it. She'd simply, and without suffering, thought of Savitha. It was the first time she'd done so, and the feeling
was like being handed a kite in a strong wind. Poornima smiled. But then
the smile immediately fell. Because in the moment right afterward, it all
rose up again: the desperate sorrow, the disorder, the mystery of her whereabouts that drove her, on some nights, to huddle in a corner of the terrace
and weep under the waning or waxing moon, the watching stars.

But she'd been free for a moment, and besides, those columns couldn't
possibly be all that difficult: those two things she knew. Those two things
she was certain she knew.

5

The first time Poornima talked back to her mother-in-law was on the morning of a marriage viewing for Aruna. She was six months older than Poornima and yet still not married. The problem, according to Aruna and her mother, was the boys. They were never good enough. One had a good job, high-paying, in Hyderabad, but he was balding. Another, tall and handsome, had a father who was keeping a woman even though his wife was still alive—and who knew if bigamy had a genetic component? Yet another was perfect in every way—job, hairline, family reputation—but he was the exact same height as Aruna, and she liked to wear a little heel whenever she went to the cinema or out to eat. "What am I supposed to do," she said, pouting, "wear chapals everywhere? Like a common villager?"

The boy coming today was from Guntur; he worked for Tata Consulting and had been to America on a project, and might even have the chance to go again. He was an only son, so the entirety of his family's inheritance would go only to him, *and* he looked like a film hero. At least, that's what one of his neighbors told the matchmaker, when he went around to inquire. "Which hero?" Poornima asked. "Is it the one in the film we saw?" Aruna scowled and shook her head. "No. Not *that* one, you pakshi. A hero in a good film."

It didn't matter which film. The house in Namburu had been aflutter since four in the morning. The stone floors in every room were washed and mopped. All the furniture was dusted, the cushions on the sofa and chairs aired out. A small puja was conducted—as soon as Aruna had washed her hair and dressed, she made an offering to Lakshmi Devi and lit incense. They were arriving at three in the afternoon but had said nothing about staying for dinner—which meant that Poornima had to make enough sambar and curries in case they did, along with pulao rice and bhajis. She was cutting strips of eggplant for the bhajis, the oil already heating on the stove, when her mother-in-law came in, yelling for her to hurry up, the milkman had arrived, and there was the milk to boil and the yogurt to set. Poornima turned down the oil and got up to get the milk pan, when her mother-in-law looked at her, up and down, and said, "When they arrive, don't show your face. Stay upstairs. We'll make up something. We'll tell them you had to go back to Indravalli for the day. Something. Just don't make a sound."

Poornima turned from the stove. "Why? Why would I stay upstairs?"

Her mother-in-law sighed loudly. "You're not—well, we don't want to bring Aruna's status down, do we? Besides, six months, seven months, and you're still not pregnant? I don't want you to rub off on my Aruna. On *her* chances. Barren women are a bad omen, and I don't want you down here."

There was silence. Poornima listened. She strained her ears and found that there was only the small, quiet sound of the oil beginning to boil, though this, too, magnified the other silence, the greater one. "How do you know?" she said. "How do you know your son isn't the one who's barren?"

The slap that followed was so powerful that it knocked Poornima backward, reeling, crashing into the stove. The milk wasn't on the burner yet, but the oil was. It splattered across the wall, dripped off the granite counter, and landed in thick, hot drops on the floor. A few drops flew onto Poornima's arm, and she could feel their sizzle, spreading like papad, hissing like snakes.

Her mother-in-law eyed her with real hatred, and then she said, "Keep acting up. Go ahead. There'll be worse. Just keep it up."

Worse? There would be worse? Kishore had said the same thing: Was it a coincidence? Or wasn't it?

That afternoon, when the boy's family arrived, Poornima was relegated to the upstairs and told not to come down until they called for her. She didn't mind. She sat in the middle of the terrace for a few minutes, away from the edge so no one would see her. It was after four o'clock when the boy's family arrived, the hour when flower vendors walked through the village, shouting and singing out the kinds of flowers they had for sale. Poornima could hear the song of the old man who sold the garlands of jasmine, plump as pillows, and just beginning to open, releasing a fragrance so intoxicating that she was certain she caught their scent on the terrace, two, maybe three streets away.

Her mother-in-law sometimes bought a long strand, cutting off the longest lengths—as long as her forearm—for Aruna and Divya (who didn't even like wearing jasmine in her hair and took it off as soon as her mother turned her head); she took a short one for her own, puny bun and gave the remainder to Poornima. Poornima, whose father, after her mother had died, had never once given her money for flowers, would rush to oil and braid her hair, wash her face, then reapply talcum powder to her face and neck, draw kajal around her eyes, and paint on a fresh bottu. And only then, only after she'd made herself worthy of the flowers, their sweetness, their beauty, would she finally put them in her hair. On those nights, after Kishore took her—not once commenting on the flowers in her hair; did he even notice them? Poornima wondered—she'd lie back on her pillow, and their scent would drift up toward her like mist, like drizzle, like the unbearable sadness of that upstairs room, her husband turned away from her, the shutters closed against burglars, but still a mild breeze sneaking in, rustling the edges of the sheet, and Poornima, lying there in the dark, her eyes open, warm, inundated by the fragrance of flowers.

The voice of the old man selling the garlands of jasmine faded, and

Poornima got up and walked across the terrace. She went into the upstairs room and closed the door. The papers were still on the desk. They were the same stack, sitting in the same place, and had been for the past two weeks. She moved aside the top page, the one with simple addition, and looked at the next one. This one had more numbers, but it also had a heading at the top of the page. The heading was in English, which Poornima couldn't read, but there were other details in Telugu. For instance, the first column had a listing of various machines, such as cars (6), lorries (3), tractors (2), combines (2), and so forth. Each machine had an amount next to it. Judging by how high the numbers were, and how all the numbers in a group—such as the group of cars—were approximately the same, Poornima guessed each number corresponded to the value of the listed machine. Next to one car, she saw it read "Dented," and was valued less than the others. The lorries, on the other hand, were all valued far more than the cars. Poornima shuffled to the next page. She was doing this out of boredom, she realized, but it was also fun, in a way. She couldn't say why, only that figuring out what the numbers meant, what the columns stood for, gave her a sense of accomplishment, of gain. The feeling itself was unfamiliar, and she wondered at it: Why hadn't she felt it when she'd worked at her charkha, or when she made a particularly tasty sambar, or even when she'd bought the two bananas, an apple, and the handful of cashews for her mother? Well, one reason was obvious: her mother died, the sambar got eaten, and the charkha, well, the charkha spun and it spun and it never stopped spinning. But *this*? This stack of papers? It was leading to something; she could sense it. She left that page and turned to the next.

The nagging from Poornima's mother-in-law and Kishore escalated. Aruna's marriage to the boy from Guntur was nearly fixed; it was just a matter of a little more haggling over the dowry and the amount of jewelry (measured in ounces of gold) each side would give the bride. Aruna's family had the dowry money, though they had to sell a small farm they owned outside Kaza for the gold. But the farm didn't bring in enough, and so every time Poornima entered a room, or left one, her mother-in law yelled after her, "That no-good father of yours said within the year. All five thousand. Well, the year's come and gone. And here we are, feeding you three times a day, without even a grandchild to show for it. No-good fathers beget no-good daughters, that's what I say. And here's my poor son, a prince, stuck with you. We should've never married into such a family." Poornima snuck a look at Kishore's mangled fingers and wondered, Who is stuck with whom?

Kishore's mode of escalation was more subtle, though also more painful: the sex became rougher. Violent. He'd grab her hair, yank her around the bed by it, slam into her with such force that her head would hit the wall behind the bed. The next day, bruises bloomed across her body, green and blue and gray and black, growing like nests, as if tiny birds were coming in the night to build them, one feather and branch and twig at a time. At the end of two weeks, Poornima could no longer see the true color of the skin on her legs and arms, and she wondered—bracing every evening for Kishore's return from work, serving dinner with as much care and slowness as she could manage without being told to hurry up, washing the dishes even more deliberately, and then climbing the stairs one by one, knowing he was upstairs, knowing what the night would hold, and even, once or twice, closing her eyes when she reached the top step, praying, hoping, that when she opened them, Savitha would be there, standing on the terrace, laughing, saying, Let's go—but wondering, wondering, she couldn't help wondering if *this* is what they meant by worse.

Kishore's work pages took on a kind of poetry for Poornima. She could've gazed at them for hours, days, were it not for chores, and for the simple fact that she didn't know what they actually *meant*. Individually, she knew what they meant, but not together: the first page was simply various payments made to Kishore's company over the past three months, added up. The second page—the one with the listing of cars and lorries—was a listing of the company's assets. The third page, Poornima realized without much trouble—based on the columns of other company names and an amount beside each name, some getting smaller, some getting higher—were the company's debts. But what did they *mean*, when taken together? Why was Kishore always shuffling them around, punching numbers into some small machine, grumbling about this or that outstanding payment? Loans. Debts. It didn't make sense. Poornima wandered through her chores in a daze for a full week, until one afternoon, while she was hanging up the laundry to dry, one of Aruna's shalwar tops was whipped to the ground by the wind, and Aruna ran up behind her, caught Poornima's arm in a grip, and swung her around to face her. "Do you know whose this is? Do you know what it's worth?" Poornima looked at her, and then she couldn't help smiling. It was so simple. Of course. That must be it. All those papers, stacked on the desk: they added up to something. They added up to what the company was worth.

And so as the stacks kept changing—with Kishore taking stacks back to work, bringing new ones, all the while completely unaware that Poornima was studying them, that she was *learning* from them—she began to see the world differently; she began to see it with a kind of clarity: there was what you owed, and there was what you could sell to pay off what you owed, and whatever was left (if there was anything left) was all that you could say was truly yours, all that you could truly love.

6

By the middle of the second year of Poornima's marriage, the nagging grew into outright hostility. She couldn't recall a single day when she hadn't been slapped or screamed at or forced to ask for forgiveness (for the smallest things, like when she dripped a few drops of tea onto the stone floor). The five thousand rupees was still outstanding, and her mother-in-law and Kishore reminded her of it every time she put a bite of food in her mouth, or drank a glass of water. "You think it's free?" her mother-in-law hissed. "You think that water's free? That pump we installed cost three thousand rupees. So *you* wouldn't have to go to the well. And where do you think we got that three thousand rupees? Where? Not from your father, not from him. That's for sure, the thief. Both of you. Thieves." But the water pump was installed the year *before* I came to Namburu, Poornima wanted to say, but didn't. Not because she was afraid; fear began to lose meaning in her life—fear was a thing she'd felt for so long, first with her father and then with her mother-in-law and Aruna and Kishore, that it took on a monotony, an everydayness that struck Poornima as being just as boring as washing dishes, or ironing clothes. Why should she be afraid? She'd left her father's house and nothing had changed. Maybe nothing ever did. She understood now that Savitha had been right to run away. She'd been right to leave. Fear was no good, but neither was the monotony of fear.

But then, all of a sudden, everything changed. It simply stopped.

There was no more yelling, no more demands, no more violence. Poornima went about her chores and they simply ignored her. Sometimes, she'd catch one or another watching her, waiting, it seemed. But for what? She didn't know, but she did know one thing: she had to get pregnant soon. She'd heard of barren women being replaced by second wives. She wouldn't mind that much—she might actually prefer it—but she thought they might send her back to Indravalli once the second wife arrived. She sometimes dreamed that they had, and when she walked into the weaving hut, Savitha was seated at the loom, waiting for her. But that wasn't true; only her father was there, and Poornima refused to see him. Even during festival days, when daughters were expected to return home, Poornima wouldn't go. Why should she? "No," she said with finality, "I won't go," and her mother-in-law cursed her under her breath, mumbling, "No. No, you wouldn't. That would save us a week's food, so why would you?"

Aruna's marriage was finally fixed—with the man from Guntur—for the end of August. The family was overjoyed. It was now July, and preparations began in earnest. There was shopping to do, invitations to send out, the marriage hall to book. Aruna was beside herself. She grabbed Divya by the arms and spun in circles, laughing. "He's so handsome, Divi, and so rich, and we'll have to live in America. That's what his father told Nanna, that he would have to go back soon on another project. Oh, Divi! Can you imagine? Me, in America. I need clothes. Amma, I need clothes. Not these ugly shalwars, but modern clothes. Amma, did you hear me?" She went on and on in this way, and Poornima was glad she would soon be out of the house.

Preparations intensified in the middle of July, but on a windless day, late in the afternoon, during tea, the matchmaker, whose name was Balaji, arrived at their door. He was invited in with great aplomb, but Poornima's mother-in-law took one look at his face and put down her teacup. "What is it?" she said. "What's wrong?"

The matchmaker looked at the nearly empty teacups, and then at Poornima. "Don't just stand there. Tea. Bring us some tea."

By the time Poornima returned, Aruna was crying.

"*Off?* But why?" her mother-in-law wailed.

Balaji wouldn't say. Only that they'd had a change of heart.

"Change of heart? But why? Why? We gave them everything they asked for."

He sipped his tea and looked at Aruna sadly. "She's a fine girl. We'll find another match."

"Another match? You fool. What happened to this one? How does it look? Practically on the altar, and *then* they cancel. Why?"

She got no more out of him, only that it was better to leave it all behind. Move forward, he told Poornima's mother-in-law. The way forward is the only way, he said.

But rumors trickled down.

The main one was that somebody had told the Guntur family that Kishore's mangled hand was a genetic condition, and any children Aruna would have might also be disfigured.

"That's ridiculous," Kishore said, infuriated. "They're idiots. Dongalu."

Poornima was serving him dinner. She scooped some rice onto his plate, and then she said, "Is it?"

"Is it what?"

"Is it a genetic condition?"

Kishore blanched; he got up from the table and left the room without a word.

"Get out!" her mother-in-law screamed. "Get out of this house. It's you. It's because of you they canceled the wedding. You're a curse on this family. It's all because of you."

Am I a curse? Poornima wondered vaguely, climbing the stairs to the second floor. She didn't go into the bedroom, where she knew Kishore would be. Instead, she stood on the terrace and looked out at the palm trees swaying in the distance, and the thatched-roof huts huddled beneath them, and then she turned to the west and watched the last rays of the sun leave the sky, as if they had no use for it anymore, and Poornima wanted to follow it, follow the sun, and she thought, What has my life added up to? What's been taken, what's been left? What's it worth? Then she heard footsteps. She thought it must be Kishore, and braced for what would come, but it was Divya, holding out a plate of rice. "You didn't get to eat," she said.

Poornima nearly cried out with gratitude.

Divya turned and went back down the steps.

Poornima idled on the terrace well into the night, and then snuck noiselessly into the bedroom. Kishore was turned toward the wall, and she thought he must be sleeping, but no, his breathing was ragged, uneven. He was awake, and he was angry. She could feel his fury. She edged to the opposite end of the bed and waited, expecting the worst, but he seemed to eventually fall asleep. Or maybe she did.

The next morning, too, was strangely quiet. Divya went to school; nowadays, Aruna nearly always stayed in the bedroom she and Divya shared. Kishore stayed home from work. He said he was feeling ill, but instead of resting, he and his mother locked themselves away in the upstairs bedroom. Midafternoon, Poornima's mother-in-law came downstairs. She looked at Poornima sweetly and said, "My dear, how about some bhajis for tea today? I feel like eating bhajis. Would you mind?"

Poornima stared at her. She'd never once heard this voice before.

There was only one potato in the house, and some onions, so she cut those up and put the oil on to heat. Her mother-in-law lingered in the kitchen and even offered to help with the chopping, but Poornima said it was all right; she would make them. The oil began to pop, and then to slightly smoke. Poornima dipped an onion into the batter. Just then, Kishore walked into the kitchen. Poornima was startled—never once, not once, had Kishore come into the kitchen.

He, too, smiled sweetly.

No, she thought in that instant. No.

None of it made sense, and yet it did.

She dropped the onion back into the batter and stepped away from them, and away from the stove. In that instant, both of them lurched: one body toward her, and the other toward the stove.

Poornima's vision blurred. She didn't know who it was that grabbed her, but she pushed them away so hard that she fell backward. She was on the floor, and they were both now by the stove.

Why are they standing there? She had just enough time to think, Why are they standing by the stove? before an arm swept something off it, and Kishore and her mother-in-law sprang away and raced to the other end of the kitchen.

She turned her head to follow them, and that was why, when the oil landed, it splattered across the left side of her face, down her neck, and caught her upper arm and shoulder. Poornima felt a fire, and then the fire, and everything with it, went out.

7

Kishore and her mother-in-law refused to pay the hospital bills, so Poornima was discharged on her second day. Only her father-in-law and Divya came to get her; when she sat down in the autorickshaw, the bandages still on her face and neck and arm and shoulder, she felt so small, so placental, that she shivered in the midday heat. Her father-in-law said, "You can stay for a day or two, but then you have to leave. It's no good for you in Namburu. It's no good. I'll go tonight and buy you a ticket to Indravalli."

Poornima nodded imperceptibly, and that slight nod sent a shattering pain up the left side of her face.

When they reached the house, her mother-in-law and Kishore were in the sitting room, and they watched her with contempt. Divya led her up the stairs, and when they reached the terrace, Poornima had her go in first and cover the mirror on the armoire. Only then did she enter. She lay down on the bed. Divya left, and then she came back that evening with a plate of food. Poornima looked at the plate of food and started to cry. Divya left again and came back with a glass of milk, and this she forced Poornima to drink.

The next day was the same. Only Divya came and went. But this time, she brought her books with her, and opened one of them, and began to study. Poornima made a sound, a squeak. Divya looked up from her book. "It's my Telugu primer," she said.

The primer was from the British era, she told Poornima; the small village school in Namburu never having had the money to buy new ones. Poornima opened her mouth slightly, the slightest amount, in an attempt to speak, but the pain shot through her like a cannon.

"Do you want me to read aloud to you?"

Poornima blinked.

The story Divya read was told from the perspective of a man on a ship in the early 1900s. The man's name was Kirby. Divya paused and said, "It doesn't say if it's his family name or his given name." Then she continued reading.

In the story, this man Kirby was traveling on a ship from Pondicherry to Africa. While traveling, he met another man, also on the ship, who was a Portuguese army colonel. The colonel, according to Kirby, was traveling to his family's estate in Mozambique. They grew sisal, the colonel told Kirby, and went on endlessly about how sisal looked (like a Mexican agave, Kirby wrote, though neither Poornima nor Divya, even with a footnoted explanation, had any idea what that was either), how it was grown and then harvested. He said the blades of the sisal plant could cut deeper than a sword. Kirby then asked the colonel, But how do you handle it?

Oh, we don't, the colonel said. The Negroes do all that.

On his last night on the ship, before he was due to disembark the next morning at Lourenço Marques, the old colonel told Kirby this story:

It happened one winter, the colonel began, when I was stationed at Wellington, near Madras. Years ago. Our cantonment, quite suddenly, was overrun with rats. Hundreds and hundreds of them. They got into the food, the beds, the artillery. And not just any kind of rat, he said, and here he cupped his hands so that they were as big around as a dinner plate. They were enormous. Well, no one knew how to get rid of them. We tried poison and traps and we even had this tribal shaman come down from the mountains, some sort of expert on rodents and scorpions and such. None of it did any good, you see. The rats went right on eating and shitting everywhere. (Here there was inserted another footnote indicating that the colonel had meant to say *defecating*.)

After about a month of this, the colonel continued, one of the young soldiers noticed that after he'd spit on the ground, a rat came around, sniffed his sputum, and looked up at him with the kindest, most concerned eyes the man had ever seen. The soldier told us about it at dinner that evening, almost joking, you see. But I could tell the young man was a bit shaken. The camp doctor heard this, and that very night he diagnosed him with early-stage tuberculosis.

Kirby noted that here, the colonel took a sip of his champagne (again, Poornima and Divya shrugged, not knowing what that was). Rats, you see, he said, putting down his glass of champagne, can detect tuberculosis well before modern medicine can. That damn rat very nearly saved the camp from an epidemic. Amazing, isn't it?

Kirby, apparently, then asked the colonel, What about the rats? What happened to them?

That's the thing. One day they all just left. Picked up and disappeared. It was as if their sole purpose was to warn us. To save the thing that was trying to destroy them.

At this point, Kirby, writing this account, said he laughed out loud but that the colonel only closed his eyes. At the end of the story in the Telugu primer, Kirby wrote that early the next morning, when the ship had docked in Lourenço Marques, they went to wake the colonel, but he was dead. Kirby wrote that laying on his narrow ship's bed, the colonel was pallid, his skin nearly translucent, and that he could almost see the blood drifting away from the colonel's heart.

That was the end of the story, and when Divya stopped reading, Poornima looked at her. A young girl, the same age she and Savitha had been when they'd first met. She then looked down at Divya's neck—brown like bark, a vein throbbing, pulsing steadily, a lighthouse beneath her skin—and then

Poornima thought about the poor colonel, and the rats, and Mozambique, wherever that was, and she didn't have to wonder what it looked like, blood drifting away from the heart.

The next day was a Sunday. Everyone was at home. Poornima could hear them moving downstairs, talking, laughing, and the vendors, mostly vegetable sellers, stopping at various doors, yelling out their wares, eggplant and beans and peppers plucked just that morning. The dew still clinging to their skins. The Krishna didn't flow past Namburu, but Poornima thought she caught its scent on the wind, could see the fishing nets flung into its waters, twirling like langas. When she closed her eyes, there were the saris drying on the opposite shore. Every color, fluttering in the river breeze, fields of wildflowers.

Her eyes, now, were often closed. She stayed in the room all day, only going downstairs to use the latrine. She hadn't bathed since the spill, and her musk and animal smell, mingled with the smell of her sweat, of rotting bandages, of copper (Had she gotten her period? Maybe. She didn't care to look.), and burned flesh, always the smell of burned flesh, assaulted her as she tried to sleep. She didn't mean to sleep. She meant to stay awake, all night, if needed. Her father-in-law had come upstairs the previous night and handed her a train ticket to Indravalli. Second class, instead of third, so she could travel in relative comfort. He hadn't looked her in the eye, but she knew he was sorry. She knew so little about him, but she knew suddenly that his life was lived in regret. He stood at the door for a moment, before leaving, and she was lying on the bed, and she thought they must look like two wounded animals, circling in a dark cave.

After he left, Poornima stared at the ticket, and then she put it under her pillow. It was the twice-daily passenger train, leaving Namburu at 2:30 P.M. and arriving in Indravalli at 2:55 P.M. Twenty-five minutes. That's all there had ever been.

She thought Kishore might come upstairs, if only to ensure that she was leaving, but only Divya came in the evening, bringing Poornima's dinner of rice and pappu, the rice cooked soft so that she wouldn't have to chew very much. After she left, Poornima closed her eyes again. It was dark when she opened them. There was a gibbous moon, so when she studied the shadowed room, she saw the shapes of the furniture, the gleam of the stone floor, the pattern of flowers on the sheet that covered her. She looked at the desk; she saw, even in the moonlight, the stack of papers, the accounting papers that had given her such pleasure to decipher, such a sense of accomplishment and purpose. It was nothing, she realized, her heart breaking. All of it was nothing. It was nothing in the face of something as simple as hot oil, and the slightest evil.

She then rose heavily, into the silver moonlight, and stepped onto the terrace. She would miss the terrace; she realized it was the only thing, along with Divya, that she *would* miss from her two years in Namburu. She walked to the edge of the terrace and looked at the first stars, and she thought of the many years she had left to live. Or maybe she had none at all. It was impossible to know. But if she didn't die tonight, if she didn't die within the amount of time a human being can readily foresee, can honestly imagine (a day? a week?), What, she wondered, will I do with all those years? All those many years? To look forward, Poornima realized, was to also look back. And so she saw her mother, as she had once been: young and alive. Sitting at the loom by lantern light, or bending over a steaming pot, or tending to one of Poornima's brothers or her sister, wiping their faces or bathing them or pushing the hair from their eyes. That's all she could recall her mother ever doing: something for someone else. Even Poornima's most tender memories—of being fed by her mother's hand on the bus trip to see her grandparents, or the weight of it against her hair while she'd been combing it—had all of them to do with her mother doing something for her child, never for herself. Is that how she'd meant to spend her life? Is that how lives were meant to be spent?

Now, Poornima looked to the future. She saw herself going back to Indravalli. At 2:55 P.M. the next day, she would step off the passenger train, walk to her father's house, and enter it. She could see him clearly, sitting on the veranda, on the hemp-rope bed, smoking his tobacco and watching her. Just as she was watching him. Perhaps her siblings would be there, perhaps they wouldn't. But what the future held most clearly—more clearly even than the image of her father—was the image of a battlefield. And no battlefield, in all the histories of man, could compare with the one Poornima now saw: blood-soaked, and littered—littered with what? She moved closer, she knelt to see, her eyes widened: it was herself. It was littered with her limbs, her organs, her feet, her hands, her scalped hair, and even her skin, shredded, mangled as if by dogs.

Poornima blinked, but it wasn't tears she blinked back. What was it? She didn't know, but she could see it—floating in the air around her, suffocating, spinning like ash.

She walked back into the upstairs room, took out the train ticket from under her pillow, and ripped it in half, then quarters, then eighths, and then she let the tiny pieces fall to the floor like confetti. She watched them fall with a certain delight, and then she turned to the armoire, opened it, and took out the locked box. There was no key that she could see; probably her mother-in-law had the key on the key ring she always kept tucked into the waistband of her sari. Calmly, Poornima gripped the statuette—the one that had been presented to Kishore for being first in his college—and slammed it against the lock. The lock broke, but so did the statuette, at the point where the figurine (of a bird taking flight from a branch) was cauterized to the engraved base. She threw both pieces of the statuette back into the armoire. The papers in the box were of no interest to Poornima, but the jewelry—only a thin gold chain and two bangles; the rest Kishore kept in a safe-deposit box at the bank—she tied into a pouch at the end of her pallu and slipped it into the waistband of her own sari; the cash (a little over five hundred rupees) she placed into her blouse, next to her left breast. Then the box, too, she tossed back into the armoire, closed the door, and stood in front of it.

The mirror was still covered with a sheet, and Poornima stood looking at the sheet, as if it held an answer. A sign. But it held nothing; it was just a sheet. She ripped it off the mirror with such force that the wind in the room shifted; her hair flew up and around her face as if she were staring out to sea. But Poornima felt none of it, none of the wind and none of the sea. She stood perfectly still in front of the mirror—it was the most she'd ever seen of herself. The mirror in Indravalli had only been a hand mirror, and while in Namburu, though she'd been living here for almost two years, she'd never really stood in front of this mirror. Or any other. But now, she stood. She saw that she was no longer a girl. And if she had ever been pretty, she certainly wasn't anymore. She stepped closer, and then she raised her hands to her face and removed the bandages, one by one. The left side of her face and neck were just as she imagined them, or worse: flaming red, blistered, gray and black on the edges of the wide burn, the left cheek hollow, pink, silvery, and wet, as if it'd been turned inside out. Her left arm and shoulder, though, were not as bad as she'd thought. They had only been splattered by droplets of oil, rather than splashed, and the splatters already seemed to be healing. But the face and neck she knew she had to keep from getting infected, which meant she needed clean bandages and iodine. With the bandages off, she looked even more grotesque than she did with them on. She recalled the doctor saying, while she was in a morphine haze, "You're lucky it didn't get you below the neck."

She'd turned her sleepy gaze to him.

"Your husband won't leave you. As long as you have proper breasts, a man won't leave you."

She'd wanted to say—had she not been in an opiate haze, had she not been content to simply close her eyes—Then I wish it'd gotten the breasts, too.

Poornima lay back on the bed and waited. She waited until the darkest part of the night, then changed into a fresh sari, drank the glass of water that Divya had left for her, and snuck downstairs, out of the house, and out of Namburu, and all of this she did with a shocking stealth and precision and cold-bloodedness, because of course she knew exactly what she was going to do, no matter how long it took her, no matter how difficult the journey, and she knew exactly where all of this had always been leading, always.

She was going to find Savitha.

8

Poornima made a rough calculation and decided that Savitha had left at around four in the morning. She guessed this because, as she recalled, on that last night, she'd gone to sleep with her arm around her, and when she'd woken up, with the sun, Savitha was gone. When did the sun rise? Maybe six thirty or seven? If that was the case, then Savitha had to have left much earlier, to avoid detection, so probably she left at four or five in the morning. Closer to four, Poornima guessed. But why not earlier? Say at two or three in the morning? It was possible, Poornima thought, but where would she go? None of the buses or trains ran at that hour, and trying to catch a ride on a lorry on the highway would've been too risky. Besides, if she'd done that, if she'd gotten into a random lorry on the Tenali Road, then she could be anywhere by now. She could be in Assam or Kerala or Rajasthan or Kashmir. Or anywhere in between. Anywhere at all. And *that*, Poornima refused to consider.

She also refused to consider the nearly two years that had passed since Savitha had left, and that that amount of time, too, could have taken her anywhere. But this Poornima chose to ignore. After all, she told herself, time was simple. Time was no kind of mystery. It was naked and unblinking; it was like the buffalo she saw plowing the fields. All it did was plod along, never wavering and without a thought in its head. Time was all her days in Namburu, and all the days before that. But geography? Now, geography Poornima considered a mystery. Its mountains, its rivers, its vast and endless plains, its seas that she had never seen. Geography was the unknown.

So it was decided: if she had left at four A.M. or thereabouts, she could've taken only one of two buses. Only two buses ran at that time of morning. One went south, to Tirupati, and the other went north, to Vijayawada. Now, here was another geographic mystery: Which one would she have taken?

Poornima considered the question, and then something floated back to her. Something so fine, so like gossamer, that it could hardly be considered a thought, or even a fragment of a thought, but it was there, she was certain it was there, and she brushed at it as if it were a spider's web, caught in the deep recesses of her mind. Poornima was by now on the outskirts of Namburu. She was going to the bus depot that was on the highway, rather than the one in Namburu, so that no one would see her. As she approached it, she saw an advertisement for amla oil. On the advertisement was the green amla fruit, with sparkling oil, lit by the sun, dripping out of it and straight into a pale green bottle. Next to the bottle was a photograph of a woman with thick, lustrous hair, taken as she spun her head, her hair fanning out toward the viewer as she turned. Presumably, the amla oil had made her hair so lustrous and thick. Poornima stared at the advertisement—she studied the perfect amla fruit, and the drops of oil, and the woman—and then she looked again at the amla. *The perfect fruit*. She waved aside the gossamer web, and then she knew. She knew where Savitha had gone: she'd gone to Majuli. She had to have.

Poornima smiled; her entire face burst into pain, but she smiled anyway. And where was Majuli? She recalled her saying it was on the Brahmaputra, and Poornima knew this much about geography: she knew the Brahmaputra was north, and so, twenty minutes later, Poornima flagged down the bus to Vijayawada, going north, and she didn't even notice when the driver and the conductor and the old woman she sat down next to gave her strange looks, revolted looks, as they stared at her face, her burns, no longer covered, but raw and pink like the sunrise.

When she got to Vijayawada, the first thing she did was go to a medical shop and buy bandages and iodine. She learned how to wrap the burns and apply the iodine from the man who was working there—an old man with glasses, who asked no questions at all about how she'd gotten the burns, as if he saw women with this exact injury every day, which Poornima figured he probably did. The only question in his mind, she guessed, was whether it was oil or acid. But even that he didn't ask, though she thought he might've been able to tell just by looking at them. Regardless, she liked him; she liked how gentle he was when he showed her how to wrap the bandage around her neck and over her cheek, and then to tie it so it was snug but not too tight. He said, "It needs air," referring to the burn, and then he said, "What else do you need?"

Poornima said she needed directions to the train station, and he nodded. This, too, he seemed to expect.

The walk, he said, was long, so it was better to take the bus. But Poornima decided to walk anyway, and along the way, she bought a packet of idlis, because they were all that she could manage to chew. Then she drank a cup of tea, standing next to the tea stall, with the men gathered around staring openly, or surreptitiously, but all of them with disgust—knowing what was beneath her bandages—and maybe a few, one or two, with shame.

When Poornima reached the train station, after an hour of walking, the sky was just beginning to lighten. The white marble floors, strewn with sleeping bodies, still shone between the array of arms and legs draped over the very old and the very young. She stepped gingerly between them, entered the vestibule, and studied the listing of trains. Obviously, Majuli wouldn't · be listed, since it was an island, so Poornima looked for all northbound trains. There were none. At least, none that left from Vijayawada.

She stared and stared at the listings, thinking she must be mistaken, but not one was going anywhere beyond Eluru. She turned and went to the ladies' counter. It wasn't open yet, and it wouldn't be for another two hours. At this, Poornima considered waiting in the vestibule, but then she thought she might be able to find out more information on the platform.

She paid five rupees for the platform ticket, and when she walked through, the entire length of the first platform was bustling. An overnight train from Chennai had just arrived. The coffee and tea stalls were steaming, the puri wallah yelled through the windows of the train, running up and down its length, vada and idli packets were piled nearly to the rafters, and even the magazine and cigarette and biscuit shops were open, along with the sugar-cane juicer shop across from it, already thronged with people. When she passed the water fountain, it was ten deep, with everyone pushing and try-ing to get to one of the six taps.

Poornima had never seen so many people. She stood for a moment, dis-oriented, and then realized she should be looking for someone to ask about the northern trains. There were hundreds of porters, everywhere it seemed, in their brick-colored shirts, but they paid her no attention, and in fact pushed her aside once or twice to make way. Poornima edged toward the wall, away from the train, and waited. Finally, after twenty minutes, the train pulled away, and everything, all of a sudden, stopped. Now the por-ters, the ones who hadn't been hired, were standing around, listless, drink-ing a cup of tea or coffee, and waiting for the next train. Poornima pulled her pallu over her head and approached a group of three who were standing near one of the wide girders. They weren't talking to one another, but they were definitely standing together.

"Do you know anything about the northern trains?" Poornima asked.

The slightest one, hardly older than an adolescent, looked her up and down and stopped just before her face. He said, "Do I look like the infor-mation booth?"

"It's closed."

"Then wait," another one of them said.

"But there's not a single one going north. Nothing past Eluru. Do you know anything about it?" she said, turning to the third man, older, with a graying mustache and a thick shock of salt-and-pepper hair.

He, too, looked at Poornima, mostly at her bandaged face, which she was trying unsuccessfully to obscure, and said, "The Naxals. They blew up the tracks past Eluru."

"So there are *no* trains?"

"Did you hear me?"

"But no trains? None? How can that be?"

The young man laughed. "Take it up with Indian Railways. I'm sure they'll be happy to explain."

Poornima walked away from the porters and back to her spot by the wall. She slid to the ground.

How long would five hundred rupees last her? Not very long. And it was too soon to sell the jewelry. She decided to stay at the train station, sleep in the vestibule, with the others, or on one of the platforms, maybe the farthest one from the signaling office, until the northern tracks were fixed, or until they kicked her out. She could wash at the taps, eat from the stalls, and as for the latrines, well, the latrines were just the tracks, anyway. Why didn't I bring a blanket? she thought, annoyed with herself.

Still, once she decided to stay, the first thing she did was buy a small water jug, for the purpose of washing up, and then she sat down, next to the Higginbotham's bookstore stall, and tried to look like she belonged there, like she was waiting for a train, or for someone—someone dear to her, someone *on* a train—to arrive. The stall had a niche, behind a stand of magazines and comic books, and Poornima found that she fit perfectly into this niche, as long as her legs were pulled to her chest and wouldn't be seen. From this vantage point, looking up, she was amazed by how few people looked down. None, as far as she could tell during her first few hours in the niche.

After a time, she got up to stretch her legs and walked up and down the bridge that stretched over the platforms, with stairs leading down to each. From here, she could see the long sinews of the trains coming and going, the roofs over each of the platforms, and the tracks—how many were there?

Maybe twenty, maybe more; she'd never seen such a thing, she'd never even known that so much commerce, so many people, and so much travel existed in the world—stretching in every which direction like the lines on the palm of a hand.

This was her daily schedule: sleep on one of the platforms, or the vestibule, check the train departures first thing every morning for anything going past Eluru, and if there were none, buy herself a packet of idlis and a cup of coffee or tea, depending on her mood, and then walk or huddle in the niche behind Higginbotham's.

It wasn't until the beginning of her second week that she met Rishi. He was a slim boy about her age, maybe a little younger. She had noticed him before, lurking on the platforms, at their very edges, and studying everyone who passed him. He studied them so keenly that she wondered if he wanted to draw them, or rob them. But he never did, at least not that she could see. He was there every day, just as she was. He'd studied her, too, once or twice, though she'd ignored him and had kept walking. Still, he must've known she was mostly living behind Higginbotham's because one afternoon, he came over and began to examine the stand of magazines and comic books. He picked up a *Panchatantra* and flipped through it. Then he picked up a film magazine that had a woman in a red dress on the cover. When he put that one back on the stand, somebody Poornima couldn't see yelled out, "Hey. Hey! You. Either buy it, or don't. But don't get your mother's hair grease all over it." The boy backed away from the stand—Poornima could see his sandaled feet take a step back—but then he swung his head and looked right at her.

Poornima jumped. Her heart stopped. Was he the police?

"What happened to your face?" he said.

Poornima pulled her pallu down over her forehead, nearly over her eyes, and didn't say anything.

"Are you deaf?"

She shrugged.

"Let me see." He came toward her; Poornima pushed deeper into the wall. He knelt a little, but gently, with a kind of grace. He wasn't the police; that much Poornima knew, though she kept her face lowered and raised only her eyes. He looked in them, and then he said, "Your neck, too? Your father or your husband?"

Poornima was quiet for a moment, as if she was trying to decide, and she said, "No one. It was an accident."

The boy nodded, and then he said, "It always is. My name's Rishi. What's yours?"

Why was he talking to her? What did he want? She clearly had no money, but he didn't seem frightening. He seemed more like a brother than anything else. Still, she didn't respond, and after lingering a few moments, he shrugged and walked away. She watched him: he walked forward, still where Poornima could see him, and then he went and talked to somebody unloading burlap sacks from a goods train, and then he bought himself a cup of tea. He looked in Poornima's direction once or twice, as if making sure she was still there, and then, when he'd finished his tea, he waved at her, as if he'd known her all his life, as if she were an old friend he was seeing off at the train station, and then he walked right past her, out of the vestibule and into the world.

But he was back again the next day. And the next. And the next. And each time, he waved at Poornima when he came in the mornings and waved again when he left at night. She began, surprisingly, to look forward to seeing him. If he happened to pass her in the middle of the day, as he often did, seeing as they both wandered the same ten platforms, then he didn't wave; he didn't even look at her. They nearly bumped into each other once, on the passenger bridge over one of the platforms, and yet he didn't so much as acknowledge her. How odd, she thought. That evening—after they'd bumped into each other on the bridge—she sprang up when she saw him approaching the exit, on his way to wherever he went every night, and she said, "Poornima."

He looked at her and smiled, and she felt a rush of relief and warmth.

After that, they walked and talked together almost every day. She told him about Kishore, and her mother-in-law, and even about Indravalli, and a little about her father. Then she said, "Where do you go every night?"

He straightened his back, and his voice grew serious. "I have a very important job."

"Oh? But you're here all day. Is it a night job?"

He seemed to consider this for a moment, and he finally said, "I work here. I'm working now. I go in the evenings to report back to my boss."

"You're *working*? But all you do is walk around."

"It just looks like that. You don't know anything."

Maybe I don't, Poornima thought, but she knew when someone was working, and Rishi certainly wasn't. "What is it that you do?"

"I find people."

"Like who? Like lost people?"

He shrugged. "How long are you going to stay there? Behind Higginbotham's?"

"Till the northern trains start running."

"The Naxals blew up the tracks."

"Why do you think I'm still here?"

"Do you have someone up north? Someone waiting for you?" he asked, his voice taking on a strange curiosity.

"Yes. In a way."

"The tracks could take weeks, months. Why don't you just go around?"

That had never occurred to Poornima. Why hadn't it ever occurred to her? Something so simple.

"You're lying."

"I'm not lying. About what?" she said.

"You don't have someone waiting for you. I can tell. I can tell you're alone."

Poornima scratched at her bandages. The itchiness had begun, and she could hardly sleep or eat or do anything for how maddening it was to not scratch. "How can you tell?"

"I help girls just like you," he said. "Girls who are alone. I help them be safe and make money. Just until they're ready to leave. Like when the tracks are fixed, for instance. But most never leave, they like it so much." He asked Poornima if she wanted a cup of tea, and she said yes.

"What do they do?"

"Office work. Like a secretary. Or they work in a fancy shop. Or sometimes in a sari store. Things like that. Easy work."

"And you've helped lots of girls?"

Rishi nodded. "Oh yes. Hundreds. Probably more. I know every single girl who walks through this train station. I have one of those memories, you see. I know them all. And I know which ones could use a job like that."

Poornima was silent, and then she said, "Every one?"

"Not a single girl gets on or off any train in this station without me knowing. I remember their faces. I never forget their faces. Sometimes, I talk to them, just like I'm talking to you, and then they take the jobs and they always make a point to come and find me and thank me."

"I've never seen any girl thanking you."

He sighed loudly. And then he said, "Why would you? Sitting like a mole behind Higginbotham's. Anyway, I have work to do. I can't stand here and talk to you all day. Take the glass back when you're done," he said, referring to her teacup. He turned away, but not very convincingly. He started to walk down the platform.

"Wait," Poornima yelled after him. He stopped a yard or two away from her, and she thought he might be smiling, but she couldn't be sure. It was just a sense she had. Though why would he be smiling?

When he turned to look at her, his face was serious. He said, "What? I have things to do."

"Every girl?"

"Yes. That's what I said."

"How long have you been here? At the train station?"

"Why?"

"Just curious."

He thought for a moment. "Maybe three years. Four."

Poornima felt a shiver go through her, and she thought, What if he did? What if he *did* see her? "Did you happen to see a girl, not quite two years ago? She would've been a little taller than me. And wearing a blue sari, patterned with peacocks. A beautiful smile. From Indravalli?"

Rishi considered for a long moment. His eyes began to spark. "What else?"

"She was thin, but not as thin as me. Straight hair, but with small ringlets at her forehead. Probably she was going north, too."

"Did she have pretty lips? And did you say the sari was blue?"

Poornima's eyes also lit up. "Yes! And her name was Savitha. Did you see her?"

"Savitha? Did you say Savitha?" Rishi smiled—a wide smile that plumped up his thin face, as if his cheeks had sprouted for just that smile. "Why didn't you say so earlier? Of course I know Savitha."

"You *do*?"

"Yes, it must've been two years ago. Now I remember. And she was from Indravalli. Are you from there, too?"

"What did she say? Where did she go?"

"Not north. Where did you get the idea she would go north? She's right here. In Vijayawada. I got her a job."

"Here? In Vijayawada?"

"Yes. Right here. Come on, I'll take you to her." He smiled again, and this time Poornima noticed that one of his teeth was discolored: one of the lower ones, in the front. She looked at it and wondered if he was lying.

9

They left the station by the same way Poornima had come in, nearly two weeks earlier. They walked for what seemed like hours, through the Green Park Colony and Chittinagar, and then they entered an area with run-down homes and shacks. The tea stalls seemed dirtier, and the eyes of the men followed them, rimmed with red. They saw Poornima's bandages and turned quickly away.

"Do you have to have those?" he said.

"Have what?"

"Those bandages."

Poornima felt the need to scratch again, the moment she thought about them. "Well, yes, of course I do."

"Savitha might mind them."

"Why would she?"

They walked on. By now, there were no more run-down houses, but only empty lots. Poornima could tell they were getting farther away from the Krishna. The wide-open lots were inhabited only by pigs and feral dogs and heaps of trash. At the edge of one of these garbage-strewn fields was a massive house, much bigger than anything else in the area, and much better maintained, too. They turned into the drive. "Savitha is *here*? She works here?"

"Sort of," he said enigmatically.

Rishi didn't ring the bell; they walked right in. As soon as they did, Poornima heard shuffling coming from the second floor. She looked up into the open balcony and saw maybe five or six girls, her age and even younger, milling for a moment, and then turning and walking away. She didn't see Savitha, though. Rishi said, "Come on," and led her deeper down the first-floor hallway. At its end was a door, and when they entered it—knocking this time—a thin man with large spectacles was sitting behind a desk. He had skin the texture of jackfruit, maybe from a childhood disease, Poornima thought. He looked up and eyed her, and his expression of boredom turned to distaste. But the edge of his gaze held more than distaste, and Poornima nearly stepped back and fled, to see such bold and ready ruthlessness.

"What is that?" he said, not looking at Rishi but clearly addressing him.

"Train station, Guru."

"Are you stupid?"

"You said we were short, Guru. So I thought maybe—"

"Is that right? Is that what you thought?"

Rishi lowered his head and nodded.

"Well, take it back," the man growled. "She's ugly. And those bandages. Who'd pay for that? Don't you have any sense? No one does. That's the problem. And guess what that Samuel did? Left without a word. Took one of the girls with him. Now what am I supposed to do? Nobody to do the books and one less girl. And you. Bringing *that* around. Get rid of it."

Poornima looked from Rishi to the man behind the desk. She thought of her money, and her jewelry, and she thought she might never have another chance. "Do you know my friend? From my village. Rishi said—" she began.

The man was scribbling in a book, a logbook of some sort, and when

Poornima spoke, he looked up at her as if he was amazed, perplexed that she had a voice. He made a slow fist. "I said, get her out of here."

"He said you did."

He put down his pen, and she could see the anger rising. Constricting his mouth, his nose, and finally his eyes into pinpoints of rage. "You know, I've seen monkeys more attractive than you."

Rishi grabbed her arm, as if to pull her out of the room. Poornima shook him off. She thought of the weaving hut, the morning after Savitha left, and she thought of how she must've walked out, all alone, into the night. She wondered whether she had turned around, just before leaving, and stood at the door, searching for a reason to stay, and yet hadn't found one. Nothing, not ever, would be emptier for Poornima than that thought. "I can do books," she said.

The man looked at her.

"I can do books. Accounting. I've learned."

The man laughed. He said, "Since when do village girls learn accounting? Where did you say you were from?"

"I can. I'll show you."

The man looked at Rishi and Rishi looked back at him. Then they both looked at Poornima. The man then turned the logbook around to face Poornima and said, "Go ahead."

Poornima studied it. They just seemed a jumble of numbers at first, with letters heading most of the columns, with what had to be dates on the left-most column. But the longer she looked at them, the more she realized there was a pattern: the numbers under some of the letters were always bigger. And the dates, she saw, were the previous month's dates. Then she realized what the letters were; they were initials. Three of them were *S*, followed by a number. Cold dripped down her spine. "Wouldn't it be better if you knew more? Like, if it was the same man, over and over again? And what days he was coming. And whether for the same girl. If you tracked that, you could charge more."

There was silence. A dog barked. "So you can," the man said. He looked at her, as if for the first time. "What else can you do?"

"I can cook, and I can clean, and I can work on the charkha."

Guru signaled with a wave of his hand for Rishi to leave the room. Once he'd gone, he looked at her with sudden interest, but interest laced with cruelty, with calculation.

"Guru," he said. "That's my name. We have more of these. Six others. You have to do all of them. Where are you staying?"

"At the train station."

"There's a room in back. You can stay there. Nothing in the room will belong to you, but we can try it for a few days. Are you willing to try it for a few days?" His tone sharpened, pointed at her like a dagger, and Poornima realized he was no longer talking about the books, or account keeping. She nodded.

Then he said, "What happened to your face?"

"Nothing," Poornima said. "I had an accident."

Guru smiled, horribly. Then he sat back in his chair and said, "Oil? Or acid?"

She was given a windowless room in the back, on the first floor. There was a cot on the floor, a framed picture of Ganesha over the door, and a small refrigerator in one corner. There was an attached bathroom with a latrine and a sink with running water and a high strip of window, which Poornima couldn't reach. She stood and stared at the unreachable rectangle of light. Then she examined the bathroom; she'd never been in a room with an attached latrine or running water. She hid the money and jewelry under the cot and then went to take a bucket bath.

When she came out and tried to open the outer door, she found that it was locked. She pushed on it, banged and yelled, but there was no sound on the other side. She stepped back and stared at the door. Maybe it had locked by accident? But it couldn't have; she'd seen the metal rod on the door handle, and how it had to be pushed into a set of grooves to lock. What did that mean? Were they imprisoning her? *Were* they? The thought pushed a scream out of her throat so loud that the frame of Ganesha fell off the wall. She flung herself at the door. She grew hoarse from yelling and crying; her hands stung from pounding on the door. Nothing. Not a sound from outside. She slumped against it and closed her eyes. When she opened them, she saw the refrigerator on the other side of the room. She rose unsteadily and looked inside. There were two bottles of water and a bowl of glistening fruit: guavas and apples and sapota and grapes. She closed the refrigerator and banged on the door again. Still, nothing. When she'd exhausted herself, she went and lay down on the cot and forced herself to sleep.

She had no idea how much time had passed when she woke up. For a moment, she was afraid. Afraid of what? she asked herself. Being locked in a room? The door never opening again? The door opening? Suddenly, none of it felt much different from the years she'd spent in Namburu, so she went to the refrigerator again and took a hesitant sip from one of the bottles of water. Then she took another, longer sip. She was hungry, so she reached for one of the fruits, but then her hand, of its own accord, simply stopped. Paused. Just as she reached for an apple. She held it there, motionless, wondering why, and that's when they came back to her, Guru's words: Nothing in the room will belong to you. Why had he said that? It seemed—with her hand still hovering near the fruit—a strange thing to say. But was it? Maybe this is a test, she thought, with sudden clarity. Maybe he wants to test whether I'll take any of the fruit. It seemed a perfectly reasonable test for an accountant: to see if they would steal from their employer. Take what had been clearly stated didn't belong to them. But she was hungry, and she thought for a moment she would take the fruit anyway, but then she thought, If Savitha *is* here, eating an apple—an apple—might spoil my one chance of finding her.

She closed the refrigerator door.

She sat in the room for three days without eating. At first, she felt a slow, growing hunger that soon gnawed at her stomach. Doubled her over in pain.

And then weakness. The hunger was a beast, and she willed it to be still, restricting herself to the cot as if chained, drinking great gulps of water. She slept fitfully but stayed in bed well into late morning. By the middle of the second day, her skin was hot and feverish. The water did no good. She wondered if she was ill. She seriously considered eating the fruit—what if they never opened the door?—but then she thought of Savitha. She was here. Poornima only needed to pass this test; she was here. She settled back on the cot and thought about food. That did no good. So then she thought about hunger. In Indravalli, there had been plenty of days when she'd gone hungry, giving her share to her brothers and sister, but there had always been a little for her, even if it was only a handful of rice and pickle. But *this* hunger: this hunger was a ravaged land.

The weakness spread. She was tired from the exertion of going to the bathroom, of lifting the water bottle. On the third day, her skin ceased to function. A drop of water landed on her arm, and her entire body convulsed from the impact. It was as if she no longer had skin, and the water had landed on raw, exposed tissue. She didn't take a bucket bath on the third day. She could hardly stand. But her body began to emit an odor. She thought her burns might be infected, or the bandages were rotting, but it was neither: it was her pores. It was not her usual sweat; that smell she knew. This was more piquant, intense, and absinthal. The sheet on the cot was sticky with it, and yet the peculiar scent of her famished body, every one of her limbs afire, felt to Poornima as if hunger were the most natural state, the truest one. She hardly even wanted food; food became an abstract thing, a memory for which she felt mostly apathy, and sometimes hatred.

On the morning of the fourth day, the door opened.

Still on the cot, Poornima opened her eyes and didn't bother to get up. It was Guru. He looked at her, visibly disgusted, and said, "What is that *smell?*"

She continued looking at him, and then she closed her eyes. She said, "I didn't eat them."

He went to the refrigerator, looked inside, and said, "So you didn't," and then he turned to her. "I wouldn't have cared if you had."

She opened her eyes again.

"Is that what you thought I was after? To see if you'd eat the fruits?" He laughed. "You village girls are all so amusingly stupid. They wouldn't have lasted past the first day, anyway. No," he said. "No, what I wanted to show you, what I wanted you to *appreciate* is what I own." Poornima began to sit up, confused, but he said, "No, no, don't sit up on my account. In fact, lie back down, and turn over." She lay down again, but remained on her back, watching him. "If you're going to work for me then I need you to understand what I own. I own *you*," he began. "I own the food you eat. I own your sweat, your stink. I own your weakness. But most of all, I own your hunger." He was standing above her, looking down. "Do you understand? I own your hunger. Now," he said, unbuckling his belt, "turn over. I don't like faces. Especially not yours."

She began working for him the following day. Her desk was next to his, but smaller, so he could watch over her. But he was rarely there. She was usually alone, and she left the door open, looking up at every girl who passed by it.

None of them was Savitha. At least, none at this location. Poornima wasn't allowed to talk to them—Guru watched her keenly when he was there, and when he wasn't, the cook, named Raju, watched her—but every time one of the girls came downstairs, Poornima nodded or smiled. They mostly ignored her. Some of the younger ones, or newer ones, would look back at her sadly, or bravely, and then they would go back upstairs. There were thirteen girls. But *were* they girls? Poornima wondered. Of course they were. None of them was probably older than sixteen. But there was something missing in them; some essence of girlhood had left them. What was it? Poornima thought about it every day during her first few weeks at the brothel. Innocence, certainly. That was obvious. And they were damaged. That, too, was obvious. But there was something else. Something finer.

And then she had it. It came to her while she was watching one of the girls trudge through the house midafternoon, just after she'd woken up, on her way to the latrines. She was rubbing her eyes, and her face was swollen with sleep, or maybe fatigue. Her gaze was even, and indifferent, as she stood at the back door, looking out. And it was when Poornima saw this gaze, this indifference, that she understood: the girl had lost her sense of light. It was all the same to her, to all the girls, really: light and dark, morning and night. But it wasn't an outside light they'd lost a sense of, Poornima realized. It was an interior one. And so *that* was the aspect of girlhood they'd lost: a sense of their own light.

Poornima thought of light, and then she thought of Savitha. There were six books she had to track and balance and audit against the money that was coming in. They'd even given her one of those little adding machines Kishore had used. The machine made everything much, much quicker. Even so, she worked diligently, all the while trying to figure out a way to go to the other brothels, to see the other girls. By now, she knew Rishi had been lying, back at the train station when he'd said he knew Savitha, but Guru ran nearly all the brothels in Vijayawada, and Poornima decided she couldn't make her way north until she knew for sure. And so she stayed, and she waited.

By her ninth month working at the brothel, Poornima had only managed to visit two of the other locations, asking to go along with Guru when he collected. "I'm not one of the girls," she said. "I want to drive around a little." He agreed reluctantly, though she sensed that he'd come to trust her. She never stole money, she never asked for money, and she never made a mistake in the books. He came to confide in her at times and even began giving her a small salary. She realized it was because of her scar that he trusted her, in the small way that he did. It was odd, but it was true. She was no longer wearing bandages, but the burn had healed and left scar tissue that was shiny and wide and blisteringly pink. It made her look damaged, harmless, and, most important, pathetic.

One day, Guru came in complaining of the cost of buying food and clothing and sundries for the nearly hundred women and girls in the brothels. "Thousands of rupees I spend per month. Thousands. All they do is eat."

Poornima didn't say anything. She knew for a fact that he made over one hundred thousand rupees a month off the girls. In some months, he made two lakhs.

"For instance, just the other day, a girl tells me it's her birthday, and could I buy her a sweet. Her birthday! I said, You'll get a sweet when you do ten men in one night. That's when you'll get a sweet."

Poornima nodded.

"Every day. Every day they eat and eat."

She went back to her work; it was common for Guru to complain, and she'd grown used to it.

"And the audacity. One time, this one girl says to me, I want a banana. So I say, I buy you rice. Go eat that. And you know what she says?"

"No. What?" Poornima hardly looked up.

"She says, But I like to eat bananas with my rice. With my yogurt rice. Can you believe that? A banana! The audacity."

Poornima's head shot up. She stilled her thoughts, she evened her voice. "Oh," she said. Then she said, "What happened to that girl? The one who asked for the banana?"

Guru shrugged. "We sold her."

"Sold her? To whom?"

Guru looked up. His eyes narrowed. He said, "You think all we have are these shitty brothels? You think you're doing *all* the books? Our main income is from selling girls. To rich men. To men in Saudi. Dubai."

Poornima took a breath. She told herself, Don't let him see. He won't tell you if you let him see. "But that one," she said lightly, "the one who wanted the banana. Where did she go?"

"I think she was part of that big shipment we made. A year ago? Some rich man in America. Get this: he wanted girls to clean apartments. Apparently, over there it costs serious money to hire people to clean. To *clean.*

Common Dalits. It was cheaper for him to *buy* them. He owned hundreds of them. Apartments, I mean. Some place called Seetle, Sattle. I don't know. But he paid good money for them."

Poornima could feel the air around her cooling. She could feel a great wooden door creaking open. "How do you get there?"

Guru started to laugh. He started to howl with laughter. "It's far. It's far, far away. You'll never get there."

Poornima laughed with him, but she knew she would.

Savitha

1

Savitha knew she wouldn't get the banana, not at first, at least. But what would it take to get something as simple, as small, as a banana?

She'd find out.

Savitha also knew she had to deal with the leader of the ring, named Guru. No one else. He came around occasionally to check on his goods, as he called the girls. The first time was within a few weeks of her arrival. She'd left Indravalli in the early hours of the morning, on the same day she was to marry Poornima's father. Her body hurt. She'd been crouched in the corner of the weaving hut for three days. She hadn't wept, she hadn't blinked (not that she was aware of), she hadn't hoped or prayed or felt pain, nor had she had a single thought. Not one. Well, maybe one. Her only thought had been, Which is better? This? Or being dead? Or are they one and the same? Before leaving the weaving hut, and the sleeping Poornima, she'd untied all the tiny knots of the sari she'd been making for her, not yet even half completed, stretched out on the loom like a shroud, and folded it into eighths, and then tucked the cloth into the inside of her blouse, against her flat chest.

Then she left Indravalli, knowing it was forever.

When she got to the bus stop—out on the highway, not the one in town—the first bus that pulled up was the one to Vijayawada. It was empty, except for the conductor. Not even the farmers were headed to market yet. Savitha didn't have any money, not a single paisa, so when the door of the bus opened, she looked up at the driver, not at all pleading, but with a look that was stern, deliberate, and she said, "No one will possibly find out if you give me a ride."

The bus driver looked at her, up and down, and then he laughed and closed the door and drove away. A lorry was her only chance. She waited a few more minutes until one came into view. It drove off, not even slowing, as did four others, ignoring her utterly, until the sixth one. The sixth one was painted intricately, a Ganesha on top of the windshield, in the middle, with a scene of a tranquil lake with a hut and cows on one side and a bouquet of roses on the other. Two fresh limes dangled from its front bumper, for good fortune. Along the inside top of the windshield was draped a length of red streamers, sparkling even without the sun. Savitha hailed the driver, stepping onto the edge of the road, and when he slowed, she saw that he was young, hardly older than her. Closer up, once she'd climbed into the cabin, she saw that his teeth were the most brilliant white she had ever seen, whiter even than the temple on Indravalli Konda, though his eyes were bleary, red, maybe from the lack of sleep or dust or drink.

"Where are you headed?"

"Depends," she said. "How far are you going?"

"To Pune."

"Then that's where I'm going."

He smiled, and this time, Savitha wasn't so sure of the brilliance of his teeth. Their whiteness, yes, but not their brilliance.

It took less than ten minutes, bumping along on the Trunk Road, past the shuttered roadside tea shops, and the dark huts, and the dewy fields of rice, and the sleeping dogs, for the driver's hand to leave the steering wheel. It didn't inch along the seat, as Savitha might've expected, but simply took flight and landed on her thigh. "I'm in no hurry," he said. "Are you?"

Savitha took a breath.

She understood, in that very instant, that a door had been opened. Not today, but three days ago. What was this door? she wondered. Why hadn't she ever known it was there? She had no answer. Or maybe she hadn't wanted to know the answer. Regardless, it was now open, and she was through it. Poornima's father, of course, had been the one to open it, the one to push her through, and she felt rage, an intense and terrible rage toward him—for no other reason than that he hadn't asked her what *she* wanted. He hadn't said, There is a door. Do you see it? Do you want me to open it? Do you want to see what's on the other side? But now it was done. And now, she realized, that's all she'd ever be in the eyes of men: a thing to enter, to inhabit for a time, and then to leave.

They drove on. The lorry driver's hand inched up her thigh. They drove across the Krishna and turned onto the national highway.

Well, if that were true, then something else also had to be true. She didn't have to think long on it to figure out what it was; it was like it had been waiting there all along, alongside the road. And it was this: there was yet another door. A smaller door, a more formidable one. A hidden one. But through this other door, she knew, lay the real treasures: her love for Poornima, her love for her parents and her sisters. *These* treasures gleamed: the feel of cloth, the one against her chest, yes, but really, all cloth. How it lay like a hand (not the lorry driver's, but a tender one, wanting nothing) against your skin, protecting you, softening with time. They shone through the night, these treasures: the memory (already a memory) of her father's hands, the way they reached with such fear, such longing, the taste of yogurt rice with banana, the way it was creamy and sweet, both at once, the fill of her heart, the way it swelled but never broke.

"Stop here," she said.

The lorry driver's hand paused, nearly at her crotch.

"Here?"

"Right here."

"But we're hardly past Vijayawada. You said Pune."

She looked at him, at his dark lips, the top one nearly completely curtained by his mustache. Then he smiled, as if she might smile back. But she only looked some more, at the red of his eyes and the white of his teeth. He slowed the lorry but didn't stop. Savitha looked out the window. A mangy dog lay next to a garbage heap; farther down, a chicken scratched at the dirt. He'd swerve to avoid *them*, she thought. Anybody would. And then she thought, I hold the key.

She lifted his hand from her thigh and wrenched it, hard, at the wrist. He gasped, slammed on the brakes. The lorry tilted and then screeched to a halt.

"You bitch. Pakshi. Get out."

When she did, the lorry pulled away with a loud squeal and a cloud of dust. Savitha stood on the national highway and looked to the east and to the west. Toward the east were the outskirts of Vijayawada. They'd mostly skirted the city, but it would be easy enough to go back. Back. That didn't seem very smart. To the west were Hyderabad and then Karnataka and then Maharashtra and then the Arabian Sea. Not that Savitha knew any of this; she knew only that Pune was to the west, and beyond was a sea. She sat right down, on the dirt, on the edge of the highway, and wondered what to do. There were more vehicles now, mostly lorries. She could hail another one, hope for a better man. Most any one of them would take her to Pune, if Pune was where she wanted to go. What did they speak there? Marathi, of course. Which, of course, she had no idea *how* to speak. What if she asked them to take her to Bangalore? They spoke Kannada there. Close to Telugu, but not quite. She turned her head and looked toward Vijayawada again. It was wiser to go back, she decided. It was better to first make some money, and to make money it was best to stay where she knew the language. And really, if anyone in Indravalli went looking for her, which she doubted they would, somewhere as obvious as Vijayawada would be the last place they'd look. Or so she guessed. But this she knew: it was better to be wise than to be smart.

Everyone called him Boss, or Guru, but his real name was probably something different. He was thin, with huge spectacles, and wiry, and seemed weak, but his physical aspect was a foil. This Savitha could see plainly in his eyes. His eyes: boring through her as if through rock, through mountain, through the Himalayas, looking not for metals or minerals or gems, but for *girls*, poor but pretty girls, which she came to understand was just another word for profit.

The first time he came around Savitha was still drugged. She'd made it so simple for them; it was almost laughable. She'd walked back into Vijayawada. For three weeks she'd gone to various tailoring shops and seamstresses, looking for work, and in the nights, she'd slept next to a gutter in the goldsmiths district, scented by the coal braziers used to filigree the shining yellow metal during the day, teeming with rats and pigs at night. One rat had tried to nibble on her ear as she slept. She'd eaten whatever she could find: the insides of discarded banana peels, a half-gnawed roti, a slice of coconut from the Kanaka Durga Temple. Toward the end of her first month, she'd gone to a tea stall, on a narrow alley off Annie Besant Road, and stood on the edge of a group of men, looking up at the soot-grimed walls of the close buildings, the narrow strip of sky, glowing with sunrise, and the clotheslines, crisscrossing between the buildings, slicing open the morning sky. She wondered what to do. A man came up behind her, one she hadn't even noticed in the huddled group of men, and he offered her a cup of tea. Savitha looked from the steaming, sugary cup of tea to his face. He was middle-aged, well dressed in clean pants and a shirt; his hair was neatly oiled and combed.

"Go on. Take it."

She hesitated.

"Are you waiting for someone?"

"Yes. My husband."

"Where's your mangalsutra?"

She shrugged, and he laughed. And it was then that she realized her mistake: her hands should've instinctively gone to her neck. But he only laughed some more, good-naturedly, and said, "Go on. This stall serves the best tea in the city."

She took a sip, and then another, and then another. Then she drained the glass. She felt light-headed at first, which she took to be from the lack of food, but then when she opened her eyes, she was tied to a hemp-rope bed in a damp-smelling concrete room with no windows. She was tied at the wrists and the ankles. And no matter how much she strained and screamed, no one came; the rope didn't give. After what seemed like days, someone entered the room, a boy, she thought, but couldn't be sure because it was dark inside the room and dark outside the room. He ran his hand over the bed, then over her face. When he found it, he pinched her nose shut until she opened her mouth, then he threw another bitter liquid into it, this time without the benefit of tea.

She dropped again into a deep sleep.

Three or four or five days later, or maybe a month later, the door opened for a second time. This time, a thin yellow light seeped in from outside the door, and Savitha saw that it was a little girl. She was lugging a bucket, far too heavy for her, splashing water on the floor and over the front of her torn frock. Savitha was still hazy in her thoughts, her body still limp, but she told herself, Talk to her. Talk to this girl. Tell her you'll do anything, anything. Her mouth opened, or so she assumed, but nothing came out. Savitha willed harder, she closed her eyes, she focused on the fog, the heaviness, she told herself, Speak. "Untie me," she finally managed to whisper. "Please."

The girl seemed not to hear. She went about raising a wet cloth to Savitha's legs, her crotch, her underarms, her chest. My chest, Savitha thought. Was the strip of Poornima's sari still there? Was it? "The cloth," she croaked. "Is it?" By now the girl had found it. She raised it to her face, seemed to sniff it once, then threw it into the corner. Savitha let out a long wail. Animal. Wounded. The girl still paid her no attention. She went about her work, the damp cloth now wiping down Savitha's neck, her arms. When she reached for her hands, Savitha grabbed the girl's forearm. She yanked her closer, so she could see the child's face in the dim light of the half-open door. She looked into the girl's eyes; they returned her gaze, but they were unmoved, blank, gray, as if the concrete of the room had blown like sediment and settled into them. Savitha's alarm pushed through layers of confusion, rage, incoherence, and flame, and she said, "Can't you hear me?"

The girl let out her own wail, though hers was even more animal, more wounded. And it was then, at *that* sound, when Savitha truly began to understand her bondage, her imprisonment, the totality of its vision, the completeness of her fate. And that she'd been neither smart nor wise: the girl was a deaf-mute, and the boy had been blind.

She flailed. She strained at her wrists and ankles, managing only to tighten their grip. She beat her head against the hemp, she screamed, she wept. She bit and snapped against the rope with her teeth. Too far away for her to cut through, but the ends she caught and gnawed until her gums bled. She tasted copper and thought, Good. And then she thought, How long will it take to bleed to death? Out of my gums? The drugs she spit out, gagged on, retched every time the boy poured them in. That's when he started injecting it—mostly by plunging the needle into her stomach, but if she squirmed too much, straight into the side of her buttocks. But even in her haze, her bafflement, Savitha could see clearly the edges of the bed, the dark corners of the room, and in the dank of the windowless walls, the beauty she'd lost: sunlight, wind, water.

In between bouts of sleeping, sweating, waking, and vomiting, there were other memories, floating in and out, above and beyond, like breath. There was the shimmer of the temple on Indravalli Konda, the perfume of freshly cooked rice, the shouts of flower vendors, spilling petals on the streets, there were the words of an owl, there was the feel of the loom, the feel of thread, the feel of form, taking shape, *becoming* something. She could've woven a river; she could've woven a sea. Why was she lying here? Why?

The door opened, soon after the girl had cleaned her again. This time it was a man she'd not seen before. Although, in truth, she was bleary-eyed, weak, sodden, and high, her limbs long ago gone numb, so really, it could've been her father.

But it wasn't her father.

This man—who she learned in time was the one called Guru—let the light spill in. Savitha squinted. He approached the bed with a small smile. Then he laid a knife at the edge of the bed, just beyond her reach. Despite her frailness, a sliver of something feral, a shard of some lucidity, sliced through her consciousness. Savitha lurched for it, nearly tipping the bed over. She rocked violently from side to side, side to side, until the knife fell to the floor with a clang. Guru ignored her. He walked to the corner of the room, where Poornima's half-made sari still lay, and nudged it with the tip of his shoe. He bent a little, taking a closer look. He held his face away from the cloth, as if it were rotting meat, and then he smiled and said, "I know this weave. So distinctive. You're from Indravalli, aren't you?" Savitha said nothing. He walked back to the bed. His smile widened. She looked up at him, called him names, she begged; she sensed what was to come. "You stink," he said placidly. Then he said, "There's nothing worse than a woman who stinks." He picked up the knife. He studied the blade intently. After a long moment, he said, "Maybe there is one thing. Just one. And that's a woman who won't listen." He lowered the blade and ran the tip of it along her cheek, her neck. He yanked back the folds of her sari; her blouse fell away in tatters. He traced the edge of the knife against her breasts, under them, between. "Not much to them, is there," he said, looking down, and then he said, "You'll listen, won't you? Won't you, my dear?" He looked into her eyes, almost kindly, and then he spit in her face. The spit, in the midst of her grogginess, her fear, just as she turned her head to avoid it, landed at the edge of her mouth and on her cheek. Guru rubbed it over more of her face. "A smudge, you see," he said lightly, and then got up and left.

The thick glob of spit dried and puckered on Savitha's cheek. He'd been chewing betelnut; she could smell it for hours.

They untied the rope but kept her locked in the room. They made sure she was hooked—if the boy with the needle was even a few minutes late, she pounded on the door, shivering and beseeching and mad, skin alight, on fire—and then, when she was good and hooked, they made her go through withdrawal. When they finally let her out (a month later, two?), Savitha had lost nearly ten kilograms, and her face was gaunt and gray. Large clumps of hair had fallen out. She was bruised, her ankles and wrists inflamed and red, not having yet healed. The madam took one look at her and clucked with disapproval, as if Savitha were a child being naughty, misbehaving, come home late for supper.

Savitha bent her head, believing she was that child.

Her first customer was a middle-aged man, maybe forty or forty-five. He worked in an office; Savitha could tell just by looking at him, slacks and a neat shirt, a gold watch, clean toes. There was a faded strip of ash across his forehead—had he conducted the puja that morning, or had it been his wife?

The man was furtive at first, but then he sat down next to her, on the edge of the bed, and said, "Will you give me a kiss?"

Savitha looked up at him. "I don't know how," she said. The statement so guileless that the man seemed to almost wilt when he heard it. "Here," he said finally, "let me show you."

After that, the mechanics of it all became routine: the five to six customers she had per day, the constant clucking and recriminations from the madam, the talking and laughing and teasing and silence of the other girls, whose names Savitha tried to remember but couldn't, as if her mind had jellied, relented, forfeited. Relinquished something essential—kingdom, subjects, throne—while even the blood in her veins collapsed, not wanting, any longer, to carry the enormity of memory, the sorrow of new names.

But something remained, a constant, a comfort, and it was this: the cloth on which she lay. While the men pushed into her, pressed her face into the sheet—rough, cheap, bought at one of the tawdry stalls on Governorpet—Savitha closed her eyes and pressed her face, her back, her knees, her palms, deeper and deeper and deeper. The scent of woven cloth, threadbare with use, with semen, filled her nostrils. She held back tears. She held back thoughts of Poornima. She held back her girlhood, squandered on heaps of garbage. She held back her father, her mother, her sisters, her lost brothers. She held back the loamy scent of the Krishna, the laundresses laughing, the temple deepa quivering, the dark of the weaving hut, forever mourning. Though what she did let loose, let soar like a bird out of a cage, was the flight of her hands, weaving.

She allowed herself to recall that one thing.

Once, while still a small child, she'd gone to the cotton fields outside Indravalli, on the way to Guntur. Her mother had worked for a summer in the fields, and Savitha had trotted behind her, jumping for the bolls, wanting to help. She'd been far too short, but one had floated down from her mother's hands and Savitha had caught it and squealed with delight, as if she'd caught a piece of a crumbling cloud. When she'd yanked her mother's pallu and held it up like a prize, her mother had barely looked at her; instead she'd said, "Keep it. It's what your frock is made from." At those words, Savitha had stood still in the middle of the cotton field, hot under the summer sun, and had looked down at the boll in her hand, soft, full of seeds, and then she'd gazed up at the rows and rows of them, round white moons held aloft to the sky, so exquisite, so out of reach. Then she'd looked down at her frock, a faded pink, frayed at the hem, dirty, but still a frock. But how? she'd wondered. How could this little piece of fluff with the little brown seeds become my frock? She'd thought it was a secret, a secret kept by the adults. Or magic, more likely. But a mystery. Always a mystery, even after she grew up and began sitting at the charkha and then sitting at the loom and then sitting next to Poornima, eating dinner together, which, by her weaving, at least in some part, the purchase of food, *food*, had been made possible. So, an even greater mystery: from boll to cloth to food to friend.

And this mystery remained with her. All through the years. From then until now. She held it close while at the brothel, tucked away inside her pillow. Along with Poornima's half-made sari (she'd screamed for it in one of her drug-fueled rages, and someone had—not out of kindness but to shut her up—found it lodged in a corner of the concrete room, lifted it with their toes, and flung it at her face).

There, then: the mystery of cloth, and the cloth itself. She felt both, burning—as mysteries do—inside her pillow.

2

The second time she saw Guru was a few months later. One of the girls was sick from an infection. A customer had given it to her, and she lay in bed with a scalding fever, a wide, blistering rash on her thighs and crotch, unable to swallow even a single sip of buttermilk. The girls crowded around her. A doctor, one of them yelled. There was a scampering. The madam pushed her way to the front. "It's a Sunday," she said, without much regret. "There'll be a surcharge."

A Sunday.

There is such a thing as days, Savitha suddenly realized. There is such a thing as time.

Her mind pricked. Something small, behind the eyes, grew rigid.

Guru arrived later that afternoon. The madam had phoned him and asked him to come. The girls gathered around again. This time, Savitha noticed that his shoes had a slight heel, and that the betelnut had colored his teeth orange. "You call me for *this*," he said.

The madam kneaded her hands. "It's the worst I've seen."

He studied the girl's wan face, her lips split and bleeding from fever. "Was she one of the popular ones?"

"She is," the madam said.

Guru then studied her some more, turned on his elevated heels, walked to the door, and said, "Let her die."

Savitha watched him leave the room. The girl whimpered in her sleep, as if she'd heard the words. Though she couldn't possibly have. Not through all those layers of heat and withering and waste. Let her die. The words hung in the air for a moment, and then they began another journey, this time snaking through Savitha's own layers of heat and wither and waste. Her eyes grew wide; they ached with new light. There was a door, she remembered, a hidden one. Where all her treasures lay. And it remained closed, through the tea stall and the concrete room and the drugs, through the men and the men and the men. And it was through this door that the words found their way.

She looked around the room.

It seemed to her, looking now, that they were all simply children, waiting to die. And in the next instant, she thought, No. No, we're all old. Old, old women, ravaged by time, and waiting to die.

And it was this thought that brought the others. An avalanche of others—not in their number, but in their precision.

The first one was this: she couldn't stay here. It wasn't an obvious thought, not to her. Since Poornima's father had raped her, she'd floundered in something like life, but not life itself. A veil had fallen when he'd held his hand over her mouth. A fadedness, too, had fallen, when he'd pried her legs open. A branch had snapped—a branch from which all things grew, from which every banana, every hope, every laugh sprouted—when she'd looked into his face, and, in a small way, seen her friend's. After that, what did it matter where she lived, or ate, or breathed her lesser breaths? What difference would it ever make? So that now, when the thought came to her that she needed to leave, that she *must* leave, she realized, with surprise, that she was beginning to live again. That it *did* matter. That this again was life.

Her second thought: in order to leave, she had to get past Guru. She recalled, a few months ago, that one of the customers had wanted to use a wooden pestle, and when Savitha had run out of the room, horrified, the madam had yanked her back inside and said, "It would be a shame if someone snapped your father's fingers off, wouldn't it? Or if your sisters ended up where you are?" The madam hadn't gathered those things on her own. Guru had. That much she knew. And yes, she'd been barely conscious for the past few months, but she'd been conscious enough to notice that this was no singular house or madam or undertaking. Not at all. It had its leader—Guru—and it had its lieutenants, like the madam, and it had its foot soldiers, like the man who'd offered her the tea, and the boy who'd injected her, and the girl who'd cleaned her, and the one who'd gone to Indravalli, asked around, and had made sure that no one would come looking for her, or at least that no one had the money or the power or the pull (all three, one and the same) to look for her.

Her third and final thought was this: she needed an advantage. There were only a few clear advantages in the world. She obviously had no money, her only skill was weaving, and she could barely read or write. That left only one thing: her body. My body, my body, she thought, looking down at the now used-up husk of the girl she'd once been, the chest still flat, the hands still big, the skin still dark. She moved then to the mirror—a small round mirror, framed by green plastic, hanging by a nail on a wall opposite the bed. She'd not once looked into it, not once, but now she took it down and studied her face. Her eyes, her lips, her nose. The curve of her cheeks, the sweep of her lashes. She moved the mirror closer, then farther. She tilted it; she straightened it. She looked. And there, just there. What was that? "Stop," she said out loud, into the emptiness of the room. "Hold it there." And so she held it there. And that was when she saw it. Had it always been there? That lamp glowing from within. How had it survived all these previous months? How had it held on? No matter, it was greater than her body, it was greater than all else. She laughed, for perhaps the first time since the night in the weaving hut, to see it there. To know it was hers.

Over the next few days, she watched the other girls in the brothel; she stared into their faces, their eyes, five who'd been there longer than Savitha, one who had arrived only the previous month. And none of them had it. Not one. Theirs had been extinguished. But hers, hers.

So now she had two advantages: she had her body, and she had her light.

She bided her time. On every full moon night, she looked up at the sky.

It took the better part of a year, but one winter evening, when Guru came to check the account books, she waited outside the madam's door. He was saying something about having hired a new accountant, someone trustworthy, he thought, and then he laughed, and then the rest of the conversation was muffled. When he came out, Savitha stepped in front of him. Guru was taken aback, or so she guessed by the slight quiver she saw at the edge of his lips, though he said and did nothing more to indicate his surprise.

"Do I know you?"

So that's how many girls he had: more than he could remember.

"Savitha."

"Savitha?"

"I'm the one you spit on."

He seemed to consider the statement, the words themselves, and the fact that they'd been spoken. *To him.*

"I'd like a banana," she said.

By now, the madam had come to the door. Her eyes blazed. She laughed nervously. "A joker. It's nice when one of the girls is funny."

Savitha braced her feet to the floor. She willed her body taut. Her eyes blazed back. Guru seemed amused. He rocked on his elevated shoes, eye to eye with Savitha, and said, "You get enough rice."

"I do. But I'd like a banana to eat *with* my rice. My yogurt rice."

He laughed out loud, for a long while. And when he finished, his voice dropped; it settled like stone. "Come with me," he said. "Let me show you how you can get that banana."

She followed him inside. He sent the madam down the hall and closed the door behind her. Then he walked to the desk in the center of the room and opened one of the large books stacked in a far corner. Savitha had never seen a book that big, the pages filled with lines and columns and numbers and all manner of scribbles. "You see this," he said, pointing to a row in the middle of a page. She leaned over. No, she didn't see. It looked to her like random markings. "This is how much you make in a month. And you see these? These numbers here are what you cost me. The difference is my profit. You see?"

Savitha nodded.

"Very good. Then you must also see that for every banana you want, all you have to do is take on one more customer. One banana, one customer. You see?" He looked at her.

Savitha looked back. "I see. I'd also like to know how to leave here," she said.

He sat down on the chair behind the desk. He folded his hands. His look was one of sorrow, or maybe sweetness. "Forget what I said about a woman who won't listen. The worst thing is a woman who knows what she wants." He rose slowly and came around the desk. His heels clicked on the stone floor. "Let's start here," he said, and led her to a cot in the corner of the room. Savitha lay down on her back, but he turned her over and took her that way. "I don't like faces," he said.

Over the next months, Guru sought her out whenever he came to the brothel. It wasn't very often; usually he had the books delivered to the main house, where the accounts were kept. Somewhere outside of town, Savitha was told.

He'd asked for her by name.

Each time, he'd ask her how many bananas she'd earned that month. Six, she'd say, or five. You like them that much? he'd ask. They keep me from forgetting, she'd say. Forgetting what? Savitha would only smile and burn brighter.

In the spring of that year, Guru summoned Savitha into his office. It had been nearly two years since she'd left Indravalli. This time, as she looked around the room, she saw that the books were gone; there was only him, behind the desk, waiting. "Sit down," he said. And when she did, he said, "There's a Saudi prince."

"Saudi?"

"It's a country."

"Is this a story?"

"Sort of. Yes, yes, it is. He wants to buy a girl. Young, not too young. You might be just right."

Savitha listened.

"A lakh rupees. We'll split it two ways. A year or two over there, and you'll be free."

Savitha's eyes widened. Fifty thousand rupees! She could get all her sisters married; she could buy her parents a house, a castle! But wait. Why would he share the money with her? Why would he give her a single paisa?

"The thing is . . ." Guru continued, hesitating, though Savitha had never before seen him hesitate. "The thing is, he has interesting tastes."

"What kind of tastes?"

"He likes amputees."

"What's an amputee?"

"Someone who's missing a limb."

Savitha shook her head, confused. "But I'm not missing a limb."

He looked at her. A long, cruel look.

"No." She laughed, chilled by the realization of what Guru was suggesting. "Never."

But he continued looking. He waited. She jumped up, breathed with effort. "You're worth about a quarter of that to me," he said. "Twenty-five, let's say. Do you know how long it will take you to buy your way out of here?"

Savitha thought of the book, the markings, the figures. She thought about what a banana cost. "I don't care. I'm not—"

"So the question is," Guru said, interrupting her, "do you want to be worth what you are, or do you want to be worth more?"

There seemed no greater question in the world.

Savitha looked down at her hands, and as if prophetic in her gaze, when she asked, "Which limb?" he said, "Any limb. A hand, let's say. Either one. You choose."

The operation was scheduled to take place two days later, but was then moved up to the next day. Less time to change my mind, Savitha thought. Regardless, she lay in bed all the night before, cradling her left hand, letting it wander over the ridges of her body. How can they take a hand? How can a hand be taken? she wondered. The palm, the fingers, the crescent moons at their tips. The warmth of blood beneath the skin, already curtailed, lost. The ends of a body as beautiful as its beating center. She decided in that moment, resolutely, lying in bed, No, I won't do this, I won't let them. But then she gazed into the dark of the room, into the dark oblivion of her waiting sisters, their waiting dowries, and knew she would. Knew she had to. She would let them buy it—her hand; she had nothing left to sell.

3

It was called a general anesthetic, but it felt to Savitha as if a light had been turned off, as if night had crashed through her like an anvil. When she woke up, the stub of her left arm was bandaged. The doctor beamed with pride and said, "Cleanest one ever. It looks almost pretty." When the bandage came off, Savitha sat in her room and stared at it. What did they do with my hand? she wondered. Where did they take it? If someone paid for a stub, then maybe someone else paid for a hand?

Regardless, in the end, she realized, it *had* come down to the body.

She held back tears. She could never again sit at the loom, or the charkha, but why would she need to? With fifty thousand rupees she could buy all the cloth in the world. Silks and chiffons and gold-bordered pottu saris. Saris she could've never before imagined, but now could buy as gifts for her sisters on their wedding days. With that thought, she searched in her pillow and took out Poornima's half-made one. She held it to her chest; she buried her head in its folds. What reason was there to be sad? It was just a hand. Imagine Nanna's surprise, she thought. Imagine his delight. All that money. And yet, and yet the scrap of a sari she held now, she knew—the knowledge grottoed in her heart, hidden in a cove, reached only by the darker waters, the quieter ones—was the truest offering. What did they matter, the ones to come? What did they matter to her? What mattered was that once, long ago, a line of indigo thread had met a line of red, and out had poured a thing of beauty. A thing of bravery.

She lifted her head and noticed a dampness. She was crying. And the cotton, as cotton will, had soaked up the tears.

Savitha waited for her ticket to Saudi to arrive. She tried to find a map, but she couldn't. When she asked the madam where it was, she said, "In the desert." So it was near Rajasthan. That wasn't so far. Though it did occur to her that far might be the best place to be. She had been wrong to turn back, to come to Vijayawada, where she could still, in a certain wind, scent the waters of the Krishna. And that scent would then plunge her into a terrifying and quarried understanding of how little she'd managed, how corrupt her fate: she'd come all of twenty kilometers from Indravalli. What would've happened if I had gone to Pune? she wondered. She looked at the space at the end of her left arm and thought, Would I still have you? But now she was going even farther, and to go far, and then to return, *with money*, was, she decided, what the crow had told her that long-ago day: Let them eat you, let them, but be sure to eat them back.

Money. Money let you eat them back.

She was no longer considered one of the regular prostitutes, but one of the special ones. What did that mean? Savitha wasn't quite sure. She didn't have to take as many customers, that was one thing, because mostly, as it turned out, the fetish for an amputee wasn't all that common; most of the men preferred one of the girls with both hands intact. Though the customers she *did* have paid more, and were much more talkative than they had been, as if her missing hand were an expensive conversation piece, as if it lent her an added ability to understand their deepest selves, their darkest fears. Savitha was happy to listen. In fact, she became such a good listener that she could sense a man's sorrow—the *source* of it—the minute he entered the room. It was easy. A man with a nagging wife held his head unnaturally high when he entered. A man who'd been unloved as a child waited for her to speak first. A man who had no money—who was perhaps spending the last of it on her—held on to the doorknob for longer than he should.

She once had a customer who confessed to having been in jail. For killing my brother, he said, though he said nothing more about it. But he went on to tell her that after his third year in jail, he'd escaped and lived as a fugitive for more than twenty years. In Meghalaya, he said, in the forests. He said he'd been the pampered eldest son of a wealthy family. Wheat merchants. I had no idea how to cook even rice, he said, let alone live in the wilderness. But he learned to make his way in the forests, he told her, and he began to realize certain things.

"What things?" Savitha asked.

But at that point in the story, he stopped. Savitha waited. She watched him. He didn't *look* like a fugitive, though she had no idea what one would look like. She'd expect them to at least be wild-looking, haunted in some way, but this man looked quite serene, contented even, as if he'd just had a refreshing bath and a nice breakfast.

At last, after almost ten minutes of sitting in silence, the man, with graying hair and dark eyes, by turn tunnels and then becoming the smooth faces of cliffs, said, "By my fifth year in the forest, I realized I could no longer feel. Not just that I couldn't feel pain or loneliness or lust. Not just those things, but that I could no longer even feel my own heart. Do you understand? It was beating, but it might as well have been a stone, beating against another stone."

By his eleventh or twelfth year, he said, he was no longer human. He said, "I'd catch an animal, in a trap or with a crude bow and arrow, and kill it without a thought. Strangle it, snap its neck, while I looked into its eyes, and not feel the slightest thing. Not even victory. I would bash its head in with my bare hand, and it felt like I was cracking a nut." As he neared the twentieth year, he said, he could recall no other life than that of a fugitive. He had memories, he told her, of the time before he was a fugitive. Vague memories of being in jail, even vaguer of being a son, a brother. "It was as if," he said, "it was what I was born to be: a fugitive. Not just that. But that I was *born* a fugitive. Do you understand?"

This time, Savitha did, a little.

"Every so often, I met other fugitives. Sometimes tribals. But they generally left me alone. They asked no questions. Questions are for the living, and they could very clearly see that I was dead. At the start of my twenty-fourth year," he said, "I began talking to the universe. Not just talking to it, but commanding it. I could make clouds part. I could make fish swim to me, swim into my hand with nothing in the hand besides desire. I could make wind stop blowing. I remember one night, deep in the forest—I couldn't ever be near a ranger station, or a village, even the smallest—I was asleep, and was awoken by a strange rustling. When I sat up and looked around me, there was a cobra, staring straight back. I'd fashioned a kind of hatchet, so I reached for it. But the cobra was faster. It caught my hand just as I touched the hatchet, and it said, 'You can't kill me twice,' which is when I knew it was my brother. And then the cobra said, 'Find out something for me.' I waited. I thought he, it, would ask me to find out whether our parents were all right, or whether fate and chance were in battle or in collusion, or whether our cycle of suffering would ever truly end, but instead, the cobra said, 'Find out for me the depth of the forest floor.'

" 'The depth?' I said.

" 'Yes. I've tried, you see. I've tried to snake my way all the way down; that's what we do, after all, we snakes. But I can't seem to find its floor. It's as if I could keep going and going and going. That maybe there is no end. But there has to be. Maybe it goes to the core of the earth, or maybe somewhere even darker. Or hotter. Don't you think?'

" 'No, I don't,' I said.

" 'Neither do I,' the cobra said, and slithered away into the forest."

Here, the man—who was clearly no longer a fugitive, as he was sitting in Savitha's room—looked at her, maybe for the first time, and said, "That's when I walked out of the forest. The very next morning. Because you see, the cobra didn't want an answer; it didn't want anything, certainly not to know the depth of the forest floor. What it wanted was to reveal to me that there is no end to guilt, no end to the prices we pay, that we are the forest, and our conscience, our hell, is the forest floor."

He looked at her. She thought he might be waiting for her to say something, but no, he was just looking at her.

"I went to the nearest ranger station that morning. That very morning. Walked right through the doors and told them who I was and what I'd done. At first they didn't believe me. Some guy who was saying he'd lived in the forest for twenty-five years—why would they? They didn't even think it was possible. But after some discussion among them, they drove me to the police station in Shillong. And there, they *had* to call it in. So they called the police station in Guntur, but they said that the old courthouse, where all the criminal case files would have been kept, had burned down long ago, years ago, and that their own files from that time, kept in boxes in a musty back room, had been chewed through by rats, so really, there was no record of me at all. Anywhere. The constable put down the receiver, looked at me, and explained everything the Guntur police had told him, almost apologetically. And then he said I was free to go."

"What did you do then?" she asked.

"I came home," he said. "But by then, both my parents had died. From heartache, some said. But that's what people want to believe. It's more romantic that way. If I had to guess, I'd say my father died from rage and my mother from boredom. They were childless at the end of their lives, it's true, even after having had two sons. I wish I could've apologized to them for that. I wish for many things. But they must've searched, too, for the forest floor."

And with that, the former fugitive, who was now a customer, and yet had not once touched Savitha, his face as placid as the surface of a still lake, said, "So how did you lose your hand?"

4

The ticket for Saudi never arrived. Guru called her into his office three months after her operation and said the prince had found somebody more suitable. More suitable? Savitha asked. What's more suitable?

"Apparently, a missing leg."

"He told you that?"

"*He* didn't tell me anything. His people did."

Her left hand—the phantom one she'd been feeling over the past few weeks—clenched. It drew phantom blood. "What about the money?"

"Forget about that measly one lakh. I have a better deal."

Savitha was seated in front of his desk, but she still slumped. She was tired. She was tired of deals. Every moment in a woman's life was a deal, a deal for her body: first for its blooming and then for its wilting; first for her bleeding and then for her virginity and then for her bearing (counting only the sons) and then for her widowing.

"Farther away, though," he said, twirling a pen in his hand.

She waited for her exhaustion, her despair, to pass. Then she said, "Farther is better."

"A temporary visa first. Then they'll figure out a way for you to stay. Or you can come back, if you want."

"What do they want me for?" she asked, afraid of the answer.

"To clean houses. Flats. Apparently, they have to pay maids so much over there, it's cheaper to buy them from here."

"But how will I—" she began, but Guru, before she could finish, said, "I told them you'd work twice as fast."

"Where?"

"America. Someplace called Sattle. Good money, too."

Unlike Saudi, *America* she knew. Everyone knew America. And it was indeed far away. Far, far away. On the other side of the earth, she'd once heard someone say.

"How much?" she asked.

"Twenty thousand. Ten for you, ten for me."

"That's hardly anything! You said yourself I was worth more than that."

Guru put down the pen. He leaned back in his chair and smiled. "Dollars, my dear. Dollars."

But why would Guru split the money with me? Why would he ever have? That was the first thing that passed through Savitha's mind, sitting across from him, watching the avarice glow in his eyes. The second was, He won't, of course. Still, what bothered her was not that he was lying, which didn't really matter, nor that she had been so slow to see it, but that she, *she*, had said the word *worth*.

It was a Telugu man who'd bought her, Savitha learned. In this town in America, she was told, he owned hundreds of apartments and a handful of restaurants and even a cinema hall. Maybe I'll finally get to see a cinema, she thought, not with excitement or bitterness, but with a kind of shame. She'd always have to sit to Poornima's left, she realized, so that they could hold hands during the scary parts. The man in America had two sons and a daughter. The daughter was married to a doctor, a famous doctor, the kind who made women's breasts bigger or their noses smaller. Savitha had never heard of such a thing, had never known there were doctors who did such things, but wondered whether the extra nose bits went to the same place her hand had gone, and whether the extra breast bits came from that same place. The two sons helped the father run his many businesses, and Savitha didn't know whether they were married. The man in America had a wife who was from Vijayawada, which is how they'd come to know of Guru, and she was exceedingly devout. She was involved in good works all over the city, giving money to the poor and the sick, and every year, she donated ten lakh rupees to the Kanaka Durga Temple, along with a new set of gold ornaments for the deity.

Then she learned of a thing called the exchange rate.

Guru, out of this deal, would make over thirteen lakh rupees. That was a sum Savitha couldn't even imagine, and she smiled with him when he said, "We could *buy* Indravalli, you and I." After a moment, she asked him why her, why someone with only one hand, why not one of the other girls, one of the ones with both hands; they would certainly agree to go to America, and they would also clearly make better maids. Guru's eyes sparkled. "That's the beauty of it," he said. "Only *you* can go." Apparently, this all had to do with something Guru had mentioned earlier, something called a visa. There were visas to do different types of things, such as one to visit a place, and another to work in a place, and another to study in that place. And then there was one to get treatment.

"What kind of treatment?" Savitha asked.

"The kind you're going to get," Guru said. "At least, that's what they'll tell him. To whatever official." Then he nodded at the stub of her left arm, resting on her lap. "They'll say you need to enter America for a special operation, one only they can perform. One doctor here, a doctor there—their son-in-law, maybe—will vouch for your need for *American* medical treatment. And once you're there, well, the rest is easy."

"But will I get the operation? Will they give me a new hand?"

He looked at her with something like incomprehension, maybe even a trace of contempt. "Of course not, you fool. There *is* no operation. You're going to clean houses."

So she was going to clean houses. That was fine. That was better than sleeping with men. But something Guru had said kept echoing inside of her. No, *echo* would indicate it was his voice she heard. It was not. It was her own, and it repeated, over and over and over again: Only you can go.

Only you can go. What did those words mean? They meant that of all the girls in all of Guru's houses, only she could go. And why was that? Because she was the only one with a hand missing—the others might be prettier or stronger or sweeter; they might be lighter skinned or bigger breasted or have longer and thicker hair, plumper and rounder hips; but only she could go.

But what did that *mean*?

Savitha smiled.

It meant that she had leverage. It meant that she had power.

"I won't go," she said to Guru a week later.

His eyes widened in alarm. He laughed nervously. "What do you mean, you won't go? Think of all the money."

"I am."

He was an animal in the dark, she thought. His eyes scanned the night forest for movement, sound. "You're afraid I won't give it to you? How could you? It's just that I won't get the money until after you're there. Upon receipt. It's like goods, you see."

It wasn't *like* goods, she thought.

"I'll go on one condition," she said.

He relaxed into his chair. He lifted his arm in munificence.

"My little sisters. I want you to give my parents enough money for their dowries. I want you to give them enough money for a new house. I want you to give them enough money to last the rest of their lives."

He roared with laughter. She sat very still. He looked at her face, then at the strength of the one hand resting on her lap, and he stopped. "All right."

"I want you to do it before I leave. And I don't want them to know it had anything to do with me."

He nodded.

"And one other thing," she said. "I want you to loan me a car."

"Why?"

"Because once you say it's done, I want to make sure it is."

She went in the middle of the night. She asked the driver to go up Old Tenali Road, and then told him to stop a few hundred yards from her parents' hut. How will I know? she wondered. How will I know if he gave them the money? I'll know, she thought, just from looking at the hanging vegetable basket. She walked up the stinking hill, keeping off the main path, so she wouldn't be seen, and along the backs of the huts.

Indravalli Konda loomed in the distance. The temple floated at its center, a lone and beating heart. Its colors changing in the moonlight, according to her glimpses of it: buttermilk and pumice, then mother-of-pearl, then the froth of the sea. The deepa wasn't lit, and so the rest of the mountain, its contours, was lost to the sky. When she passed by one hut, a sleeping dog woke at the sound of her footsteps and barked into the night. An emaciated goat, tethered to an emaciated tree, stiffened with fear.

The moon was high, and when she finally came upon her parents' hut—the one she'd been born in, and all her brothers and sisters—she crept along the back of it quietly, meaning only to peek inside, but there was no need: it was empty. Only a dried gourd and a rat-chewed blanket in one corner.

She, too, stiffened and ran. Down the hill, her breath a fist through her body. All manner of thoughts, as she ran, all of them culminating in the one: they're dead, he's killed them to get out of paying.

She slammed into the side of the car. The driver jerked awake. "Ask. Go ask," she hissed. "Ask them what happened."

He cursed his luck for being on duty tonight, and then drove around until they reached the highway. There, a tea stall was still open. Inside, behind a false door, was whiskey and moonshine. "Crazy bitch," he muttered, and partook, asked a few questions, and then came back outside.

She was slouched in the backseat so no one would see, but sprang to attention like a coil. "What did they say? *What?*"

"They've moved," he said, the scent of whiskey filling the front seat and then the back. He started the car. They drove again, this time away from Old Tenali Road, to the other side of the village. Hardly five minutes away, but the houses richer, bigger, no longer thatch but concrete. He stopped at the end of a road Savitha had only walked by, not ever having known anyone wealthy enough to live in one of the dhaba houses. "That one," said the driver, pointing to the third house on the left, painted pink and green and yellow, with still-green mango leaves stretched across the front door. There was a gate, locked, and she stood outside of it and saw a figure sleeping on the veranda, on a hemp-rope cot, a thin blanket over them. Through an open door, three more figures slept on beds. Beds!

When she came back to the car, she said, "It isn't them. There are only four people in that house."

"One of your sisters is already married. Last week."

"She *is?*"

She told him to wait a moment more and went back and stood at the gate. She studied the dim interior of the veranda, the rich moonlit marble floor, the sleeping bodies—still skeptical. A breeze swept past her and into the house, and with a rustle, the figure on the veranda threw off the sheet. And in that moment, she saw the fingers, gnarled and noble and lovely, more beautiful than broken. And then she knew.

The driver turned toward Vijayawada, but she said no, there was one more place she needed to go. He sighed loudly and turned the car around again.

Poornima was married by now, of that Savitha was certain. She thought vaguely of asking the driver to take her to Namburu, but *where* in Namburu, and was that even the boy she married?

That hut was the same. The same thatched roof, the same dirt floor, the same dusty and stunted trees. Four small figures were asleep on the ground, on the same mats, under the same thin sheets, with forlorn faces peeking above them, impoverished even in the moonlight. Another, larger figure was asleep on the hemp-rope bed, and from him, Savitha averted her eyes, allowing them to rest, just for a moment, on the nearer structure, the weaving hut. She gazed at it with sudden emotion, maybe even longing, for what she had left inside, for what she had been, and then she turned to the driver and said, "Let's go."

5

She left for America two months later. All of the necessary documents had been witnessed, notarized, fingerprinted, and all manner of other words Savitha had never heard before. Guru took her to Chennai on the train, and from there, she was to be accompanied by an older woman who was to pretend to be Savitha's mother. The older woman was indeed probably her mother's age, maybe a little older. Savitha never quite understood who she was, how she was related to the people in America, or why she'd agreed to accompany her, but she was, in her way, the perfect choice: she was grave, her sari was simple yet impressively well woven, humble to look at, and she wore round spectacles, which gave her an air of seriousness, and more important, gave her an air of concern—which was exactly what she should feel for a beloved daughter about to travel halfway around the world for hand surgery.

In Chennai, Savitha put on a cast, so no one could see that her stub had completely healed, and then they boarded a plane. Guru had explained it to Savitha—that she would travel to America on a long bus that could fly through the air. She had been confused, and still was, even as the plane taxied down the runway. And then: it lifted into the air. The old woman—the one who was supposed to be her mother—sat beside her. She had hardly spoken to Savitha, merely nodded when they met, and now, once they were on the plane, she'd inserted what looked like tiny cotton balls into her ears, with wires coming out of them, and seemed completely absorbed or asleep or maybe just unwell; her eyes closed the moment they sat down. Savitha thought that she might have an ear infection. One of her little sisters, who was prone to ear infections as a baby, had always needed to have cotton balls, dipped in coconut oil, stuffed in her ears to ease the ache and her crying. But now, as the plane lifted off the ground, Savitha grabbed the woman's hand and stared frantically from her to the window and then back again. The plane climbed higher and higher; Savitha swallowed back her racing heart. The woman opened her eyes, looked down at her hand, took out one of the cotton balls with the other hand, and shook Savitha off as if she were a fly. Then she said, speaking Telugu with a Tamilian accent, and without a trace of a smile, "This is the best part. Enjoy it."

What did she mean by that? Did she mean that this was the best part of the plane ride, or that this was the best part of all that was to come? Maybe she meant this was the best part of all of it: the plane ride, what was to come, and all that had come before.

Regardless, after an hour or so, after Savitha had stared, unblinking, at every cloud that floated by her oval window, she leaned back in her seat and fell into a deep sleep.

When they landed at Heathrow, the first thing Savitha noticed was that it smelled like nothing, absolutely nothing—as if not a single animal had passed through here, nor a single flower bloomed—and then she noticed that it was cold. So cold that it seemed to be spilling out of the walls, climbing out of the floor. She asked the woman if they were in America. The woman said, No, we're in England. Why did we stop here? she asked. Because it's halfway between India and America, the woman said. They sat in the transfer lounge, which Savitha only registered as a long, crowded room with row after row of orange chairs. There were also a few shops, which were so brightly lit that they scared her away. She sat in one of the orange chairs and looked at the other people in the lounge. They, too, scared her. She noticed a few Indians, but mostly, the people around her—sleeping or eating or reading or talking—seemed to her like giants. Tall and un-wieldy and oily. Some of them pale giants, some of them burnt, crisp giants, but all of them towering over her, even over the woman who was supposed to be her mother. Where had they all come from? Where were they all going? It felt to Savitha as if the world was full of them, these giants, suddenly, and that she and the old woman and Indravalli and Vijayawada were all merely their playthings, kept locked in a box in a hotter part of the world.

After that, after boarding another plane and after more hours upon hours had passed, during which, whenever Savitha woke and blinked into the dark of the plane and into the dark of the world beyond, she thought that maybe she was dead, and that this was the afterlife: all of them headed in a long bus to whatever was next, and around and beyond them was only stillness, and stars, and below, far, far below, only some gigantic moving mass, by turns white and then gray and then only black, reflecting the stars but darker, angrier than any night sky, and when she pointed to it and asked the woman, in alarm, What is that? the woman hardly even glanced at it, never even took out her cotton balls, and as she closed her eyes again, she said, "Water."

The next morning, or what Savitha presumed was morning because the woman said, "Go brush your teeth," they landed again. This time, when Savitha said, Is this America? the woman said, Yes.

They were at JFK.

They stood in one long line and then another. Then they sat down in another transit lounge. This one had blue chairs. Otherwise, it was just the same: the same lack of scent, the same cold, the same giants. "What city are we in?" Savitha asked. "Are we in Sattle?" No, the woman said, New

York. And then she told her to sit right there, don't move, and went off to make a telephone call. Savitha could see her in the distance, standing at a pole with a telephone attached to it. The woman put something into the telephone and pressed some buttons and started talking.

Savitha was nauseated, or maybe just lonely, so she closed her eyes and tried to think of Poornima, of her sisters, of her father, of anything that had perfume that she could inhale. Her mind swirled, but she was so tired, so depleted of memory, that nothing came to her. Not one thing. So she leaned down and opened the suitcase that Guru had given her to pack her few things, and she took out Poornima's half-made sari and held it to her nose. She breathed. And there, even after coming all this way, to the other side of the earth, there was the scent of the loom. The scent of its picking stick. The scent of the rice starch used to dampen the thread and the scent of the charkha and the scent of the fingers that had wound it on the charkha, perfumed with turmeric and salt and mustard seed, and there, just there, was the scent of Indravalli Konda, and the deepa, the oil burning low, drenching the cotton wick as if with rain, with typhoon; she buried her face deeper and out rose the scent of the Krishna, winding its way through the mountains and valleys and into the sea.

When she raised her head, the woman seated across from her was watching her.

Savitha averted her eyes, but the woman kept looking.

The woman who was supposed to be her mother seemed to be saying her good-byes. Savitha wished she would come back quickly, but then the conversation seemed to take another turn, and the old woman began talking animatedly again. Savitha looked over, and when she did, the strange woman across from her, one of the giants, her hair the color of jilebi, and with round spots on her face like a ripe banana, leaned across toward Savitha, gazed at the cast on her arm and then into her eyes, and said, "Are you okay? Do you need help?" Savitha had no idea what she'd said, so she only shook her head, and then nodded, and then waited, hoping the jilebi-haired woman was satisfied and would leave her alone. She considered getting up and going to the woman who was supposed to be her mother, but she'd specifically told Savitha to stay put and watch their bags.

"Do you understand English?"

Savitha smiled and nodded again.

The woman smiled back. And it was then—when the woman smiled, when she revealed her tiny teeth, not at all giant, but dazzling, pearls, the most luminescent pearls, as if the oyster who'd made them had been in love during their making—that Savitha saw how gentle the jilebi-haired lady was, how concerned. Gentler and more concerned than anyone she'd met in a long, long time. Maybe ever. And Savitha thought, Maybe I've come far enough away. Maybe I'm in a good country. Maybe I'm in a kind one. Just then, a loud announcement came over the PA system and Savitha jumped, but the woman seemed unafraid; she reached inside her purse and took out a small white rectangle of paper and held it out to Savitha. Savitha took it, not knowing what else to do, and then the woman picked up her purse and her bag and walked into the mass of people that had gathered when they'd heard the announcement. Savitha watched the woman, inexplicably sad at her departure, and then she looked at the card. It had letters, maybe her name, and then more letters. She stared at it and stared at it, and when she looked up, the woman who was supposed to be her mother was walking toward her. Savitha had no idea what the letters spelled, but she knew enough to slip the card into the inside of her cast.

6

When they landed in Seattle, a man came to collect them. On the plane from New York, Savitha had looked out the window and seen the sky in front of her brushed with strokes of deep orange and rose and rust, but when she turned around, so was the other side. Though ahead of her it was brighter, the reds fiercer. West. They were heading west.

Savitha stepped through the sliding doors into the open air (after what felt like a lifetime) and saw that it was midday. The sun was high and warm. Lines of cars, shiny and silent, drifted by her; a few were stopped and had one or two people standing next to them, loading luggage or embracing or standing expectantly. One couple even kissed, and Savitha looked away in embarrassment. A few were standing at a far end, smoking. Otherwise, it was empty. There was no noise or clamor or porters or horns. There was not one policeman blowing his whistle, shouting for people to keep moving, nor a single person haggling with a taxi driver or laughing or eating from a cone of peanuts, dropping their shells on the ground, birds pecking among them for food, dogs sniffing at blowing wrappers and the discarded rinds of an orange or a mango, not even idle young men, standing in groups and watching the women and smoking beedies and spitting betelnut. Waiting for life. Here, there was nothing but a silent, ordered sleekness.

She looked up at the sun again.

It, too, was quiet. Not blazing and insolent and angry and rowdy, like it was in Indravalli, but tempered, emasculated. She didn't know if she liked this sun. She doubted it was even the same one.

It was then that a black car, the windows so spotless they shone like a mirror, pulled next to her and the woman who was supposed to be her mother. The man who'd come to collect them, named Mohan, stepped out. He was older than Savitha, maybe thirty, though she couldn't be sure, because he, too, was a giant. The first Indian giant she'd ever met. He was not exactly fat or puffy, though certainly there was something cherubic about his face. He was muscular, though, like the images of the cinema heroes Savitha had seen on posters, when she'd passed a handful of times along the Apsara or the Alankar. She saw them again now, those heroic muscles, curved, firm, rising from Mohan's arms, his chest, while his neck and his hands held taut with their power, their magnificence, nearly discomfited by their rising and falling. Savitha found it disconcerting: this well-fed, well-tended extravagance, this health.

Nevertheless, what struck her most about Mohan was his melancholy. Eyes and lips turned by some sorrow, some blunder, the sad slope of his stride as he came around the car, reached for their few bags. His gaze paused at Savitha's cast and then continued up her stomach and breasts to her face.

"Is that all?" he asked in Telugu. The old woman nodded, and they climbed into the car.

It smelled like a lemon.

Below the scent of lemon was the smell of coffee. Both thick and bitter, Savitha thought, and then she searched the car and saw a white cup with a white lid. Mohan's hand hovered near it even as he drove: first on a curved road out of the airport and then down a wide road that was the blackest one Savitha had ever seen, with more cars than she had ever seen. They drove in silence—with the old woman sitting next to Mohan and Savitha behind her. After a few minutes, Mohan turned on the radio. It was a kind of music Savitha had never heard before; it had no words. At times, the music soared to a lofty peak, like being on the top of Indravalli Konda, and at other times it was gentle, yet controlled, like lapping water. She wanted to ask what it was, but the silence in the car, too, seemed controlled and inflexible.

After twenty minutes or so, Mohan pulled off the many-laned road to a smaller one. On this road, Savitha noticed low, flat buildings; there were cars parked along this street, and the storefronts (or so she guessed by the genteel window displays) were not at all like the storefronts in India. In India, they were choked with colorful streamers and the windows piled high with merchandise and the whole crowded with people yelling and pushing and shoving. Here, they seemed hardly occupied. Only their lighted interiors revealed a few customers, any sign of life. Halfway down the street, Mohan stopped the car in front of a long building, lined with doors, and he and the old woman got out. She leaned into the car—as Mohan was getting her bags—and said, "Stay here," and then she seemed to waver, or sway with a kind of discomfort, or guilt, and added, "Be careful."

Be careful of what? Savitha wondered.

She watched them. What is this place, she puzzled, with its series of doors, though the old lady and Mohan ignored these and instead entered the only glass door, more prominent than the others. They were inside for maybe ten minutes, and then Mohan walked the old lady to one of the regular doors and said, "See you tomorrow." When he returned to the car he looked at Savitha shyly and said, "Come to the front if you'd like." She got into the front passenger seat, and now, now she felt the true enormity of this new country. It could only be felt from the front seat, she realized, only from the wide window and the unobstructed light.

The music came on again.

They drove over a bridge, though from Savitha's seat, it looked to her more like a bolt of unfurled silk over a layer of mist. Above Savitha, from the little mirror Mohan had looked into earlier to take fleeting glances at her, dangled a thin yellow tree-shaped decoration. Lemon! So that's where it was coming from. Then the road curved, and suddenly, before Savitha, were the tallest and shiniest buildings she'd ever seen and the bluest stretch of water and the greenest mountains. "Is this Sattle?" she asked.

"*See*-attle," he corrected her.

They neared the buildings, rising out of the earth like blazing rectangles, reflecting the sun, and then cut along their right-hand flank and went down another black road with many lanes, for quiet mile after quiet mile, until Mohan said, "Are you hungry? We can stop."

"Yes."

"Not for long. There's a McDonald's, Taco Bell up there."

Savitha looked where he was pointing. He saw the expression on her face, and he said, "No, not Indian food, but it's not bad."

She turned to him and said, "Do you have bananas here?"

He was startled by the question, she thought, because he slowed the car, and then he met her gaze. He was unused to looking at women. Maybe not all women, she thought after a moment, maybe just women with a certain openness, a kind of curiosity, perhaps even that radiance she had glimpsed long ago, bearing itself up behind her eyes like a crumbling fort, an embattled army. They stopped at a massive building with many parked cars, and he went inside, and when he came out again, he handed her a bag.

Inside the bag were bananas.

There were six of them. The biggest bananas she'd ever seen, worthy of giants. She took one and tried to give the remaining five back to him. "They're yours," he said.

In all her life, Savitha had never possessed this many bananas at once.

That first one she ate in the car. With only one hand, she'd learned to use her teeth to rip open the end of the banana, opposite the stem, and as she did, she felt Mohan watching her. She offered him one, but he said no. She was about to eat a second one, with a vague sense of bafflement, awe, repletion at the thought that she even *could*, when Mohan stopped the car. He parked in front of a building that was four stories tall, cream-colored with chipped brown windowsills and a brown roof. Many of the windows were open, and from them fluttered all colors of curtains. Some seemed to be sheets, torn in places, tie-dyed, others were flags; a few had broken blinds. A small tattered awning over a sagging door in the center of the building indicated the entrance. Next to the front door were three rows of cubbyholes, some with bent or rusted metal flaps. "What are these?" Savitha asked.

He looked at her curiously. "Mailboxes," he said in English.

"What are they for?"

"Letters."

She studied them, many bursting with browned envelopes that seemed to have been set out in the sun and rain for weeks, months. "But why don't they take their letters? Don't they want to read them?"

"No. Not these kind of letters."

What kind were they? she wondered. Savitha had not once gotten a letter (From whom would she get one, and why? She could hardly read.), but she thought if she did, she wouldn't leave it out in the sun and rain, she would tear it open and stare at it, relish the slant of the letters, the way they'd written her name (*that* she'd known how to read and write since she was three years old), the feel of the paper, which she knew would be very different from the paper scraps she'd collected from the garbage heap, and the color and the beauty of ink. But when they went inside, Savitha's reverie ended. They climbed a musty stair and then walked down a musty hallway. Mohan carried her one suitcase—though it was practically empty; what was there to put in it?—and Savitha carried the bag of bananas. At the end of the hallway, Mohan opened a door, with the assurance of knowing it would be open, as if he lived there, and inside the small room was another man, also Indian but older. He was watching something on television, holding a glass—the chair on which he was sitting, the glass, a small table to hold the glass, and the television being the only four things in the room. He looked up when they entered, at Savitha with barely concealed contempt, and then he said, in Telugu (was *everyone* in this country Telugu?), "A stub to clean houses. I suppose next he'll buy a one-legged man to ride a bicycle."

Mohan stammered something in embarrassment and glanced at her once, for a moment that felt to Savitha as if he were at war, or had just returned, and then he left. She didn't see him again for three months.

7

The older man took her up another flight of stairs. He'd taken one look at her suitcase and her bag of bananas, and then had looked away without a word. Savitha carried the suitcase in her right hand and the bananas in the crook of her left arm. At the top of the stairs, the man opened a door that led into a room smaller than his own. On the floor of this room, laid out on the mildewed and stale-smelling beige carpet, were three cots. He pointed to the farthest one, on the side of the room opposite from the door, and said, "That's yours," and then he said, "That's *all* that's yours." He closed the door behind her.

Savitha took two steps into the center of the room—still holding her suitcase and her bag of five bananas (and the peel of the one she'd eaten)—and saw that there was a tiny kitchenette in one corner of the room and a door to the bathroom in the other. She looked at the cots. They were positioned in the shape of a U, with the one in the middle beneath the only window in the room, one behind her, against the wall with the front door, and hers, next to the bathroom door. The cot by the front door was neatly made, with the pillow fluffed and centered and a small, cheap suitcase like her own resting at the foot. The sheets of the one in the middle were in complete disarray, the pillow half flung, and there was no suitcase in sight, only clothes and toiletries and hair things tossed in every which direction as if it were the wreckage of a ship, and the beige carpet a sea.

The first thing she did was to take out Poornima's half-made sari from her suitcase and look at it. From boll to thread to loom to this, she thought. And then she thought, I made you. She tucked the cloth into the inside of her pillowcase. Then she slid off her cast and placed the little white rectangular card back inside its hollow. She placed them against the wall. After a time— during which Savitha tried to take a bucket bath, but there was no bucket in sight, only a long white rectangular hole (was everything in this country white and rectangular?)—she washed her face and drank a glass of water and ate another banana. She lay down on her cot, but as soon as she did, there was a sound at the door. A girl entered, and she said, "Who are you?"

The girl's name was Geeta, short for Geetanjali, and she was talkative.

"I'm named after the film," she began, in Telugu. "Did you see it?"

Savitha shook her head.

"My amma saw it a few months before I was born. It was the first movie she'd ever seen. She said she didn't really follow the story, not really—she was only thirteen or fourteen—but she said that when she came out of the cinema theater, back into the world, it felt new. Polished. Like it was a different world, and that anything could happen. She said she practically skipped home. Back to the little hut she lived in with my nanna, on the edge of a jute field, neither of which they owned. She said she felt the same way when I was born, that the world was somehow new. That I'd made it new. So she named me Geetanjali. Isn't that nice?"

Savitha had to agree.

Then Geeta laughed. A tinkling laugh that cut through Savitha's fatigue, the fog of the long plane ride. "It's funny, though, isn't it? It's still the same old world. They're still in that same hut, leasing that same farm. And here I am, just a housecleaner and a whore."

Savitha blinked. She got up from her cot, her legs unsteady.

A whore?

"Didn't they tell you? Maybe they didn't. Anyway, it rains a lot here. Rain is the only sound in this country. If *you* make any others, if you talk to anyone, if you even open your mouth to speak, they'll come for you."

"Who'll come for me?"

"Who brought you here?"

"Mohan."

"No wonder," Geeta said knowingly, laughing again. "You're lucky. He's the nice one."

Geeta told her that Mohan was the younger of the two sons. The older one was named Suresh, and he was more like his father, cruel, slapping them around to show them who was boss, as if they didn't know; he worked them long hours, sometimes through the night if an apartment or office building needed to be cleaned by morning, so they wouldn't have to go even one day without collecting rent on it, as if they didn't have tens of thousands, maybe even lakhs of dollars in the bank, Geeta said; Suresh came around whenever he wanted, he had his favorites, of course, she added, but he'll come around at least once, try you out. She glanced at the stub and then the cast, and said, Well, maybe not you.

Then she told her a story. The story was about Mohan and Padma.

"Who's Padma?" Savitha said.

Geeta nodded toward the third cot, the unkempt one. "She says they make her clean other people's toilets, but they can't make her clean her own. But she's the prettiest. She could've been a film star." This Padma, as it turned out, was in love with Mohan. "Stupid. Idiotic. What chance does she have with him? With the son of the man who *owns* us."

"What's his name?"

"Whose?"

"The father's."

"Gopalraju. Are you going to let me finish?"

It was about six months ago. Geeta had just arrived. From where? Savitha wanted to ask, but thought she would wait. Padma had already been here for more than a year and had already fallen completely and utterly in love with Mohan. The problem (other than the obvious ones of caste, class, ownership, enslavement, and opportunity) was this: Mohan refused to sleep with her. The father and the older son had already been by, but the younger wouldn't even look at her. But why? But *why*, Padma kept lamenting. Geeta said Padma tried everything: she borrowed Geeta's new hair clips, the ones her mother had given her before she'd left for America; she tore the sleeves off her blouses and sewed up the ends, to show off her pretty arms; she tried to wear her hair down like the American girls they saw on the streets as they were being driven to and from the cleaning jobs, but they had no shampoo, and they were forbidden to go to the store, or anywhere for that matter, so her hair hung like the greasy ends of a scruffy broom, and no one noticed, least of all Mohan, but she kept it that way, hoping, until Vasu (the man from downstairs, who managed the building, but mostly managed the girls) said, Unless you're going to mop with it, put it up. It went on like this, with Padma trying to lure him more and more desperately, dropping things on the floor and bending to pick them up slowly, ridiculously slowly, in low-cut blouses, or wearing a horrid bright orange lipstick that they'd found left behind in one of the apartments. It made her look like an orangutan, Geeta said, laughing. None of it worked, you see, she said, until one day, he came by the apartment drunk. He was only there to pick us up and take us to a cleaning job. Usually he waited for us in the car, but that night, he came to the apartment, he took one long look at us, from one to the other, and then he stumbled to my cot, lay down, and began to cry.

"Cry?" Savitha asked.

"Cry. Actually *cry*, more like sobbing," Geeta said.

When he'd finished sobbing—during which time Geeta and Padma began to panic, wondering if they'd been at fault, and if so, if Gopalraju would go and demand the money their parents had been paid for them, money, as they both knew, which was long gone by now, used already to pay off debts, or to pay the dowries of their other daughters—he sat up and asked them for a glass of water. Padma ran to get it. He drank it down, and then he said, Do you have any vodka?

What's that? they asked, and he said, Never mind.

Here, Geeta paused.

"So what happened?" Savitha asked.

"Nothing," Geeta said. "Nothing, until we got to the building we were supposed to clean. It was the middle of the night, you see. And he gave me the key, and he said, Go on up. So I did. But I watched for Padma, wondering what was happening, but also knowing, and when she finally came up, disheveled, maybe twenty minutes later, I said, What happened? And she said, He took me. In the back of the car. But she didn't look altogether happy when she said it.

"I mean," Geeta said, "I know he forced her, I know he didn't make *love* to her, but I thought she'd be happier. So I asked her. I said, I thought you wanted him to. Yes, but it was cramped, she said, and his breath was awful. He reeked. And then she said, And here's the other thing: When he was done, he dragged me out of the car; I'd barely had a chance to put my clothes on again. He dragged me out, and he pushed me to the ground, and he stood staring down at me. I thought he would kick me, but instead he dropped to his knees, right next to where I was sprawled, but he wouldn't look at me, he wouldn't, he looked only at the ground next to me, and then somewhere into the dark, and then he reached up to where I was lying on the grass, and he took each of the buttons of my shirt, open, because I hadn't had time to do more than pull up my pants, and he buttoned them. One by one. Gently, like they weren't buttons at all, but beads of rain. Not even my mother, she said, was ever that gentle."

And then what happened? Savitha asked.

Nothing, Geeta said. Then we went back to cleaning.

What about Padma? Savitha said. Does she still love him?

Geeta laughed, and then she said, She loves him even more.

When Padma came in late that night, dropped off after a cleaning job in Redmond, she looked over at Savitha and said, "New girl?" Savitha nodded.

She was indeed pretty. But she knew it, and she said, "Oh," and then went into the bathroom and closed the door.

The next morning, just as Geeta had said, it was raining. Savitha was picked up with the others. When she'd come out of the bathroom (Geeta had showed her how to work the shower and explained that there was so much water in this country that no one took a bucket bath) wearing one of the two saris she'd brought along, Padma had laughed, and Geeta had said, "They don't want us wearing those. We stick out too much," and lent her a pair of black polyester pants and a gray-and-pink checkered shirt. The shirt, Savitha noticed, was cotton and felt good against her skin. She checked the threading, even though it was clearly machine made. When they handed her a pair of old sneakers to wear, Savitha looked at them and then at Geeta and Padma. They stared back. "She can't tie them," Padma announced glee-fully, as if she'd solved a riddle. Geeta tied them for her and told her she'd find her Velcro ones. "What's that?" Savitha asked. "You'll see. You'll be able to tie your shoes with your teeth," Geeta said, laughing. My teeth, Savitha thought, and wondered how tying a shoe could be like peeling a banana.

They were dropped off, and each of them went to clean different apart-ments. Padma and Geeta first showed her how to use the various mops and brooms and brushes, the sprays, the vacuum cleaner. None of it was difficult—running the vacuum cleaner was even fun—but it was hard to do with just one hand. She was slow. When Padma and Geeta came for her an hour later, she'd hardly even started. But within a week, she was almost as fast as they were. At the end of two weeks, recalling what Guru had said, that all she had to do was work twice as fast, Savitha sometimes finished before them.

The apartments were always empty. That made it easier. The tenant who'd moved out, usually a student at the university, would've been gone for only a day, sometimes only a matter of hours, and Savitha always, upon enter-ing, stopped at the threshold of the apartment. She stood still and smelled the room. The houses in Indravalli never had a smell, because the windows and doors and verandas were open to the world, and every scent in the world was a scent of theirs, and the small windowless huts always smelled of the same thing, poverty. But here, the smells were subtler. Was it a boy or a girl who'd lived here? That was easy enough to tell. But underneath. Underneath, there was so much more. What did they eat, how often were they home, how often did they bathe, did they like flowers, did they like rain. She could sometimes even tell what they had been studying. She thought one boy might've been studying the stars, because they were drawn in great detail on his walls, at the height he must've been. He liked milk, cheese, dairy, she guessed, and he didn't bathe very often. Another girl was probably study-ing the arts, she thought, by the scent of paints and oils, and she must've liked rain and sun, because every window had been thrown open.

All this within minutes of entering the apartments.

By the end of the month, she was cleaning almost a dozen of them a day, but she no longer took any great pleasure from guessing at the previous occupants. There was always another to clean, and then home to a plate of rice and pickle, maybe pappu if one of them had the energy to make it, her only hand trembling from exhaustion, unable to lift even a bite of rice to her mouth, and then to sleep. Walking now into the empty apartments, she scanned them quickly, assessing in the first sweep how much work needed to be done. She saw—on the carpets and the walls, sometimes on a shelf—the places where furniture or picture frames or potted plants or books had once been, and once removed, had left the square or the circle or rectangle brighter, untouched by feet and dirt and damage, more luminous than the space around it. Savitha stared at the spot of brightness in the middle of a dull, gray room and wished she were that space, the protected one. Instead, at the end of a few weeks, at the end of many apartments, she understood she was the pallid part, the discolored one. She was what absorbed the dirt and the dis-tress. What was fatigued by sun. What lay, like a hand, over brightness.

8

She'd been in Seattle for two months, but she'd never before seen the man who came to pick her up—in a bright red car—one Saturday night in December. Only Vasu had ever driven them, picked them up. And with each passing day, the walls of the apartments closed in; the air grew thinner. She ran to open windows, and stuck her head out, starved for cold, for feeling, for the fall of rain.

Unlike Vasu, the man in the bright red car was tall, a few silver hairs at his temples. He had the beginnings of a belly, and though not nearly as muscular, he was clearly Mohan's brother. He said, "Get in," in Telugu, and then drove her to a low building on a side street. Savitha had been trying to learn her letters, studying street names and signs, but she couldn't see any, it being too dark or the area too industrial. A flickering white light seeped from a distant streetlight. The area was deserted, and when Suresh turned off the headlights, they were plunged into a deep darkness. Her eyes adjusted and she saw that the building he'd parked in front of had a thin line of light at the seam of the door and the sidewalk. It glistened in the dark like a knife.

Inside, they passed through an area lined with boxes to a door at the back and to the left. Suresh knocked, and a voice said to come in, and even before she saw him, Savitha knew it was the father, Gopalraju, the one who'd bought her. He was not as old as she'd expected him to be, his hair unnaturally blue-black, clearly colored, but his face wide and alert, flushed with the same peculiar raw, cold light that came with success, wealth, that she'd seen in Guru, except Gopalraju's face was even sharper, more calculating. He looked at her for a long moment, and then, with false tenderness, he said, "Getting along all right?" She nodded, though she knew it wasn't truly a question. Not really, not in a concerned sense. More precisely, she knew it was a statement, followed by a *different* question entirely. The statement was this: You *will* get along all right. And beneath that statement, just as Geeta had said, was this: If, perchance, you don't get along all right, if, perchance, you feel like talking, like telling, like running, like shouting, if, perchance, you feel coming upon you any kind of despair, distaste, if you feel the need to find a phone, to stop a person on the street, to scan the sidewalks for a policeman, and if, perchance, you feel descending upon you breathlessness, madness, a desire for revelation, then you will no longer be all right. And so this, in turn, was the true question: Do you understand? he was asking. Do you?

Then he saw her stub.

His lips curled up, ever so slightly, in what she knew was disgust, and he closed his eyes, just for a moment, and in that moment, he looked almost ecclesiastic, almost beatific, and Savitha thought they would simply let her go, back to her empty cot, her pillowcase tucked with a half-made sari, a small rectangle of paper, back to the apartment where Padma and Geeta were sleeping, dreaming.

"Be careful. Might poke your eye out," he finally said, still looking at Savitha, but clearly talking to Suresh. She turned to him, and he was laughing, and it was then that she saw she wouldn't be led back, that what lay ahead was another door, behind Gopalraju, and it was through this door that Suresh pushed her. It was dark inside, and when he turned on the light, there was only a roughly made bed, a squat fridge, and some bottles strewn on a corner table. There was a small bathroom on one side. The smell of stale beer, which Savitha didn't recognize, hung in the windowless room, though the other smells she did recognize: unwashed sheets, shit, semen, salt, sweat, cigarettes, a kind of anguish, a kind of listlessness, a kind of gloom, all of which had a scent, all of which had a shape, all of which sat hunched in the corners of the little room.

He told her to get on the bed. And then he did, too. When she lay on her back, he said, No, you'll do the other thing. And so she turned, but he said, No, no, that's not what I mean. Savitha looked at him, confused, and then he showed her what to do. He had a bottle of something clear that he smeared over her stub, and then he showed her. He said, Like this, and then he got on the bed. On all fours. He told her to go in and out, and when she did, he said, Oh, yeah, like that, like that. A pain hit somewhere behind her eyes, and she turned away. But the pain was thunder, it broke and it broke. And he said, Yeah, oh yeah, yes, just like that. And she began to cry, willing it to end. Praying that it would. But he said, Keep going. And so she did, and so it broke.

She closed the door of the small bathroom. The light made her dizzy so she turned it off. She felt her way to the sink and washed up, scrubbed and scrubbed with a little cake of soap, her brown skin reddening all the way up to her shoulder. Then she turned off the water and was about to leave, when she heard something. What was that? She listened. It was coming from the toilet; it seemed to be humming. She leaned closer and listened, and it was. The toilet was humming! Just for her. It was humming a simple song, a child's song, but it was humming it for her. Savitha smiled into the dark, and then she knelt next to the toilet and she gave it a hug. She hummed along. Such a simple song, such simple notes, and yet so exquisite. She knelt and she hummed. The cool of the porcelain and its song; the cool of a river and its gurgle.

He was lying on the bed and smoking. Her legs were weak, and maybe he could see that, because he said, in Telugu, "Come here. Sit down." So she walked to the end of the bed and sat at its edge. He looked at her for a long while, and then he said, in English, as if she could understand, "I wasn't raised here, you know. I was raised in Ohio. You know where that is? I was on the track team. You know what they called me? Curry in a Hurry. Mohan was on the wrestling team, and they called him Curry Up. They didn't think anything of it, the kids. And I would laugh along. There was so much to laugh about back then. But I wanted to punch them. Every time someone said it, and they laughed, I'd laugh, too, and stare at their mouth, and I'd imagine grabbing its edges and ripping it open. Nice and wide."

He took a sip from a bottle that had been resting on the corner table. He sank deeper into the bed with a contented sigh, and he said, again in English, "How'd you lose that hand, anyway?"

He closed his eyes for a moment, and when he opened them, he sat bolt upright. His eyes widened, and he said in Telugu, "Hey. Hey, watch this."

There was a fly on the table. It jerked here and there. He was watching it intently. Savitha too. He took the cigarette out of his mouth. He held it poised above the table, not near the fly, but a little away, as if he knew where the fly would veer. And it did. It inched right toward his hand, which was still as a statue. Savitha had never known a man to be so still. To wait so patiently. For what? She didn't know, but his stillness seemed to her a state of fallen grace. A form of dark worship. Then, in a flash, his hand swept down and he caught it: he trapped the fly under the burning cigarette. Savitha blinked. He couldn't have. She looked again, and sure enough: there was the fly, a slight sizzle, a flailing of this or that limb, and then it was still. As still as Suresh's hand had been.

He laughed out loud. "No one else can do that. No one. I've been able to do it since I was five." He looked at her. "The key is: your hand has to move before your mind even tells it to move. That's the only way to kill a fly."

He lifted the cigarette, the fly still caught on its end, its body no longer distinguishable from it, and dropped the butt into the ashtray. His smile, too, dropped, and he said, "Let's go." When he pulled up to her building, he said, "I'll be back in a week or two."

When she got back to the apartment, she stood for a moment and looked at Padma's and Geeta's sleeping faces.

We were once children, she thought; we were once little girls. We once played in the dirt under the shade of a tree.

Then she turned away, the nausea rising in her throat. She showered. She smelled burning flesh, though was there enough to a fly to be called flesh? She didn't know, and she stopped wondering. After her shower, she drank a glass of water, went to her cot, and took out Poornima's half-made sari. She looked at it, she looked at it hard, and she thought, In a week or two. He'll be back in a week or two. And then she thought, but of course there was enough to it. There had to be. There was enough to everything to be called flesh. Even the smallest creature. The poorest. The most alone. And yet. And yet, he'd be back in a week or two. She looked at the fragment of sari in her hand, and she thought, I am not that girl in that room. I am not. I am this; I am indigo and red. And to be here in a week or two, and a week or two after that, and a week or two after that, was to surrender to what the crow had warned against, had always been warning against, it was to surrender to being eaten piece by piece.

She didn't sleep that night, thinking. And she stayed thinking all the next day: while she cleaned apartments and one floor of an office building and a few rooms of a residential hotel. When she got back to the apartment, late that night, she ate, thinking. Padma came home after her. Still pretty after a day of cleaning, Savitha thought, but all that prettiness came to nothing. Just a made-up girl wearing orange lipstick, heavy kajal, cleaning the houses of strangers, and waiting for a man who would never come.

Savitha was quiet, and Padma must've noticed, because she said, "What's with you?"

Savitha looked at her as if she'd never seen her before. "What keeps you from leaving?"

"Where would I go?"

"Back to India."

"Where would I get the money? Besides, India's no prize. Nothing there. My father used the money he got for me to buy a motorcycle."

Savitha was silent.

"Why? Are you thinking about it?"

"No, but you. You're just so pretty."

That made her smile, touch her fingers to her hair, and Savitha smiled back, imagining Padma believed her.

She was wrong.

The next time she took out Poornima's half-made sari, a few days later, she gasped: a long swath was ripped from it. Torn, the weaving mutilated, the tear uneven. Who'd done such a thing? She looked inside her pillowcase and then in her cot. She looked at the remaining piece, a third of it missing. Gone. She sat for a moment, and then she jumped up and scoured the entire apartment: the kitchen cabinets, the bathroom, the hall closet, Geeta's and Padma's things. Padma! She must've told someone Savitha had been asking about India, about leaving. And they'd . . . they'd what? She slumped again on her cot. They'd taken a piece of the only thing that meant anything to her. And why would they do that? Why wouldn't they take the whole thing? "Why," she said to the walls. But the walls said nothing back.

I have to be more careful, she decided. Much more careful. The sky seemed to agree: the rain came harder; the air grew heavier.

9

Over the next weeks, she lay in bed every night and thought about the journey from India to Seattle. She dissected every moment, every document. When she and the woman who was supposed to be her mother had first arrived at the airport, in Chennai, the old woman had taken out two strips of paper and two small blue books and handed them to the lady at the counter. The strips must've been their tickets, because the lady at the counter had stamped them and handed them back. The blue books she'd only glanced at before handing them back. Then what? Then nothing, until they'd arrived in New York. Here, the whole process had been reversed. Here, Savitha recalled, they'd stood in a long line, and this time, the old woman had shown the tickets and the two small blue books to a man. The man had stamped the blue books but not the tickets. What were those books? Savitha had no idea, but she knew she needed one: the blue book. She also knew she needed a ticket. And for both of those? She knew she needed money.

Her heart sank.

Because she realized that even with money and a ticket and the blue book, she obviously still couldn't leave. Not at all. They knew her family, they knew they were in Indravalli, and if she left, well, anything could happen to them. Gopalraju had paid a lot of money for her, more than she could imagine—she was an *investment*, something Savitha knew only in terms of cows and goats and chickens. And why would anyone let their cow or goat or chicken simply walk away? They wouldn't. Never. And as for her family: they could be killed. She knew that, she knew that as she knew her love for them: in her gut. So she would stay.

Toward the end of her three months in Seattle, there was a knock on the door. Savitha panicked. Vasu usually barged right in, using his key, so it wasn't him. It was a Wednesday night, and Padma and Geeta weren't home yet. What if it was Suresh? But he usually picked her up at one of the buildings, and took her to the room, and handed her the tube with the clear liquid. Those were the nights she came home well after Padma and Geeta were asleep. A few times, afterward, she'd vomited on the sidewalk when he'd pulled his car away; one time she'd held her stub over a flame.

Another knock. Who could it be?

She stood by the door and listened. Nothing. Then a shuffling of feet. Not going away, not yet. She waited. There was no peephole, though in some of the apartments she'd cleaned, she'd noticed the hole in the door. Now she wished she had one.

On the third knock, she turned the knob silently, as quietly as possible, and peeked through the crack.

It was Mohan.

She opened it wide, and he stood there sheepishly, not moving. She waited at the open door, wondering if he, too, had come to take her to the room.

He smiled shyly, maybe even sadly, and then he handed her a brown paper bag. When she opened it, there were six bananas inside. The bananas, the sight of them—their smooth yellow skins, their defiant firmness, their subtle beauty—made her laugh with pleasure. She looked at them and she looked at them, and when she finally looked up, Mohan was looking back at her.

"In America, they cut them lengthwise and put ice cream in the middle," he said.

She tried to imagine that and couldn't. "I like them with yogurt rice," she said.

They stood for a moment, and she invited him inside (though she felt funny about the invitation; it was his father's building, after all). He said, No, maybe another time. Maybe next week, he said, and then he left.

That night, Savitha had two helpings of rice and yogurt and banana. The first helping so sweet and creamy and divine that tears streamed down her face. Geeta laughed, and let her have a little of her portion of rice. The second helping—Geeta's kindness, Mohan's kindness—made her think of Poornima, and more tears came to her eyes, though these, she knew, were for different reasons.

"Let's go," Mohan said.

He'd come to an apartment she was cleaning, and he stood by the door, as if the carpet were wet, which it wasn't, or as if there were other people inside, which there weren't.

"But I'm not done," Savitha said.

He looked around the lit room once, let his gaze pass perfunctorily from one end of the room to the other, and then he said, "It's fine."

She climbed into the same car in which he'd picked up her and the old woman from the airport. It was still flooded with the scent of lemon. She didn't know where he was taking her, but he'd turned away from the direction of her apartment. He was quiet, almost morose, but she hardly noticed. She was looking out the window, at the nighttime streets. She'd only ever been driven from cleaning jobs to her apartment and back again, ten, twenty minutes at a time, but now, she sensed, they were *drifting*, a word she'd never associated with her life, never associated *with* life, life being only a constant doing; doing so that there could be eating and sleeping and surviving. But now, now, on a wide street, and on a wide and drizzly night, to glide under the traffic lights and to watch people sitting in brightly lit rooms and to imagine the smell of those rooms, the warmth, the chatter of the people inside or of the television or of nothing at all, just the silence, but to imagine it, sitting in a fancy, lemon-scented car, and with nothing ahead, and nothing, not really, behind, it was enough to make Savitha's heart swell, enough to make it ache with something like happiness.

They eventually turned off the wide main street and started to go up a hill. They wound through dark streets. The wind picked up, and she asked if she could open the window, and when Mohan didn't respond, or maybe didn't hear, she fidgeted with some buttons on her door until the window rolled down, with a smooth, thrilling ease, and the breeze lifted her loose hair (with only one hand, she could no longer wear her hair in a braid), and the drizzle sprayed her face, set her shivering with delight, and the shadowed leaves swayed above her and beside her as they drove past, moving as if wedded to the night, as if dancing with the wind.

No, she couldn't remember a night so wondrous, here or anywhere, and when she turned to Mohan, nearly laughing, she saw that he was unscrewing the cap of a small bottle, lifting it to his mouth, and it was then, when she saw the gold liquid in the bottle, tipping, when she saw his face wince with the first sip, it was then that she knew she was mistaken. None of this was true. Not in the least. This night, this drizzle, this uphill climb. None of it was her own. It was his. He *owned* her, and that was the only true thing.

She rolled her window back up; the walls closed in again; she closed her eyes.

When she opened them, the streets were even darker, and they were still climbing. Eventually he pulled the car onto a small embankment, off the side of the road, and he turned the engine off. He took a long pull from the bottle, and when he saw her watching, he held it out to her. Savitha thought about her father, then she thought about Poornima's father, and then she took the bottle. It went down like fire—her first taste of whiskey—and she coughed and sputtered until Mohan laughed and took the bottle back. She thought then that he must be unused to laughter, or at least unused to laughter not tinged with sorrow. The whiskey reached her stomach, and then her eyes floated and bobbed along on a warm sea. When they focused she saw that they were on a high ridge, and below them and beyond them, all the way to the dark horizon, was a field of lights. The lights spilled like beads on black velvet. "Which way are we facing?" she asked.

"West."

West, west.

She studied the lights, and she thought that somewhere below, just below, must be her apartment. Beyond the lights, in the distance, was a strip of solid black. "What is that band without lights?"

He looked up, clearly drunk by the way his head wobbled, and he said, Where? She pointed into the distance. He followed her arm and said, "Water. That's water." She remembered the bridge they'd gone over and yet, in her three months in Seattle, had forgotten they were so close to water. All she knew were walls. Even on sunny days, the light was gray, slanting dolorously into dirty apartments. The dust motes spun in place, having nowhere to go. She stared into the black mass before her, that strip of dark, and though she knew all about washing machines now, she wondered if that black mass had ever had laundresses on its shores, if saris had ever fluttered there like flags.

"You know when I had my first drink?" he asked into the dark, in Telugu. She took another drink from the bottle.

"I was eleven. Almost twelve. Behind the carousel at the state fair." Now he was switching between Telugu and English, and Savitha struggled to understand. "Went with my friend Robbie and his dad. His dad thought it was time, so he bought us beers." Then he was silent for a long moment. "We moved the next year. Nanna sold the motel, bought another two. I'll build us an empire, he said. An empire!" He looked at Savitha, and he said, "I guess you're it. I guess you're the empire."

The whiskey was gone. Mohan flung the bottle into the backseat and leaned his seat back. How did he do that? Savitha wondered, pushing against her seat to get it to lean.

"Open that," he said, pointing to the glove box.

She fiddled with it, and when it popped open, there was another bottle inside. She handed it to him, and he held it close, without opening it, as if it were a talisman, an object of great beauty.

Into the silence of the car, he said, "I stopped wrestling at sixteen. Just stopped. Suresh must've asked me a million times. Still does. Why, he'll say. Why'd you stop? You were good, Mo, really good. You could've made it to the state finals. The nationals." He stopped and looked at Savitha. He asked in Telugu, "Do you understand any English?"

She shook her head no.

He continued, this time only in English. "He picked me up after school one time. Just that once. There was a girl sitting in the backseat, about my age. I looked at her, and then I asked, 'Who is she?' He didn't even turn his head. Said, 'Just go in there, Mo. Just go with her, wait for her to be done, and come back out. Nothing fancy.' By then, he'd pulled the car up to a clinic, and we just sat there in the parking lot. The three of us. By then I understood. I said, 'Why can't you go?' He waited. I didn't think he'd answer, but then he said, 'They might recognize me.' So I took the girl in there and talked to the nurse. I knew what she was thinking, the way she looked at me. She gave me pamphlets on contraception and abstinence and all that. I must've turned beet red.

"When the girl came back out, she was carrying the same pamphlets. Couldn't speak a word of English, but she clutched those pamphlets as if they were a hand. Wouldn't look at me. Wouldn't raise her head. I didn't know what to say. I was a kid. We both were. I finally stammered something about getting her some water, and she said, 'No, thank you, sir.' Can you imagine that? Sixteen, and she calls me sir."

He laughed.

"After we dropped her off, I said, 'Who the fuck is she? What's she doing in our building? What'd you do to her?' He looked at me, long and hard, and he said, 'What do you *think* she's doing in our building? Huh? What do you think we do, Mo? How do you think we make it in this country? Make it big. You think Dad got us where we are *without* girls like her?' "

The drizzle turned to rain.

"Girls like her," he repeated, and then he grew quiet. In Telugu he asked, "What did you understand?"

Savitha said, truthfully, "I understood the word *girls*."

He looked at her with what she thought was real longing, or real loneliness, and then he ran his fingers slowly down the side of her face, and he said, in English, "You are an empire. You're more than an empire."

Savitha looked at him and she wanted in that moment to tell him everything, absolutely everything, but instead she took the bottle from his hands, saw the liquid tilt against the raindrops, the distant lights, drank as her father would've drunk, and then she smiled.

It was the following week. He came to another apartment, on Brooklyn Avenue, and without a word he lay her down on the carpet. He kissed her arm and then her throat and then her mouth, and even though she had been kissed many times before, she thought, So this is what it's like to be kissed. The give of the carpet was on her back, and he pushed the hair from her face, and then he unfastened her blouse. It didn't fall completely open, only to one side, and on this side he took her breast into his mouth. She cradled his head in her hand, and Savitha saw, in the quiet black of his hair, his first coarse gray. A window swayed above their heads and then a thick cloud shifted and light flooded in, fell onto her face. He took off her pants, her underwear, both a size too big because they had to share clothes and Geeta was bigger than her, but he seemed not to notice, nor to care, because he was kissing her stomach. He laid his head against it, as if listening for voices, and she cradled his head again, keening to him, wanting him to continue, but no, he wouldn't. Not yet, he said. She felt first impatience and then despair. Please, she almost said, in English, in Telugu: *please*. But he waited, held himself above her, looking down. No, he said again, no, I want to look at you first. The full fiery brown gleam of you. She rolled her head back, and he held her away like that, poised above her, poised perfectly, heartlessly, and the light beyond her shivered, nectared and alive.

They sat together afterward in the fading light. Under the window, on the floor, their legs outstretched and touching. Neither spoke. Savitha wanted to take his hand, but he was sitting to her left. She looked at her stump, resting on her thigh, though Mohan hardly ever seemed to notice it. Instead, he reached for his pants, took out his wallet, and said, "Here. I want to show you something."

It was a small photograph, and though it was creased and yellowed, she saw immediately that it was Mohan and Suresh, as boys. "How old were you?"

"Eight and fourteen."

She studied them: the too-long hair, the round eyes, the expression of irrepressible wonder on Mohan's face, tilted half toward his older brother, half toward the camera, his smile unabashed and absolute, and Suresh not smiling at all, but with an adolescent seriousness, or maybe an adolescent stubbornness, but still with his arm around his little brother, holding him close, though not too close. "Where's your sister?"

"She took it. We were on vacation. The only vacation we ever took. My dad wanted to show us Mount Rushmore. This was back when we lived in Ohio. '*That* is greatness, kids,' he said, 'when your face is chiseled onto the side of a mountain.' I don't much remember it. Mount Rushmore, I mean. But what I do remember is that place," he said, nodding at the photograph.

Savitha looked deeper into it, past Mohan and Suresh, and at the stand of trees behind them, and maybe a river or a lake in the near distance. "What is it?"

"Spearfish Canyon. We just drove through, but I remember it was perfect. It was the most perfect place I have ever been."

She stared some more. It didn't look like much; it didn't look half as awe-inspiring as Indravalli Konda. "Perfect how?"

He was silent. And then he shifted his arm and wrapped the fingers of his right hand around her stump, as completely and as naturally as if she, too, had a hand. "There is no way," he said. "There is no way to explain a thing that is perfect."

Savitha considered the photograph. "Was it like flute song?"

"What?"

"This place. Was it like flute song?"

A small smile played at the edge of his lips. "Yes. In a way, it was." Then he said, "I never thought of it that way. But yes, it was flute song."

"What is it called again?"

"Spearfish Canyon."

She broke the words down into parts and said them to herself. Spear. Fish. Can. Yon. Then she said them out loud. "How do you spell it?"

"Other side," he said. And when she turned the photograph over, there it was: written in blue ink: S-P-E-A-R-F-I-S-H C-A-N-Y-O-N. When she handed it back to him, he said, "Maybe we can go one day," and she nearly laughed. Why, she didn't know, couldn't say; only that she felt no joy.

10

She had been in Seattle for over a year. Sometimes, when Vasu drove her from apartment to apartment, they would pass the university, and Savitha would look out the window of his old beige car, at the waiting or the walking or the laughing students, and she would look especially at the girls. They were her age, sometimes older, and she looked at their skin, the fall of their hair, the slope of their shoulders, both of their hands, and she would think, What is your name? Where do you live? Do you live in an apartment I've cleaned?

If Mohan knew about Suresh and the room and the bottle of clear liquid, he didn't let on. He was usually silent, or he would tell her stories in English, or he would make love to her and then he would make her coffee. Even if they were in an empty apartment, with not a pot or pan in sight, he would run down to the corner store, buy instant coffee, boil water in the microwave, and then settle on the floor with her, drinking weak coffee out of a Styrofoam cup he'd found in his car.

Once, he had neither a pot nor cups, but the previous tenant had left a

small plastic flowerpot on one of the windowsills. Savitha saw Mohan looking at it, and she said, No, that's disgusting. But he cleaned it out in the
sink, and boiled water, and they passed it back and forth, the slight scent of
dirt mixing with the strong scent of coffee.

Of course, she didn't tell Geeta or Padma about either Mohan or Suresh.
None of them talked much about the brothers. But one night, after they'd
found a bag of half-rotting capsicum at their door, probably left by Vasu,
Geeta cut out the inedible bits and made a curry of capsicum and potato.
They had it with rice, and then they had yogurt with rice, and as Savitha
was peeling her banana, Padma said, "Where did you get that?"

She couldn't tell her the truth, and so she said, "Outside the door. Just
like the capsicum."

They ate in silence, and after they'd washed up, they lay on their cots
and Savitha heard a distant bellowing, and she said, "What is that?"

"It's for the fog. It's to warn the ships."

"Fog?"

A thick mist, they told her. Ships can lose their way. Savitha remembered
the early-morning mist over the Krishna; she could've ladled it out like
sambar. And then she thought about ships. There must be a port nearby, she
guessed, and there must be sailors and captains and passengers and wonderful
things from all over the world coming to that port. Like spices, maybe, or gold.

"Mohan came by earlier," Geeta said to Savitha. "He said he needed to
take you to a job in Ravenna. I told him I could go, but he said no, it could
wait."

Savitha was quiet, but Padma sighed into the dark.

"You should tell him," Geeta said, giggling as if she were a schoolgirl.

Padma turned in her cot, sighing again, humorless.

Their breaths deepened, and into the dark, Geeta said, her voice now
serious, "What are you afraid of? I mean, hasn't the worst thing already
happened?"

There was silence. Savitha felt for Poornima's half-made sari, wondering over and over whether she should hide it before she left in the mornings. Wondering *why*.

Padma and Geeta finally seemed collapsed into a restive sleep. But Savitha lay awake. Geeta's words broke through her thoughts; they held like a weight over the room. The night, too, was a weight. She wondered for a time whether she felt jealous, not of Padma, obviously, but of what was to come. Suresh, she'd learned, was married, but Mohan wasn't. She knew he would be, one day soon, to some appropriate girl from some appropriately wealthy family. She would be Telugu, and she would be charming. That, too, she knew. But she wasn't jealous. She'd known the conditions of their affection all along. Affection? No, not affection; but was it love? Maybe it *was* love, and that thought, as she lay on her cot on the floor of a run-down studio, was the one that saddened her. She turned away then, *physically* turned away from the thought, and faced the wall.

She thought of a story her father had told her, long ago. She'd been just a girl, and all day she'd played among the stunted trees near their hut, watched as the laundresses passed by, bundles of folded clothes balanced on their heads. It had been evening, and the chores had been done, and even her amma had come and sat on the ground, at the foot of her husband's bed, oiling Savitha's hair (there weren't any other daughters yet). In the story, Nanna had been Savitha's age, maybe even younger, and being the youngest and too small to start on the loom or the charkha, he was instead sent every morning to the milkman's house. Now, the milkman's house, her father told her, was almost four kilometers away, and there was no money for a rickshaw or a bus, so he had to walk.

"I was sleepy, always sleepy and stumbling along," he said, "but my favorite part was to greet the cows. They always stood waiting for me, their wet noses against their pens, and just then, just then the sun would come up and the tops of their fuzzy, funny ears would be all aglow, as if they were little hills, lit from behind. During the day," he continued, "it was a pleasant walk. Through the fields and toward the river. But in the morning, early

morning, while it was still dark, maybe three in the morning, maybe four—
so he could get the choicest curds, discounted for him because the milkman felt sorry for him, felt sorry that so little a boy had to come so far—the
fields were awful. They were awful and frightening."

"But why?" Savitha asked, the scent of coconut oil mingling with the
night air.

"Because I was just a boy," her father said, "and because it was dark, and
because that's when all the fears come out: when you're a boy—or a girl,"
he said, patting her head, "and when it's dark. So anyway," he went on,
"one morning I was on my way to the milkman's house when I stopped in
my tracks. Just stopped, right in the middle of the path. You know why I
stopped?" he asked Savitha.

She shook her head, her eyes wide.

"Because I saw a bear. Or a tiger. I couldn't tell, you see. It was dark, as
I said, and even though I could almost reach out and touch it, even with
my child's arm, I didn't dare. Who would? But it held me, it held me in its
gaze. Its eyes were yellow, I could see them, and they didn't blink, or they
blinked in the exact same moments that I blinked. At any rate, in that
gaze, I was frozen. Absolutely terrified. And as I stood there, not moving,
it stood there, too, not moving. Just stood there, gazing at me. Waiting to
eat me."

Savitha gasped. "What happened, Nanna?"

"Well," her father said, "we stood looking at each other, breathing, unmoving, its yellow eyes slowly turning red. Orange and then red. And then
more and more red. By this point, I'd found a small hollow near me, just a
few steps away, and so I backed away from the bear or the tiger, ever so quietly, and I settled into this hollow. I would wait till sunrise, I decided, and
then make a run for it. Or more likely, I hoped, it would leave and go back
to the forest or the jungle or wherever it had come from. Besides, by then,
I figured, the farmers would start coming out to their fields, and maybe one
of them would have a stick to scare it away. Well, these were the thoughts
going through my head, but mostly, there were no thoughts, just fear."

And then, much to Savitha's surprise, her father laughed out loud. "And you know what happened next?"

Savitha stared up at him.

"The sun came up. That's what happened. And then you know what happened after that? I saw that that big bear or tiger or whatever other monster I'd imagined was nothing but a tree. A tree! It was just a tree. A dead tree." He laughed some more. "It was the dark, you see. It was my imagination."

"So there was no bear? There was no tiger?" Savitha asked, a little disappointed.

"No, my ladoo," he said. "It was just a tree. Like most fears, it was nothing. Nothing."

Savitha lay in the dark and thought about that story. She hadn't thought about it in many years, but she thought about it now and realized: But my fears aren't nothing. My fears for my family, for their well-being, are real. They *are* a bear. A tiger. And if I were to leave—well, she couldn't even finish that thought. But why did I think of the story about fear on the very heels of thinking about love? she wondered. Was it obvious? Of course it was. She'd never known one without the other: she'd always feared for her father's health, his drinking, her sisters' marriages, her mother's endless days. And with Mohan. Well, with Mohan, it was even clearer—there could be no love *without* fear. The two had always been bound for her, she realized, fear and love, always, but just there, floating on the edge of wake and sleep, another thought drifted up, as if from the cloth that was tucked into her pillow: the thought that maybe there had been one exception. Maybe once, just for a short time, in her girl-hood, they had been separate. For a short time (she was already snoring, beginning to dream), she had loved Poornima, and in that love, she had felt no fear.

Suresh came and took her to the room and then Mohan came and then Suresh came. Then Mohan came and they had sex in an empty apartment, and once in an office building. This pattern followed her around like a lost dog. Months went by. She once sat on the edge of the bed and watched

Suresh open a bottle of beer, and she said, "Can I have one?" He looked at her, astonished—perhaps that she had spoken at all, something she avoided, broken as she still was by him and the room and the bottle of clear liquid and the act—and handed her one. And so, yet another pattern: beer with Suresh, coffee or whiskey with Mohan. She found herself alone one night, in the studio, and could hardly sit still. She went from the window to the kitchen to the bathroom and back, and realized that what she really wanted was a drink. The thought stopped her cold. She stood at the window and thought about her father, about his destruction, and then she thought about the blind boy, and how she'd lain in her cot and stared at the locked door, waiting for him to arrive with the needle. She swore it off in that moment. All of it. And never again touched the beer or whiskey she was offered.

At the end of July, on a warm and cloudy afternoon, Mohan came to pick her up and said, "I have a surprise." They drove on a wide road again, this one next to the water, and then he parked on a busy street, between a blue car and a red car. She would always remember that: that he'd parked his black car between a blue car and a red car. The restaurant he took her to was the most colorful room Savitha had ever seen. The booths were bright red, cinema posters lined the walls, and the counter was blue. Blue and red again, she thought. When they sat down—Savitha still bewildered because he had never brought her to a public place before, and what was more, she'd never actually *been* in a restaurant before, ever, with or without Mohan— she looked around her at the other patrons, laughing and chatting, utterly at ease, and slid into the corner of her seat. She surreptitiously tucked in her blouse so no one would see how loose it was and concealed her stub under the table, and then she watched the happenings in the restaurant, the clatter and the conversation and the steaming plates of food going past their table, all with a kind of reverence, a wide-eyed wonder.

When the waitress came to take their order, she looked at Savitha with what seemed to her like ridicule, or maybe pity, and then she turned to Mohan. He ordered something Savitha couldn't understand, and when it arrived, the waitress set the shallow oval bowl down in the center of the table, between them.

Savitha looked at it. "What is it?"

"Don't you remember? I told you about it. It's called a banana split."

She looked at it, and there it was! A banana! "But what is that?"

"Ice cream."

"No, on top."

"Chocolate. And that's whipped cream."

"And that?"

"Strawberry sauce."

"Those look like bits of peanut."

"Yes."

"What about the thing on the very top?"

"It's a cherry. Have you ever eaten a cherry?"

Savitha shook her head, and so he insisted that she eat that first, and when she did, she decided it was the strangest thing she'd ever tasted. The texture like a lychee, but the taste more a sweet, syrupy alcohol. Then she took a bite of the banana with a bit of ice cream and chocolate and dipped the tip of her spoon into the strawberry sauce so she could taste all of them together. She also got a bit of the white, fluffy weightless substance, and it all took a moment, but then she closed her eyes. It was the best thing she'd ever tasted. Was it better than banana with yogurt rice? No, but it was more extravagant. It was hard to even think about both of them together. Yogurt rice with a banana was like life, simple, straightforward, with a beginning and an end, while the other—the banana split—was like death, complex, infused with a kind of mystery that was beyond Savitha's comprehension, and every bite, like every death, dumbfounding.

Mohan watched her intently, taking only a bite or two, and then he said, "It's hard to leave you, at times like this."

"Times like what?"

He didn't respond. He instead reached over and wiped a bit of chocolate from her cheek, and he said, "I have to go to the airport soon."

"Oh," Savitha said, hardly listening, focused on the banana split.

"Another girl."

Savitha looked up. She was listening now.

"A cleft lip, I think."

So another medical visa.

"Where is she from?"

"How should I know?"

"I mean, is she Telugu?"

"Probably. But we make a point not to know."

Savitha felt a rush of cold air. She held the spoon steady. "I don't under-stand. You make a point *not* to know?"

He lowered his voice to a whisper, though Savitha saw that there was no one seated near them. Besides, they were speaking in Telugu. Who could possibly understand them? "Otherwise," he said, "well, otherwise, in case of trouble—" He stopped, and then he said, "Not here."

So she finished the banana split and he paid the bill, and when they got back to the car, she said, "Are you saying—"

"Just that, in case of trouble, no one knows any of the other parties. No one can rat anyone out."

"So you don't know where—where this girl is coming from? Her village?"

"No."

"Her family?"

"No."

"How did your father get her, then?"

"There are middlemen. The world is full of middlemen."

"What about that old lady? The one who pretended to be my mother?"

"Not even her," he said. "Least of all her."

Savitha sat back in her seat.

Her thoughts whirled: I'll need money; where do I get money; and how, how will I leave; the little blue book; the little blue book; medical visas;

stupid, stupid, why didn't I pay more attention to signs, to roads, to English; a girl with a cleft lip; Nanna, you're safe; Nanna, you were right, it wasn't a bear, it wasn't a tiger, it was all in my head; should I tell Padma and Geeta, I can't, I can't; cleft lip; I remember someone with a cleft lip, that girl, the daughter of one of the laundresses, she crawled and fell down the well by accident, or did she; airport, should I go to the airport; banana split; death, being here will be death; the little blue book; idiot, why didn't you plan better; but Nanna, I didn't know, I didn't know it wasn't a bear, a tiger, not until now, not until sunrise, not until this moment, I didn't know.

Her thoughts whirled and whirled, spun in great gusts, and at their center, in their precise and perfect center, there was absolute quiet, and in that quiet, there was only one thought: I can leave.

11

S he waited. She stilled her mind, and she waited.

The next time she saw Mohan was two weeks later. He came to an apartment she was cleaning, a studio like hers but much prettier, with fine wood
floors and shining white cabinets. He made her coffee. She took a sip, waited,
took another sip, and said, "Did you pick them up?"

"Pick who up?" He was distracted, fiddling with a loose faucet in the
kitchen. She couldn't see his face, but she could see his hands, and she focused on them. "The girl. The one with the cleft lip."

"Not yet. Postponed. Some issue with the visa."

She watched his hands, and then she looked around the apartment. "This
place is nice, isn't it? I wish I could live here."

Mohan turned to face her. He said, "I could try to get you in here. I could
talk to Nanna."

Savitha nearly went to him. She nearly cried out. It is love, she thought,
it is love.

Only a few days later, after she'd gotten home and was heating up rice, there was a knock on the door. She put the rice back in the pot, washed her hand, and went to answer it. Suresh. A pain stabbed her middle. When they got to the warehouse, Savitha looked again at the desk where Gopalraju had been sitting the first time she'd been here. This time the chair was empty, pushed in, and all the papers were piled neatly next to a big computer. The desk, she saw, had three drawers down one side of it. None of them had a lock.

When they entered the room, he kissed her roughly and then handed her the bottle of clear liquid. She rubbed it over her stub, and then she closed her eyes. She'd done this so many times that she could do it by feel. But behind her closed eyelids, there was a different vision. And in this vision, she saw a collapsed building. She couldn't see what had made it collapse, but she saw that not only that building, but all the surrounding buildings, and all the houses around the surrounding buildings, they were also collapsed. And it went on: beyond the houses, there were slums, and these, too, were rubble. And then followed the factories and the garbage dumps and the fields: flattened. She didn't know what had caused this collapse, all the way to the horizon; she didn't need to. She only needed to see the ruin, *know* the ruin, know it would never end.

When Suresh went to the bathroom, she slipped out of the room and rifled through the first drawer of the desk. And then the second. And then the third. Nothing. No little blue books. Where could they be? Anyplace. A million other places. Probably not even in the warehouse. She ran back inside, and when she did, Suresh was coming out of the bathroom. He looked at her, and then at the open door. "Where'd you go?" he said, his voice even.

"I heard a sound."

He raced past her and checked the warehouse and then outside. He came back and said, "Nothing." He eyed her suspiciously, sternly, and then he took two steps, to where she was standing, and slapped her, hard, and said, "Next time there's a sound, *I'll* check."

When she got back to the apartment, she sat on her cot for a long while. She listened to the night sounds: Padma's and Geeta's breathing, the swoosh of cars, the rustle of leaves, the burning of stars. Then she took out the remaining strip of Poornima's half-made sari and brought it to her face. She cried out.

Geeta sat straight up. "What? What is it?"

Savitha whisked it behind her. "Nothing. A bad dream." Padma didn't wake. She looked from her to Geeta, who'd fallen back on her pillow, and then brought it out again: even in the dark it was plain to see: Another piece. Gone. Now it was hardly the size of a towel. *Now* she understood. Now she knew. The pieces were a warning. They were a message. The pieces said: Stop. But how? How did they know? And how many pieces were left? How many till the last?

She looked at the cloth, as if for an answer. "From boll to thread to loom to now," she whispered into it. And then, "We're leaving, you and I."

She waited. She wondered about the blue book.

She asked Geeta in a whisper one morning, after Padma had left, "You need it to go places? What places?"

"How should I know?"

"You mean if Vasu can't pick me up. If I take the bus."

"*No*, not like that. You need it to get on a plane. To go to another country."

Savitha was astonished. Relieved. She looked at Geeta. "How long have you been here?"

"Five years."

"How old were you?"

"Seventeen," she said.

Savitha nodded. Around the same age I was when I met Poornima, she thought. And then she thought, But where will I go? Certainly not back to India; she didn't have the money. Or the blue book. But she didn't know anyone here. No one. Except—there was that one lady, the jilebi-haired lady, the one with the teeth of pearls. It was something, at least; *someone*. When Geeta went to take a shower, Savitha took out the white rectangle of paper and looked at it. Her name was Katie, Katie something. And under her name was a string of letters. No phone number, but there was an address: New York, New York. Twice. And to the east.

A few days later, she saw a young woman, with a kind face, coming out of one of the apartments, and she pointed to the string of letters. "What, please," she said.

The young woman looked at her, perplexed. "Excuse me?"

"What this?"

The young woman looked at it. "That's an e-mail address."

It was Savitha's turn to look perplexed.

"Do you have a computer?"

Ah. Savitha nodded, and thanked her.

A computer.

Well, she didn't have a computer, and she couldn't head west; Mohan said there was only the ocean to the west. And north, south? What was there to the north and south? She had no idea. But east. It would have to be east.

She began carrying Poornima's half-made sari with her. Every day. Mohan noticed it once, on a clear, cold day in mid-September. "What is that?" he asked.

"Nothing," she said, stuffing it back into her pocket. "Just something someone left in one of the apartments."

He looked at her, hurried into his clothes, and said, "I have to go. Pick them up."

"Who?"

"The girl with the cleft lip."

Savitha nodded. After he left for the airport, she took out the half-made sari, folded and refolded it, smoothed it with her one hand. She was now even more careful. Clutching it in her hand as she slept, never letting it leave her sight, even while she was in the shower. Still: nothing. Nothing. But she knew it would have to be soon.

On a Thursday evening, by now late in September, Mohan came for her again. He took her back to the park, the one overlooking the lights, the beads, and the band of water, and then he asked her what apartments she'd cleaned that day and took her to the one on Phinney Ridge. By now, she'd taught herself some of the street names and had learned to read a few signs, like Stop and Exit and Merge. Merge—she liked the sound of that one best. She'd also learned her numbers and how to write her name in English letters, and she'd asked Mohan how to spell his, and then she'd asked him how to spell Seattle. They hadn't gotten much farther than that.

She watched him now, in the kitchen, making coffee. She remembered the first time she'd seen him, and how he'd gazed at her cast, knowing it was false, but still with genuine concern and curiosity. And how he'd bought her her first American bananas. And how he'd wooed her, in his fashion, in this place. In the intervening years, though there was so little she knew about him—since most of his stories were told to her in English—she'd come to sense that there fluttered in him some fragile being, some lone and broken creature, beating its wings against some lone and broken heart. And if she had to guess, she would say he had no idea what to do with her either, with *this*. But that, too, was as it should be. There was no answer. He was raised for different things. Different ends. Things maybe even he didn't understand. But she? She knew what she was raised for, even with one hand, she knew: she was raised for the loom, the cloth, the magic of thread, the magnificence of making a thing, of wrapping it, like a lover, around your body.

And so it was—with hardly any hesitation—that she reached over and took out his wallet from the pocket of his pants. Why wait any longer? There was a little more than a hundred dollars, $112. Over six thousand rupees! It would certainly get her to New York. It would have to.

Just as she tucked the stack of bills into her pocket, she noticed lodged between them the photograph he'd shown her, the one of Spearfish Canyon. She considered it for only an instant before ripping it in two and stuffing the half with Suresh back into his pocket. And the half with Mohan, along with the money, into her own.

He dropped her off. Not this time, and never before, did they kiss good-bye.

She had to leave *that* night, that very night, before Mohan opened his wallet, before her love for him stopped her.

And so she did. She crept out of the apartment—after she was sure Geeta and Padma were asleep—and eased down the stairs. Nearing Vasu's apartment, she saw the crack under his door was dark. Still, she trembled as she passed it; her left foot landed. Her right. A creak.

The lights came on.

Savitha stopped; she held her breath. Footsteps. Go—go now. She bolted down the remaining stairs. She opened the front door with a crash.

She knew east. East, she knew. She ran.

Poornima

1

It wasn't easy for Poornima to get to shepherd the cleft-lipped girl to Seattle. That was what the Telugu word for it meant, *shepherd*. No, it was extraordinarily difficult. And required such meticulous planning, persuasion, and sheer ingenuity that she'd laugh to herself at times; with the effort I put into it, she'd think, I could've laid railroad tracks across a mountainous country, or built bridges across a watery one.

Most of the two years it took felt to Poornima like she was wasting time, precious time, time she counted out in minutes, seconds, but she knew she had to be still. It was stillness, she learned, that at times was the greatest movement. She would find Savitha, she knew that much, but she also knew that it would take enormous amounts of patience to understand what she *didn't* know. For instance, all she really knew was that Savitha had been sold to some rich man in America, in a city called Seattle. She didn't know where Seattle was, or how she would get there, or even what was required to travel to a place like America.

How *did* one cross the borders of a country?

Once Guru had revealed to her Savitha's whereabouts, Poornima did nothing. She waited. She knew that if she raised any suspicion in Guru's cruel mind—that she knew Savitha, or was looking for her—Poornima was certain he would sabotage every link to her and would turn Poornima out of the brothel immediately. So she waited a good three months—long, frustrating months—and then, very casually, on a hot, languid yellow morning, when even the fan seemed to stumble with fatigue, she looked up from her accounting books and her calculator, and she said, "A new cinema came out at the Alankar. I saw it last night. The crowd was a hundred thick. I saw one woman get pushed to the ground."

Guru barely nodded. He was chewing betelnut and reading a newspaper. "Another woman had her blouse torn off. The animals."

Guru looked up from his paper. He cringed, subtly, as he did every time he saw Poornima's face. No one ever got used to it, she noticed, not even she. It had healed completely, but the half that had been splashed by the oil was still bright pink, and against her brown skin, her face looked like a rotting flower. The entire left side was misshapen, hollowed out like a mine, revealing something too raw, too naked. But it wasn't just the pink, edged with an island border of white, the center cratered, dark, as if small animals lived inside; there was another aspect that was far uncannier. Poornima thought it might be her smile, and how it twisted her face grotesquely—children paused in their play and looked at her in fright—and so she stopped smiling altogether, but it wasn't that.

It was something else entirely: it was something beneath the face. Or rather, it was something *raging* beneath the face. It was a light, a fire. And it burned. Even as the hot oil on the surface of her skin cooled, capitulated, the fire within grew brighter. And that was what was truly uncanny, untoward. It was tragic to be a burn victim—oil, acid, dowry disputes, cruel in-laws, all that—though what was expected next was a humble, pained exit, feminine in its sorrow, in its sense of proportion. In other words, what was expected was invisibility. For the woman to disappear. But Poornima refused, or rather, she never even considered it. She walked down the street, she held her head high, she wore no mangalsutra, she had no male escort, she was iron in her purpose, imperial in her poise. And what was more, and what was uncanniest of all, was that all this, all this fire, began raging *after* she was attacked with hot oil.

Of course, Guru saw none of this. He saw only the burn, and the deformed face, and squirmed with discomfort.

"They filmed the songs in Switzerland," Poornima continued. "Switzerland! In the snow. That poor heroine, dressed in that tiny bit of cloth, having to dance and sing in the snow and cold."

"What did you say the name of the movie was?" he asked.

"I'd like to go there one day," Poornima said, sighing. "Wouldn't you?"

"To Switzerland? Why? Plenty of mountains here. I've heard there's some mountains two hours north of Delhi."

"I know. I know. But the mountains in Switzerland are different. Don't you think?"

"No."

She paused. "How would I get there, anyway?"

He turned back to his paper. "Switzerland? I guess you'd get a visa and a plane ticket, like everywhere else."

"A visa?"

"It lets you travel out of the country."

"How do you get one?"

"Well, you'd have to start with a passport first."

"A passport? What's that?"

Guru crumpled the paper down so that she could see his eyes, and he said, "Like anyone would let you into their country with a face like that."

"Just to visit. Just to see the mountains."

He groaned loudly, and then he explained to her what a passport was, and about the Indian government, and then about the visa, and about the Swiss consulate ("Wherever that is," he said. "Good luck finding it."), and then about how all this took inordinate amounts of time and documentation and photo-taking and fingerprinting and "Money! Most of all money. And that's *before* you buy the plane ticket, before you even get there. And from what I hear, Switzerland isn't exactly cheap," he added.

Well, Poornima thought, I'm not going to Switzerland.

Still, she was undeterred. And as Guru had said, she started by applying for a passport.

The months wore on. Poornima paid them no mind. She did her work and by then had rented a room a little away from the brothel, but on the bus route. Sometimes, she walked the five kilometers to work, and on the hottest days, or the wettest, she treated herself to an autorickshaw. She ate simple meals that she cooked on a small gas stove, shopping for the evening's vegetables on the way home and buying packets of milk, which she stored in her landlady's refrigerator. She used just enough oil to fry up the vegetables, never more. On Sundays, she walked around Vijayawada, looking into shop windows or drifting toward the Prakasam Barrage, or climbing up to the Kanaka Durga Temple. She never went inside. She once splurged and agreed to twenty rupees to take a boat ride on the Krishna. The boatswain was a lithe young man, not yet twenty, with coppery-bronze skin and the blackest and thickest head of hair she'd ever seen. He ran up to her as she walked along the shore, and said, "Look at her. Just look at her. Don't you want to sail on her? Doesn't she look like what life should've been?" He was pointing to the river, and with its sparkling waters, the sparkle even mightier because there were clouds darkening the waters downriver, the Krishna did indeed glitter like a gem, like a promise.

She talked him down from thirty rupees to twenty and climbed onto his rickety boat. "Did you build this yourself?" she said.

He laughed. She liked his smile. She liked that he looked right into her face and didn't once flinch.

He navigated to the middle of the river, and here the water suddenly turned choppy. She held on to the sides of the boat, while the boy pushed back toward shore with his long pole for an oar. The clouds were now racing upriver, and she watched as the billowing gray masses crowded above them, colliding and roaring like lions, and she said, "Hurry," and the boy only laughed, and said, "Are you scared?"

Yes, she thought, yes, I am scared.

The water now tossed them like a coin, and they landed with a thud, and then the first raindrop landed. On her arm, and as big as an apple. There was nothing else for a moment, the briefest pause, and then, as if the heavens had tired of playing, of flirting, they opened with a vengeance so sudden and so powerful that Poornima was thrown against the lee of the boat. She caught the sides, scraping her hands. The boy was now struggling against the pitch of the waters. His pole so curved against the current that Poornima thought it might snap in two. She saw his muscles, wet and taut. She saw his hair, dripping like a forest around his face. And both of their clothes, soaked through. She thought of her father in that moment, and she nearly laughed: I might drown in the Krishna after all, Nanna, she said to him. Just twenty years too late for you.

The boy finally heaved them out of the middle of the river and then pushed them toward shore. The rain seemed to abate, just a little, though there was no longer any distinction: her skin was as wet as the river that was as wet as the storm that was as wet as the sky. When they reached water shallow enough to see sand, she jumped out. She waited for the boy to drag his boat to higher ground and found that her fear had left an exhilaration, a lightness of body she had never before felt, and she tilted her face to the sky. The rain, the rest of her years.

She paid the boy twenty-five rupees, and his smile grew even wider, impossibly alluring, and she walked back through the wet streets, jubilant, though she never again took another boat ride.

Her passport arrived. She'd taken the blank forms to a local scribe, near the courts, and he'd filled them out for her. He'd then told her she needed to get photos taken and instructed her on where to submit the forms and the photos. She went back to the courts, months later, passport in hand, and searched the crowd of scribes for the same one who'd helped her before. "Now," she said to him, "how do I go to America?"

A visa, then. That's what she needed. The scribe had explained it to her, much more clearly than Guru had, and so she went back to her flat, deep in thought. She cooked herself some rice and plain pappu and had it with a bit of tomato pickle, then she had yogurt rice, washed up the few dishes, and sat down by the window. Her second-floor flat looked out onto a peepal tree, and beyond that, a man had set up an ironing stall. He was there on most days—thin, with a tired face, graying hair, his iron steaming with red coals, his long fingers dipping into a bowl of water, sprinkling it on the creases of shirts and trousers to crisp them, the edges of saris to smooth them. Poornima had watched him on occasion, but today was the first time she *noticed* him, how rapt he was, how completely consumed he was by the ironing—of what? What was that? A child's frock. It was a child's frock, and it utterly engrossed him. She watched him a little longer, watched him fold the frock, ever so gently, and then place it on a pile of already ironed clothes. He took up the next item. A man's shirt. Poornima then looked up and down the street. There was a cow at one end and a stray dog picking at some greasy newspaper thrown on the ground on the other; a rickshaw wallah was taking a nap on the opposite side of the street. A cool evening wind was rustling the leaves of the peepal tree, and there was the scent of something frying, maybe pakora, from one of the nearby houses. The sky was yellow, thick like ghee, as it cooled into evening, into night's blue mood, and Poornima came finally to see the unavoidable: that she didn't have the money for a visa. She'd used all the money and jewelry she'd stolen from the armoire to pay for the passport. She didn't even have enough for a tourist visa, and she knew no one in America who could sponsor her. That left Guru. And though she was infuriated, she saw no other option: she was far more dependent on Guru than she had imagined, than she would've liked, but she needed him now more than she ever had before.

She obviously couldn't tell him she *needed* his help; he would never give it to her. She had to appeal to the only thing he loved, and she lacked: money. Her opportunity came a few weeks later. She was checking a list of expenses for the previous month—routine odds and ends, like a new hot-water geyser for one of the brothels, the cost of repairing a gate that had rusted, and official payments like the one for a new phone line, and unofficial ones, like the bribe that had been paid to the telephone company administrator to nudge their application for the new telephone line—when she came across an expense that was huge, eight lakh rupees to be exact, but had nothing listed beside it. No name or company or even the initials of a name or a company. Poornima guessed it was a bribe to a politician; only that would explain the extraordinary amount and the fact that it was left blank and untraceable. When next she saw Guru, she asked, "That eight lakh rupees. From last month. Do you know who it was paid out to?"

He had come to check up on a new girl who'd just arrived. A farmer's daughter. The farmer had committed suicide, and the mother had sold the daughter to pay off debts. Poornima saw her only in passing, sitting alone in a room, hardly more than twelve or thirteen. Her face was round, and she wore a glittering nose ring. Poornima imagined that the mother had given her that small piece of jewelry, and that she'd said, Remember me by this, remember your father. But probably it was only a cheap ornament, a tawdry carnival item that had been bought for a few rupees. Though the glitter was real, and it made her face, in the dark room, glow like banked embers.

Guru was on his way to see her when Poornima asked him. He stood at her door, his teeth and lips orange from the betelnet, and said, "Oh, *that* money? Fucking Kuwaitis. They wouldn't pay a single paisa for the shepherd. Made me pay, the rich bastards."

"A shepherd? A shepherd for what?"

"For the girl."

Poornima looked at him. "What girl?"

"Look, can't sit here talking to you all day. You don't need to know."

"But I need to balance the books. Know expenses."

He glanced in the direction of the farmer's daughter's room and said, "On my way out." When he came back, twenty minutes later, his face was calm, and he smiled and said, "Usually, we split the cost with the buyer, but they wouldn't split."

By now, Poornima had figured out most of it: a young village girl, bought by some foreigner, certainly couldn't travel alone. She would clearly need a shepherd, someone to deliver her. But who were these shepherds? "Middlemen find them for us," Guru said. "Someone who knows English, obviously. Airports and all that."

"That's it? Someone who knows English, and they get eight lakh rupees for two days' work?"

Guru shook his head in disgust. "It's thievery, plain and simple. But you're not just buying two days' work, or English, what you're buying for eight lakhs is discretion. Or, shall we say, a bad memory."

Poornima shook her head right along with him. But her thoughts were elsewhere. English, she was thinking. English.

That very night, she rode the bus to Governorpet and asked around. There was a good English school on Eluru Road, the college kids told her, and so she got on another bus to Divine Nagar. She enrolled in a conversational English class starting the following week.

She thought about all the English words she knew, which were the same ones everyone knew: *hello*, *good-bye*, *serial*, and *cinema*. She knew the words *battery* and *blue* and *paste* and *auto* and *bus* and *train*. She also knew the word *radio*. Those wouldn't help her much. She knew the words *penal code section*, also from the movies, the ones with courtroom scenes. Those certainly wouldn't help her. She knew the words *please* and *thank you*. They might.

The class met three times a week, from seven to nine P.M. During the first class, they covered most of the words Poornima already knew, and some she didn't, and they learned simple sentences, like "My name is" and "How are you?" and "I live in Vijayawada." Those were all fine and good, but by the end of the week, they hadn't learned a single thing that would help her while traveling, in airports, or to function, even for one or two days, in a new country. When she asked the teacher about this, about when they would learn things like asking directions or reading signs in an airport or interacting with the officials at passport control (which the scribe had also explained to her), the teacher—a young woman who was a newlywed; Poornima could tell this because she wore a fresh, fragrant garland of jasmine in her hair every evening, and she looked at her watch constantly, and as it neared nine P.M., she would be flush with what could be only expectation, joy, newness—looked at Poornima curiously, averting her eyes from the scar, and said, "This is a conversational English class. You want the one for businesspeople."

"Businesspeople? Why?"

"Because they're the ones who travel," she said.

So Poornima transferred into the class for businesspeople. This class had five men in it, and Poornima. The teacher was a middle-aged man, maybe forty, with a prominent nose and an excitable manner. He would leap around the class like a grasshopper, explaining various words and their meanings and engaging them in conversation. By the end of the fourth week, Poornima was elated. She was able to have this conversation:

"What is your name, madam?"

"Poornima."

"What is your business?"

"I am accountant."

"I am *an* accountant," the teacher corrected her.

"Yes, yes," she said. "I am an accountant."

"How was your flight, madam?"

"Very good, sir."

"Did you fly from Delhi or Mumbai?"

"I fly from Delhi."

"I *flew*," he said.

"Yes, yes. I *flew* from Delhi," she said smiling, resplendent, unaware of the five other men in the class, staring at her face in horror.

The course was four months long. At the end of the four months, Poornima knew the names of major airports (Heathrow, Frankfurt, JFK), and she knew the words *gate, transit, business, pleasure, no, nothing to declare*, and lots of other business phrases she hadn't even imagined, like "In for a penny, in for a pound" and "Let's seal the deal" and "Bon voyage" (which wasn't even English!). She would walk home after class, or ride the bus, and speak to the passing scenes. She'd say, "Bird. Hello. I am learning English." Or she'd say, "Tree. Do you know English?" Once she saw a cat prowling around an alley near her flat, and she said, "Cat. You are looking thin. Drink milk." On the last day, the teacher gave Poornima a pocket-size Telugu-English dictionary for being the best student in the class. She received it in front of the other students—all of them still unused to the burn scars on her face— folded her hands, and said, "Thank you, sir. With me, I will take it America."

Once the class was finished, there was nothing more to be done. Poornima considered taking another class, an advanced class for businesspeople, but she didn't have the money to enroll, so she waited, saved most of her salary each month, and carried the Telugu-English dictionary with her everywhere, as if it were an amulet, a charm that would take her to Savitha faster. It did nothing of the sort. In fact, she had to wait half a year before she saw another large payout. This one was for five lakh rupees. No name, no notations. She seized the opportunity. She said to Guru, "Another shepherd?"

He groaned. "They'll finish me, with their prices."

"How much do you make on the girls?"

"None of your business," he said, looking her squarely in the eyes, as warning, as admonishment. The funds were kept separately, Poornima had noticed, off the books.

"I was just thinking," she said, ignoring his look, "that I could go. Take the girls. You'd only have to pay for the ticket."

"*You*," he said, and laughed, "with that face? And not a lick of English?"

"But I do know English."

"What?"

"I learned in school. In diploma college. When I learned accounting."

"Where are you from again?"

"Ask me. Ask me anything."

Guru didn't know enough English to ask her anything beyond "What is your name?" and "What is your caste?" but the next day, he brought in an English-language newspaper, *The Times of India*, and said, Read that. She did, and explained that it was about two tribals in Jharkhand who'd been beaten to death for being Christian. He looked at her, amazed. Apparently, he'd already had someone, an acquaintance or a man at the newsstand, read the article and tell him what it was about. "Diploma college, you say?"

Poornima nodded.

He was still skeptical, until Poornima started speaking to him exclusively in English, convincingly enough for Guru, who hardly knew it, until he finally said, "There is this one girl. Going to Dubai. But you'll have to get a passport."

Poornima jumped at the chance, hiding from him the fact that she already had one.

He warned her: This is unorthodox, he said. And then he corrected himself: Actually, he said, it's not done. He took a deep breath. "We're supposed to keep everything separate. So no one knows anything, all the way up the line. But do this one, let's see." He chewed his betelnut. "Don't talk to her. Don't answer her. Don't have a *conversation* with her, you understand? You don't know her. And you especially don't know me. Who am I?"

"Who?"

"Exactly." And then he said, "I'm a stranger. The girl's a stranger."

"Okay, but who is she?"

"The farmer's daughter," he said.

2

They left the following month. The girl's name was Kumari and she was wearing a new sari, a fancy one that was yellow with a green border. Poornima noticed that she'd washed and oiled her hair that morning, powdered her face with talcum, and still wore the nose ring, still glittering against the russet of her skin. She looked like a doll, one that Poornima would see in the shop windows during her walks.

The story was that they were sisters, going to visit relatives, though with her scarred face, it was nearly impossible to tell Poornima's age. "I never even thought of it before now," Guru exclaimed, joyous at the prospect of saving the five or six lakhs he would've had to pay another shepherd. "You're perfect. Perfect. And you're so ugly, they might not be able to look at you long enough to ask all those questions."

Poornima hoped so.

Then he said, "You mention me, you utter the first syllable of my name, and I will kill you myself."

She nodded.

Guru even saved money on the train trip to Chennai, as he simply had his driver take Kumari and Poornima to the train station in Vijayawada and drop them off. Naturally, Poornima knew everything there was to know about the Vijayawada station. She bought the girl a chocolate bar at the Higginbotham's, glanced at the niche behind the magazine rack, and then boarded an overnight train to Hyderabad. From there, they took an airplane to Mumbai, barely a two-hour flight. Even so, it was the first time on a plane for both of them, and when they hit turbulence midway, Kumari looked over at Poornima, stricken, green like the green ends of her sari, and said, "Will we fall out of the sky?" Poornima looked back at her, thought of Guru's orders not to speak, and thought, What could it hurt? And though she, too, was terrified, she said, "Of course not. Planes are like birds. They never fall out of the sky."

In Mumbai, they boarded another two-hour flight to Dubai. When they passed through customs and immigration, their passports stamped with barely a glance, barely any questions, there was a man waiting for them in the arrivals meeting area—he was Indian, and humorless. He said there was a car waiting and led Kumari away. But just as the girl turned, the sun struck her face, shone against the nose ring, setting it ablaze. And it was then, with the small jewel spinning like a sun, that she turned to Poornima, and said, "Birds do. Sometimes."

"What?"

"Fall out of the sky."

Poornima watched her go, her eyes warming with tears. So that's how it can hurt, she thought.

She spent a few days in Dubai, at a cheap hostel, so that passport control in India wouldn't start asking questions. What questions, she didn't know, but Guru had given her dirhams and said, "Stay there. And don't talk to anyone." No one talked to *her*, so it was easy, and three months after she returned to Vijayawada, she took another girl to Dubai. Two months after that, she took a girl to Singapore. She also finally saved up enough money to register for the advanced English class for businesspeople. It was taught by a different teacher, another middle-aged man she didn't like as much, but she liked that there was another woman in the class this time, a stylish woman who wore skirts and jeans and who'd already been to many places, like England and America, on business. "What kind of business?" Poornima asked. "Computers," the woman said. Poornima had never seen a computer, or heard the word, but she was too embarrassed to ask any more questions.

Finally, toward the middle of the year, it happened.

Poornima, when Guru told her, sat speechless. She sat without blinking. She stared at him, her body suddenly weightless, exhilarated, and she thought of the night after the boat ride.

"Did you hear me? I know it's not Switzerland," he said, laughing. "But you might like it. Everyone else does."

America. Seattle.

They needed another girl. The girl they'd bought last time, Guru told her, was the hardest worker they'd ever seen. "And get this: the hardest worker, and she only has one hand," he exclaimed. Poornima nodded, hardly listening. She was going to America. She was going to Seattle.

"Savitha," she said that night, into the dark of her room, "Savitha, I'm coming."

3

The preparations for this trip were far more complicated than for the other trips. Much stronger rules, Guru told her. The girl Poornima would shepherd, Madhavi, had a cleft lip. Another medical visa, he added. Then he laughed and said, You two might as well be on a billboard for medical visas. Still, it took months to gather all the documentation, witness them, and submit them, and then to travel back and forth from the American consulate in Chennai. Even so, they rejected Poornima's visa initially, and she had to reapply for a tourist visa, which they delayed again, at the last minute, after they'd bought their plane tickets, so that now Guru had to pay change fees and a bribe to a consulate official, and he grumbled incessantly, but she knew it was still lucrative for him, even after all these expenses.

While they waited for the visas, Poornima slowly began selling away her things. She didn't have much, only a cot and the stove, some dishes, and a small suitcase she'd bought to store her clothes. She sold the cot for a hundred rupees and slept on the mat that had been underneath. She kept the stove for the time being but promised it to her landlady when she left. The suitcase, made of a flimsy, dented plastic, which she'd bought for sixty rupees at Maidan Bazaar, she threw out, and bought herself a new one. "Made for foreign," the man at the shop said, slapping the side of the suitcase. She carried it home, filled it with her few clothes, took out all the money she had in the bank—everything she'd saved since paying for the passport—hardly adding up to a thousand dollars, once converted, and put that, too, into a secret side pocket of her new suitcase, and then she waited.

On the morning of their flight, there was one final delay: Madhavi. She refused to come out of her room. There was no lock on the inside, but she had shoved a broom or a stick into the handle of the door, and rebuffed all their pleas to come out, or to let them in. Guru waited, cursing her mother and father, all the way to her great-great-grandparents, and when Poornima asked to talk to her, he said, "No. No, you don't talk to her. Your only job is to deliver her." But when, after five minutes, she still hadn't opened the door, he relented. "Fine. Talk to her. Tell her another five minutes before we break it open." As it was, Madhavi hadn't offered a word of explanation to the madam or the other girls, but when Poornima leaned into the door and said, "Madhavi, open the door. Open it. Don't you want to go to America? Everybody wants to go to America."

There was a slight shuffling, and then a whimper. And then a thin voice said, "I do."

"Then what is it? Come out."

"I'm afraid."

Poornima stepped back. Of course she was. She had no idea what awaited her in America. "Don't be afraid. I'll be there with you."

"But that's what I'm afraid of," she said.

"What?"

"You."

"Me?"

"Your face. It scares me. I had a dream, when I was little, and I saw a face just like yours."

Poornima laughed out loud. And then she grew silent. She said, "Madhavi," and then she stopped. She felt something rise inside of her, something bitter, something angry, and she spit out, "You fool." She heard the girl back away from the door. "You fool," she cried again, and heard the girl whimper. What a fool you are, she thought, fuming. What fools we all are. We girls. Afraid of the wrong things, at the wrong times. Afraid of a burned face, when outside, outside waiting for you are fires you cannot imagine. Men, holding matches up to your gasoline eyes. Flames, flames all around you, licking at your just-born breasts, your just-bled body. And infernos. Infernos as wide as the world. Waiting to impoverish you, make you ash, and even the wind, even the wind. Even the wind, my dear, she thought, watching you burn, willing it, passing over you, and through you. Scattering you, because you are a girl, and because you are ash.

And you're afraid of *me*?

She went to where Guru was waiting and said, "Break it down." When he looked at her uncomprehendingly, she said, "The door. Break it down."

They left in the afternoon, in mid-September. Chennai to Mumbai to Doha to Frankfurt. In Frankfurt, they waited five hours in a busy transit lounge. So far, Madhavi had avoided her entirely, wedged into the corner of her window seat and hardly speaking. She hadn't eaten on the plane, only picked at the food. When Poornima told her to eat, she said, "I don't like it." In Frankfurt, Poornima watched people coming and going. Travelers from all different places, hurrying home or away from home. The transit lounge had no windows, but Poornima raised her face to the ceiling and thought she could scent the mountains of Switzerland, she was so close. She then looked over and saw that Madhavi was staring at a display of pastries at the coffee shop near where they were sitting. She said, "Wait here," and went and bought one for her.

She watched the girl eat.

It was as deeply satisfying as if she were her mother, watching the way her eyes glistened when she reached for the pastry, how she broke off the sugary dough piece by piece, wanting it to last, and then nibbled the pieces with such pure and ravenous delight that Poornima nearly took her head in her hands, held it to her chest.

They flew into JFK in the dark early-morning hours, and just before they landed, Poornima leaned over Madhavi, sleeping now, and looked down. She saw a field of thick stars and she thought the plane must be upside down; how else could there be stars below them? But then she realized they weren't stars, they were lights, and her breath caught in her throat, her chest ached, to think a country could be so alight, so dense and dazzling. Once they landed, though, they were herded into a long line for immigration, and when Poornima reached the border control agent, all her English left her. She stammered through her responses, barely understanding the man's accent. She wondered if she'd even learned the right kind of English. He hardly seemed to notice her responses, though. He was bald, with the thickest shoulders Poornima had ever seen, and a stern face, and skin so white that Poornima could see the little pink pinpricks in his nose, and the blue and purple capillaries in his cheeks. He had the dainty rose lips of a baby, and Poornima thought his voice might be soft, but it was harsh, and deep, and he said, "How long are you staying?"

"Three weeks," Poornima said.

"Where you headed?"

Headed? "Pardon me, please?"

"Where are you traveling?"

"Seattle, sir."

He studied her face, and Poornima dared not look away, but she was suddenly conscious of her scars in a way she had never been in India. He stamped their passports and waved them through. The man at customs was the opposite of the man at immigration. He was so black he shone. Poornima could see the gleam of the fluorescent lights reflected in his face. He avoided her face, though, and said, "Anything to declare?"

This, Poornima understood. "No, nothing to declare," she said triumphantly.

They took a small train, and then, as they were walking toward their next gate, jostled and harried, people brushing past them rudely, Poornima slowed to study the gate numbers. The crowds and the newness and the enormity of glass and light and sound were overwhelming, but just as they neared their gate, Poornima stopped in her tracks. Madhavi bumped into her from behind, and some man in a suit gave them a dirty look. "What," Madhavi said. "What is it?"

But Poornima didn't hear. She was looking at a glass case. Overcome, broken, by the bowl of fruits on top. One of them a banana.

She stared at it. Could hardly believe its beauty. The perfect yellow of the sun. The biggest banana she'd ever seen, and yet flawless in posture. Arced like a bow, her gaze an arrow.

She spoke.

Look where I am, she said to the banana. Look how far I've come. We were in Indravalli once. Do you remember? We were so young, you and I. And the words of a crow were our mother and our father. Look where I am. For you. For you, I've come this far. I've lost no hope. I take this girl from slaughter to slaughter—because of that hope. Because it's made me cruel. But I have not lost it. Do you remember? We were children, you and I. And look at you now, unbendable and strong. Shaped like a machete, pointed at my heart.

She would've stood like that for days, but Madhavi nudged her, and two hours later, they boarded the last plane, the one bound for Seattle.

They landed in Seattle midafternoon. When they came out of the airport, Poornima took a deep breath and felt as if it were her first one in days. And though they had not been outside of the airport in New York, the air here felt colder and brighter. A car waited for them. Black and sleek.

Out stepped a man who glanced at each of them perfunctorily and then lifted their bags into the open trunk. He was handsome, Poornima thought, and though he was clearly Indian, he seemed unlike any Indian man she'd ever known. Too brawny, she thought, too sad. Though against his stature, his vigor, she imagined that she, with her burned face, and Madhavi, with her cleft lip, must look like circus performers, or carnival acts. And he their keeper.

They entered a wide road, and it reminded her of the road leading out of the airport in Singapore, and she realized, with something like awakening, like freedom, that this was the last road, the one that would take her to Savitha.

4

"Wʜat's your name?" the man asked Poornima in Telugu, out of the silence. But no, it wasn't silence. Poornima realized in that moment that music was playing, from the car's radio, but the music had no words. It could've been a hum, carried on the wind.

"Poornima," she said. "And she's Madhavi."

He nodded, or so Poornima guessed, or maybe he was just hanging his head with that awful sadness he seemed to carry in his eyes, around his neck. "What's yours?"

His hand reached for the radio, and as he turned up the music, she saw in it such strength, such wholeness, that she almost took it. Held it in her own. And he seemed to sense it, because he looked over at her, and she saw in his face a fineness, a fallenness, that of great ruins, and he said, "My name is Mohan."

Immediately, Poornima could tell two things about him. The first was that Mohan was an alcoholic. The signs were all there: the eyes rimmed with red, the barely submerged anguish, just beneath the skin, the hands that fluttered, or hung limp and useless, not knowing their purpose without a bottle in their grip, the gray skin, the gray gaze, the gray, celestial waiting—for the next drink, for the next clink of bottle against glass, for the next ethereal rising. The second thing she knew was that his heart was broken.

And these two things, she realized, were her best weapons.

Besides, she understood, in this new country, that she had to confide in someone, and Guru had mentioned only three people, and even then, only vaguely. The first was Gopalraju, the patriarch, but Poornima doubted that the man who commanded this vast network of apartments and money and girls would in any way lead her to Savitha. In fact, he would most likely do quite the opposite. She'd also once heard a brother mentioned. But who was he? What was his name? Would he be beneficial? It was impossible to know.

And so she chose Mohan. They hadn't spoken any further on the drive from the airport; he'd driven her to a motel, brought her suitcase around to the passenger side, and said, "You'll stay here until your return flight."

Poornima remained in the car. "What a strange city," she said, peering out the windshield. "From the plane, the islands looked like floating banana leaves, waiting for rice."

He eyed her impatiently. "You coming?"

She turned her gaze to him, shook her head.

"You're not leaving *today*, are you?"

"No, my flight's in three weeks."

"Three *weeks*," he said, running his hand through his hair. "The shepherds usually leave in a day or two."

She watched his hands, the sorrow he held in them, as surely and as firmly as he would a glass, a lover. "They've been asking more questions. At border control," she said.

"On the Indian side?"

"Both," she lied. "But I have a thousand dollars. Is that enough for this place?"

He sighed heavily, marched to the back of the car, threw her suitcase into the trunk again, and dropped into the driver's seat. He looked at Madhavi in the rearview mirror—Poornima had hardly heard her breathe since they'd climbed into the car—and then he looked at Poornima. She couldn't quite decipher his expression. A mixture of curiosity, maybe, but also a vague protectiveness, she thought, perhaps from her scarred face and neck. She tilted her face imperceptibly to the left, to reveal the center of the burn. He studied her face some more, but he didn't seem at all to be pitying her, which she'd come to expect. Nor did he seem disgusted, to which she'd also become accustomed.

"I'm still monitoring you. Every day for those three weeks. Don't think I won't," he said, and drove them to a small, one-room flat in a different part of town, more residential, with peeks of dark blue water between some of the buildings. He and Poornima took an elevator to a flat filled with light, even though clouds were gathering to the west, which was the direction the apartment faced; it had wood floors and spotless white cabinets. She looked around the room and said, "Here? We can stay here," knowing Madhavi would never be allowed to remain with her.

"The girl comes with me."

"Where will she stay?"

"This is your first time being a shepherd, isn't it?"

She wanted to smile, but knowing her face contorted grotesquely, she only nodded.

"You'll need food," he said, looking around the empty apartment. "I'll get you a blanket, some dishes."

"Rice and pickle will be fine."

"There's a small store two blocks from here. Don't go any farther than that. They'll have rice. No pickle. You have to go to an Indian grocery store for that." He seemed to be considering that statement, and Poornima wanted to ask him where the Indian store was, but she knew he wouldn't tell her; her burned face was far too conspicuous to frequent a small store where the Indian community probably gathered and most likely gossiped. Who is she? they'd ask, and then look around for an answer. "Do you know English?" he asked after a moment.

"Yes," she said proudly, lifting her head, "I know English."

He seemed unimpressed, and said back to her in English, "I'll bring them over tonight."

What surprised Poornima was that there was no snow. It was the middle of September and she was in Seattle, and yet there was no snow. She'd heard endless stories over the years about how cold it was in America, and how the snow reached to your waist, and how the cars just went along anyway, slipping and sliding on the snow and ice. She had to admit that she was a little disappointed. Not only was there no snow, it was actually *hot*. Not as hot as Indravalli or Vijayawada, certainly, but it must be over thirty, she thought, opening the two windows of her one-room flat, fanning herself, taking off the thick brown men's socks she'd bought in Vijayawada, specifically for the trip, in anticipation of a cold country.

She was also surprised, by the time she returned from the corner store—with a small packet of rice and some vegetables and salt and chili pepper and a container of yogurt and a few pieces of fruit, along with a bar of soap and a small bottle of shampoo—that the country was so empty. In the two blocks to the store, she'd seen a few cars drive past and a plane overhead, and heard a distant honk, but there hadn't been a single person on the streets. Not one. Where were they? Did anyone even live here? she wondered. Did they all go to another city to work or to school or to shop? And where were the children? She'd passed a small park, but that, too, had been empty. It frightened her a little, the quiet, the emptiness, the loneliness of the streets and the sidewalks and the houses, standing so abandoned, built for people who never passed or never stayed. It wasn't till that evening, while she waited for Mohan, that she saw a few lights come on inside the neighboring houses, and every now and then saw a figure pass in front of a window; Poornima nearly whooped with joy to see them.

All through that first afternoon, though, she held herself back. She clenched her fists and kept herself from bursting out of the door and running up and down the streets looking for Savitha. Yelling out her name. What good would that do? None. She had to be systematic, and for that she needed Mohan.

He returned that evening with a sleeping bag (which he had to show Poornima how to use), a pillow, and a bag containing a pot, a pan, a few utensils, and some plastic plates and cups. Poornima looked at them, piled on the kitchen counter, and said, "How is the girl? Madhavi?"

He eyed her sternly. "Why?"

"I traveled halfway around the world with her."

"You no longer have anything to do with her," he said. "Forget it." He turned and walked to the front door. When he reached it, Poornima forced her voice to thicken, to break, and said, "They're loved, you know. You think they're not, because they're poor, or because they were sold, or because they have a cleft lip, but somebody loves these girls. Somebody longs for them. Do you understand? They're loved. You can't possibly know that kind of love."

He glared at her with what seemed to her like murder, and she blanched, falling silent, but then his gaze seemed to ebb in some way, and he said, his voice disquieted, "She's fine."

"Then show me where she lives. What could it hurt? Take me now, in the dark. She can't be far, can she? I just want to see."

She held her breath. She thought he would refuse again, but he looked at her for a long moment. "This once. Just this once. After this, shut up about it."

She didn't think it possible, but the streets were even quieter than they had been during the day. She rolled down her window, better to see the street names, but she couldn't make out a single one in the dark, or else Mohan drove so fast past them that she didn't have a chance to read them. The ones she did glimpse—with her limited English—just looked to her like a jumble of letters. So she began focusing instead on the turns he was making, the number of streets between each turn, and the slope of the streets and the look of the houses and the reach of the trees. Even flowerpots, on the edge of porches, she memorized.

Finally, after ten or so minutes of driving, they reached a narrow street that was long and lined with what looked like cheap apartment houses. He drove to the middle of the street, eleven houses in, on the left, pointed to a window on the second floor, and said, "There. See? The light's on. She's fine." Poornima, in the few seconds before he sped up again, noted every feature she could of the shadowed building: the tattered brown awning over the front door, the lighted windows, six across and each hung with cheap curtains, a tree with flat, dark green leaves at the edge of the building, one of its branches angled toward the window that Mohan had pointed out, Savitha's window, maybe, the branch twisted, trying to reach inside. Would it look the same during the day, or was it a trick of the light? She needed more. She looked for a star, any star, but the sky was now completely smeared with clouds. They were waiting at a traffic light, at the end of the street.

"Are the stars here the same as in India?"

"More or less," he said.

"So the North Star," she said, her voice relaxed, as if only mildly curious, making conversation, "it's behind us?"

"No, it would be there," he said, pointing ahead of them.

She said, Oh, as casually as she could manage, and smiled into the dark.

That night Poornima tried to sleep. She said to herself, You can't go out in the dark, in a strange town, in a country not even your own, in which you arrived all of ten hours ago, looking for one particular building and for one particular person in that building. So she tried to sleep. But she couldn't. She was jet-lagged, and the time difference between India and Seattle was twelve and a half hours, so basically, night was day and day was night, though Poornima didn't know any of this. She only tossed and turned in the sleeping bag, rolling some along the smooth wooden floor. Around three or four A.M., she began to doze, but she was jolted awake. She felt a sudden chill. What if Savitha had already been sold to another ring? In another city? What if the trail was dead? What if this was the end, and she'd lost her scent forever?

Her breathing became ragged; she got up and drank a glass of water. She went to the window. It was raining; streaks of water maundered down the glass. She remembered then, looking into the dark, the rain, something that had happened long ago, a few months after she and Savitha had met.

It had been the monsoon season. She and Savitha had gone to the market. It had been a Sunday, and most of the shops were closed, but the tobacco shop was open. Poornima's father had rolled the last of his leaves the previous evening, and so, before lying down for his nap, he'd told her to go to the market and fetch him two rupees' worth of tobacco. Savitha had arrived just as Poornima had been getting ready to leave, though both of them, of course, had been barefoot—Savitha because she had no shoes, and Poornima because her flimsy sandals (passed down from her mother) would've been useless if it started to rain, getting caught, or ripped, in the muddy sludge. Still, they had taken their time walking through the market— the sky overhead had been overcast, but there was no rain. Not yet.

Poornima remembered that they had stopped and peered into the window of the bangle shop, with its row after row of colorful glass bangles, a color to match every shade of sari. "Can you imagine," Poornima had said, breathless, "having ones to go with *every* sari?" Savitha had only laughed, and had led her past the paan shop and the dry goods store and the grain mill, all of them closed.

They'd entered the produce market, and the vendors had eyed them sleepily. They squatted on the ground, bits of dirty plastic tarp held at the ready, for the coming rain, to cover their heads and their capsicums and their squashes and their cilantro. They'd been able to tell that Poornima and Savitha had no money to spend—vendors always could. At one turning—as they'd followed behind a bullock cart hauling unsold produce back to the farm—a tiny round eggplant had fallen out of the cart. Savitha had squealed with delight and run and picked it up. "Look, Poori! What luck."

Yes, Poornima had thought, what luck.

They'd been nearly home when the rain had started. Poornima had thought they should run for it, but Savitha had pointed to a nearby sandalwood tree. She'd said, "No, let's wait under there." And so they'd huddled together under the tree's branches and watched the downpour. It had been a squall, and Poornima had known it would soon pass, but she'd hoped—in the way she'd once hoped that a handful of fruits and cashews would save her mother from cancer, from death—that the rain would last the rest of the days of her life. Why? She couldn't say. It hadn't made sense. But it was true: Even as they'd both shivered with cold. Even as their hair and their clothes had dripped with rain. Even as her father had waited, and she'd known he'd be furious when he saw the damp tobacco.

There had been a gust of wind then, and the leaves of the sandalwood tree had shuddered, and cold, fat raindrops had splashed down their necks and backs. Tickled their scalps. They'd laughed and laughed and laughed.

The rain had poured harder. Come down in relentless sheets. Savitha had put out her arm and drawn Poornima deeper under the tree. To protect her from the rain. At the time, Poornima had shivered and felt it to be true: she *did* feel protected, she felt safe.

But now, standing at the window of an empty apartment, in Seattle, holding an empty glass, Poornima laughed, half mocking, her lips trembling, her eyes growing hot, and she thought, How foolish. How foolish we were, how foolish *you* were, she bristled, to think you could protect me from rain. Against such a thing as rain. As if rain were a knife, as if it were a battle. And you, my shield. How foolish you were, how stupid you are, Poornima thought, nearly weeping with rage. With anger at Savitha's ignorance, her infuriating innocence. To find herself in this place, passed like a beedie between the hands of men. Don't you see, we were never safe. Not against rain, not against anything. And you, she railed, all you thought to do was huddle under that indifferent tree. As if, against rain, against my father, against what remained, all we had to do was stand closer. Stand together. As if, against rain, against fate, against war, two bodies—the bodies of two *girls*—were greater than one.

"You fool," she cried into the dark, and bolted out of the apartment into the night.

5

It took her more than five hours to find the building Mohan had showed her. She was soaked. She'd left her apartment a little before a muddled sunrise, and now it was nearly eleven o'clock. It had stopped raining, but she and her clothes were still damp, cold; she settled on the stoop of the building and waited. Of course, she knew Mohan would come to check on her, but her only strategy was to blink her eyes and proclaim innocence. "Oh," she planned to say coyly, "I didn't know I *had* to be here. It's my first time shepherding, after all."

In the first hour, only two people came out of the building, neither of them Indian. After the first person came out, she slipped in through the swinging door and considered knocking on every apartment, but when she snuck up to the top of the first flight of stairs, she peeked around the corner and saw an old Indian man sitting in a drab room, his chair tilted toward the half-open door. He was seemingly absorbed in the television show, but Poornima knew better—he was policing the stairwell. She abandoned her plan and went outside again. In the second hour, a man parked a small lorry in front of the building and came to the door holding a box in his hands.

He pushed one of the buttons and said, "Package," into the wall, and the door began to buzz. He went inside.

Poornima tried the same. She avoided the button that read 1B, as that was what the door of the Indian man's apartment had read, but she pressed the buttons to the other apartments. Most of them didn't answer or weren't home. One did answer, and Poornima, in her accented English, said, "Are you Indian, please?" The other end was silent for a moment, and then a woman's voice said, "What is this about? I just got a package."

Poornima sat back down on the stoop.

She waited until five o'clock in the evening and then started on the hour's walk home, made even longer because she got lost twice. She showered when she got back to the apartment and made rice, and when she heard the knock on the door, she knew it was Mohan, come to check on her. He hardly stayed five minutes; he scanned the room, and then her face, and then he left.

The next day, she was smarter: she took a packet of rice for lunch and got to the building at seven in the morning. She did this for three days, and finally, on the fourth, she realized she must be there during the wrong times, and so on the fourth day, she got there midafternoon and stayed late into the night. This time, she knew for certain that she would miss Mohan, and that simply pleading ignorance might not be enough; she decided she'd buy something on her way home, something she'd desperately needed, to show for her absence. She hoped it would be enough.

A car slowed in front of the building. Poornima crept into the shadows, away from the streetlights and the ones spilling from windows, and waited. She couldn't see the driver, but someone got out of the car, and as they approached the building, Poornima saw that it was Madhavi. She walked slowly up the drive, bent somehow from the last time she'd seen her. Poornima waited until the car pulled away, and when she revealed herself, feigning concern and delight, she saw that Madhavi's expression was grayer, more tired under the sallow bulb hanging over the entranceway, or maybe from the long day of cleaning. When she noticed Poornima, Madhavi's eyes widened. "Akka! What are you doing here?"

Big sister. She'd never called her big sister before. "How are you? Are they treating you well? Are you getting enough to eat?"

Madhavi shrugged. "Why are you here?"

"Come," Poornima said, hoping there was a back way, "let's talk inside. Have some tea."

Her face darkened. Her voice grew panicked. "No. No, you can't. No one is allowed inside. They warned us."

Poornima made her eyes go kind. She nearly smiled. "It's me, after all. Mohan showed me where you lived, just so I could visit you."

"He *did*?"

"Didn't he tell you? Anyway, how are you getting along? Do you live with other girls? Are they nice to you?"

She shrugged again. "They're all right."

"Are they Telugu? What are their names?"

Madhavi looked around and behind her. "I'm not supposed to tell."

"You act like I'm a stranger," Poornima said gaily. A car drove past, and they watched its red taillights disappear down the street. Poornima's vision burned with that red; she felt Madhavi shivering beside her. "Is one of them named Savitha?" she asked.

"No."

Poornima searched her face. "Are you sure?"

"I'm cold, Akka. I'm so cold. I want to go inside."

Poornima gripped her arm. "I'm no stranger; you know that, right? I may be the *only* one who's not a stranger."

Madhavi nodded and ducked into the building.

When she got home, after stopping at the corner store, Mohan was waiting for her. He was making coffee. "Where were you?"

"Coffee? This late?"

"Where were you?"

"How long have you been here?" she asked.

"Where? At this hour?"

"I needed these," she said, holding out a packet of sanitary pads.

"It doesn't take an hour to go two blocks."

"I stopped to rest at the children's park. Cramps." She grinned sheepishly, tilting her face just enough.

"No more going out," he said, pouring the coffee into a strange metal cup with a lid. "I'll pick up what you need from now on." He asked for the keys—both for the front entrance and the door to the apartment—and pocketed them. He then pointed to the pot on the stove. "There's some left. If you want."

There was enough for nearly a full cup of coffee, but Poornima saw, after he'd gone, that he'd also left his coat. When she lifted it, a small book fell out. She went through the other pockets and found only change, a few receipts. She looked again at the book. It was odd—unlike any she'd ever seen. After her wide, flat accounting books, this one was minuscule, hardly bigger than her hand. When she opened it, she found that none of the lines went to the edge of the page; they all stopped short, and each was spaced differently. How strange, she thought. Was it the Gita? No: this one had an author, and an English title. It was tattered, clearly read through many times, but one page in particular was especially frayed, dog-eared and worn.

Poornima turned to this one and began to read.

The next morning, after a long night's sleep—even after drinking the coffee—Poornima considered her options. She hadn't learned much during her time in Seattle, but she'd learned this: Savitha was not living in the same apartment as Madhavi. Madhavi had been scared, undeniably, but she hadn't been lying. So where was Savitha? She pondered that question; she'd pondered it for years. Mohan, too, she'd learned something about: she'd convinced him to show her where Madhavi lived, certainly, but she knew, just as she knew Savitha was here, *here*, that she could never—no matter how many lies she told, no matter how pathetic she looked—convince him to show her where any of the other girls lived.

And there was one other thing she'd learned about Mohan: she'd learned that he liked poetry.

She studied the dog-eared poem—called "The Love Song of J. Alfred Prufrock"—a few times and decided that she hated it. Or at least, she hated what she understood of it. The first few lines didn't even seem to be in English, though the letters were the same. And though she had no idea who Michelangelo or Lazarus or Hamlet were, the person writing the poem— presumably the man with the unpronounceable name in the title—seemed weak to her. Utterly feeble. Why was he writing the poem? Why bother? Why not just come right out and ask his question, whatever it was? Then no one would have to drown at the end. Regardless, she read it with great interest, wondering what Mohan saw in it.

When he came to check on her that evening, she held it out to him, along with his coat. "You left them here last night," she said.

He took them, seeming bewildered, and stuffed the book back into one of the pockets of the coat. Poornima waited for him to reach the door, and then she said, "It's about regret, isn't it?"

"What?"

"That 'Love Song' poem. The one you like so much."

He half turned; Poornima saw his grip on the doorknob loosen. "You read it?"

"Why not? I like poetry."

"You do?"

"I'm starting to."

He turned to face her; he took a step deeper into the apartment. "Somewhat. But it's also about courage," he said, after some hesitation. "It's about the struggle to find courage."

"And if we don't? What happens? We drown?"

He smiled. "In a way."

"You don't think this, this Puffrock is weak?"

In that moment, Mohan's eyes flashed with a sadness so intense, so violent that Poornima felt it—the sadness, the violence—flare against the back of her own eyes. Then it receded just as quickly as it had come. "I think he's just like you and me," he finally said.

Poornima looked at him. No, she thought, you're wrong. You're wrong. He's nothing like me.

6

Madhavi might still be able to help her.

That was what Poornima considered that night, after Mohan left. She couldn't be certain, but Madhavi, isolated as she was, as all the girls must be, might still have been taken to a different location initially—as a kind of holding cell, until space opened up in her current flat—or maybe the girls sometimes rode together, and she'd seen one or another being dropped off at various other apartment houses, or maybe the girls talked, or one of them mentioned a street, a neighborhood, *anything*.

It was her only chance.

She waited all the next day. Since she no longer had keys, she surveyed her own building and found an unlocked back way, by the trash bins, and she had to leave the door to her apartment open. She estimated that Mohan nearly always arrived between four and eight P.M. What did he do during the day? How many shepherds did he monitor? How many girls did they own? Did *he* know Savitha? She had answers to none of these questions; she knew only that she had to wait until after eight, after his departure, before setting out for Madhavi's.

He was late that evening. He arrived near nine o'clock, offering no explanation for his delay, and yet, in some way, he seemed more conscious of her, softer in the way he studied the room, her face, the disarray of the sleeping bag, her few things spread across the floor. It was as if their conversation about the poem had awakened in him the *possibility* of Poornima, the possibility of her existing as anything other than a purveyor of girls.

"Need anything?" he asked.

"Vegetables."

"I'll bring some when I come tomorrow."

"Stay for dinner."

His gaze darkened, perhaps with revulsion at the request, perhaps in surprise, though Poornima understood suddenly, very distinctly, as though after a clarifying rain, that here was a man who was very alone, who knew very little beyond that aloneness. He left soon afterward without a word.

It was after midnight when Madhavi was dropped off at her flat. Poornima waited again in the bushes, at the border of the apartment house in which Madhavi lived and the one next to it, to the north. This time, the girl seemed unfazed by Poornima's abrupt appearance as she passed through the thin light of the entranceway. Poornima looked at her and saw that there was no point in asking how she was doing; it was obvious that she had hardened. That in the space of a week, she had reached a slow and stoic resignation. A week. How little time it takes to sever the spirit, Poornima thought, if the spirit is disposed to severing. Above them, clouds obscured the moon, the stars; a nearby streetlight flickered.

Madhavi sighed. "Are you here about that girl again?"

"You met her? Do you know something?"

"Please, Akka, stop coming around. If anybody sees us—"

"Look, just tell me if you know where the other girls live. Any of them."

"I *don't.*"

"They've never dropped someone off at another apartment house? You've never ridden with another girl? *Talked* to another girl? They've never taken you to another location?"

Madhavi shrugged and looked away.

"You have, haven't you? Who? Where does she live? What did she say?"

"Not another girl. Just . . ." Here Madhavi trailed off, and Poornima nearly burst; she clenched her fists to keep from shaking it out of her.

"Just what?" she asked gently, steadying her voice.

"Well, he took me to a room once. Different from the ones we clean."

"Where was this room? Were there other girls in it? Other people?"

"No."

"Who took you?"

"Suresh."

Who was that? Poornima wondered. The brother? They stood silent for a time, Madhavi avoiding her eyes. "Where was it?"

"I don't know. I don't know."

"Was it close to here?"

"No."

"Close to the airport?"

"No."

Poornima searched her mind for other landmarks, other sights that Madhavi might know. "Was it near that tower? That thin one? Was it near water? Or was it in the middle of the tall buildings? How about the college? Did you notice a college?"

"Akka, *please*."

"Anything? Do you remember anything?"

Someone on a bicycle passed without seeing them. Wind rustled the leaves of the nearby tree. Poornima heard a dim and distant moan, coming from the direction of the sea. "There was something round nearby," Madhavi said slowly, forlornly, into the dark.

"Round?"

"Like a cricket stadium. But bigger. Much bigger."

How did this girl know about cricket stadiums? "And what else?"

"There were not many people. None. It was empty."

"This entire country is empty."

"And the buildings had no windows."

Poornima nodded. She would've smiled, but she didn't want to scare the girl. Instead she looked into the hushed shadows: the low clouds, unmoving, the streetlight, now gone out, the silent streets, the wearied face, the lifeless body. She recalled then the delight in Madhavi's eyes as she'd eaten the pastry—on that day in a wholly different life—the sugary dough crumbling between her fingers. Poornima took a deep breath, a deep American breath, and she thought, Such a quiet country, and yet so much to cry for. She could think of nothing more to say, and so, before leaving, before walking into the night, she said, "Be careful," knowing that care had already been squandered, that care—for this girl, for her journey—had already, long ago, been scattered and spent.

Poornima started early the following morning. She arrived at Third and Seneca, after asking no less than a dozen people how to get to the stadium, and waited for the 21 line. She took it to where she was within sight of the stadium, and then, not knowing where else to start, walked back to Third Avenue. On one side of the street were warehouses, and on the other were railroad tracks. She looked at the warehouses: no windows, and not a single person. But Madhavi had not mentioned railroad tracks, which Poornima guessed she would have had she noticed them. So she walked deeper into the rows of long, single-story buildings, all of them painted either gray or beige. She took her time, slowly reading the few signs on the outsides of some of the buildings, peering into the windowed garage doors. She kept close to the sides of the buildings, studied every car parked along them, and scanned around each corner. She knew she was conspicuous, even with her western clothing and a scarf draped over the side of her face to hide the scarring, but only Mohan knew her face—that was her biggest advantage. Besides, she concealed herself the best she could

when the few cars drove past her, knowing she could spot his car a kilo-
meter away.

She walked for hours. The maze of warehouses went on and on. Some of
the alleys between the buildings had no names, so Poornima would reach
the same warehouses from the other side, having walked in a wide circle.
She lost her sense of direction, so when she came into a clearing, she looked
for the tops of the downtown buildings to indicate true north. Two men
slowed—one in a pickup truck and another in a blue sedan—and asked if
she needed help. Poornima pulled the scarf higher across her face and shook
her head. She heard a freight train go by and thought suddenly of the train
she hadn't gotten on in Namburu. She thought of the torn pieces of the
ticket, fluttering to the ground. What if I *had* gotten on that train? she wondered. What would I have become? She was unused to such a thought—a
thought that had no end—and so she shuttered it, slammed it closed, as if
it were the door to a house that was haunted.

She left when the sun swung to the west. She was hungry and tired
on her bus ride back. It was possible she wasn't even in the right place, she
considered; it was possible Madhavi had meant another neighborhood
entirely, but it had now been a week since she'd arrived, and she had only
two left. She returned to the warehouses the following day, and every day
for the next four. It wasn't until the fifth afternoon, after walking for hours
through an increasingly heavy rain, that she turned a corner—along a gray
building advertising radial tires and other car parts—and saw it: she saw
the black car. It was Mohan's, that much she knew immediately, but from
where she was standing, she couldn't quite see the entrance to the building.
She walked the long way, around the massive warehouse that faced Mohan's
car, and emerged on the other side, hiding against one wall. She was now
closer to the door but farther from his car. There was one other car, red,
parked in front of Mohan's, and this, she guessed, belonged to either the
brother or the father.

She waited, shivering, in the cold rain, but not a single girl came out of
the warehouse or went in. At three o'clock, she returned to the bus stop,

knowing it was an hour's ride home. The rain picked up in the evening, after Mohan left, so she waited until the next morning—she bought a flashlight and thicker socks, and when she arrived, she saw that this time neither car was parked in front of the building. She tiptoed to its entrance and squinted to see through the darkened glass door. Nothing. She tried the flashlight and saw a few meters into what she guessed was a vast room, piled with boxes, and with the outlines of maybe a desk at the far end. There were no other rooms that she could see. She walked around the building, looking for an unlocked back way, or a loading dock, like she'd seen in so many of the other warehouses, but this one was only metal siding on all sides; she listened for sounds, voices; she thought she might try to break open the lock on the door, but as she stood examining it, a car passed along the adjoining alley.

If Savitha *did* live here, it occurred to Poornima, crouched against the side of the building, why would she be here during the day? She would be cleaning houses during the day.

That night, when she returned, the warehouse was even darker and quieter than it had been during the day. She knocked on the door, waiting for a light to go on. She walked around the building, slamming her fists against the sides. She tried to break open the heavy lock, and then the glass of the door, but it was reinforced, and neither the plastic flashlight nor the weight of her body did any good. Where was she? Where was she? Poornima stared at the door, gave it one last kick, said to the dark, unbreakable glass, "Not here," and left.

On the bus ride home, after midnight, she looked down at her bruised arms, her gashed elbows and hands, her broken flashlight, and realized the thing she had known all along: Mohan was her only hope.

She bought a bottle of whiskey—the most expensive she could find at the corner store—and then she spent the afternoon making rice and dal and eggplant curry (the fattest eggplants she had ever seen, and which cooked nothing like the ones in India) and potato cutlets, though the hot oil frightened her so much that she made just enough for Mohan and turned off the stove. But even with the scents of the food and the bottle of whiskey set out on the counter Mohan refused to stay for dinner. He left without a word, before she could think of anything more to convince him.

Poornima grew desperate.

She paced the small room, looking out of the window, up and down the street, every minute or so. She remembered, back on her street in Vijayawada, the man who'd been ironing the child's frock, and the sleeping rickshaw wallah, and the cows and the dogs poking among the small garbage heaps, and the vendors calling through the streets, and she was struck by a sudden and violent homesickness. She nearly bent over with it, but straightened her back at once. For what, she admonished herself, angry with herself for even this slight moment of weakness. For brothels and charkhas and men and mothers-in-law? Is that what you're homesick for? She smoothed down her blouse and jeans, unused to wearing them, and which, again, she'd bought in Vijayawada specifically for her trip to America, and took a deep breath: she recalled suddenly the one thing that had made his eyes flicker, the only thing, in the two weeks that she had known him, that had given him pause.

She left the whiskey on the counter, and when he arrived the next night, she said, "I won't drink it. You might as well take it with you."

He looked at the bottle and hesitated, and when he did, she said, "Who is Lazarus?"

"What?"

"Lazarus. From that poem. The one you like. Puffrock said something about being Lazarus."

His face softened. Or maybe it was only his lips that seemed to lose something of their severity, their density. "You remember that?"

"I've been wondering."

"He's from the Bible. Jesus brought him back to life, after he died. After four days, I think."

"Was he being tested? Like Sita?"

"No, I think it was Jesus who was being tested. Or maybe his believers. But not Lazarus."

Poornima looked at him. "Why do you like it? Because you think Puff-rock is like you and me?"

"*Proof*rock. And yes, and because it's such a lonely poem."

"You should open it," she said, nodding toward the whiskey.

This time, there was no hesitation. He poured himself a half glass of whiskey, the gold-brown liquid sending up the strong scent of deep forests and woodsmoke and something Poornima couldn't name, but recalled, maybe that thunderstorm, she thought, the one that had caught her on the Krishna. He settled under the window and placed the glass in front of him. He took a sip.

Poornima watched him. She thought he might leave after finishing the first glass, but he poured himself another. She said to herself, Wait till he finishes this one. Wait till the end.

When he did, she said, "Your days must be long."

His head was leaned back against the wall. He seemed to nod, or maybe she only imagined it.

"Are there other shepherds? What do you do after leaving here?"

"Homework."

"Homework?"

He avoided her gaze. "I take classes. At the university." He raised the bottle again and studied the label. "Where did you get this? I thought I told you not to leave the apartment?"

"For what? What are you studying?"

He laughed, poured another glass. "That Puffrock poem. Other poems, too."

"But—"

This he drank in one great gulp. "You can tell a lot about a parent from what makes them laugh. When I told him, middle of high school, that I wanted to study literature, he laughed for three days, and then he said,

'Engineering or medicine. You pick.' That's the best part of being an Indian kid," he said. "We get to pick." Then he looked at her sternly. "He doesn't know about the classes. No one does."

They sat in silence then, he against the window, she against the wall by the kitchen. Nothing stirred, not inside, not outside. Poornima shut her eyes. She could sense him watching her.

"These," he said into the dark, "these are my favorite lines from the poem: 'And indeed there will be time / To wonder, "Do I dare?" and, "Do I dare?" / Time to turn back and descend the stair'."

He went on to explain each of the lines, each of the *words* in meticulous detail, and about when the poem was written, and about how the time it was written related to the forces of fear and boredom and modernity, just before World War I, and he even told her about the author himself, and how he had been an immigrant, too, except to England, and Poornima wanted to ask about Michelangelo and Hamlet, but instead, she said, "What else made him laugh?"

There was silence again, and she thought he might be annoyed by her question, but when she opened her eyes, Mohan was asleep, the glass still clasped in his hand.

She had one week left.

Savitha

1

The bus was in the mountains when Savitha opened her eyes. She had been dreaming of Mohan. Nothing in particular, nothing she could name, not even in the moments after she woke up, but she had a sense that he'd drifted through her dreams, without touching them, like a ghost, or a scent. But then she was jolted from half sleep, and she looked around her frantically, seeing clearly the road, the mountains, the strange faces. The flight. Had there been footsteps behind her? She hadn't looked. She'd run wildly from bus stop to bus stop, hailing buses just as they'd pulled away; the third local bus that passed her opened its doors; Savitha said, breathless, "New York?" and the driver had laughed and said, "Not quite. You want the Greyhound. I'm going past the station, though. Get on!" At the bus station in downtown Seattle, she'd stood and stared at a map of the United States. She'd found Seattle, knowing there was only water to its west, and then she'd looked for New York. Her gaze had traveled east and east and east. Where could it be? She thought she'd missed it and started again. This time she didn't stop, and there it was, on the other side, with only water to its east. She'd said to the man at the ticket counter, "How much New York?"

He'd said, "Lady, first you gotta go to Spokane, and then you gotta get on another bus to New York." And then he'd said, "Thirty dollars."

She hadn't understood the first part of what he'd said, but she'd understood that the ticket to New York was thirty dollars. All that way for only thirty dollars!

She'd glanced at the doors to the station, clutched her ticket in her hand, and seated herself in a chair farthest from the entrance; her eyes never left it.

How long would it take her to get there? And what would she do when she did? How would she even begin to look for the jilebi-haired lady with the pearlescent teeth? None of these questions had answers, not yet, but once she was on the bus, pointed away from Seattle, and the fear and the adrenaline had stopped racing, and her heart had stopped pounding, she realized, looking out at the silhouettes of the pine trees and into the dark of the mountains, the road a bolt of cloth draped over them, that sometimes *leaving* was also a direction, the only one remaining.

They went over Snoqualmie Pass, though Savitha had closed her eyes again by then. Just before she did, the swing of the bus's headlights caught a clump of purple wildflowers at the base of one lone pine, as if it were an umbrella over the shivering blooms. They passed a long stretch of water on her side of the bus, but the water went on for so long that Savitha thought she might be imagining it in her disorientation, her near delirium. When she woke finally, near sunrise, the mountains were dark, blanketed with trees and farther away. The sky was steel-gray and thick with clouds. There was just enough predawn light that Savitha saw the young pine saplings all along the road, gray-green clumps that held close together and seemed to spin like dervishes in the early-morning songs of birds and wind and even the swoosh of the bus as it sped past them.

Savitha shifted in her seat, her muscles stiff, and she realized with a start that there was a woman seated next to her. Where had she gotten on? She couldn't recall the bus stopping, but maybe she had switched seats in the night. Savitha looked at her. She was fast asleep, her head lolling toward

Savitha's shoulder. She was as young as Savitha, maybe younger, with fingers littered with silver rings, all except one thumb and one pinkie. There was a tattoo in the triangle between her right thumb and index finger, a symbol Savitha didn't recognize, but it was a faint tattoo, a watery blue-green, and Savitha sensed, looking at the young woman's sleeping face, the fine lines around the eyes and the lips already forming, that she hadn't intended it that way, that she'd intended the tattoo to be a rich blue, a blue with density, depth, the ocean at night, but that it hadn't worked out that way. Nothing had.

The bus stopped near sunrise, and all the sleeping passengers were herded off. Savitha's first thought was that maybe they'd already arrived in New York. She'd gotten on at one in the morning, and it was now a little after six. Could it be? But then she looked at the sign above the main door: S-P-O-K-A-N-E. She went to the map again and saw that she wasn't even out of the state, let alone in New York. A profound tiredness enveloped her. At this rate, it would take her months to get there! She rubbed her bleary eyes and wanted to ask about the bus to New York, but the ticket counter was closed until eight. On the signboard, it listed only two departure times: one to Seattle and the other to a town called Missoula. She checked the map again; Missoula was to the east, Savitha saw, not by much, but east, and was scheduled to leave in two hours. Maybe she would have to take that bus and transfer again? She didn't know. She wanted to wait at the bus station for the ticket counter to open, but she saw that the coffee stall inside the station was also closed, and she was hungry. When she walked outside, she looked up and down, and then at every car in the parking lot; she looked for a red car and a black car and a beige car. The streets were dry and cold. It was a mountainous cold, one Savitha had never grown used to, and she pulled her sweater tighter around her shoulders. She'd stolen it, the sweater, from Padma, along with the small plastic knapsack, where she kept her remaining eighty-two dollars, the ripped photograph, a change of clothes, the white rectangle of paper, and what remained of Poornima's half-made sari. The fragment she'd wrapped gently in old newspaper and placed at the bottom of her sack. The bus station was a two-story redbrick building; outside was a row of trees like the trees that had blanketed the mountains all along the highway, and beyond the trees were some buildings, tall but not nearly as tall as they had been in Seattle. It was not yet seven A.M., but Savitha still saw a few people wandering around, not as if they were going anywhere, but simply wandering. That struck her as odd for such an hour, but they paid her no attention, almost as if she were invisible, and continued on their way.

In the parking lot of the bus station, to the right of the row of trees, a man leaned against a yellow car, smoking. There was a woman sitting inside the car, smoking as well, her arm resting on the open window, but neither talked nor looked at the other, like strangers, in fact, though Savitha could see that his thigh was touching the tip of her elbow. Another man was standing against the eastern wall of the bus station, squinting at a newspaper. She stood and watched the light of the sun emerge from behind the distant mountains and bathe him in its glow, his pale white skin turning a burnished gold. She crossed the street and walked in the direction of the buildings until she saw a restaurant. Savitha went inside and sat down in one of the booths. There was a menu resting on the table, filled with pictures, and when the waitress came, Savitha pointed to the one that looked like three little dosas, all in a row. She took a sip of her water and waited. When the plate arrived and she took a bite (with the spoon, fumbling, not knowing how to use either the fork or the spoon), she realized that they weren't dosas, not in the least. They were sweet! And inside them, instead of potato curry, was the same white fluffy, weightless substance that had been *on* the banana split. How odd. What a mysterious country, she thought, how small for all its vastness. But they were good, and she was hungry.

Before she left the diner, she bought a bag of chips, a bottle of water, and a package of what looked like little cakes.

She walked back to the bus station and sat on a bench outside, facing the row of trees but with a view of the street and the parking lot. It was fifteen minutes to eight, and she tried to stay awake until the ticket counter opened. She watched the drift of the low, round clouds rising out of the edge of the earth with the sun. To the west, the mountains, caressed now by morning light, turned pink and green and charcoal, the clouds above them also low, seeming to gather and gaze at those hills as if they were children. Savitha looked at the mountains and the clouds and thought, This is the most I've seen of this country. This is my widest view. And then she thought again of Mohan. A pain blossomed in her stomach and spread, thin and blue as ink, to her chest. She focused again on the mountains, the clouds, but they were distant and preoccupied. She concentrated instead on the street and the parking lot. At one point, a tiny swirl of tumbleweed rose into the air, spinning like birds. It was nearly transparent, whirling in the gust, carried by its own buoyancy and the slightest exhalation of wind. Savitha closed her eyes—just for a moment, she told herself—and fell into a light sleep.

She was woken by a car horn, or maybe a voice, and saw that it was a little after eight. She jumped up, cursing herself for falling asleep when they could be here, *here*, and ran inside, clasping her ticket stub. She went to the counter, held out her ticket, and said, "Hello, madam. When is bus to New York?"

The ticket lady, a black woman with crimson lipstick and silver glitter on her eyelashes, blinked, as if orbiting her two moons, and then she looked at Savitha's ticket. She said something Savitha couldn't understand. "Pardon me?"

The lady turned away and then brought out a chit of paper. On it, she wrote, *$109.* "But I have ticket," Savitha said.

The lady shook her head and said, "That's only to Spokane. *This* is the cost of a ticket to New York." She pushed the chit of paper toward Savitha, and she took it. Another small white rectangle of paper.

She walked out of the bus station.

Along the side of the bus station was a curved road, and beyond it, another parking lot. And beyond even that were yet more buildings and yet more parking lots. Savitha looked and looked at the endless, unbroken pattern, despairing, and then she noticed that she was still clutching the chit of paper in her hand, dampening it with the sweat of her palm. She threw it into a trash bin. The clouds, since the early morning, had fattened, and scuttled lazily eastward; Savitha watched them with envy. She walked with a lurch to the southern end of the station, and then to the northern. She sat again on the bench outside, listless, wondering what to do. Then she got up and walked again.

She walked for some minutes until she reached the edge of a river. Here she sat down on another bench and tried to keep herself from crying. She hugged her knapsack to her chest, as if it were the only hope left to her, and she realized, with something nearing heartbreak, that it was. She had no idea what to do, how to get more money. She'd clearly misunderstood the man who'd sold her the ticket in Seattle, and now she thought, Even if I hadn't eaten the sweet dosas in the restaurant, I still wouldn't have enough money. I never did. She felt a stabbing pain at the end of her stub, a phantom pain she had not felt in many months. She shook out her arm and considered walking some more, but her tiredness returned, more parched, depleted, so she merely sat and looked at the river.

As it neared midafternoon, more people arrived at the river. There was a jogger or two; one man was peeling an orange; a few mothers stood in a group, watching their children at play.

Savitha blinked as if waking from a deep sleep. She was hungry, but she thought she should save her chips and cakes. She didn't dare spend the money she had remaining. She drank water from a fountain and walked back southward, though away from the bus station; that was the first place they would look for her. She turned the corner. There was a long street, leading into a cluster of buildings. Cars were parked along the street, and as she drifted toward the buildings, she caught sight of the license plate of one of the parked cars. Savitha stopped in her tracks. She glanced up and down the empty street, then she bent down and read it again slowly. She was not mistaken: the letters added up to the words *New York*. She sat down, right there on the curb next to the car. What was she doing? She was waiting. What was she waiting for? Anything, she thought, I'm waiting for anything.

Her stomach growled. She succumbed and ate the chips and the two tiny cakes.

After an hour or so, an elderly couple came walking toward her. The woman was wearing pink pants, just past her knees, and a yellow shirt that read *New Mexico, Land of Enchantment.* All Savitha could read was the word *New,* and she counted it as a good sign. The woman's silver hair was curly and cut close to her head. She wore pink lipstick that she'd tried to match with her pants, but clearly hadn't, in a gauche way, and Savitha thought she must've always been so, even as a young woman, on the edges of beauty, at the very walls of prettiness, but never quite inside. The man was wearing a baseball cap and jeans and a checkered shirt, and they were obviously married. And had been for many years, since their youth, Savitha thought, noticing the familiarity, the distance, the dull ache between them. When they reached Savitha, they looked at her inquisitively for a polite moment, and then they saw her stub; they turned, suddenly self-conscious, hesitant, to their car. The New York car. The man took out a set of keys.

Savitha jumped up. "Pardon me, sir, madam. New York? You go to New York?"

They both looked at her again, befuddled, and then the woman let out a small whoop, and she said, "Oh, honey, this is a rental car. We're not going to New York. We're heading down to Salt Lake."

Savitha stood there and watched them.

"Show her, hon," the woman said. "Show her on the map."

The man brought out something from the glove compartment and unfolded it into a wide piece of paper. He laid it out on the trunk of the car, and all three of them bent over it. "Here," he said. "This is where we are." Then his finger traveled south and east, and he said, "And this is Salt Lake City. This is where we're headed." He looked at Savitha; Savitha looked back at him. She held her stub away, behind her back. But he seemed to no longer

see her stub. He seemed instead to sense how confused she was, how crestfallen, and, as if it would comfort her, he trailed his finger to the very edge
of the map and said, "And this is New York."

They all turned back to the map, and by now Savitha had realized the
couple was headed mainly south, not east. But she didn't want them to leave;
she liked them. She could tell they were parents, that they knew a kind of
love that was limitless and hopeless, both at once. She grew desperate; she
considered, at the very least, asking them for some money, but was shy, embarrassed, and didn't know how. And then, again with a rare kindness, the
woman looked at Savitha for a long while, and said, "Maybe she can ride
with us, Jacob. Come over to Butte with us."

He shook his head. "That's all mixed up, Mill. She'll be a tad closer, but
Spokane's a better spot for her." He stopped and said, "What's your name,
anyway?"

Savitha nodded and smiled.

He pointed at himself and said, "Jacob." He pointed at his wife and said,
"Millie." Then he pointed at Savitha.

She smiled again, wider, and said, "Savitha."

"Saveeta," he said.

Savitha looked at the mountains in the distance, standing like sentinels,
like guards against the east. The old man followed her gaze and said, "A tad
closer is a tad closer, I guess; come along if you want to."

She turned to them. First to him, to decipher what he'd just said, and
then to the woman. She was smiling. A little of the pink lipstick on her teeth.
"Come on now," she said, "get in," and motioned to the rear door. Savitha
stood for a moment, unsure what to do. She understood by now that they
weren't going to New York, despite their license plate. She also understood,
in that moment, her piercing aloneness, her billowing sorrow—she had no
money, no food, and no road behind her.

She climbed into the backseat.

The couple chatted between themselves for some time. At one point, the
woman said, "Where you from, honey?"

Savitha didn't understand what she'd asked, so she said, "Yes, yes."

The woman opened a bag of peanuts and offered them to Savitha. She could've easily eaten the whole bag, but Savitha politely took one and said, "Thank you, madam."

"Call me Millie," the woman said, and then leaned her head back and was asleep a few minutes later. Savitha heard her softly snoring.

The man drove in silence for a long while. They were in Idaho now, and the clouds grew thicker, huddled close against the horizon, and were laddered against the distant mountains, now to the east and to the west. The mountains themselves, Savitha noticed, were streaked with tendrils of blue and red. The valley between the bowl of mountains, the one they were passing through, was green and fertile and reminded her of the fields around Indravalli, fed by the Krishna.

The man popped a peanut into his mouth. He raised his eyes to the rearview mirror. "Spent many of my days out here," he said, clearly talking to Savitha, though she had no idea what he was saying. "Fishing. The Bitterroot, Salmon, every little creek and stream. Spent most of my twenties and thirties back there in Coeur d'Alene." He pointed out the passenger side window. "Right there, right down there is Trapper's Peak. Spiked, like this." He showed her with his hands, his elbows guiding the steering wheel. "Can't look at it too long, though. It'll break you up inside. That's how some mountains are."

His eyes in the mirror were watching hers.

"What is your story, anyways? How'd you end up on that damn sidewalk? And how in God's name did you lose that hand?"

She met his gaze and then looked down. She liked his voice. She liked the way it summoned her, summoned even the uncomprehending, the wandering parts of her.

"I couldn't even take a guess. Not one. And what are you? All of twenty?"

She wanted to tell him something, maybe something about Poornima or her father or Indravalli, but there was nothing she could piece together that would've made sense to him, and so she was quiet, listening.

"Well, I know accidents happen. I know all about that. I've had my share.
I could tell you stories. Boy." He stopped; he shook his head. Savitha's eyes
lit up. She understood that word: *boy*. She began to listen even more carefully. "I got one," the man said, his voice rising. "I got a story for you. It's
about a little boy. Little. I'll say he was about four. He and his mama and
daddy lived in Montana. Just them. Just the three of them. His father was
a ranch hand. One of those cattle ranches with hundreds and hundreds of
heads. One of those ranches where you could spend an entire year just fix-
ing the fences, let alone calving and vaccinating and culling and weaning.
A big place. You get the idea. Well, one day, when this boy was four, his
mama up and ran off. With some traveling salesman that came around,
maybe, or a heavy machinery salesman. Hard to say, because immediately,
before the boy could say boo, he was sent to live with his grandparents in
Arizona. Tucson. His daddy put him on a bus, by himself, and sent him
down to the desert. And you know what happened? I'll tell you what happened: the boy found his spot. He loved it, the desert. His grandparents lived
in a little house surrounded by dirt and sand and cactus, no fences, and with
a yard that ended far away, in a low range of blue and purple and orange
mountains. Well, the boy couldn't get enough of it. He'd play, but mostly
he'd sit and watch those mountains. He'd watch them so close it was as if
he expected his mother to walk right out of them. Walk out, take his hand,
and lead him away. Not back to Montana, mind you, but deeper into the
desert.

"Some time after the boy moved to Arizona, his grandparents hired another boy to work for them. Older. A teenager. Just someone to come
around and help with the chores. For instance, they had a detached shed
that needed to be cleaned out. Out back. And they wanted help with building a porch. The sides would be braided thistle, to keep the sun out during
the day, but open to the west, facing into the mountains and the sunset.
They joked with their grandson. They watched him staring into the
mountains—coming in only for the hottest part of the day, when the sun

was directly overhead—and they laughed and they said to him, When that porch is built, we'll never see you again.

"Well, the teenage boy—let's call him Freddie—began with the porch. He built it in a couple of weeks, and then he moved over to the shed and started in on that. He must've seen the grandson dozens of times, talked with him, even answered a question or two the little boy had for him, but he'd never shown any particular *interest* in him. He was a teenage boy, after all, and the grandparents thought having a bit of company must've been nice for their grandson.

"And it was. It was. But the third week in, Freddie called the little boy over to him. It was just about sunset. The boy's grandparents had finished their dinners, and they were sitting out on their new porch with iced teas and smoking. When the boy walked into the shed, hardly any light coming through the door, Freddie coaxed him into a corner, took the boy's arm, and he said, Shhh.

"Well, you can imagine what happened next. And it kept happening almost every day for the next month. And during all that time, the boy heeded Freddie's words. He never made a sound, not one, but in the evenings, in the desert quiet, he could hear his grandparents, sitting just a few feet away on the porch. They'd laugh, they'd bicker, but mostly, they'd just talk of this and that. The weather, for instance. Or the cactus out front that had bloomed last year, but not this year. Or their small aches and pains, the ones that come with age. And the boy, from the shed, as Freddie did what he did, would listen with all his might. He'd listen to the voices of his grandparents. Although, to tell you the truth, they ceased to be his grandparents. They were just voices now, voices that he listened to with such intention, such *intensity*, that he slowly lost his own power of speech. He spoke less and less, and one day, toward the end of the month, he stopped speaking altogether. His grandparents were mystified; they never understood why. They thought it was from his mother leaving him and the move to the desert. But the boy knew why. Maybe not at the age of four, but later. He came to understand why: he came to understand that the most magical words, the only words that mattered, were the ones spoken by his grandparents. While they sat out on the porch—grown old now, their concern for the bloomless cactus, or the clouds, or the pain in their knees filling the night sky. Filling it like stars. You see, the boy knew, *knew*, even at the age of four, that he would never in his life sit on a porch as his grandparents did. He would never sit with another person and speak of small things. Or great things. Or even the most effortless things. And that *that* was what Freddie had taken from him. The boy knew this; the boy knew this as he knew those mountains, as he knew his mother would never come out of them."

There was silence. A silence so deep that when Savitha closed her eyes, she felt a warm wind brush against her face. Why is there a wind, she wondered, in a closed car?

"And you know what's most interesting," the man continued. "It's not what happened to the little four-year-old boy. No. He just grew up like the rest of us. A grown man by now." He paused; he seemed to Savitha to be studying the road. "Living somewhere, I guess. Mostly unhappy, like the rest of us, but mostly getting by. But you know what's most interesting? What's most interesting is what happened to Freddie. The boy who built the porch. He went off to college eventually—using the money he'd saved up from his odd jobs—and then, in one of his college classes, he met a pretty gal by the name of Myra, and they got married. After graduating, they moved to Albuquerque, and then to Houston. Freddie got a job at an oil company, paid good money, and he and Myra had three children, two boys and a girl. Before you know it, they had a five-bedroom house in the suburbs, and two cars, and eventually, even an in-ground pool."

The old woman let out a little snort, adjusted in her seat, and went right on sleeping. The man looked over at his wife and, as if he were talking to her, as if she were awake, he said, "Now, as I was saying, Freddie had three kids. Two boys first, and then a little girl. Freddie Jr. was the oldest boy, and he was his namesake, all right. Took after his dad, and did everything with him: they went hunting and fishing, threw the ball around. In fact,

Freddie Jr. got so good that his Little League team went to Williamsport one year. Well, one summer, the two boys, Freddie Sr.'s two boys, went to stay with their grandfather, Freddie's dad, and his new wife back in Tucson. He'd been widowed, you see, and had married a woman he met while golfing in Palm Springs. He still lived out in Tucson, and besides, it was only for a couple of weeks. So the two boys got on a plane, just the two of them, and headed to the desert. Sound familiar?" He let out a laugh, and then he said, "As you can imagine, it was boring at first for them. They sat around the house and watched television or played video games. Their grandfather, you see, had a large plot of land just west of town, but unlike the first little boy, these boys weren't at all interested. They found it dull. But eventually, a few days in, a boy about their age, a neighbor of the grandfather's, came over and the three became fast friends. He showed them how to have *fun* in the desert: how to hunt for Gila monsters and go sand sliding and dig for whiptail eggs. The neighbor boy only went home for dinner, and sometimes not even that. In fact, toward the end of the two weeks, Freddie Jr. and his brother didn't even want to go back to Houston.

"Well, on their last day in the desert, the neighbor boy came over, as he always did, and they wandered around out back. The grandfather and his wife were inside, making sandwiches for lunch. And right then—right when the grandfather was putting mustard on the slices of bread—they heard a huge explosion. I mean, massive. It rocked the house; it knocked the butter knife out of his hand. Frames fell off the walls; the lights swung from the ceiling. They thought it was an earthquake, or a bomb of some sort. But it wasn't that. It wasn't that at all. When the grandfather ran outside, he saw a huge plume of smoke rising from the edge of his property. The very edge, and he also saw flames. He ran at top speed, which, given his age, was remarkably fast. But they say that, don't they? They say in times of incredible strain, emergency, in times that require great acts, the human being is strangely capable of them: these great acts. But he wasn't fast enough. You see, the three boys had been playing with matches, and they had been near a propane tank. I don't want to be overly graphic, you understand, but they weren't near it anymore. The neighbor boy had second-degree burns; Freddie Jr.'s younger brother was also burned, but not as bad. But Freddie Jr. Now, Freddie Jr. had third-degree burns. The explosion burned away every layer of skin he had, and then it reached into his bloodstream, damaged organs. He was in the hospital for over two weeks, suffered terribly, and finally died of sepsis. He was thirteen. And his father, Freddie Sr., he was at his son's bedside every one of those days. He refused to leave, I mean *refused* to leave: even after the boy died, he just went right on sitting. He went into some sort of shock, they say. His hair turned completely gray in the two weeks he was at the hospital, and when he punched a hole in one of the hospital mirrors, a shard sliced a major nerve and he was never able to fully lift his right arm again. Of course, the grandfather was broken, too. He blamed himself, naturally. He died a few years later, but he'd died long before then. The surviving brother was never the same either. He refused to speak for the first couple of months after his brother died—does *that* sound familiar?—and when he finally did start talking, it was mostly to buy drugs."

The man was quiet again, in a way Savitha had never known: the silence a substance, water, the air in the car a lake of light.

The man smiled into the rearview mirror, but he didn't say anything for a moment. Then he said, "What is your name again? Saveeta? Well, Saveeta, I'm not a mulling man, but don't this strike you as—oh, I don't know— unnerving? All right, sure, sure, you could say these things were random, not at all linked, that life isn't *poetic* like that. Hell, maybe it was all the mother's fault. The one who ran away with the traveling salesman. But I've got my money on poetry. On its symmetry, sure, but also on its *inadequacy*. Its meanness. Its slaughter of lambs along with the lions. Everything of value. Don't you agree?" And then he stopped, and then he smiled again. "You're a pretty one, you know that? You're Indian, aren't you? You all brown up real nice in the sun. I've noticed that. Real nice. Yes, you do. Don't they, Mill?"

His wife woke with a start and said, "Huh? What was that?"

He laughed a little and ate another handful of peanuts.

2

They dropped Savitha off in the main section of Butte, Montana. The old man said, "Stay on the ninety. You got that? Ninety. That should get you over to New York or thereabouts." Then they each embraced her, the old man and the old woman, and they wished her well and gave her the remainder of the bag of peanuts. The woman waved as they pulled away. "Good luck," she said, the last of her hand out of the window waving like a flag. Where were they going? What was their hurry? They'd told her, certainly, but Savitha hadn't known what they were saying. She'd wanted to say to them, Maybe I can come with you, just for a while, but that, too, she hadn't had the words to speak. Where they'd left her was in downtown Butte.

She thought, They won't come *this* far, will they?

The town was ringed by mountains. She was on the corner of a sloping street, sloping down to the south and the west, and sloping up toward the north. To the east, which was where Savitha focused her gaze, there was another huge mountain. But this one, unlike the others, wasn't whole. Its face had been mined, skinned from the nose down, and all that remained was pink, exposed flesh, throbbing in the coming twilight. She turned away

and looked along the sloped streets and saw that most of the brick buildings around her were shuttered. Her heart sank.

She ate one peanut at a time, trying to make them last, and wandered up
and down the streets. She couldn't have known this, but many of the streets
in downtown Butte were named after gems, minerals, metals, some shining
thing that had once been hidden deep in the bodies of the surrounding
mountains. She walked from Porphyry Street up to Silver. At Mercury, she
turned and stood in front of another brick building, this one lighted. Inside,
people sat on high stools and laughed and talked, and Savitha felt such a
pang that her eyes watered. She saw plates of food, and tall glasses shot
through with golden light, as if they, too, were mined from the hills. But
standing outside, despite the heaping plates of nachos and buffalo wings and
french fries, all she smelled was stale beer: cutting through the brick and the
glass and the slope of the street, the stand and measure of her body, and
reaching inside of her, through her. Suresh and the room and the bottle of
clear liquid. She wanted to cry out, put her fist through the window, but instead she swallowed, pushed back bile, let out a smaller sound—that of an
animal trapped in a distant cave, a faraway hollow—and hurried down the
street.

At its base, she saw a sign. *Rooms, $10.*

It was musty, the sheets grayish and rumpled, not very clean. But there
was a shared bathroom at the end of the hallway, and the shower was hot.
She washed the clothes she'd been wearing in the sink. She hung them to
dry by the tiny, dirty window in her room. She saw, in the falling light, that
the mountains looked higher, closer, more sinister. There was something
white and shining at the top of one, and she wondered if it was a deepa.
When she slept, her sleep was dreamless, and she held the knapsack to her
chest all through the night.

In the morning, she understood.

She understood that she had sixty dollars remaining. She further understood that sixty dollars would either get her six nights in a dingy room in Butte, hardly a third of the way to New York, or back to Seattle.

She took the room for another night, and then another.

At a coffee shop on the third morning, she sat down without a word on the round stool at the counter. She'd only eaten a prepackaged sandwich and a stolen apple on the previous day, and felt weak with hunger. The waitress passed by her a dozen times, though, without even a glance, until Savitha finally motioned to her, and then pointed to a little girl's plate of eggs and toast and sliced banana. When she returned with a glass of water and utensils, Savitha said, "Coffee, please, madam."

The man sitting beside her laughed. "I thought you was mute," he said, "and then out you pop with 'coffee, please.'" He laughed some more.

He paid his bill and left. The seat was empty until Savitha was almost finished with her toast, saving the banana for last, when another man sat down next to her. This one looked more stoic, she thought. He was old and black and his woolly hair was gray at the temples, balding on top. Savitha had never been this close to a black person before, and with each of their arms resting on the counter, she saw that they were nearly the same shade of brown. Her skin more yellowish-brown, and his more reddish-brown. The thought was a comfort to her, though why should it be? He saw her looking but said nothing.

He was eating from a plate stacked with what looked like uthapams, though these were only dough, without the onions and green chilies and tomato and cilantro. He poured a brown syrup on them, and when he caught her looking again, he pointed to her banana slices and said, "Sometimes I like some of them on top. Chocolate chips, if I'm feeling frisky. But not today. Today I'm feeling simple."

His voice was deep, with a slight, subterranean roar to it, somehow pained but mostly good-natured. He seemed to sense her pleasure at the sound of his voice. He said, "We're two fish out of water, aren't we? Out here. A black man, and what? Indian? Out here. Where you headed?"

She understood the word *Indian*. She smiled and nodded.

"You speak English? Enough to order you some breakfast, I know that much. Excuse me, excuse me, young lady," he said to the waitress as she walked by. "Can we get more coffee over here?" The waitress poured them more coffee, and Savitha was delighted, not realizing she could get another cup, grateful that he'd had hers filled along with his. "Rapid City. That's where I'm headed. You know Rapid City? I have a daughter out there. About your age. Nothing but a mess. A mess and a half. How did I raise such a mess? Her mother's white. Maybe that's what it is, but I don't know. She was just born a mess."

No, Savitha thought, not at all stoic.

"I'll tell you what, though. Not much else out there, but that Spearfish Canyon is nice. Only been once. She's not one to stay in a place long. But I'll tell you what: that Spearfish Canyon is something else. You understand me? I'm headed down on the ninety. You?"

Savitha's head shot up.

The man seemed startled. "You too? Where, though? Where to?"

"New York," she said, hardly listening. She knew those words; she knew the words *Spearfish Canyon.*

"New York," he guffawed. After some thought, he said, "Might be better off on the eighty, but this'll get you there eventually, I suppose."

Savitha nodded vaguely. The perfect place, Mohan had said.

"You got a car? Are you driving?" He motioned with his hands, as if positioned on a steering wheel.

Savitha shook her head. "Bus," she said, rummaging in her sack.

"Bus! Sweetheart, there's no buses to New York from Butte. Who told you there was?"

Savitha looked up; she sensed a crisis. And where was that photo? Where? She watched the man's face, wondering if hers, too, flushed darker with heat. She delved again into the sack.

"Might do better in Rapid City. You might. At least you're headed the right way. Might be able to connect up through Chicago. Eventually. Who told you anyway?"

There! There it was.

Savitha looked at him again, and it struck her that there was nothing as concerned as this man, not just for her, but for all girls of a certain age, maybe, or for those with a certain ache. She held the ripped photograph out to him and pointed to the back.

His eyes grew wide. He flipped it to the front, and then stared again at the back. "You know Spearfish Canyon too?" he asked. "You got people there? Why didn't you say so? I thought you said New York. Hell, Spearfish Canyon is on my *way* to Rapid." Then he looked, for the first time, or so Savitha thought, at her stub. His gaze didn't linger, nor did it turn away too soon. He handed the photograph back to her, took a sip of his coffee, smiled real wide, handed the waitress a twenty, indicating both their checks, and said, "Want to come along?"

Come? Yes, she nodded, yes.

On the drive out of Butte, stone spires rose up out of the mountains. Trees grew from sheer rock. Beyond, the mountains stretched out, flattened. The road curved past vast ranches and farms, and bales of hay dotted the land. Sunlight sparkled off the wheatgrass, lighting the very tips like candles.

"No," the man was saying, "no, I can't tell her anything. Not a thing. She knows it all, or thinks she does. Has since the age of two weeks, give or take. Half of her family is white. But the other half is black. And I say to her, I say, Look. Look what we've endured. What we've survived. You are a part of that survival. That endurance. I say, Your great-great-grandparents were slaves. They picked cotton in—"

"Cotton," Savitha said, smiling wide, suddenly listening.

"Don't smile like that," the man said. "Don't smile. It ain't shit. Anybody, and I mean *anybody*, says the words *cotton* or *plantation*, or hell, the word *ship*, you run the other way. You hear? You think you're not black, but when it comes down to it, when it comes down to cotton, you are. Everybody who isn't white is black. You understand? Now, like I was saying—"

Savitha looked out the window and watched the fields and the mountains and the sky. The ridges first softened as they drove east—the valleys like bowls of golden light—and then the peaks rose up again, muscled and towering. There is no way to explain a thing that is perfect, he'd said.

Toward midafternoon, the man stopped in one of the towns and split cheese sandwiches with her out of a cooler he had in the backseat. He handed her a soda, and then he unfolded a paper napkin and filled it with potato chips. She took it and began eating the chips one by one, but he signaled to her and said, "Like this." She watched as he disassembled his sandwich and placed a thick layer of potato chips over the slice of cheese, and then replaced the bread on top, and then bit into it with a loud crunch. Savitha did the same and after her first bite decided she'd never again eat a sandwich without potato chips tucked inside.

They were in Spearfish by late afternoon. The man stopped at a gas station, and he seemed sad. He said, "You don't have an address? A phone number? They'll pick you up, won't they? This is as good a place as any, I guess. Pay phone over there. Maybe your people can find you somebody going east. Maybe not *New York*, but east. You'll get there. You'll be all right, won't you?"

Savitha looked at him.

He took out his wallet and handed her a ten-dollar bill. "Get you something to eat," he said, and then he left.

It was not yet dark. She stood, undecided, at the gas station for a few minutes. No one pulled in or out, and so she walked to the corner and looked up and down the street. On the opposite side was a car dealership. There was a liquor store next door. There were low hills in the distance, dotted with clumps of trees and dry grass. Was *that* the canyon? On the opposite side, to the southwest, was more of the town, and so she headed toward it. There were brick buildings here as well, just as in Butte, but these were all open and unshuttered. Better maintained. Some of the buildings were freshly painted, she could see, and people roamed around among them, families, some of them pushing strollers or with older children running ahead of them. It seemed a nice town, one where night fell slowly and comfortably. She thought of staying in one of the hotels, seeking out the canyon in the morning, but they all looked expensive. One had a blinking sign out front that advertised rooms for $79.99.

She only had fifty dollars left.

Savitha turned away from the closed doors of the warm rooms. She was not yet hungry, but she knew she soon would be. With the ten dollars the man had given her, she went into a small shop and bought a banana, an apple, a loaf of sliced bread, and a bag of potato chips. She put her purchases into her knapsack and walked back toward the gas station, hoping to get back on Interstate 90 and to the next big town with a bus station. On her way, she passed a bank and a restaurant and a hardware store. She stood at the window of an art gallery and looked at each of the paintings. There was a sculpture in the center of the gallery of a bird about to take flight; Savitha compared it to the only other sculpted birds she'd ever seen, the sugar birds, and decided that they had been prettier. On the next block there was another art gallery; this one had a display of native Sioux quilts in the window. She studied these even more carefully—the thread, the bold colors, the integrity of the weaving, the patterns and the workings of the loom. So different from the saris made in Indravalli, she thought, and yet cloth just the same. She wondered who'd made them and how far the quilts had traveled to be in this window.

At a nearby park, she stopped at a wooden bench and carefully assembled her potato chip sandwich, making sure there were two even layers of chips, and then she pressed the bread down around the edges so the chips wouldn't fall out. She ate her banana next. She saved her apple for later.

There was more traffic back at the gas station. She didn't run up to any of the cars; she waited by the door, a little away, and spoke only to those who smiled or looked kindly in her direction. One woman, her short dark hair neatly cut, rummaged in her purse and then looked up at Savitha, smiling. Savitha smiled back and said, "You go canyon, madam? You go ninety?" The woman seemed to panic and slipped quickly into the gas station without a word. A few minutes later, another woman emerged from the station, herding her two children. The children were holding candy bars, and all three were laughing. "Pardon me, madam," she said. "Canyon? New York?" All three of them—the woman and the two children—stood and stared at Savitha's face, and then, all of them, all at once, lowered their gazes and gawped at her stub. Finally the woman said, "Sorry. I don't have any spare change," and hurried the children away.

Savitha thought she might have better luck with a man, so she picked an old man, his hair white, his face wrinkled and friendly. He looked at her and held the door open, thinking Savitha meant to go inside. "No, sir. No. You go canyon? I come?" The man's face was confused for a moment, and then closed in some way, Savitha thought, somehow slammed shut, and he said, "Do your business somewhere else, for god's sakes. Families come through here."

There was no one else for a long while. It was getting darker. She went inside and asked to use the bathroom. The large man behind the counter, with gray eyes and a suspicious stare, looked at Savitha for a moment, brought up a large block of wood with a key attached to it from under the counter, and said, "Out back," and then, "You Mexican?" Savitha smiled and took the key. When she came back, the man was busy with a customer, so she set the key on the counter, by the cash register, and left.

Now, along with the falling light, the wind had picked up. It wasn't particularly cold, but it whipped her hair, her loose clothes pulled taut in the gusts. She stood undecided, watching the road, which was empty, and the hills to the northeast, which no longer seemed low, but towering and severe. A truck pulled into the parking lot, but no one got out. She looked up and saw the first stars; beyond the pools of the gas station lights, there was only cold, unnerving night. She decided it was best to walk back into town and at least find cover in the small park. She gathered her knapsack and started past the gas pumps. The door of the truck opened. Two men got out. Savitha didn't particularly notice them, only saw that there were two of them as she walked past; she was chilled suddenly, Padma's sweater hardly thick enough to hold back the night. She'd cleared the farthest pump when she heard footsteps running up behind her.

She turned; she'd nearly passed through the last pool of light, but she turned.

3

The baby-faced one smiled first. His smile so genuine and carefree, his approach so guileless, that Savitha thought he might embrace her, as if they were long-lost friends. "Don't go," he yelled out. "Hey, where you going? Don't go."

"Let her go, Charlie," came a bored voice. Savitha then saw the second man, behind the baby-faced Charlie. The second man was bony, with a thin face and long hair, stringy and to his shoulders, and dark hollows for eyes. They came toward her slowly, but with an electric charge in their walk; she had the sudden impulse to run, and she nearly did.

But then, in the next moment, the baby-faced one was beside her. She smelled the alcohol, even before he grabbed her arm. "Don't go," he said, the words no longer a request but an order. Savitha tried to squirm out of his grip, but he tightened it and smiled again. "Look at her, Sal. She's a pretty little thing. You a lot lizard? Whoa, now. My, my. Feisty. My uncle Buck gave me a hamster just like you. When I was five. Shot himself in the head. Uncle Buck, I mean, not the hamster." And then he laughed, and then the man named Sal came up beside them, into the pool of light, and it was only now that Savitha saw it was not just alcohol, it was something else that drove them, that seemed a ruthless engine inside them.

"What's your name?" the baby-faced one asked.

Savitha understood the question, but was too panicked to answer.

"Where you from?"

Savitha shook her head. "No English," she said.

She realized instantly that it was the wrong thing to say.

Charlie's smile widened, though his face took on a quieter, sinister quality. "Is that right? No English? Hey, Sal, did you hear that? No English."

They all three stood like that, looking at one another, and Savitha, for the flash of the tiniest moment, thought the baby-faced one would simply let go of her arm, and she would continue on into town, back to the small park. But it wasn't true: something glimmered in Sal's eyes. He said, "Hold on, now. What do we have here," and then he said, "Lift up that arm, Charlie." It was her left arm, her stub, and when Charlie twisted it up toward the night sky, they both howled with laughter. "Who was it? Who bit your hand off?" Sal asked.

"I bet it was a tiger," Charlie said, still laughing, still painfully gripping her arm. "Don't you all have tigers over there?"

"Shut up, Charlie," Sal said, his face suddenly serious. "Come on. Get her over to the truck."

Charlie yanked on Savitha's arm. She jerked forward; her eyes snapped to the empty road, to the inside of the gas station, the counter. The large man who'd given her the key was turned away. She opened her mouth to shout, but Charlie was quicker: he slapped his hand over her face. Her head came to his chest, and his hand was so big that it covered her mouth and most of her eyes. He pushed her against the truck, and when the long-haired one opened the door, she thought they would force her inside, but instead, he yanked the knapsack from her shoulder. He rummaged until he found the money, then threw the knapsack into the cab of the truck. He then reached for something she couldn't see, closed the door, and said, "Come on."

"Where to?"

"You want Mel to call the cops?"

"But the truck."

"We won't be long. Let's go."

They dragged her to the back of the gas station. By now, Savitha couldn't breathe. She twisted her head this way and that, until a gap between his fingers let in air. She tried to bite and got the inside of a finger, but he yelled, "Goddammit," and clobbered the side of her head. Savitha's ears rang. "Will you shut up," Sal said, and led them to a clump of cottonwoods, a little distance behind the station. They entered the thickets, and within three or four steps came to a small clearing. Beer cans shone in the moonlight; a fire had once been built—she saw even in the low light that they'd been here many times before. "Let me see it," Sal said.

"What you going to do, Sal?"

"I said, pass her over."

It was now Sal who clenched her left arm with his own left arm, bony and cold compared to the baby-faced one's arm. He didn't bother with the hand over her mouth. Instead, he reached somewhere under his shirt, and there, in the moonlight, was something black and gleaming. He held the gun to her face. "You make a noise. One fucking noise. You understand that?"

Savitha stared at him, her thoughts stilled, her eyes wide. She was looking into it, but inside her—inside *her* was the long and dark tunnel.

"I said, do you understand?"

No, no, she didn't understand, but evil had its own vocabulary, its own language. She nodded.

"And you try to run. You try to take a fucking step."

She understood.

He let go of her arm; she stumbled back and fell to the ground. She hadn't even known he was holding her up. "Get up," he said, and when she did, he said, "Now go ahead. Put it in your mouth."

She looked at him, no longer understanding, and then she looked at the baby-faced one. And they stood like that, neither truly understanding.

"I said, put it in your mouth."

When she still stood, unmoving, not knowing what he wanted, he grabbed her arm again and shoved her stub against her mouth. It knocked her teeth into her bottom lip, drawing blood, but he kept shoving. What did he *want*? "Open it," he seethed into her face, his acrid breath greater than air. "Open it, and put it in." He pushed the gun up to her face, between her eyes, and she heard a click. "Put it in."

Now she understood. The whole night now a violence of understanding. The stars blazing like bullets.

He let go of her arm and took a step back. He waited.

She opened her mouth. She wrapped her lips around the stub.

The baby-faced one whooped with delight, but the long-haired one only watched. He nodded. His bony face white against the black of the gun, still held at the ready, pointed at her face.

After a moment, he lurched with irritation. "Not like that," he said. "Bitch, not that. You know better." And he reached over, grabbed her by the hair, and rammed her face into the stub. She choked on her own arm. Tears filled her eyes. He then pulled her head back up, and then back down, and then back up. "Like that," he said.

And so she did.

By now, the baby-faced one had unzipped his pants and was moaning at the edge of Savitha's blurred vision. She saw the movement of his hand.

But the gun. The gun didn't move. It was motionless in the moonlight, black, lustrous, untroubled, its feathers unruffled. It laughed.

You're alive, Savitha said.

The crow watched her, still laughing, in the silver and starry night. Its beak rose into the air, and there it stayed, its stillness mocking her movement.

They've taken you, haven't they? the crow said. They've taken you piece by piece. And this—*this* is the last piece. Now, in this clearing, with these strangers. I warned you, it said. I warned you all those years ago. In Indra-valli. I said, Make sure they take you whole. But you didn't listen. You didn't listen. And now look at you. You are nothing. You are a girl. You are a girl in a clearing.

The baby-faced one let out a long groan, and the bony-faced one laughed, and the crow pulled back, opened its wings, and flew up and away, and Savitha followed it with her eyes, but the rest of her dropped to her knees.

And so it was: that the fabric of something she'd never understood, had never even tried to understand, was what had enclosed her heart, what had held it with its soft and wrinkled and cottony hands; it was *this* cloth that was now ripped wide open. The two men left her there, in the clearing, and she heard the turning of the truck's ignition and then the sound of the engine going up the road, becoming, at last, only the night. Silent and unforgiving.

But how was I to know? she thought, lying on the ground. How was I to know: that it was always this: always the boll to the loom to the cloth, and then, finally, and with such fragility, to the heart.

4

There was lightning to the west. She raised her head, and at first she smiled, thinking it a gathering of fireflies, synchronized in their mirth. But when she stood up, she saw the dark clouds racing toward her. Toward Spearfish. It was not as dark as she remembered. Was it morning? The thunder rumbled. It spoke. And then one drop, and then two. She lifted herself up, saw the discarded beer cans, the old circle of fire, and she wondered, Which way is east?

She straightened her clothes, but when she took a step, she crashed to the ground in a heap. Her legs were numb. And her mind was terribly empty.

Had she fallen asleep?

The storm was coming fast now. The thunderclouds racing across the prairie, over the Black Hills, into the Dakotas. She watched them with such interest, such longing, that they seemed as if they might bend down to her, the clouds, low and rushing, and carry her off in their embrace. But they paid her no attention and gathered ominously, growing darker and heavier with deluge. The lightning now struck from the west and the south, some from the north. Savitha watched it; the lightning her father's hands, reaching for her. Nanna, she said, was I ever the one with wings? But then the thunder crashed, and she stumbled out of the clearing, around the back of the gas station—the wind whipping around her, swirling with the strength of a sea—holding on to the walls, blinded as she was by wind, by rain, by sudden storm.

There was no one behind the counter. The key was where she'd left it.

She opened the door of the bathroom, saw her reflection in the mirror, in the light through the open door, and slammed it closed as she crumpled to the floor. And here, then: another clearing. Her money was gone. Her clothes were gone. The photo and the small white rectangle of paper were gone. Even the remaining loaf of bread and the potato chips and the apple were gone. But of all the things that were gone, that they had taken, it was Poornima's half-made sari that pinned her to the floor.

The rain started. She could hear it, clambering like little feet over the metal roof, hurrying on their way. To where?

East, she thought, east.

And what was there to the east? Nothing. Just as there had been nothing to the west.

She began to sob, and the sobs became a wail, and the wail became a low and gentle hum. She looked over, humming. Another toilet. It, too, was humming. She crawled over to it and put her arms around the cool porcelain. She smiled. But then the strong stench of urine reached into her head, cut her reverie with a knife, and it snapped her back—or was it the jiggling of the door handle that snapped her back? She didn't know, but she saw now that there was so little to be done. The single naked bulb above her ached, in its lonely, buzzing way. Her skin, illuminated by the bulb, shrieked with sorrow. Her thoughts folded and unfolded in pain. For it was here, under this white light and in this horrible stench, that Savitha realized how lost she was. How mislaid. How all the beacons of the world, standing all in a row, couldn't save her.

Poornima

1

It came down to this: her only chance of finding Savitha was to invoke her. Talking about poetry was well and good, but Poornima was running out of time, and what was the worst Mohan could do? Ignore her? Throw her out of the apartment? Deny knowing Savitha? Put her on an earlier flight back to India? Quarantine her until that flight?

None of those was worse than neglecting to use the last and only weapon she had.

That evening, she dispensed with preparing dinner, and when Mohan arrived, she simply handed him a glass. She waited for him to take his first sip of whiskey, pushed her gaze toward him, and said, "I became a shepherd for one reason. And one reason alone. To find someone."

Mohan studied her, nonplussed. He gestured toward her face. "Him? The guy who did that to you?"

Poornima hardly heard him. She spoke out into the room, dauntless now, insentient, and as if she were alone. "He doesn't exist for me. No, the person I'm looking for is my friend. Her name is Savitha. That's who I'm looking for, why I'm here."

Mohan seemed to shudder at something she didn't understand, and though his face was lost in the gray gloom of the far wall, Poornima felt his shudder through the floor, suspended in the air between them. Into that air, he said, "How do you know her?"

Poornima looked up. "She's from my village. The last time I saw her was four years ago."

He held his face against the light, away from it, as if they were locked in battle.

"Do *you*?"

"No," he said, and Poornima knew he did.

"I have to find her," she continued. "I need your help."

He swirled the whiskey in his glass. His body stiffened. He looked at the floor. "She left."

"What?"

"Two days ago."

"Two days?" Poornima felt a scream, a hot pulsing pain, rise to her throat. Two days! "Where? Where did she go?"

Silence.

"You have to know *something*."

"She took a bus. That's my guess."

"But to *where*? Where? These, these girls—they don't know anybody, any other places. They don't even know English. Where *could* she go? And without money."

Silence again.

Poornima's mind raced. Her plane ticket was through JFK. In one week's time. What was better, to stay here or to go to New York? What if Mohan didn't let her stay? What was the *point* of staying? When Savitha was gone? She knew, she knew already: if he made her go, she would simply walk out of the airport when she got to New York. And she would keep walking. Would anybody stop her? Could they? And even if they didn't, what then? Where would she go? How would she begin? Such a big country—how long would a thousand dollars last? No matter: she would meet her from the other end. And then she thought, enraged, She was here. She was here the whole time and I didn't find her. I was looking in the wrong places, walking the wrong streets. For *two weeks*.

"Money, she had."

She looked up at him, as if waking from a deep sleep and surprised to find him there. What was he talking about?

"What money?"

"She took it. From my wallet. Not much. Won't get her very far."

"But how far? Where?"

"And half a photograph."

"Where would it get her? Tell me."

"I don't know why she took *that*," he said.

"A photograph? Of what?"

"Some place I told her about. Me as a kid."

"What place?"

"Spearfish Canyon."

"Is that a city?"

"Near a city. In South Dakota."

"Where is that?"

"Midway. Not quite."

Poornima looked away, and then she looked back at him. "What did you tell her about it?"

Mohan shrugged. He said shyly, "I don't know. Nothing much. Just what I remembered. That it was a perfect place. That's how I remember it from when I was a kid. That it was perfect. That's what I told her. But then—but then she asked me the strangest thing."

"What?"

"She asked me whether it was like flute song."

"Flute song?"

Poornima's voice trailed off. Her face hardened into a kind of resolve, a purpose, a slow cooling, as of lava, a firming, as of the desert after a rain. And so it was: her face took on the characteristics of landscape, of natural forces, of tectonic plates and pressure and finding of place, of settling into a destiny. It no longer mattered: the logic of a thing. What mattered was the conviction in the pit of her stomach, burning its way through her body: Savitha was there. If she wasn't there, she was nowhere. And that Poornima could not abide. She had traveled half the circumference of the earth, and traveled all these many, many years. And for what? To miss her by two days? No. No, *that* she would not abide. Out of the darkness, she said to him, "I have one week left here. And then I get on a plane to New York. And you will never see me again. But I will pay you. I will give you my entire savings. Will you take me? Will you take me to this Spearfish Canyon? You don't have to, I know that. But will you?"

Mohan began to chuckle, but then his face pulled back. He was quiet. He eyed her with disbelief, but also with a kind of awe. "I can't. I have to be here. You know that. You're talking about leaving in a few days. I couldn't possibly."

"Not a few days. Tomorrow. Tonight, if you can manage it."

Now he did laugh out loud. But it was a sad person's laugh, not very deep, as thin and unconvincing as pond ice in spring. Afterward, there was silence again. They sat on the floor, facing each other, in a silence that was heavy, that hung like mercury. "You're not serious," he finally said.

She'd been wrong: She had one weapon left. She had the poem.

"These are the stairs, Mohan. She's two days gone. There is no time. There is no time."

The room spun. It spun like a charkha. He rose unsteadily, took his car keys from where he'd placed them on the counter. He said, "Twenty hours, give or take. Pack a bag."

2

They left the next morning. He picked her up at seven o'clock and they drove east. Poornima packed not just a bag but all her few things, as if she was leaving for good. They took Interstate 90, and Mohan explained the numbering of the interstates to Poornima, though they couldn't find much else to talk about. They drove toward Mercer Island, and Poornima thought they must be going the wrong way, going as they were over water, but Mohan told her it was right, it was east, toward South Dakota. They then drove over the dense, green Cascades, on through Cle Elum and George and Moses Lake, and then came into the eastern part of the state, the hills now spread before them like immense reclining women. At Coeur d'Alene, there were more mountains, these not as lofty as the Cascades, but sloping gently, forested on either side of the highway. The sky now, Poornima noticed, opened like a curtain, stretched endless and blue. Silver-tinged clouds, wispy at their edges, dense and gray at their centers, floated eastward. She pointed up toward them and said "Maybe rain." Then she said, "Lolo. That's a funny name."

Mohan seemed deep in thought, and the wordless music in his car, the same kind of music she'd heard when he'd picked them up at the airport, played on and on, and she grew drowsy.

They passed through Missoula and Deer Lodge and Butte and Bozeman. At Livingston, they stopped for coffee. Without ever discussing it, they both understood they would drive through the night. The sky clouded over some more, but Poornima looked into the horizon and thought she could see to the ends of the earth, its curving unto itself, feminine and aching. Cattle grazed in the far, far distance, sprinkled on the golden and green rolling grasses like strewn mustard seeds. Ranch houses and trailers dotted the hills at long intervals, set deep into the tapestry, and she thought them lonely, though defiant in their small conquering. They'd bought sandwiches at a gas station in Garrison for lunch, but for dinner, Mohan said they should stop, and pulled into a roadside restaurant outside Crow Agency. They ordered coffees, which were hot and had a thick, mineral taste. After she asked what various items on the menu were, never having seen the words *steak* or *meatloaf* or *burger*, Poornima ordered a grilled cheese sandwich and mashed potatoes. Mohan ordered a cheeseburger and french fries. They ate to classic cowboy songs playing on the restaurant's jukebox, and though Poornima was grateful to finally hear music with words, she couldn't understand a single one. They filled up again after dinner and drove on as the sky behind them bruised pink and orange and gray. Before them, the blue deepened, widened like water.

It was only then, once they left 90 and got onto the 212, that Mohan mentioned Savitha again. He didn't look at Poornima but spoke into the dark of the road. "What if she's not there?" he asked.

It was such a simple question, yet she had no answer. She could feel the fury moving up her throat. The frustration that she'd pushed back these last few days. All this way, and for what? Two days. Two days. She grimaced. What *if* she wasn't there? What then? She looked for her all along the highway, as they passed through towns, into the hills and the vast ranches, as if life granted such a thing. As if life granted such a thing so lovely and effortless and miraculous as seeing Savitha standing on the crest of a hill, or ambling along the street in one of those small towns. "I don't know," she said, and she didn't know: in this whole wide world, after all this searching, she no longer had a place to begin.

She began to cry then. She hadn't cried in years, but now she began to cry. As if all the ravening of all her years had, in that moment, come down upon her. She choked for breath, sobbed. "I don't know," she said, unable to stop the tears, and buried her head in her hands. She felt Mohan's hand on her arm, and he held it like that until she raised her head, wiped her tears.

"She couldn't have gone much farther," he said.

"How do you know?"

He paused, still staring unblinking at the road. "Because I only had about a hundred dollars in my wallet."

Poornima looked at him. She wiped away tears. The wind, howling past the car, ceased.

"And she had to have gone east."

"Why?"

"Or south."

"What about the others?"

"Puget Sound is to the west. Maybe there, but probably not. Water is too uncertain. And Canada's difficult without a passport."

She didn't take her eyes from him. "You've given this some thought."

"No," he said, smiling weakly. "None at all."

After the Crow and the Northern Cheyenne reservations, the road veered south-southeast toward a town called Broadus. They were nearly there. Hardly two more hours, Mohan said. "We'll wait till morning," he added, "to go to the canyon."

Poornima turned. "Morning? No, as soon as we get there."

"What's the point? It'll be dark."

"Dark is the past four years," she said.

Mohan shook his head. The first stars blinked awake, though Poornima only glimpsed them through passing clouds, gathering heavily to the east and south. There was a flash of lightning far to the south. It was after midnight when they neared Spearfish. "Are we almost there?" she said, needing to use the bathroom.

"Just a few more miles," he said.

When they reached the outskirts of Spearfish, she saw a gas station. "There," she said. "Stop there."

The lights of the town shone in the distance. And then, she knew, was the canyon.

He pulled in, and Poornima jumped out of the car. A storm was coming. The lightning was close now. There were no more stars. She felt the gray dense weight of the clouds, hanging above yet close to the earth. For now, they held their rain, crouched in place.

She glanced up again and then sprinted into the gas station. The man behind the counter rested his thick forearms on the counter. His left one had a tattoo of a woman in a short dress, kicking up her long legs, reclined in a martini glass. Poornima looked at it, and then at his gold chain. She scanned the room. She didn't see a bathroom. "Pardon me, please."

"Around back," he said, turning away, clearly disgusted by her face. "Might want to wait, though. Some Mexican gal's in there now."

Poornima understood that the bathroom was outside the building and raced out of the door. "And bring that key back," he yelled after her. When she got outside, she tried the handle, but it was locked. She looked around, waiting. She could no longer see Mohan or the car, but she heard it idling. Across the street was an auto repair shop. Next door to the gas station seemed to be some sort of warehouse. The storm clouds were overhead now. The wind lifted her hair, swirled the strands in great and roguish kites. A drop of rain landed near her foot, and then another on her head.

She jiggled the handle some more.

There was a flash of lightning. The gas station went white, bright as bone, and then, as if a light had been switched off: black.

Car lights swung like a cradle. She squinted when they swept over her.

She shivered, to be so exhausted, so alive. A car pulled up. It was Mohan. He rolled down the window and yelled out, "Looked at the map. We're close."

"How close?"

"Just southeast of here." He smiled. "You've been waiting this whole time?"

The clouds thundered. They both looked up at the boom. Then, in that instant, the clouds broke, and the rain poured down. She raised her face to it, cooling all the fires.

"All this time?"

She nodded. She looked at Mohan. He was shaking his head and laughing. The world felt so slick, as though it had washed over and out of her: time, the organs weighted with hunger, the memory of a slippery hand, holding yogurt rice and banana to her starved lips. Finally the handle of the bathroom door turned. She smiled, suddenly shy, as if she and Mohan were two lovers, come upon each other in a grove, in a garden, under summer showers.

"Not much longer," she said.

Acknowledgments

My gratitude to:

Amy Einhorn, Caroline Bleeke, Sandra Dijkstra, Elise Capron, Amelia Possanza, Conor Mintzer, Ursula Doyle, Rhiannon Smith, Zoë Hood, Rick Simonson, Charlie Jane Anders, Nancy Jo Hart, Theresa Schaefer, Nichole Hasbrouck, Sierra Golden, Mad V. Dog, Dena Afrasiabi, Jim Ambrose, Sharon Vinick, Arie Grossman, Elizabeth Colen, Hedgebrook, the Helene Wurlitzer Foundation, Lakshmi and Ramarao Inguva, Sridevi, Venkat, Siriveena, and Sami Nandam, Kamala and Singiresu S. Rao, and the ones who stood with me on the prairie: Abraham Smith, Srinivas Inguva, and Number 194.

My deepest gratitude to:

Barbara and Adam Bad Wound, for the Badlands.